G. J. Whyte-Melville

Digby Grand

An Autobiography

G. J. Whyte-Melville

Digby Grand
An Autobiography

ISBN/EAN: 9783337122263

Printed in Europe, USA, Canada, Australia, Japan

Cover: Foto ©Raphael Reischuk / pixelio.de

More available books at **www.hansebooks.com**

DIGBY GRAND.

An Autobiography.

BY

G. J. WHYTE MELVILLE,

AUTHOR OF

"THE INTERPRETER," "GENERAL BOUNCE," "KATE COVENTRY." ETC.

NEW EDITION.

LONDON:

LONGMANS, GREEN, AND CO.

CONTENTS.

DIGBY GRAND

AN AUTOBIOGRAPHY.

—◇—

CHAPTER I.

'THE MORNING OF LIFE.'

'GRAND and Buffler to stay!' says the 'prepostor' of the Lower Remove-Remove, as he darts into our hall of learning on his humane errand. Right well do Grand and Buffler know what that simple sentence indicates; and ere the messenger of Fate, in the shape of a short and dirty lower boy colleger, or 'tug,' has departed, they evince by a simultaneous hitching of the waistband, and wistful expression of countenance, their very disagreeable anticipation of the discipline to follow. Gravely the construing proceeds, as it has proceeded from time immemorial within those classic walls, and whatever 'Henry's holy shade' might think of it, I can imagine the pagan ghost of heathen Horace would be somewhat aghast, could his repose in the realms of Pluto be disturbed by the blundering schoolboy's version of his polished stave.

Let us hear how Bullock-major renders the dreaded Ode. *Justum et tenacem propositi virum*, begins the much-enduring master, giving to the thrilling stanza that harmonious roll which shows that much and often as his favourite has been murdered to his unwilling ear, he still clings to him with all a scholar's devotion—'*Justum*,' &c.—'Bullock-major, go on!' Up starts the electrified disciple, with all the readiness of a professor, but

4

deep are the misgivings at his heart, and clouded the impression on his brain; for Bullock-major, though as stalwart 'a stroke' as ever feathered an oar round Lower Hope, and as straight a bowler as ever skimmed the emerald sward of the lower shooting-fields, is yet modestly aware of his own deficiencies, and has a wholesome horror of being, like Grand and Buffler, 'in the bill.' At it he goes, however, with changeless intonation and nasal twang—'*Virum*, the man'—pause—'*justum*, just'—pause—'*et tenacem*, and tenacious'—(Bravo, Bull! says the next boy on the form, a scapegrace of some eleven summers)—'*propositi*'—a solemn pause—dark grows the master's brow—'Go on, sir, *propositi*'—Bullock grows desperate: '*propositi*,' of his proposition.' Hear him, melodious minstrel of Rome's palmiest days!—'Sit down, sir!—put him in the bill—next boy go on.' And the unfortunate Bullock-major embarks in the same boat with Buffler and myself.

Ah! those were glorious days, notwithstanding the 'bill,' and all its horrors; some of the happiest hours that I, Digby Grand, have spent in my chequered career, were passed at dear old Eton; with just enough of school and school discipline to make the relaxation of play delightful, with every kind of amusement the heart of boy could desire—with boating, cricket, football, hocky, paper-chases, and leaping parties, or as we call them 'levies'—and above all, with that abundance of congenial society, and those cordial friendships, so delightful to youth. No wonder that the old Etonian's heart still warms when he catches sight of the walls of 'College'—no wonder that he remembers, with a vividness after years can never obliterate, each characteristic of the long past scene. The dreaded Hawtrey, 'my tutor,' by turns loathed and beloved; 'my dame,' an object now of ridicule, now of affection; Windsor Bridge, Mother Tolliday, the weary and well-informed Spankie himself; the 'ticks up-town,' the 'sock-shop,' the triumphs on the water, won with sculls and oar—the glories of the sward, when an Eton eleven sacked the second-best team of the Marylebone Club—all and each of these images are clung to and remembered in many a varied scene and distant land; ay, such early impressions as these will return to the imagination of the wanderer, even when the dearest and holiest ties of home are for a time forgotten. But let me also look back through the long vista of years gone by—let me live once more in memory the joyous days of spring, when the heart was merry and the step was light,—when the breeze of morning kissed an open brow, as yet unseamed by care, and lifted clustering locks, unthinned, unbleached by time—when to-morrow was as though it would never be, and to-day was all in all—without a care, without a fear, save of the consequences of some youthful scrape, ending in the fatal catastrophe of corporal punishment.

I was brought up a 'dandy'—that was the word in my younger days. From the time I left the nursery, the first lesson inculcated on my youthful mind was, 'Digby, hold up your head, and look like a gentleman.' 'Mister Digby, don't dirty your boots, like the poor people's children.' I lost my mother when still a baby; so my ideas of her are chiefly drawn from her portrait in the dining-room—a fair and beautiful woman, with large melancholy eyes and nut-brown hair: I presume it was from her that I inherited those glossy locks, on the adornment of which I have spent so much time and trouble, that would have been far better bestowed on the cultivation of the inner portion of my skull. My father, Sir Peregrine Grand, of Haverley Hall, was what is emphatically called a gentleman 'of the old school;' that is to say, his weaknesses were those of drinking a great deal of port at a sitting, swearing considerably even in ladies' society, and taking an inordinate quantity of snuff; but then he was adorned with all the shining virtues that so distinguished this same 'old school:' he eschewed cigar-smoking as a vice filthy in the extreme. His morals were as loose as those of his neighbours, but his small-clothes were a great deal tighter. He had his hair dressed by his valet regularly every morning—and then *he knew his position* so well, and he took care every one else should know it too. Nevertheless, though an ill-judging, he was an indulgent father to me; and I do believe his dearest wishes were centred in myself, his only child. Not that he thought much of my morals or my intellect, but he took care that I should be a good horseman and an unerring shot; and as some fathers would wish their children to be distinguished in the different

walks of public life—as warriors, authors, orators, or statesmen
—so was it poor Sir Peregrine's dearest hope that 'Digby should
be a man of fashion—by Jove! the sort of fellow, sir, that
people are glad to see, and a man that knows his position, Dr
Driveller—that knows his position, sir. I recollect many years
ago, when I was a young fellow, the women called me Peregrine
Pickle; I could do what I liked then, anywhere, and with any
of them, but I never forgot my position, sir—never forgot my
position.'

    'Very true, Sir Peregrine,' said the worthy doctor, who would
have assented equally to the most preposterous proposition, if
made by my father,—'very true; when Digby leaves Eton, he
must go into the army.'

    'But not the Line, papa!' says the precocious urchin alluded
to. 'Fortescue-major, at my tutor's, says the Line is very low,
and most Eton fellows go into the Guards. I shall go into the
Guards, papa.'

    'Hold your tongue, Digby, and hand me the biscuits. Doctor,
ring the bell, and we will just peep into another bottle of
port.'

    Such was the substance of our usual conversation after dinner
when I was at home for the holidays, and such it might have
remained, without ever approximating the desired end, had it
not been for an accidental circumstance, which procured me a
friend whose energy urged upon my father the necessity of taking
some steps with regard to my entrance into life, and through
whose instrumentality I obtained a commission in her Majesty's
service.

    Everything at Haverley Hall was conducted upon a scale, to
say the least of it, of lordly magnificence; and as during my
boyhood I never knew a wish ungranted, or a request refused,
which had for its object the further circulation of the coin of
the realm, my boyish idea naturally was, that my father's resources were inexhaustible, and that, to use a common expression, 'money was no object.' How could I tell the lengthy
conferences in his private room from which our old man of business, Mr Mortmain, used to emerge with a darkened brow and
a drooping chin—had for their object the furtherance of sup-

plies, and for their argument the still-to-be-solved problem of making two and two equal to five ;—how could I tell that from sheer mismanagement and love of display, year after year a goodly rent-roll was diminishing, and a fine property alienating itself from its natural possessor? Come what might, Sir Peregrine must have three servants out of livery, to say nothing of a multitude of giants in plush and powder. Though he seldom or never got upon a horse, the stables must be filled with a variety of animals, good, bad, and indifferent. Hating standing about in the cold more than anything, he was not by any means a constant attendant at Newmarket ; and when there, wished himself anywhere else in the world ; but that was no reason why every list of acceptances, for every doubtful event on the Turf, should not be adorned by the name of one of his race-horses, selected from a string which he never saw, but of whose length he might judge by that of his trainer's bill. One of my first scrapes as a boy was not remembering how 'Euclid' was bred, having confounded that gallant animal with a mathematician of the same name. As for going out in a carriage with less than four horses, Sir Peregrine would rather have walked, gout and all, than compromised 'his position' by such a proceeding ; and as all his ideas with regard to dinners, entertainments, house-keeping, &c., were upon the same scale, it would have required, indeed, the fortune of a millionaire to support this style of magnificence.

From my father's increasing indolence as he grew into years, the management of the shooting and the stables came into my hands at an age when the achievements of most boys are limited to an occasional rabbit slaughtered by favouritism with the keeper's gun, or a stolen ride on the unwilling pony, that goes to the post, carries the game, and does the odd jobs ; but long ere I had mounted the tailed coat and stiff cravat of incipient manhood, I could knock over wild partridges right and left, and ride my own line to a pack of fox-hounds, as well as many who, although double my age, had perhaps less experience in these accomplishments. Before I left Eton, I used to make my own horses, as the term is ; and as my father never grudged me anything I desired, in the way of extravagance, I had but to gain

over the trainer, to obtain as a gift any of his thorough-bred
horses, that in our united wisdom we should choose to condemn
as too slow for racing. I always found this species of request,
as involving no immediate outlay of ready money, to be granted
most willingly; and it was after a gift of this description that I
sallied forth one morning in early spring for the purpose of riding
a four-year old, fresh from Newmarket, over every fence that
should come in my way, and thereby perfecting him as a hunter
against the ensuing season.   Oh! the delight of a glorious gallop
over grass, on a fine morning, the easy swing of the free-going
animal beneath you, to which every muscle and joint of the
horseman instinctively adapts itself; the fresh and exhilarating
breeze, created by the rapid motion; the constant change of
scene as you scour along over upland and meadow; the 'middle-
distance,' as painters call it, wheeling into ever-varying beauty:
then the reflective flattery, reciprocated by the flying pair; the
'how well I ride *you*, and how well you carry *me*;' the association of ideas, and recollections of the many good runs you have
seen, and the many more you hope to see, if you are a hunting
man,—as, ten to one, if you really enjoy this sort of thing, you
are,—all this makes a morning gallop one of the pleasantest
sensations experienced by youth and health; and it was with a
full appreciation of its delights that I sent the four-year old
along on the morning in question, solitary, and, as I thought,
unseen.   I sped my flight like a sea-bird on the wing.   Everything was most successful at first; my young horse was in the
best of humours, and appeared to enjoy his lesson as much as
his instructor.   We bounded over the park-rails like a deer;
we disposed of the Ha-ha—an ugly obstacle enough, in our
stride: we went in and out of a rough, tangled, double hedge,
that skirted the plantation on the hill, as cleverly as if our united
ages had been double their real amount; and when, flushed with
success, I turned his head for the vale, a fine grass line of exten-
sive pastures, I felt as if nothing could stop us.   But horses,
like men, may be somewhat too thin-skinned; and as I neared
the highroad, I spied a strong overgrown fence, through the
thorns and briers of which we should have to force our way;
and thick, tangled, and dark was the forbidden leap.   I went at

it fast, thinking the pace might send us through like a bullet; but, rapidly as we approached, my young horse, when within a stride of the fence, came round upon his haunches with a quickness all his own, and which might have unhorsed many a tolerable equestrian. One more chance I gave him, and then proceeded to coercive measures. The blood of his ancestors was roused, and the battle began in right earnest—the rider applying whip and spurs with sustained vigour—the animal backing, rearing, and plunging, in a manner that threatened soon to put a period to the contest in the downfall of one or both. At last I forced him into the fence : and as he fell upon his head into the road, and recovered himself without unhorsing me, I found myself face to face with an elderly man in undress uniform, whom I immediately recognised as General Sir Benjamin Burgonet, commanding the district, accompanied by a young aide-de-camp, likewise in the livery of her Majesty.

'Well saved, my lad, and devilish well ridden too,' said the jolly General, a large heavy man, with a red face and double chin, perfectly resplendent with good living and good humour. 'Got a good horse there for a light weight ; and I'll be bound to say, you make him go. I've been watching you,' added he, as if that fact alone made me worthy of knighthood on the spot. I took off my hat with my best Eton air, and introduced myself to the General as young Grand ; adding, that I had the honour of meeting him at a review last year, and concluding by a cordial invitation to breakfast, at which meal I was sure Sir Peregrine would be delighted to see him. It turned out that the General was returning from some duty of inspection, and being an old friend of my father, was actually on his way to pay him a visit ; nor, although he had breakfasted once, was the jolly commandant loth to indulge in a second morning meal.

As we rode into the grounds, I communicated to my companion the desire I had long entertained of entering her Majesty's service ; and ere we reached the Hall, the old officer, who had taken a great fancy to me in consequence of the exploit he had so unexpectedly witnessed, made me a faithful promise that he would use all his influence with my father to induce him to consent to my leaving Eton immediately and entering

the army, and that his own interest, which was great at the
Horse Guards, should be strenuously exerted to procure me a
commission.

His visit produced the wished-for effect, and instead of
returning to Eton, I remained at home, nothing loth, as may
be supposed. It was barely a month after the General's visit
that his promises were redeemed, and his exertions on my behalf
crowned with success. I shall not easily forget the day ; it was
one of our large dinner-parties, when the host of country neighbours came flocking to Haverley, like eagles to the slaughter.
My father was very great during these solemnities, and royalty
itself could not be more magnificently condescending than was
Sir Peregrine to his humbler guests. These dinners, like the
tides, and other important evolutions of Nature, depended
chiefly on the moon, as our roads, like all county highways and
by-ways, were most execrable, and the different tea-boys and
helpers, who officiated as body-coachmen on these occasions,
were apt to diverge into fancy driving, after their liberal potations of Haverley ale, heaven knows how many ' strike to the
bushel,' to use a professional term for extreme potency. Then
in order that the ' convives ' might get home before ' morning
should appear,' dinner was ordered at six precisely, at which
hour the good folks would punctually assemble to go through
agonies of shyness by daylight in the drawing-room. On the
day in question, my father appeared earlier than usual in that
apartment, and I saw by the care with which he was dressed,
and his determination to be ready to receive his company—for
the earliest guests had not yet arrived—that the character of
courteous host was to be acted to perfection. He was still a
fine-looking man, though bent and shrunk, and must have been
very handsome in his youth. His thin white hair was powdered, and his deep white neckcloth folded with a precision it
had cost his valet twenty years to acquire. His black panta-
loons fitted tightly as a glove on those well-turned limbs, which
had not yet lost their grace and symmetry. He was still vain
of his foot, and huge bunches of black ribbon, tying the low-cut
shoe, made its proportions appear even tinier than those which
Nature had accorded. A voluminous white waistcoat covering

a portly figure—for still the waist increases as the shoulders fall—and an enormous frill, completed my father's 'get-up.' And as he stepped forward from the hearth-rug, to welcome Mrs Pottingden, the doctor's lady, with the air of a sovereign receiving a princess, he looked what he really was—a gentleman of the old school.

Mrs Pottingden wore a turban, and was mightily afraid of my father. She rejoiced in six daughters, who went out two by two; and these were the two gawky ones.

My father says he is 'glad to see Mrs Pottingden looking so well, and her charming girls;' and being slightly deaf, does not hear the good lady's reply, that 'the weather is beautiful,' and 'Averley,' as she calls it, 'looking charmingly as she came up the approach;' for the sound of wheels going round to the stables is again heard, and our most pompous of butlers announces, 'Major and Mrs Ramrod! and Miss Arabella Ramrod!' and the same salutations are again exchanged, with this difference, that the new arrivals vote the weather cold and disagreeable, and ask after Sir Peregrine's gout. The latter inquiry is high treason, only Mrs R. had forgotten it was so; but my father is courtesy and blandness itself, for the sound of wheels is continually heard from every description of vehicle,—landau, chariot, brougham, dog-cart, and nondescript conveyance with a pair of shafts and a head; and Mr Soames, the butler, is breathless with the numerous announcements he is compelled to make. The Hickses, and the Johnstons, and the Longs, and old Lady Daubeney, and Admiral Portfire, and Squire Harpole of 'the Hills,' and fat Mr Sheepskin, the lawyer, and little Mr Stubbles, the curate—in they pour, ready and willing to pay their court to Sir Peregrine, and make play at the good things with which his table is so well provided. Heaven defend me from marshalling such a party in to dinner; bad enough is it when the order of precedence is duly emblazoned on the veracious page of Burke or Debrett; but who shall endeavour to cope with the difficulty of giving satisfaction, when Mrs Ramrod's indignation is roused at the affront put upon her in following Mrs Hicks into dinner, when everybody knows that Mrs Hicks's uncle is only a barrister, whereas her (Mrs Ramrod's) grandfather was a Master in

Chancery? (poor Ramrod! you will have it all to-night ere sleep visits your pillow); then, again, Admiral Portfire ought to have taken Mrs Long, who is a baronet's daughter, instead of making a rush for Mrs Johnston, whose only qualifications are youth, beauty, and good humour, as that ancient mariner well knew when he secured her companionship at the dinner-table. In short, there was no end to the outrages on all the decencies of precedence ; and as I knew my father piqued himself much on his management of proprieties on such occasions, and his know-ledge of every one's ' position,' I anticipated with dread the irrit-able discussion that would arise on the morrow, when we talked over the events of the preceding evening.

But they settle down, for the present, over soup and sherry ; and, through the Babel-like confusion that prevails, I catch my father's courteous tones, as he bows his shining head now to deaf old Lady Daubeney, now to voluble Mrs Long, while he slices the turbot, and dispenses the precious pearls of his condescension in due share to every guest. He is telling a story of the Prince of Wales and Carlton House to Lady Daubeney ; and she thinks, good soul, that he is discoursing of an eminent firm in the city, which has lately failed, and sits—listening it can hardly be called in one so devoid of hearing—with an expression of interest and commiseration upon her countenance which is perfectly irresistible.

Sir Peregrine, though pompous, is seldom at fault, and he cleverly diverts his conversation to his fair neighbour on the other hand, leaving the old lady perfectly satisfied with the share she has borne in the dialogue. And now little Mr Stubbles, commiserating her isolated position, and emboldened by sherry, hazards a remark across the table, to the effect that ' the weather to-day was remarkably cloudy for the time of year.' The attention of the company is forcibly arrested by her ladyship's loud and irritable interrogative, and poor Mr Stubbles, in rising confusion, repeats his unfortunate discovery. Again the old lady ' begs his pardon, she did not quite catch what he said ;' and the victim, ready to sink with shyness, a third time publishes his meteorological observation. He has at length succeeded in exciting her curiosity, and, leaning back, she desires one of the stately footmen standing behind her chair to fetch her ear-trumpet out of the drawing-room. The instrument arrives, and Stubbles is again placed on the rack. I never saw a man blush so blue. The old lady adjusts her acoustic auxiliary with the nicest care, and repeats her inquiry : and when Stubbles, wishing that the earth would yawn and swallow him, has stated, for the fourth time, his observation about the clouds, my well-bred father himself cannot resist a laugh at the ' Humph ' of disgust and disappointment with which the old lady receives the washy substitute for what she hoped would prove a real ' bran-new bit of news.' That dinner, which my young impatience thought interminable, at length came to a close ; and as I was ruminating, half asleep, over my claret, and feigning an interest in the lively poor-law discussion carried on across me, by my neighbours on either side, Major Ramrod and old Hicks, the door opened, and Soames, walking gravely round the table, presented me with an important-looking missive, adorned with a huge official seal; above the address I read, with an indescribable thrill of excitement, the talismanic words, ' On Her Majesty's Service.' The whole thing flashed upon me in an instant, and long ere I had deciphered the formal announcement from the adjutant of the 101st Regiment of Foot, informing me that ' the Queen had been graciously pleased to appoint me to an ensigncy in that distinguished corps,' and that he, the adjutant, ' had the honour to remain my obedient humble servant.' I was aware that the transformation had taken place, and the bumper of '19, filled by a mere schoolboy, would be emptied by an officer in Her Majesty's Service. I passed the letter down to my father with an air of military carelessness, and strove to preserve a becoming bearing of unmoved stoicism, during the congratulations that followed from all present. They drank my health, and success to me in my profession ; and I went to bed that night feeling more thoroughly ' the soldier,' than any veteran that ever obtained his long-expected medal as a receipt in full for the wounds and dangers of a hundred fights.

A gallant and distinguished regiment was the 101st Foot, and a well-drilled and efficient depôt did they possess, then quartered in the north of Scotland, the regiment itself being scattered over some five hundred miles of frontier in Canada West; and as I drove into the barrack-gates, and marked the alert sentry, the lounging guard, and the smart non-commissioned officers hurrying about, my Eton impudence was impressed with a feeling of respect for my future corps; and with a bashfulness the fifth form had not totally eradicated, I walked up to a tall erect sergeant, who was pacing to and fro on the parade, and requested to be informed which were the adjutant's quarters. His quick eye had detected my name on the portmanteau, then being lifted off my post-chaise, and ere he replied, he drew himself up still more, and *saluted his officer*. That salute made a man of me; and I am convinced I grew two inches during my conversation with this respectful warrior, as he ushered me into the presence of my former correspondent and obedient servant, Lieutenant and Adjutant Tompion, who, with Major O'Toole, the commanding officer, was poring over a large interlined volume in the orderly-room. I took it all in at a glance; the boarded floor, the deal table, the stand for measuring recruits, the extreme bareness of walls and furniture, the few articles of necessity, looking, as in fact they were, capable of being packed up in five minutes, the only litter consisting of two or three single-sticks, a pattern knapsack, and the orderly-room clerk, a sort of knight-templar—half warrior and half scribe. From these my astonished eyes travelled over the persons of commanding officer and adjutant; the former a jolly-looking round little man, close-shaved and clean, in most unmistakable plain clothes, having nothing military-looking whatever about him: the latter a gaunt weather-beaten officer, with enormous hands and feet, clad in a threadbare blue coat, and much worn pair of seales, without sword or sash, or any offensive weapon, save a stupendous pair of brass spurs, and whose duty seemed to consist in keeping one of his huge fingers pressed on the folio before him, and agreeing cordially with the major in all his proposals.

'O Mr Grand!' says the Major; 'how do you do, sir? We expected you yesterday. Hope you have had a pleasant journey. Tompion, you wrote to Mr Grand to say when he was to join?'

'Yes, sir; I wrote to inform Mr Grand his leave would be out on the 31st.'

I apologised for the mistake, saying I understood I was not to join till the 1st.

'Never mind,' said the Major; 'when you have been with us a little longer, you will find out we always get as much leave as we can, so you have only begun on the usual system. But I see my horses waiting. Good morning, Mr Grand; we shall see you at mess, at half-past seven; no occasion to come in uniform, as I suppose your baggage is only just arrived. We shall not trouble you much with drill for a day or two, till you are fairly settled. Tompion, you will show Mr Grand his quarters, and anything worth seeing about the barracks; I leave him in your hands. Good morning!' and the jolly major swaggered off for his afternoon ride.

'Come,' thought I, 'these are very pleasant people I have got amongst; I think I shall like it. And now to see what sort of a fellow Lieutenant and Adjutant John Tompion is.' Accordingly as I walked across the barrack-yard with my new acquaintance, I endeavoured, by asking him a few questions as to the customs of the service, to gain some little insight into my new profession; but no; Tompion, though an excellent adjutant, and as steady a drill as ever overlooked the 'awkward squad,' blundering through the 'goose-step,' had not an idea beyond his own duty, and that of the sergeant-major. I gave him a capital cigar, one of a lot that I had bought from Hudson, for the express purpose of joining with, and I thought he was disposed to look upon me in a more favourable light after this demonstration; but it was with a sort of dull surprise, as that of one who should see a child unbreeched handling a dice-box, or Tom Thumb struggling with an eighteen-foot salmon-rod; and I have no doubt that I must have appeared a mere baby in the veteran eyes of Lieutenant Tompion, who had been twenty-five years in the service, working his way, without friends or purchase-money, up to his present position. Be that as it may, he seemed relieved to hand me over to the attention of the quarter-master, a much fatter and more communicative individual, to whose good-nature and activity I owed the comfort of getting my things unpacked, and my bran-new goods and chattels shaken down, for the first time, in my own barrack-room.

'Dandy' Grand, as I had been at Eton, and still was, never in my life was my toilet for the dinner-table more carefully arranged than on that day. Boy as I was, I had shrewdness enough to know the advantage of first impressions; and I felt that from that evening I must take my position in the regiment I had entered. Accordingly, as I walked across the barrack-yard to what was termed the 'little mess-room'—the apartment in which the officers met before dinner—I glanced down at my neat and well-arranged toilet, and congratulated myself on having hit off the happy medium between foppery and carelessness that was most appropriate to a man-party. Long ere half the introductions to my new comrades were completed, the bugles marshalled us into dinner with the appropriate air of 'The Roast Beef of Old England;' and it was with a most confused notion of the different individuals, owning the names of Smith, Brown, Guthrie, Random, Captain Levanter, and Dr Squirt, that I took my place for the first time at the mess of the 101st Foot.

Cordiality, mirth, and jollity reigned paramount; later in the evening, perhaps, there was a shade of 'tipsy revelry;' but in the presence of Major O'Toole, who sat at the right hand of Ensign Spooner, president for the week, and who told some most marvellous stories to his admiring audience, everything was conducted within the bounds of propriety. Constant were the calls—'Mr Grand, the pleasure of a glass of wine,'—'Grand, a glass of wine with you;' and as all these convivial challenges had to be replied to, and my new comrades pledged in the standard mess-wines, strong port and sherry, a more seasoned brain than mine might be excused for owning, in a slight degree, the influence of so many bumpers as I was obliged to quaff.

Some of the officers, then quartered at the depôt, had seen a good deal of service in India, the Peninsula, and elsewhere; and after Major O'Toole had taken his departure, which he forbore from doing until *we* had swallowed an infinity of his wonderful anecdotes, and *he* his full share of the 'Prince Regent's allowance'—as a certain quantity of the mess-wines is termed—a chosen few of us gathered round the fire, and ordering a fresh supply of port, proceeded to make ourselves comfortable for an extraordinary sitting in honour of a new companion-in-arms.

' He's no flincher,' said old Brevet-Major Halberd, a veteran tanned into mahogany by hard service, and a most religious adherence to port wine and brandy-and-water in every climate of the globe—'he's no flincher, that lad,' as he eyed, with marked approbation, the steadiness with which I filled my eleventh bumper of port.

' I think he'll do, at least for a young one,' replied Ensign Spooner, a beardless warrior, some two years my junior, but whose six months' seniority in the Army List gave him all the advantage of comparatively an old hand.

I marked his flushed countenance and wandering eye, as he made his remark, and thought to myself, ' Dandy Grand will see you out, my boy, or his Eton education and his bill at " The Christopher " goes for nothing.'

' But, Major,' said Captain Levanter, resuming a conversation that our move to the fireplace had interrupted, 'you never finished that outpost story ; and I daresay Mr Grand and some of our young ones would like to hear it.'

' By all means, Major,' was the unanimous cry ; ' let us have a yarn of the Peninsula.'

If the proverb, *In vino veritas*, has any truth, the officers of the British army must be indeed devoted to their profession, as whenever they exceed their ordinary moderation in the pleasures of the table, their discourse invariably turns to what they call ' pipe-clay,'—a term which must be explained to the civilian to mean all and everything connected with the stirring scenes, the lights and shades of military life.

' Well,' said the Major, ' if you young fellows like to hear it, you are welcome to the story, though it tells sadly against myself, since I was outwitted, by Gad !—outwitted by a Frenchman ! But this was the way it came off. You were all children then, except my old friend Squirt ; and he looked older than he does now, for he had not mounted a wig in those days. But I was, even at that early period of history, a lieutenant in a regiment of light infantry ; which, from one cause and another, was so short of officers, that I found myself, one fine morning, in command of an important outpost, close to the enemy's lines. There was a mill near my position, and a rapid stream, pretty deep, too, which

looked to me a tempting sort of a place to throw a fly—a sport,
my boys, that, in my humble opinion, beats cock-fighting!
Well, I was smoking my weed, after a light and wholesome
dinner off a piece of black bread and the outside of an onion,
when a brown, dirty-looking fellow, who swore he was a miller,
and who talked Spanish, and stunk of garlic like a true "patriot,"
asked to have an interview with "my Excellency;" and with many
compliments, and a great deal of translating by signs—for my
knowledge of Spanish was not equal to my taste in sherry,—he
begged of me to allow him to place a couple of planks across the
stream, to enable him to carry his sacks to the mill. I never
suspected a "plant" of any kind, and gave the beggar leave to do
what he wished, more particularly as I could see the men grinning
at his cursed volubility, and my bad Spanish and queer gestures,
and I was in a hurry to get rid of him. Off he went, apparently
very well satisfied; and in an hour's time I saw a couple of
planks had been placed across the mill-stream, and a very commodious foot-bridge constructed by their means. Whether my
old colonel thought me too young for "the situation," or whether
it was accidental, I know not, but I was providentially relieved
that very evening by my own captain—poor fellow, I saw him
afterwards killed at Badajoz,—and the very first thing he did, on
reconnoitring his ground, was to kick the miller's planks into the
stream, and put two extra sentries within sight of the spot where
he had made his foot-bridge. Would you believe it?—the very
next morning his post was threatened by a squadron of chasseurs,
who, finding themselves unsupported, retired, after exchanging a
shot or two ; and a large body of French infantry marched down
to the exact spot where the foot-bridge had been erected, commanded by the Spanish miller in person, attired in the uniform
of "Capitaine of the Deuxième Leger." The clever rascal had
disguised himself as a Spaniard, and a miller to boot, and having
to do with a young one, almost succeeded in his ingenious plan of
forming a means of transport for his company, which he hoped
on the morrow to lead to victory, in a brilliant affair of outposts.
That fellow was born to be an actor,' concluded the Major ; 'and I
daresay he is one by this time, for a Frenchman can turn his
hand to anything. Pass the liquor, Spooner, talking always
makes me so devilish thirsty.'

That evening, like many others in the 101st Foot, concluded with broiled bones, brandy-and-water, cigars, songs, and choral accompaniments, wofully out of tune. I have, even at this distant period, a dim recollection of an imposing war-dance, performed round the mess-table, to the heroic air of the 'British Grenadiers,' and of our carrying Spooner to bed, in a sort of triumphal procession, in which, as the soberest of the party, I bore the huge silver candelabrum and its load of wax-lights. After parade at nine the following morning, I again met my comrades, Spooner included, clean, fresh, and merry, as though they lived on toast-and-water, and went to bed at ten o'clock.

Let me pass over the first two months of military life, taken up, as it was, with my initiation into all the mysteries of war,— 'goose-step,' 'extension motions,' 'manual and platoon exercise,' and all the other intricacies of what is termed 'squad drill.' My principal instructor was a stalwart sergeant of the light company, whose heart and soul were bound up in the profession he had adopted. 'Carry the butt of your firelock half an inch more to the rear, Mr Grand,' would exclaim this warlike enthusiast; 'half an inch, sir, makes all the difference ; and no object in nature is more beautiful than a well-carried musket.' How people's ideas of the picturesque must vary !

However, the two months soon passed over, and I was judged capable of being dismissed my drill, and taking my duty ; but in the short period which I had spent in the society of my brother officers, I had gained an insight into their several habits, and into the character of the regiment, which convinced me that 'Dandy Grand' was destined for a higher flight than a marching corps in country quarters ; and already I nourished hopes of obtaining an exchange into some crack cavalry regiment, or—summit of my ambition !—an appointment to the 'Guards.' The fact is, the 101st was a slang regiment ; even the best of them, as I considered him, Captain Levanter, the only officer who, in my secret heart, I deemed a fitting companion for Sir Peregrine's son,—even he was given to driving tandems, and such other vulgar accomplishments ; and one of my first triumphs, was the winning ' a pony ' of the captain, as to the feasibility of driving a pair of hired horses, harnessed tandem-fashion, in and out of the barrack

B

gate, a very awkward turn, placed at an acute angle with the
street, a feat which I accomplished in a trot, according to the
terms of the wager. Levanter never paid me, but was good
enough to grant me his friendship ever after,—a boon of which I
have no doubt he over-estimated the value,—and we soon became
inseparable companions. The older officers shook their heads at
our escapades, but amongst the young ensigns and lieutenants we
were perfect demi-gods. I bought two very clever horses, which
he and I drove by turns, to the admiration of the High Street. I
won a pigeon-match of Mr M'Dookit, the sporting lawyer of that
locality. I rode Major O'Toole's black mare, for a bet of half-a-
crown, backwards and forwards over the gate that led to our
parade-ground ; and, as I was better dressed, smoked better
cigars, and drank more wine than any member of the mess under
the rank of a field officer, it is no wonder that I was considered
rather 'a great card' at the depôt of a marching regiment in
country quarters.

The weeks slipped away pleasantly enough : one day will serve
for a specimen of the rest, as they varied but little in the nature of
the pursuits and amusements they afforded. A struggle to get up
and be dressed in time for parade at nine, was the invariable
commencement. I buckle my sword-belt and tie my sash as I
run down-stairs, and make my appearance on parade in time to
salute the Major before the officers proceed to inspect their
respective companies. The rear-rank of No. 2 is my especial
charge, and I walk down the front and up the rear with the air
of a perfect martinet. Brown's knapsack is hung too high,
Smith's pouch is put on too low, and Murphy is sent to drill 'for
unsteadiness in the ranks.' The Major walks down, and compliments me on the progress I make in my duty. The bugles
sound—the band plays—the four companies we boast of form,
and march past, saluting Major O'Toole as if he were the Duke
of York ; the officers fall out, the parade is dismissed, and I go
to breakfast. When that elaborate meal is finished, Levanter
kindly accepts one of my cigars, links his arm in mine, and we
proceed down the town to play out our match at billiards, in
which he gives me five out of a hundred, and wins by a stroke.
(Levanter can play billiards better than any man in England, and

what I have learnt of this crafty game I owe to his tuition, though I must confess my instructor did not teach me gratis.) The admiring Spooner looks on, and in his regard and affection for myself, loses a five-pound note, or as he calls it, ' a fiver,' to my antagonist. We return to the barracks to readjust our toilets before appearing at ' the gardens,' where our drums and fifes will delight the fair admirers of the military with all the last year's waltzes and polkas, and an occasional quick-step or ' gallop;' and here I devote my attentions to Miss Jones, the fort-major's daughter, a crafty young lady of two or three and thirty, with whom I fancy myself in love. Miss Jones hovers undecided between Levanter and myself, but thinks she has the most chance with the young one, and, as she herself would say, ' rather inclines to Grand.' Like all boys, I am not very good at love-making, and the more I find I care for Miss Jones, or ' Fanny,' as I begin to call her to myself, the greater difficulty I have, notwithstanding much encouragement on her part, in telling her so. On the afternoon I am now describing, I got rather further than usual, and found courage to inquire ' for what fortunate individual Miss Jones intended the small nosegay of violets she was carrying? ' Oh, my! Mr Grand, I 'm sure I don't know. Pa asked me for one, and I wouldn't give it him. Are you fond of violets?' Of course ere I escorted Miss Jones to her home, with its green blinds and brass knocker, one of the half-withered, earthy-smelling violets had found its way to the inside of my blue coat. But we had not yet got much farther than this sort of harmless flirtation.

' Are you nearly dressed, Grand?—the trap is at the door,' said Levanter, some half-hour after our return from the gardens, as he made his appearance in my barrack-room, ' got up' most elaborately in plain clothes adapted for a very smart dinner party. He was a fresh-coloured, good-looking man, above the middle size, and inclined to be stout; and as, with his dark hair immensely brushed, his whiskers curled to the very tips, a stupendous white neckcloth, gold-embroidered waistcoat, and blue coat with gilt buttons, he burst into my room, he looked a handsome fellow enough, but wanted a something I could not describe—a sort of finish, to give him the real air of a gentleman.

'Let me put on my driving coat,' was the reply, 'and then forward.' Another five minutes saw us bowling along outside the town with a pair of quick, high-stepping horses, my property, the leader at an easy canter, the wheeler trotting some twelve miles an hour, on our way to ex-provost M'Intyre's villa, to which we had been invited, on the occasion of one of that municipal grandee's great feeds.

'What snobs these fellows are,' said Levanter to me; 'you and I dine with this provost because it suits us, but he is a very vulgar dog, and I should cut him if I were to meet him in London.'

'I do not agree with you,' was my reply. 'This man is an unaffected business-like fellow, a good specimen of a plain, hospitable Scotch tradesman, and he sets up for nothing more. Where there is no pretension there can be no vulgarity, Levanter; and while I respect such a man as M'Intyre, there is nothing I have such a contempt for as a fellow who likes to be thought a greater man than Nature and position have made him.' This, I fear, was an unintentional thrust that my companion did not half relish, as I saw the colour settle for an instant in his cheek, and his brow darken with a scowl I had before noticed when anything occurred to displease him; but he was a man of the most perfect self-command, and if my unlucky observation had made him an enemy for life, he would not have allowed his feelings to be discovered for an instant by the expression of his countenance. He was facetious and agreeable as ever during our drive, and ere we arrived at the ex-provost's villa, we were chatting in our usual familiar and unconstrained manner.

The dinner went off as dinners do when sped by Highland hospitality; and Levanter and I got into our tandem to drive home, with heated brains, and spirits somewhat too much exhilarated for that particular mode of progression.

As we rattled along by moonlight on our way to the barracks, and smoked our cigars at an hour when a cigar is most enjoyable, the conversation unfortunately turned upon the merits of my leader, a high-bred impetuous animal, that I fondly imagined would be capable of distinguishing himself in a hunting-country, and of whose jumping prowess I now boasted to my companion

with intemperate eloquence. Levanter, who seemed more inclined to be argumentative, and less good-humoured than usual,
rather nettled me by the taunting manner in which he doubted
the powers of my horse, and, I imagined, by implication, the
nerve of his owner. Young, reckless, and excitable, and more
particularly now, when my blood was heated by the unusual
strength of my potations, and my spirits half maddened by the
exhilaration of 'the pace,' the moonlight, and the night air, this
was more than I could stand; and as I felt the devil rising within
me, I only longed for some opportunity of giving vent to the
wild excitement that was boiling in my veins. Hotter waxed our
argument as we galloped on, and ere we neared the town, personalities were freely exchanged, though with a sort of mock-
civility, that to a listener would have been inexpressibly ludicrous.
At last, stung to the quick by the cool reply of Levanter to some
proposition I made about the horse in question—'Perhaps he
might, if you had nerve to ride him'—I burst out, 'Nerve! will
you have nerve to sit still, if I drive him at the turnpike gate?
I'll show you whether he can jump.'

I thought Levanter's cheek turned a shade paler in the
moonlight, as he caught sight of the gate we were now rapidly
approaching, looking most forbidding with its series of strong
white-painted bars; but though his lip quivered for an instant,
he only said, 'Drive on, and try; but hold them straight.' And
ere the words were spoken, we were too near to be able to pull
up at the pace we were going, even had we wished it. I shouted
to my horses, and flogged the wheeler, who appeared inclined to
waver in his desperate career; the calumniated leader pulling
hard, and pointing his ears at the obstacle which he seemed determined to overcome. We were close upon the gate,—I heard
Levanter draw his breath hard, and felt the tension of the muscle
of his leg against mine, I saw my leader's back, as he rose high
in air, and surmounted the barrier; I heard a tremendous crash,
and two fearful bangs against the bottom of the dog-cart, as my
wheeler strove to follow his example—and in another instant I
was lying in the middle of the road, the surface of which, white
as chalk in the moonlight, seemed spinning round and round;—
one grasp with my hands, to endeavour to keep my position

on what appeared a sloping and revolving plane, and that is all I can recollect of my ill-advised attempt to jump a turnpike-gate in a tandem.

If there is a dangerous period for youth—if there is a time when the morbid feelings of a false and fevered passion—the creature of the imagination, and not of the heart—exercise their most unbridled sway, it is surely when the frame is languidly recovering from a violent and dangerous illness; when the brain has been excited by fever, the reason weakened by debility, and the affections roused by conscious helplessness. Heaven help the youth, if in addition to all this, his recovery should take place, as mine did, during the balmy sunny days of a late spring, and be attended, as mine was, by a handsome woman, who has made up her own mind on a subject, in the carrying out of which it requires two to constitute a 'quorum.' Let the victim, besides all this, drink green tea and read Byron; let him find himself quoting largely from *The Giaour, Parisina*, and the *Bride of Abydos*, whilst he eschews with a conscious sensitiveness the bantering pages of *Beppo* and *Don Juan*, and we may safely vote him in that hopeless, helpless state which our astute brother Jonathan describes by the graphic title of a 'gone 'coon.' And so was it with me. Picked up by the turnpike man and Levanter, with a fractured wrist, a sprained shoulder, and a concussion of the brain, I was carried into the fort-major's house, which overlooked the scene of action, and to which the master happened to be returning from a late sitting at mess. My companion escaped, as was but just, with no greater injury than a black eye and a scraped shin; but the unfortunate wheeler was so much damaged that it was found necessary to destroy him; whilst the leader, the *teterrima causa* of all, kicked himself clear of everything, and galloped scathless home to his own stable. Of all these facts I was informed in due course of time; as my first attempt at consciousness was some six-and-thirty hours after the 'smash,' when I found myself lying bandaged and helpless on a sofa bedstead, in the major's sitting-room; while Fanny's long dark ringlets trailed over my face, and I felt her breath upon my brow, as she busied herself about my couch. I was not sure that all this was real; nor was it till at least a week afterwards that

I was able to recollect any of the circumstances connected with the accident, or, stranger still, the events that took place some hours before it.

By degrees, I got better, then stronger, and at last, thanks to Squirt's skill and Fanny's nursing, I was able to sit up; but healed as were the outward wounds in my attenuated frame, an internal injury had been inflicted during my recovery, which it took me many a long day to get over—ay, which embittering as it did my earlier years, was remembered as a gloomy warning in after life, to the stifling and destruction of the purest, holiest feelings of my heart.

I need not now be ashamed to confess that I loved Fanny Jones—ay, loved her with an energy, an infatuation, in my then state of weakness, which was little short of insanity. What was she?—an old barrack-master's daughter, a garrison flirt, hardly a lady by birth, and certainly no fitting mate for haughty Sir Peregrine's son. Good heavens! he would have sunk into the earth could he have but suspected the truth; and yet I loved her. With all the enthusiasm of boyhood—with all the sincerity and single-heartedness of a child—with the romantic adoration of a dreamer, I loved Fanny Jones. She managed it very cleverly. I have since learnt it was her last resource. But she was playing with edged tools, and came not herself scatheless out of the unequal contest. In vain Major O'Toole, performing what he considered his duty, warned me repeatedly that I was 'much too thick with Miss Jones.' In vain old Halberd came to sit with me for hours after parade, and laughed at me for being 'such a spoon.' In vain the young ensigns quizzed, and whispered, as much as they dared, 'What a flat Grand was, to be hooked by such a flirt as that!' The only person that seemed to encourage me in my folly, and to assist me with his counsel and friendship, was Levanter; and I found out in time that his was no disinterested aid.

It was some weeks before I could return to my own quarters in the barracks; and as I sat with Fanny, drinking in the summer air at the open window, and enjoying the fragrance of the flowers she knew so well how to dispose about the room—as I watched her graceful head bending over the work that those long, drooping ringlets half concealed—as I noticed the smothered sigh that would sometimes break upon these long delicious silences —as I almost shrunk from that upward glance that thrilled to my very soul—the poison gradually but surely worked its insidious way into my being; and ere my convalescence was declared established—ere I was removed by the doctor's fiat from that cherished scene, I had poured my love-tale into no unwilling ear, and had plighted my faith (the faith of a scapegrace of eighteen) to Fanny Jones. Well might I have said, with the sluggard who so quaintly reproves the undue punctuality of his valet: 'You have waked me too soon; let me slumber again.' Well might I have wished to dream on, though ruin and disgrace had been the penalty, rather than be wakened so roughly, as was my lot, from that delirious trance.

I have said that Levanter assisted me much in arranging that my interviews with my lady-love might be uninterrupted; and many a time did he detain the old fort-major over his eternal backgammon-board, while she and I enjoyed our lover-like *tête-à-têtes* in what was now considered my own apartment. The captain generally appeared after parade, and kindly relieved the tedium of my convalescence by a quiet game at 'écarte' or 'lansquenet,' which, in the impossibility of the 'billiard lesson,' served well enough as a pastime to the instructor, who repaid himself to a very sufficient tune for his time and trouble. After this, he would good-naturedly devote himself to backgammon and the fort-major, by which means we were left in uninterrupted bliss, as my brother officers, who would otherwise have kindly come to sit with me, thought I was in very good hands during the long visits of Levanter.

Things went on in this way prosperously enough. Fanny and I talked over our loves and our future *ménage:* I quite made up my mind to leave the army (having been a soldier about four months), and actually determined to apply for a fortnight's leave of absence, that I might visit Sir Peregrine, on the hopeless task of gaining his consent to our marriage, when the merest accident discovered to the infatuated victim the trap which had been so judiciously concealed, and so temptingly baited for his destruction.

After my thorough recovery left no excuse for remaining any longer under the fort-major's roof, I returned to my own barrack-room—now, how dreary a solitude !—but morning after morning, directly the parade was dismissed, I sped, like a bird to its mate, down to the well-known house, there to spend the long summer's day with Fanny in her boudoir ; and how wearily passed the dull hours of that on which my duty as Orderly confined me to the barracks, when my only consolation was a crossed and re-crossed epistle from my *fiancée*.

One bright May morning, it was again my turn of duty to remain a close prisoner within the barrack-gate, to see the men's dinners properly cooked, their rooms and passages properly cleaned, and dismiss their afternoon parade *in propriâ personâ*, when, as luck would have it, Spooner, whose expectation of some visitor would keep him all day in his quarters, kindly volunteered to take this irksome duty off my hands, and the major, contrary to custom, allowed the exchange to take place after guard-mounting at ten o'clock ; consequently I was not expected at the fort-major's, and thither I sped with even more than my usual alacrity, as soon as Spooner was installed in my place. The birds sang, the flowers bloomed, and the fresh breeze blithesomely fanned my cheek, as I hurried down to the dwelling of my love. How happy I was ! I might have known by that very fact, by the exuberance, the bounding delight of my excited spirits, that a damper must be in store for this excess of joy. So has it ever been with me—so, I suppose, in this equally-balanced world, it ever is. Full of the happy surprise I should give Fanny, I stole noiselessly past the maid who was cleaning the major's white door-steps, and who was so accustomed to my presence that she never remarked me, and on tiptoe I crept up-stairs, and through the drawing-room, to the door of Fanny's boudoir. It was ajar, and on my startled ear broke the sob of my beloved one in distress. Another step in advance, and my young blood rushed to my brain, till I heard each pulsation like the stroke of a church-clock upon the nerve. My heart sickened ; I gasped for breath ; but I *would not* fall. With my hand grasping the back of a chair (her work) I steadied myself to gaze upon a sight that well-nigh broke my boyish heart. Fanny in the arms of Levanter!—her head upon his shoulder, and weeping as if in the bitterest anguish and despair! We have all a certain degree of energy—call it rather pluck—which, if we will but summon it, nerves us *to bear;* and, like an Indian at the stake, heedless of the dishonour that might be imputed to the act,—heedless of all but my burning, quenchless, eager thirst for *the truth,* to know the whole, to know the worst—I stood, unobserved, near the treacherous pair, and listened to her pleading voice. Sentence after sentence fell like ice upon my heart—sentence after sentence disclosed a scheme of guilt and perfidy, of which I, the devoted, the true, the faithful, was to have been the victim. Levanter's low tones would occasionally grate upon my ear in exculpation or commentary, proving him not only an accomplice, but the originator of the plot. Between her broken sobs and caresses, she told her guilty tale; and when, at the conclusion of a passionate appeal to his honour, to his love, to his better feelings, to marry her while there was yet time to save her from an alliance with myself—to let her stay with him, her first, her only love, in any place, in any climate, she added, with a touch of womanly feeling that half redeemed her perfidy, 'Otherwise, dear, dearest Richard, I must marry him before it is too late. Poor Grand! poor fellow, so young, so handsome, and so devoted! Ah, Richard! had we never met I could have loved him dearly and faithfully; but now'—— I rushed from the house ere a burst of grief should unman and discover me, and speeding back to my barrack-room I locked the door, and threw myself on the bed in a passion of misery which well nigh approached madness. The whole of that day and night appear to me now to have been passed under the influence of some horrid nightmare, and it was not till the bugles sounded the Reveillée the following morning that I returned to a thorough consciousness of my identity and my position. The worldling may sneer at woes such as were then mine—the boarding-school miss, with her overwrought sensibility, may wonder that I ever recovered from them; but he who studies human nature carefully—who looks below the surface—while he appreciates and pities my boyish agony, will see in my very youth the best restorative, the most potent antidote to despair.

My brother officers behaved most kindly to me in my distress. They saw I was afflicted, though they knew not, or only partially guessed, the cause. Major Halberd, whom I had the sense to take into my confidence, scouted the idea of ' calling out' Levanter, which was the first intention of my inexperience ; and ere long his judicious kindness and sympathy won from me the confession that I had had an escape for which I ought indeed to be thankful. ' Better hush it all up, my boy,' said the old campaigner : ' Levanter is gone on leave, and when you meet again, I advise you not to allude to this ticklish subject ; take my word for it, *he* won't, and this will be a good opportunity for you to break off your intimacy with him. I don't wish to say a word against a comrade, but Levanter *knows a good deal*, and you are just as well out of his hands. As for Miss Jones— whew !' And here the major gave vent to his feelings in a prolonged whistle, which clearly showed his opinion of my faithless flame. But well-meant as all this consolation assuredly was, I confess that I was not thoroughly cured till, having officiated at a board, which granted our drum-major his discharge from the service one fine summer's day, the next morning startled the town with the intelligence, that that stout, well-whiskered, and musical individual had eloped with the fort-major's daughter. Fanny Jones, who might have been Lady Grand at some future time, became Mrs Dubbs ; and it is whispered that Dubbs, since he has left his harmonious command, has taken to drinking !

It cured me of love for many a day ; and when I embarked with a draft to join the head-quarters of my regiment in America, I was once more as devil-may-care an ensign as ever made a rally from sea-sickness at the commencement of his ' life on the ocean wave.'

CHAPTER II.

WESTWARD HO!

IT is proverbially a dispensation of Providence for manning the British navy and giving thews and sinews to the merchant service, that a mania should seize upon boys of tender years, irresistibly impelling them to adopt the sea as their profession, long before Nature had given them the power of judging for themselves in 'the knowledge of good and evil.' How often do we hear the veteran seaman declare that, had he known the discomforts and miseries to be endured 'afloat,' he would sooner have spent the prime of his manhood two hundred feet down a coal-mine than within the creaking ribs of one of Britannia's 'wooden walls.' But loathsome as is the smell of 'bilge water,' and the other odours that too often emanate from 'between decks,' and uncomfortable as it most assuredly is to have no elbow-room for shaving, short allowance of fresh water for necessary ablutions, and a continually changing 'fulcrum' to stand upon whilst you draw on your boots, yet once on deck, all such petty annoyances are discarded and forgotten. You feel the wild fresh ocean breeze, the same uncontaminated current that has swept without interruption over its thousands of miles to speed you on your course ; the glittering waters are dancing in the sun ; there is beauty on the wave and health upon the gale ; and if, being a landsman, your enjoyment in all this is enhanced by the sense of variety, you are disposed to admit that, after all, a sea-life has its own peculiar charms.

' I wish breakfast was ready ; what an appetite this sea-air gives one !' said old Halberd to me, as we paced the deck of one of her Majesty's vessels denominated Government Transport No. 7 We had been fairly in blue water for nearly a week ; sea-sickness and its accompanying lassitude and misery were now completely got over ; the men came readily to the 'tub' to receive their allowance of grog, a potation seldom relished by an enfeebled stomach, and we had all settled down to the regularity of a sea life.

In that little speck upon the waste of waters were crowded together seven officers, including Halberd, Ensign Spooner, and myself—one lady, much admired, nay, adored, as ladies always are on board ship, and rejoicing in the name of Tims, whose husband, Captain Tims, was likewise a fellow-voyager—a hundred and fifty men, with a fair proportion of sergeants and corporals, and, fortunately, but few women—and the ship's company, numbering some most eccentric characters, and commanded by honest Captain Merryweather, the most jovial tar that ever paced ' his fisherman's walk, two steps and overboard,' and whose round, good-humoured face, and short, square, powerful form ever met me when I made my morning appearance with the same greeting—'Turned out early, Mr Grand!—keep all your watches below, eh ?' this piece of sea-waggery being usually followed by a sharp interrogative to the man at the wheel, ' How's her head?' 'Thank you, her head is a good deal better, and she has quite got over her sea-sickness,' is the reply coming from the pale, wan face of Captain Tims, whose emaciated form is now seen slowly creeping up the hatchway, and whose innocence and inexperience mistook the honest skipper's question as to the course his old tub of a bark was steering, for a courteous inquiry after the health of his lady-wife. Up comes the steward, an important functionary, with hair curling all over his head in a profusion of clustering ringlets that would shame a poodle, and announces breakfast. At that magical word the deck is deserted, and with many compliments to Mrs Tims, due to her early appearance, we sit down, a right merry hungry party, to our maritime fare.

' Mrs Tims, will you be good enough to beat up another egg— we want some more milk, and that is our substitute. Major, tell the steward to fry some more ham.'

' After all, salt butter and biscuit beats everything for breakfast,' says the enthusiastic Spooner, whose verdancy is a fund of amusement to the skipper. That jovial personage bursts into a hearty laugh, and promises Spooner 'soft tommy' when he gets to Quebec. The would-be facetious ensign thinks this must mean some dish composed, as he has heard the London sausages are, of an assassinated cat, and Merryweather, between his roars of laughter, tells him that he may taste 'the cat' if he fancies it, without leaving the ship; and so they ring the changes on a sea-man's vocabulary, entirely a different language from that spoken by the English nation on shore. But the steward rushes in, having seen a shoal of porpoises to windward, bearing straight for the ship, and determined, as that confiding animal generally is, to run right under her bows. This is too good a chance of variety to be lost, and we start from our half-finished breakfasts to see the rollicking strangers pursue their course, regardless of all interruptions from small shot and ball, none of which seem to have the slightest effect on the tough hides of these marine mon-sters. There is something to my fancy extremely wild in the aspect of a shoal of porpoises, bound as it were on some especial lark, with their heads all the same way, pitching and lurching through the briny element, as though they quite enjoyed the idea of having nothing to stop them between the coast of Ireland and the Gulf of Mexico. Right under our bows dashes the ungainly convoy, and I could swear that bottle-nosed laggard, the last of the shoal, and bearing, as we all exclaimed, a striking likeness to Spooner, winked at us with his roguish little eye like some ocean-hog, as he dipped his black snout into the emerald wave, and turned up his nether-end, as if to bid us farewell. Far on our lee we watch them on their course, till the dark ruffled horizon hides them from our sight, and we talk of them as folks on shore would of the coming Derby, or the late Exhibition. If 'anything's fun in the country,' surely anything is excitement at sea. What should we do without whist?—an accomplishment that in my earliest years I foresaw it was necessary to master, and the study of which I saw turned to a tolerably profitable account.

Luncheon is over in our little ocean-home, and the dead-lights are up, for it has begun to blow rather fresh, and is evidently brewing up for a gale. The cabin is small, dark, and somewhat close, but we are roughing it now, and must not be over-parti-cular, more especially as flirting Mrs Tims bears all the disagree-ables of a transport without a murmur, and is now sitting, in the most piquante of caps, teaching Spooner backgammon. Alas! poor boy, with the guileless enthusiasm of eighteen, he is drinking in deep draughts of love from those mischievous blue eyes—sport to you, Julia Tims! but death (for the present) to poor Spooner; and the only knowledge he is obtaining of the venerable game is a conviction that his most unquestionably is a hit, hers, in all human probability, 'a gammon.' The unsuspicious, accommodating Tims and myself cut as partners, and the Fates ordained that Spooner should be roused from his happy dream to join our game in the seat opposite his commanding officer, of whom he has a wholesome terror, and to endure old Halberd's rowing in no measured terms, when absence of mind or deficiency of memory shall cause the loss of a single trick. Tims could play a little; and young as I was, I had already learned that skill in all games of chance or science was the readiest method of eking out an insufficient allowance, and administering to an extravagant disposition; so, with the advantage of superior play on our side, we 'walked into' our adversaries' stakes to as large an amount as old Halberd's pay and allowances would stand.

Game succeeded game, and rubber gave place to rubber, and the commandant waxed furious. 'Good heaven! Spooner, you trumped your partner's best again! Couldn't you see the ace was out? Why, the devil, you should bottle up your king. Any one but a born fool would have played his knave.' Poor Spooner, sitting on thorns, because Mrs Tims can overhear all these compliments, and at length, utterly confused by his own losses and his partner's ire, terminates his ill-fated performance by an unequivocal 'revoke,' and the major's ire blazes forth unchecked—'Go to your cabin, sir, and consider yourself under arrest; in the whole course of my experience I never met anything like this. You laugh, Mr Grand, and well you may, for you have won a small fortune through my partner's inexplicable conduct. Nothing shall persuade me it was not done on purpose,' foamed the exasperated major; 'but I'll have a Court of Inquiry. I'll try him for his commission. I'll drive him out of the service; by Jove, I will!'

Enter the poodle-headed steward to lay the cloth for dinner; the angry commandant, whose plumes are always smooth at that interesting hour, is easily appeased, and Spooner has the good

taste, as his *chef* has the good sense, to make no further allusions
to the row, the losses, and the arrest.   Dinner progresses favour-
ably, although we are compelled to put our plates upon our knees
and our glasses in our pockets; for the gale is increasing, and
the skipper, contrary to his usual practice, and far against his
inclination, is compelled to remain on deck.   Ere our meal is
concluded, we are startled by the unearthly notes of a speaking-
trumpet overhead, followed by a faint reply, 'We are speaking
a ship'—and off we all fly to have a look at the stranger. Pitching bows under, with a double reef in her topsails, and some of
her bellying canvas aback to enable her to hold off and on, a
dirty-looking brig looms distinctly against the dark, cloudy background.   Her master, in language that none but a seaman could
understand, is inquiring his proper longitude, his own reckoning
being of the loosest description.   She is from Buenos Ayres,
bound for Liverpool, and has no more business off the coast of
Labrador, her present position, than we should have at Gibraltar.
We set her right as to her locality, and labouring on in our diverse
courses, we part, never to meet again.   She is soon lost to our
sight, for driving mists are scudding over the face of the waters,
though an occasional warm gleam of sunshine gives a magic
charm to the scene.

'What a heavenly day on shore!' says Spooner to me, as we
paced the deck, smoking our after-dinner cigars, and ever and
anon staggering to leeward when our grasp misses the stay that
should have steadied us.   'What a day in some quiet retreat in
beautiful England, Grand, with a person—I mean with a lady,
that is,' stammered the sentimental ensign—'with a woman one
really loved.'

Spooner always confided to me what he called 'his better feelings,' such as his present idolatry of another man's wife, under
the impression that my foolish entanglement with Miss Jones
would insure my sympathy in all affairs of the tender passion.
Little did he know how that unfortunate business had seared and
hardened my young heart, and changed all the softer feelings of
my nature—how regret, remorse, and above all, a feeling of
burning shame, had taken possession of me, whenever I looked
back on that season of delirium, and made me regard the sex in

the light of an enemy on whom to be revenged at every convenient opportunity. Like many other young men, I fell into that
most fatal of mistakes, 'that all women are alike.' How absurd a
conclusion !—how disgraceful a slander on many a holy, virtuous,
I had almost said, angelic being, that makes the glory and the
sunshine of a happy home !

But I am interrupting Spooner's confidences with my reflections. As they came out between the puffs of his cigar, I confess
I was startled at the length of absurdity to which a youth of
eighteen may be carried, under the influence of a dreamy imagination. He confessed to me his adoration for Mrs Tims, or
'Julia,' as he had the impudence to call her; he never seemed
to consider Tims : he wished in the ardour of his attachment
that she would fall overboard, that he, Spooner, might have the
satisfaction of jumping after her to the rescue (not a stroke
could he swim), and shutting his eyes to the probable case of
drowning and inevitable cold bath that must ensue, he seemed
to fancy such a catastrophe would be really delightful ; then
he thought of asking her to run away with him, which was
certainly not very feasible whilst we all remained packed up
in a ship of four hundred tons ; then he fancied she might get
a divorce from Tims—a quiet, easy-going husband, that suited
her exactly, and to whom at heart she was really attached—
and that he might marry her and sell out of the army ; till
at length I ventured to ask him if he had ever mentioned
the subject, or had hinted his attachment at all explicitly to the
lady.

'Why, no, not exactly,' said the suffering youth ; 'but she is
knitting me a purse, and I told her this morning that I should
hate to arrive at Quebec, and I had never been so happy as when
on board ship.'

'And did she take the hint ?' I inquired, much amused at my
companion's cautious advances.

'Why, she said she couldn't bear the sea, and was bored to
death with the ship !' was the reply ; 'but then I think she did
that to pique me !'

The burst of laughter with which I greeted this announcement, discomposed poor Spooner dreadfully ; but I pointed out

to him the absurdity of his romance, and the ridiculous mistake he was making, to suppose that the harmless flirtation, with which Mrs Tims was amusing herself, could amount to an infatuation that should lead her to sacrifice friends, home, position, and character, for the sake of a boyish greenhorn, an ensign in a marching regiment. Unpalatable as this was, it did the poor fellow good, and I was proceeding with my lecture, in my new character of Mentor, when a cheer from between decks arose that shook the old transport from stem to stern, and looking to leeward, we descried, with a thrill I shall never forget, the first land we had seen since we left the coast of Britain.

Six long weeks had we been at sea, and truly it was a glorious as well as a grateful sight. Rising like a curtain, the mist disclosed the rugged and picturesque coast of Labrador glowing in the lustre of a magnificent sunset. And oh! the richness of those varied tints to eyes so long accustomed to the weary water and the empty sky. Again and again was the cheer caught up and repeated by our delighted soldiers, and even the rough seamen cast a grim smile at that grand iron-bound coast. It is almost worth a voyage to see land for the first time. In our inexperience, we considered ourselves as fairly arrived, and from that moment began calculations and lotteries as to when we should reach our destination. The skipper alone appeared not to join in the general enthusiasm that prevailed. I observed him several times popping in and out of his cabin for constant consultation of the barometer; and I remarked that he remained on deck when, after dusk, we retired to the well-lighted cabin, and sat in for our accustomed game at *ving-et-un*, accompanied by a special bowl of punch, brewed by old Halberd, who was a very Falstaff in all matters of drink, and who knew exactly the right proportions that make rum, sugar, and lime-juice a beverage for the gods. We were so absorbed in the changes and chances of our game, that we scarcely remarked the increasing roll of the old transport, as she creaked and laboured in the trough of a heavy sea, and the constant scuffle and tramp of feet upon the deck above us; and when I turned in, as sailors call it, for the night, to share a dormitory of some four feet square with my comrade Spooner, I was too sleepy to think of anything but the disagreeables of being roused at four to keep the morning watch, a duty which I most religiously shirked on every available opportunity.

That must have been a fearful night, ay, even to the gallant hearts on deck and aloft, exposed to the fury of the gale, and striving with might and main to put in practice all that science could teach and seamanship effect, to weather the storm. Boxed up in my stifling little cabin, I became conscious by degrees that our ship was rolling and pitching more than my previous experience would have led me to suppose possible. First my dreams became more and more incoherent and disturbed—then a tremendous lurch, that nearly sent me sprawling out of my berth, roused me to a state of complete wakefulness; and there I lay, anxiously listening to the complication of noises that surrounded me, with a horrible misgiving that this might be one of those serious cases of which every one has heard and read ; and that as ships were doubtless occasionally wrecked, why not ours as well as another? This style of reasoning was not consolatory, and I had just made up my mind to put on some clothing, go at once on deck, and learn the worst—though deterred, I know not why, by a foolish sense of shame at being the first to anticipate danger—when another tremendous lurch, a fearful pause, and a vibration as though the very timbers must part, followed by a crash as if the whole deck were breaking in upon our heads, startled me at once into activity, and I jumped on the deck of the cabin, just as Spooner, in a shaking voice from beneath his bed-clothes, exclaimed, ' By Jove, Grand, there's all the steward's crockery gone ! '

I knew better; we had immediately righted, and I felt sure something must have gone by the board. As I staggered half-clothed, and with naked feet, up the chilling hatchway, I was conscious of a buzzing murmur that made my very blood run cold—' Man overboard !—man overboard !' and then for the first time I knew that it was indeed a human voice that I had heard thrilling in agony above the crashing timber and the roaring blast. It was too true ; the captain of the foretop was at that moment choking in the blackening, boiling wave. The clear cold stars looked down in pitiless beauty on the engulfed seaman, struggling hopelessly, with none to help, with none to save. I caught a glimpse of the captain's pale and horror-stricken face, and I knew instinctively that it was folly to dream of boat or life-buoy in such a sea and such a gale. How soon might not we, too, be swept into eternity! In a second of time I pictured to myself the events of years. I saw dear old Haverley in all its verdant beauty : my poor father, ay, even Dr Driveller flashed for an instant through my mind. The favourite pursuits of my youth came across me, and I could even feel with the doomed outlaw in the stirring Border ballad:—

> 'My hounds may all run masterless,
> My hawks may fly from tree to tree;'

and then I manned myself, as I thought it was my duty to meet death, come in what shape it might, as a gentleman and a soldier. Though near, his icy hand was this time destined to grasp no other victim, and in a momentary lull, I had time to obtain a view of our position, and to exchange a cheering word or two with the gallant skipper. The night was clear and bright with stars, though blowing what sailors call 'great guns,' and the first thing that struck me was the nakedness of our spars as they danced against the sky, every inch of canvass that could be spared having been taken in. At times, I could see the whole of the vessel, as it were, plunging head-foremost away from me, as I steadied myself near the poop, and tremendous was the havoc made on her decks by a succession of heavy seas—everything had been carried away—seats, blocks, spare spars, hencoops, everything that was movable : and alas! alas! the last gigantic wave that struck her had borne to his doom honest Bill Sawyer, the smartest foretopman that ever handled sheet.

'No chance of saving him, Mr Grand,' said poor Merry-weather, with a trembling voice; 'the worst of it is over now, and this gale will lull before sunrise; but it is God's providence that we were able to wear the old ship. It was impossible to tack, and this is not a night, sir, to have the coast of Labrador under your lee!'

As I went below, I found the companion-stairs and the cabin

in a state of indescribable confusion—gentlemen in all sorts of costumes inquiring what had happened, and whether 'anything was the matter?'—all seemed to have turned out except old Halberd, who lay snugly ensconced in his blankets; and when asked by Spooner who went straight to his commanding officer's cabin for orders when he thought there was any danger, 'Whether he did not mean to turn out?' replied, 'Not I; it's no business of mine; I'm only a passenger!' As I groped my way in the dark towards my cabin, a soft hand was put within mine, and a gentle voice whispered in my ear, 'Is the danger over? . . Thank you, Mr Grand: good night.' I was soon sound asleep after all my fatigues and excitement; but not before I had offered a short and fervent thanksgiving to Providence for our escape.

Could it be the same world that was melting around us in all the gorgeous brightness of a sunny noon, as one short week afterwards we glided listlessly along between the picturesque banks, whose woods, luxuriant in their verdure, fringe the noble St Lawrence! A monarch art thou of the waters, thou magnificent river: and wondrous is thy majesty to one whose homage has been hitherto paid in ignorance to the puny wave of our own Father Thames. Historic associations, natural beauty, and early recollections hallow the latter; but what shall we say of that gigantic stream, whose volume, supplied by the inexhaustible depths of Lake Erie, sweeps on through the giddy rapids, and the wondrous plunge of indescribable Niagara, to beautify the fairest portion of a continent, and only to find repose at length in the mighty bosom of the broad Atlantic Ocean! The first impression of every European on visiting America appears to be the same. Everything is on a larger, grander, and more magnificent scale than in the old country. The rivers are wider, the forests more interminable, the storms darker, the sunshine brighter, and the skies higher, than those to which they have been accustomed at home; and obtrusive as is sometimes the Yankee's noisy admiration of his unequalled States, he has, indeed, a glorious country, and well may he be proud of it.

All disembarkations are much the same, whether the released prisoners be an apoplectic alderman, with his fat wife and nume-

rous daughters, stepping ashore at Ostend, or a draft of gallant
musketeers bidding farewell to the coop which Government has
provided for a long and tedious voyage.   Beautiful Quebec glittered as usual in the sun; and our march up to the citadel, a mile
and a half, and every inch of it against the collar, convinced us
that, as the acquisition of what sailors call sea-legs is most desirable to encounter a sou'-wester in the Atlantic, so are those same
sea-legs very numbed and paralytic members to carry their owners
up a steep and gravelled hill in anything like soldier-like style.
We were received at head-quarters—the strongly-fortified and
jealously-guarded citadel—with the welcome due to a fresh arrival
of comrades to assist in 'doing duty;' and I found that my character as a 'fast lad,' and consequently an acquisition to the mess,
had already preceded me from the depôt.   My brother officers I
discovered, with hardly an exception, to be a jovial, good-
humoured, gentlemanlike set of fellows, although one and all
were tinged with a slight affectation of slang, engendered by
foreign service, and a life of almost exclusively men's society,
but which a tour of duty in England would soon and effectually
have eradicated.

We were commanded by a character in his line; and Colonel
Cartouch deserves a slight sketch from one whose youth he so
carefully instructed in all matters connected with the sports of
the field.   Cartouch had entered the service originally in the
artillery, and with some few others had effected an exchange
from that exclusive corps to the line.   He had then been in
pretty nearly every regiment in the service, mounted and dismounted—horse, foot, and dragoons; as he himself said, 'He
had a turn at them all.'   In addition to this, during a short
interregnum of half-pay, he had joined 'the Queen of Spain's
men,' where, by his own account, he saw some little fighting,
and a good deal of flogging.   In that sunny clime he had fallen
in love with and married a Spanish girl, but of what degree, or
under what circumstances, no one could tell.   And here comes
the mystery of Cartouch's character.   He was never heard to
touch upon the history of his marriage—no one knew whether
he was a widower, or if Mrs Cartouch was still alive.   Of
course, as in all cases where nothing is known, there were plenty

of stories current,—one more romantic and more horrible than another. The Colonel had a Spanish servant, a forbidding-looking rascal as man should wish to see, but who had stuck to his master, and served him faithfully through all the ups and downs of his professional career. Rumour whispered that this fellow *once* let out in his cups a frightful history of the signora's jealousy and its consequences. Tall, handsome, of a spare athletic figure, with luxuriant black hair and whiskers, an adept at all feats of grace and skill, as at all games of chance or science; an extraordinary horseman, an unerring shot, a draughtsman of no mean pretensions, and a musician of exquisite taste, the Colonel was one to make sad havoc in the female heart; and many a fair one has loved that beautiful face, with its reckless bandit expression, 'not wisely, but too well.' He knew his advantages, none better, and pushed them to the utmost; but when first I was acquainted with him, the number of his conquests appeared only to enhance his feelings of bitterness and contempt for the whole sex.

Watched by his wife with a jealousy that I fear had too much foundation, he was at last discovered. A Spanish woman roused, and more especially by such a passion, is not a character to hesitate for fear of consequences, and the young and beautiful rival—some whispered, too near a relative—fell by the wife's hand. Nor was her revenge satisfied with one victim; like a fury she turned from her sister's prostrate form upon the horror-stricken Cartouch; and the only circumstantial evidence borne by this ghastly tale is in the fact, that whenever the Colonel's neck was bared, a long, grisly cicatrice disclosed itself, extending from ear to chin, as of one who had at some time received a deadly and frightful wound in the throat. When ladies resort to extreme measures such as these, a separation is decidedly advisable, and from that hour it was said Cartouch never saw his wife again. Assuredly, his habits were not those of married life; and whether he was not happier in a state of single-blessedness and independence, it is not for me to decide. Some affected to disbelieve the whole story of his marriage and its concluding tragedy; some said the Colonel had actually run away with the sister, and deserted her as he had deserted his wife. He never touched

upon the subject himself, nor should I have liked to change
places with that man who might be bold enough to interrogate
him with regard to it; so it is impossible to say what may be
the true version of the story. All I know is, that coming unexpectedly into his barrack-room upon one occasion, I found this
hardened and sarcastic *roué*—this man of bitter feelings and iron
heart, in tears of agony, which he vainly strove to conceal; and,
hastily covered with his handkerchief, there lay on the table a
long silky lock of glossy raven hair.

With all his faults—and they were many and inexcusable—I
could not help liking Colonel Cartouch. From the first, notwithstanding the difference of our ranks and ages, we had
become constant associates and allies. Our pursuits and pleasures were similar; the Mentor, with his advantages of experience, of course far outstripping his young competitor; but then
it was his greatest delight to instruct and train 'little Grand,' as
he called me, in all those accomplishments which we deemed so
indispensable. It was the Colonel's team which I first learned
to handle, as my instructor called it, 'like a workman.' It was
the Colonel who first taught me to tie my own flies, and throw
them to an inch, although the only unwooded space around me
was the stream I was fishing. It was the Colonel who showed
me how to 'screw' and 'twist' at billiards in a manner that
would have made my old antagonist Levanter's hair stand on
end; who proved to me *why* the sound and practical whist-
player must pull through in the long run, and *why* it was
advisable to decline playing *ecarté* with a casual stranger of
whom one knew nothing—more particularly if he happened to
be a Frenchman. His explanations simplified the whole system
of drill in the field, and regimental economy in the orderly-room,
for there were few better officers than Cartouch. His knowledge
of life and intimate acquaintance with our hospitable civilian
friends, put me quite *au fait* at all usages of Canadian society; and
reaping, as I did, all these advantages from the Colonel's friendship, it was no wonder that I was above all others prejudiced in
his favour, more especially as I fancied I could detect seeds of
good, and evidences of kind feeling, in that reckless character,
for which others did not give it credit. Of course our command-

ing officer, with his tastes and pursuits, was fond of racing. A regular attendant at Newmarket when in England, he was thoroughly awake to all the combinations and arrangements which make the turf so very ticklish a science to pursue. He knew something, besides, of Sir Peregrine's trainer, and his most unsuccessful ' string ;' and this was another bond of union between us. He owned four or five thorough-bred horses, some imported from England, some bred in the States, but all possessed of racing qualities ; and garrison cups, officers' plates, and other stakes to be contended for in both the Canadas, he carried off far and near.

I have already said that I was a tolerable horseman from my boyhood, and, under the Colonel's and his trainer's instructions, I learned to ride a race very fairly for a gentleman, and, above all, to know at what degree of speed my own and other horses were going. The latter essential is only to be acquired by repeated practice ; and many were the gallops I rode round and round the celebrated plains of Abraham—the death-scene of the immortal Wolfe—at daybreak, when even in that sunny climate the air was cool, and there was dew upon the grateful turf.

A word concerning the trainer under whose fostering care I was thus so rapidly progressing, and whom I believe to have been as big a rogue as ever went unhanged. Cartouch had picked him up at Egham races, held on the historical soil of Runnymede, where a ragged, half-starved boy, with ' Newmarket ' stamped indelibly on his precocious countenance, plucked him by the skirt, and begged piteously for one of three things, employment, a shilling, or some luncheon, for he was starving. Struck by the quaintness of the demand, Cartouch questioned the little applicant, and elicited from him that he had run away from the head-quarters of racing, for the very plausible reason that he could not get enough to eat ; that he had no home, nowhere to go. ' Where are your parents ?' was the next question. ' A'nt got none,' was the reply—' father's hanged.' ' Hanged !' said Cartouch, rather inconsiderately ; ' what for ?' ' For killing mother,' was the unhesitating answer of the candid orphan. The upshot of it was, that Cartouch took him as a cab-boy, promoted him as he grew too big for that office to a groom ; and discovered one fine morning that he had walked off without a word of notice, but had taken none of his master's property with him, not even his own livery-clothes. Why he went away remained a mystery, nor was it ever satisfactorily explained ; but the next place the Colonel met him in was the Mauritius, where he was acting body-coachman to a highly respectable widow-lady. Here he expressed a desire to re-enter his former service, and was again placed in the Colonel's stable, where his knowledge of ' training,' picked up in early life, was turned to account. Since then, he had accompanied his master's horses wherever they went, and he was now *Mr* Gamblin, a very important personage, and an immense card with all the junior officers of the 101st. I believe he had no Christian name. Such was the worthy who formed the third in a highly important conclave, carried on in a roomy stable in the immediate vicinity of the Plains of Abraham.

It was just six o'clock on a sweltering summer's morning, a few days before the Quebec races—no uninteresting meeting, and one to which the sportsmen of the States were not likely to send their worst horses—'not if they knew it.' Early as was the hour, we had been long stirring, and were thinking of breakfast. I had just dismounted, after riding a gallop on Kitty Clare, the favourite for a great stake to come off next week— ' officers up,'—and Colonel Cartouch, his trainer, and myself were in earnest discussion as to the probability of success.

' Is Squire Sauley comin' ? ' demanded the anxious trainer. ' I see him at Buffaler, and he told me he should enter Fancy Jack for the Colony Plate. If he comes, Colonel, and Fancy Jack starts, we shall have a tough job to pull through. I can't get the Squire's length, Colonel ; and what's more, I don't think any man can—they're deep 'uns, are these Yankees.'

' Fancy Jack's a smart horse,' said the Colonel ; ' but the grey mare beat him last fall at Toronto, and Kitty Clare gave *her* three pounds and a beating at Montreal ; besides, Mr Grand can ride twenty to one better than Major Muffes who piloted her that time. It *must* come off, Gamblin. Don't you think so ? ' added the Colonel, appealing to me.

I certainly had great confidence in Kitty Clare ; I had ridden her several times in matches, &c., and had always won with as little as possible to spare, so that she was not esteemed by any means as good an animal as she deserved to be. This was not so difficult a matter as many might suppose ; for, with all her speed and courage, she was gentle and tractable to a degree, and had a mouth sensitive as the finest instrument, which even the black jockeys she sometimes carried were not able to spoil. Many a rouleau, to say nothing of dollars, had she put into my pocket, as well as her owner's ; and now they were betting three to one against her in consideration of Fancy Jack's performances ; and we anticipated, indeed, a golden victory. As we cantered our hacks back to the citadel, deep and earnest was our consultation as to the best means of ascertaining Fancy Jack's capabilities ; and the Colonel, with all his experience, confessed himself to be at fault. 'I can make nothing of this fellow Sauley,' said he ; and I confess he is beyond my flight altogether. I know him well, and have been down to stay with him in his racing establishment at Baltimore. He has sixty or seventy horses in training, and only black fellows to look after them, superintending the whole thing himself. I was there for ten days, and he appeared to me to be drunk the whole time ; but had I tried to get the better of him, I have no doubt I should have found out my mistake. The way he cleaned out a southerner, a fine young Carolinian, who made a series of matches with him, was, as the Squire himself would have said, "a caution ;" and Colonel Dodge, who boasts himself "a 'cute old 'coon from Mississippi," acknowledges that he cannot hold a candle to Sauley. However, the old robber is by way of being a gentleman, and we must ask him to mess, if he does come ; and I think, Grand, you will be amused with a real Yankee character. As for Fancy Jack, I am convinced my mare can beat him if she gets fair play ; and on our own course, with officers to ride, I think it will be hard if we cannot manage that. I shall not hedge a farthing.' 'No more shall I, Colonel,' said I ; and with this doughty resolution, we separated to dress for the usual morning parade.

The eventful week arrived, and with it came Squire Sauley, much to Mr Gamblin's disgust. He brought with him several

capital horses, and amongst others the renowned Fancy Jack;
but it struck me that for a gentleman making a tour of some five
or six weeks from his own home, his luggage was sparing and
simple beyond anything I had conceived possible. One tiny
valise of shining black leather, which he carried in his hand, contained the whole necessary wardrobe of this modern Diogenes—
although, unlike that amiable heathen, no one could accuse Mr
Sauley of living entirely in his tub. I had not then travelled in
the United States, and was little aware of the many crafty
inventions, such as 'collars,' 'boosoms,' as they call them, and
other trifles, which, with that locomotive nation, supersede the
necessity of carrying about a large quantity of clean linen. The
Colonel and myself received our distinguished guest on his dis-
embarkation from the steamer, and pressed on him our hospitable
offers of board and lodging, as arm-in-arm we toiled up the steep
ascent of the lower town—the Squire retaining his luggage,
which no entreaty would induce him to part with. The day was
hot, and my new acquaintance, as he expressed it, 'a thirsty
crittur;' so each hotel we passed on our pilgrimage called forth
the same observation, 'I guess I shall go in and paint.' Three
times we 'painted' accordingly, and after two 'sherry cobblers'
and a 'mint-julep,' the Squire became extremely communicative.
We talked of his country and the 'Britishers,' and the States
army, and the 'Brady Guards,' a distinguished volunteer corps;
and I was severely catechised as to my own home and family, and
whether Haverley Hall was a 'considerable clearin';' but not
one word was dropped, although I watched for it eagerly as
a cat for a mouse, concerning the all-important topic of Fancy
Jack and the coming races. No, deep as a draw-well was the
Yankee, and he had 'a pretty loud notion 'twas not *in* the
Britishers to tree *him*, not nohow *they* could fix it;' and this
idea seemed to have taken such entire possession of his mind,
that all subjects connected with racing were as studiously
banished from his conversation as though he had been a dis-
senting parson, instead of what we should call him in England, a 'Leviathan of the turf.' We had a large party that
day to dinner; but I made it my own especial study to take care
of Squire Sauley, thinking, in the verdancy of my youth, that

under the influence of good cheer and agreeable conversation, I might be able to get something out of him. He was evidently unused to a mess-table, but, like all our brethren 'over the water,' he soon accommodated himself to such customs and usages as were new to him, more especially that of drinking wine with each other in social good-fellowship—a ceremony which he found so much to his taste as to continue it after the cloth was drawn and the claret going its rounds—thereby pledging his new friends more repeatedly than is our custom in 'the old country.'

I have said the Squire's requirements in the ways of 'purple and fine linen' were of the most moderate kind, and his ideas upon the necessity of ablution seemed to be formed upon the same simple and inartificial plan. The wine had for some time been going its rounds, and grateful was the high-flavoured vintage of Bordeaux after a day on which the thermometer had stood no lower than eighty in the shade. Captain Jessamy, who always got more and more amiable and gentlemanlike as the decanters waned, was expressing to Sauley his admiration of the latter's country, his pleasure in travelling through its noble scenery, and his approbation of its excellent and moderate hotels —the only drawback to which was the very scanty allowance of the limpid element, in the smallest of basins and ewers; 'so small, sir,' lisped 'Lavender Jem,' as we called him, 'that for three days, Mr Sauley, I give you my honour, I was obliged to content myself with washing my face and hands, and nothing more.' 'Nothin' more !' hiccupped the Squire ; 'waal ! mister ; you air particular. Look at me, mister ; my name's Sauley ! I a'nt a nigger, I aint—for fifty-seven years this child ha'nt washed, 'ceptin' face and hands on Sabbath, and often not that ! G'long hoss !' concluded our informant, with roars of laughter at Jessamy's countenance pending this candid and not over clean confession.

The fun was by this time getting fast and furious, and obeying a telegraphic signal from Cartouch, I slipped out of the mess-room, leaving my Yankee friend the centre of a listening and admiring throng of his entertainers. How pure, how beautiful was the midnight sky, its myriads of stars glittering

with a radiance unknown in our duller and thicker atmosphere !
how heavenly was the mellow lustre of the moon, bathing in
floods of beauty the silver bosom of the broad St Lawrence,
and deepening into blackness the shade of its wooded banks—
as I looked down from the Queen's Bastion on one of the
fairest scenes America can produce.   Instinctively, as we lit
our cigars, the Colonel and I paced leisurely past the sentries to
that favourite spot, and as we leaned upon a gun in uninterrupted enjoyment of the sweet summer night, enhanced by
contrast with the noisy scene of dissipation we had just quitted,
I remarked on my companion's countenance a softened expression of melancholy which I had only once before seen to settle
on those chiselled features, and I knew that his spirit was with
the days that were gone by.   Yet lively and pointed as usual
was his conversation, and in a few words he informed me that
he had reason to suppose, from what his Spanish servant told
him, that there was collusion between Gamblin and Sauley's
trainer, and that he strongly suspected it was their intention to
try their respective masters' horses the following morning, and
make their own arrangements upon the result.   It was accordingly agreed that we should be on the Plains of Abraham by
daybreak, and, concealing ourselves somewhere in the neighbourhood of the course, by means of a pair of good glasses we
should discover whether Mr Gamblin was or was not to be
depended on.   Pursuant to this arrangement, the earliest streaks
of dawn saw Cartouch and myself artistically clothed in the
least conspicuous costume, creeping cautiously along a high
thick hedge that skirts the race-ground, known to many an
exhausted jockey as 'the Marchmont Fence,' and presenting the
rather unusual spectacle of two gentlemen 'touting' their own
horse.   With the skill of a practised deer-stalker, my companion
took up a position behind an impervious thicket, and drawing a
pair of double-barrelled glasses from his pocket, carefully adjusted
them for the discovery.   We had not waited long, ere, through the
early grey of morning, we made out four figures upon the plain
busily engaged in stripping two horses, one of which, even in that
light, we had no difficulty in recognising as Colonel Cartouch's
Kitty Clare—and the other, a grey, was doubtless Fancy Jack.

Small time was wasted in preliminaries ; a couple of dwarfs were hoisted into their saddles, and away they went—making running through the dubious twilight with the utmost confidence. The first round brought them within ten yards of our covert, and their identity was placed beyond a doubt,—Fancy Jack leading, and our mare well up. The important race was to be twice round, about two miles, and it appeared that the same distance had been selected for the trial. The second time they neared us, an alteration was visible in the order of their running ; the horses were abreast, but Fancy Jack was still pulling hard, whilst Kitty Clare was striding away in her usual easy-going fashion, but having apparently nothing to spare in order to keep pace with her antagonist. Up went our glasses to see the finish ; the pace increased with startling velocity ; the little jockeys, one a black fellow, set to with a will, and gamely their steeds answered to the call. Fancy Jack came with a rush, but our gallant mare kept her place at his quarters. Short the distance to the wished-for goal, but the grey horse had evidently shot his bolt, he changed his leg, the mare drew gradually but steadily upon him, and three more strides landed Kitty Clare a winner by a length.

In a short and hurried consultation, we agreed to make a considerable *détour* on our way back to the citadel, that our presence at this important contest might not be discovered. It was evident our animal was the best ; we feared nothing else in the race now that Fancy Jack was disposed of, and we agreed that if we could only discover the weights to be correct, we would back Kitty Clare for all the money we could get on before the result of the trial was made public. ' Pedro will find that out for us : I can trust the fellow with anything : and by Jove, Grand, if it only comes off, we shall walk into these Yankees " pretty considerable handsome, I estimate," ' said the Colonel, aptly mimicking Mr Sauley's very peculiar tone and pronunciation.

From that day till the race came off, I lost no opportunity of backing the mare I was to ride. It was obvious that Squire Sauley did not fancy his horse with the fanciful name, as no consideration would induce him to invest a dollar upon the grey. This convinced me more and more that he was aware of the result of the trial which had taken place with his connivance. I gathered fresh confidence, and, like Cartouch, backed Kitty Clare to win me a small fortune, particularly with one greedy individual, a shabby American from St Louis, whose capital appeared inexhaustible, and who, it never occurred to me, might be making any number of bets on commission for another.

The first day's racing, with its successes, its failures, its heat, its noise, its flirtations, lotteries, luncheons, and sherry-cobblers, must be passed over. Captain Tims was there, having journeyed from Montreal to be present; likewise Mrs Tims and constant Spooner, ever at the fair Julia's side. But, alas! Spooner was not seen to such advantage here as on 'the ocean wave.' In an evil hour, he had allowed himself to be inveigled into riding the Wild Hawk for a hurdle-race (hurdles four feet and a-half high, warranted not to bend or break!) with which the diversions of the meeting were to close. Equitation was not poor Spooner's forte, and under the solemn conviction that he should not survive the morrow's exploit, he was nervous, absent, and dispirited, or, as Mrs Tims remarked, 'a greater gaby than ever!' At last the saddling-bell rings, the stewards call for Mr Grand, who is ready, dressed, and weighed, exact to a pound—for this have I been walking miles, wrapped in clothing under a scorching sun— for this have I abstained from Saguenay salmon, and canvas-back duck, and passed untasted the amber 'Hodson's Pale,' the ruddy 'Carbonell's '25;' and this is my reward—the moment has come. Accompanied by Cartouch, I walk up the course, the cynosure of a thousand eyes, and indubitably a hero to my own company, the privates of which back 'little Grand'—through thick and thin. Kitty Clare looks perfection, and as I am lifted on her shapely back, and pass my hand in fond caress down her arching crest, the skin is soft and smooth as satin, the muscle hard and tough as steel. 'Fit to run for ten men's lives,' says the Colonel, as he walks alongside with his hand on my knee, for a few more last words. 'Never mind the others; wait upon Fancy Jack, and come at the finish,—you remember?'

I nodded intelligence, and took my place in the snorting, impatient rank. There were five others to start, but small notice did I take of any one but Squire Sauley's, whose colours I now saw close to me, worn by a man with whom I was not acquainted, an officer of a militia corps, but of whom I had heard as a practiced and skilful jockey. From him I glanced over his horse, and for an instant a horrible suspicion darted across me that this was a bigger animal than the one I had seen from my ambush on the morning of the trial. Pshaw! it was impossible; Sauley could not have two Fancy Jacks, and it must have been the difference of light that puzzled me on the only two occasions I had seen the horse stripped. But we are for an instant in line, and at that instant the flag drops, and we are off! One hundred yards always steadied Kitty Clare, and as she settled down to her stride, I was able to make a pretty good inspection of my accompanying flight. Ere we were half-way round, it was evident to me that the others, with the exception of the grey, were running themselves out. On him I waited, and the first time past the stand, much to the astonishment of the ladies, the two favourites were far behind the field. The next half-mile brought them back to us, and now the race began. One by one they faded away, and dropped off into our rear, as Fancy Jack began to force the running, and I let my mare out to live with him—faster and faster round the turn we come, Kitty shaving the posts and economising every yard of ground. I get a pull at her head without losing my place, close upon his quarters as we enter upon the 'straight run in,' and as the distance-post glances by, I sit down to make my rush. My antagonist is likewise 'setting to,' and it will evidently be a close race, the roar of the multitude falls like a dull, dead sound upon my ear, my eye is on the grey, and everything seems whirling by us, while we alone are stationary. Whip and spur are at work, and Kitty Clare runs as honest as the day; but it will not do, I feel the stride slackening—the struggle subsiding—the mare is beat! and with a thrill of disappointment I pull her up, not without difficulty, conscious that Fancy Jack has *done* me by a short half-length.

Nothing for it but to 'pay and look pleasant,'—such are the uncertainties of a pursuit on which men spend their lives and fortunes. I was dreadfully annoyed, on Cartouch's account as well as my own. In vain the latter, with his usual recklessness,

D

strove to console me by his assurances that nothing could have been better than my jockeyship—that no power on earth could have saved the race as it was run—that the trial we had witnessed had evidently been 'a got-up thing' to deceive us. I was dispirited to a degree, and could not bring myself to take any interest in the concluding sports of the meeting, the most amusing of which was poor Spooner's dreaded hurdle race, in which he distinguished himself by a series of eccentricities performed by the ' Wild Hawk,' who was not to be prevailed upon to face the first leap, and consequently had to be brought back to his stable, guiltless of any active share in the contest, which was eventually carried off by an adventurous Yankee, who having, as he declared, a 'nervous' horse, gave the animal half-a-bottle of port-wine in a sponge, and drinking the other half himself, came in a triumphant winner. But even this failed to amuse me. I was very sore at having been overreached so completely by the Yankee squire ; nor was there much consolation in the conviction at which, on putting together all we knew, Cartouch and I arrived—viz., that Sauley, having two grey horses much resembling one another, had encouraged both 'the trial' and our discovery thereof, had thrown dust in our eyes by running his inferior horse, and declining to back the actual flyer in person, whilst he took everything he could get upon him 'by commission,' and finally brought out the real 'Fancy Jack' to carry off the stakes, the bets, and the honour and glory of ' getting pretty considerably to windward of the Britishers.'

CHAPTER III.

THE CHARMS OF THE COLONIES.

'WHEN the heart of a man is oppressed with care,' sings the time-honoured muse of *The Beggar's Opera*, to the effect that there is no period when the male heart is so susceptible to woman's charms as when suffering from disappointment, no matter from whence it arises. It was natural, then, that in my depressed state of feelings I should turn for consolation to those dark eyes that had been watching my endeavours, and that would have sparkled—oh! how brightly—at my success. Charming Zoë de Grand-Martigny! sweetest of the transplanted daughters of sunny France, flourishing in a clime whose summer is even more glowing than thine ancestors' own, what a bright specimen wert thou of Canadian loveliness, no mean type of the sex! I see her now with her long glossy raven hair; her tall, undulating form : her clear, sallow complexion; and above all, those large liquid, dreamy black eyes, that might have driven many a wiser ensign than myself out of his senses. Right and left had those orbs done execution amongst the too susceptible ranks of the British army, but no one could boast, at least with any justice—for verily upon this subject man is fearfully given to lying—but no one could justly boast of having made any impression on Zoë de Grand-Martigny. Was it my fault that, like other moths, I was attracted by the light, and fluttered round, playing at sentiment till I burnt my own fingers? or could I help the foreign Zoë taking a pleasure in what she called my English *brusquerie,* and preferring my society to that of all her other danglers, probably for the very simple reason that I was less devoted to her than the rest? 'If you would have a woman love you,' said Zoë, many a year afterwards, when, like the butterfly that has been handled, the gloss and freshness were worn off our feelings never to return, ' if you would have a woman really devoted to you, beware of letting her discover that you reciprocate the whole of her affection. Anxiety and uncertainty will enhance in her eyes the value of the treasure which she is not quite certain she possesses.' This may be true, like many other uncomfortable doctrines, but it would have been better and wiser had we never been on terms to speculate in this manner on man's weakness, or discuss subjects fraught with so much danger in such company.

In the meantime we were young, merry, and thoughtless, and never was I more aware of Cartouch's consideration, and more grateful to him for his kindness, than when he granted me an unsolicited fortnight's leave after our mismanaged race, to feast my eyes on the glories and wonders of Niagara, and as fate willed it, in the company of the Grand-Martignys, who were to spend

their usual autumnal month at that miracle of nature, and sooth
to say, as the advertisement would have it, 'that resort of fashion.'
Beautiful as is every turn in the winding length of the gigantic
St Lawrence, whose waters bore us, independent of railway and
corduroy-road, the whole seven hundred miles of our expedition,
in no portion of his course is his scenery so striking, so uncommon,
so completely fairy-like, as where he spreads into what is appropriately called 'the lake of the thousand islands.' As we steamed
along that broad unruffled surface, glistening like burnished gold
in the setting sun, and studded with islands of every size and
shape, from the undulating mass, whose rocks and woods stretching away into the distance, made us fancy we were coasting the
real bank of the river, down to the tiny islet, reflecting on its
wavering mirror the single fir-tree for whose solitary growth
alone it could find room ; as we glided on through this region of
enchantment, and paced the deck by our two selves in the drowsy
air of the summer evening, no wonder that Zoë and I both felt
the influence of the hour, and that in tones lowering more and
more as we trenched further upon the dangerous ground of sentiment and romance, we breathed forth whispers that had far
better have been left unsaid, and gave way to feelings that should
rise again like ghosts of the past to embitter with their shadowy
mockery the uncared-for 'days to come.' De Grand-Martigny
was below with his three other daughters, alas! all motherless,
and never seemed to trouble himself as to what became of Zoë.
Being the eldest—such an eldest! just eighteen—she had the
control and management of the family. Her father, an indolent,
disappointed man, who looked as if his life had been spent in
struggles, one after the other, with fortune, till he was thoroughly
weary of contention, and willing to float without effort down the
stream, was in the habit of leaving everything to his eldest
daughter, which gave her a confidence and self-reliance as far
beyond her years as it was prejudicial to her interests. He, good
man, enjoying his siesta in the cabin, never seemed to think that
Zoë and the young soldier on deck might likewise be indulging
in dreams, though not quite so harmless in their tendency, and
the moon was up when we parted for the night, unacknowledged
lovers, if truth must be told. Little had been spoken that could

bear the construction of love-making, less that could mean any-thing in the shape of a pledge; but there is a language that needs not the interpretation of the lip, and we felt that we understood one another.

Youth is not prone to analyse the feelings, and is proverbially careless of consequences, so that it can secure the enjoyment of the hour. Even then I was conscious that my feelings towards Mlle. de Grand-Martigny were purely of a selfish nature; the thought of marrying her, or indeed of marrying at all, never for an instant crossed my mind. What! should I, Digby Grand, in the flower of youth and hope, with life and all its triumphs and enjoyments opening before me, delighting in my profession, and devoted far too much to the vanities of the world—should I, with my eyes open, hold my wrists out for the matrimonial fetters, and deliberately sacrifice my own liberty to give a lady hers? Forbid it, common sense! Miss Jones had given me a lesson—so in my ignorance, I thought—as to the value of woman's love. Let poets prate about 'its priceless gem,' as they call it, if they will, I knew better the worth of the article, and firmly resolved that 'I could not do it for the money.' Still it was very pleasant living constantly with Zoë, finding her taking so deep an interest in all my doings, my likes and dislikes, my profession and my pleasures, watching her graceful form, and basking in the light of her glorious eyes; so, day after day, regardless of what might come of it, looking not one hour beyond the present, I pursued my own selfish amusement and gratification, nor cared to antici-pate the time when she, with all her earnest truthfulness, should find that she had anchored her hopes upon a dream, and I should discover that, according to the old proverb, certain classes of persons, if they will meddle with edged tools, cannot always hope to escape scateless.

Who can describe Niagara? From the loftiest harps that have hymned the praise of Nature, down to that unsophisticated fol-lower of the muse who pays his artless tribute to her glories in those glowing stanzas, commencing—

'Niagara! Niagara! you are indeed a staggerer!!!'

—vide the album kept for inspection at the Falls—that wonder

of the world has indeed suffered enough at the hands of scrib-
blers to insure an immunity from the pen of an unlettered soldier,
whose military career commenced ere the Horse Guards required
from the astonished subaltern, before he is eligible to command a
troop or company, a fund of information that would almost obtain
a position of a Senior Wrangler. The calm Lake Erie, the
whirling rapids, and the rush of the cataract, these are not to be
embodied in sentences and syllables. When the painter's brush
can realise the most gorgeous conceptions of the painter's intellect
—when the poet is able to weave the brightest colours of his
dream into a form of words that shall satisfy himself, nor leave
aught wanting to the imagination unsatiated and unsatiable,
then may we hope to read a description worthy of the indescribable Niagara—but not till then.

'What do you expect to see?' said Major Halberd to me
before I started for the Fall—'the sea tumbling down from the
moon? If you anticipate anything short of this, you will not be
disappointed!' And truly I was not disappointed. But majestic
as was this masterpiece of Nature in her sublimest mood, and
deep as were my feelings of awe and admiration in contemplating
this miracle of the waters in all its phases—in short, in doing
Niagara, which takes at least a week—there was room left in my
heart for softer emotions than those of a mere tributary worship,
and as Moore sweetly sings—

> 'If woman can make the worst wilderness dear,
> Think, think what a heaven she must make of Cashmere;'

so may I confess that many a noonday ramble, and many a
moonlight stroll, beneath the roar of the cataract was rendered
doubly picturesque and doubly delightful by the companionship
of Zoë de Grand-Martigny. How is her memory interwoven
with the scene—how vivid the impressions of all that we saw
together—how dim and indistinct all that was not brightened by
her presence! Hardly can I call to mind the crowded hotels, the
disappearing dinners, at which the hungry guests came and went
with the rapidity of the figures on a magic lantern—the well-
dressed visitors from the States, a motley crowd, with their
sallow, spare, long-haired intellectual-looking men, who might

be such a fine race, if they would only not gorge their food so rapidly, and trust their digestion so entirely to tobacco, and the pretty, delicate, small-featured women, almost French in their faces and figures, and most unmistakably Parisian in their costumes—all these have I forgotten, or at least but indefinitely remember. Ay, even the usual expedition to Termination Rock, which it is necessary for every visitor to make who piques himself on his love of adventure, and which for the benefit of those sensible individuals who have not undertaken it, I can describe as being like getting *inside* an enormous wave with no very clear idea how to get out again. Even this peep behind the curtain of the Horse-shoe Fall is fading from my mind ; but the moon-lit nights, the gleaming waters, and the sighing fir-trees, all of beauty in the sky and fragrance in the breeze, all these impressed with Zoë's gentle, mournful image, steal back upon a world-hardened heart, like gleams from some other, higher, purer, better state of existence.

And we parted in that fairyland, parted as those who dare hardly hope to meet again. That mourning brow, that eager face, so wan as it looked its last farewell, how has it haunted me in the dark night-watches of many an after year—how have I been startled by that well-remembered countenance, thrusting itself upon me, with its calm, pleading expression, in many a scene of revelry and riot in the brilliant castle-hall, as on the solitary mountain top, still grieving, still forgiving ! The idol may be shattered in the dust, but the infatuation of the worshipper shall outlive his faith. The lake of the thousand islands glittered again before me, but oh ! how changed, as I steamed back to rejoin my regiment, and a lock of raven hair, a plain jet bracelet that had encircled her dear wrist, were all that remained to me of Zoë de Grand-Martigny !

Other scenes were opening before me, almost another world, for no two seasons can present such a striking contrast—nothing can be so different as summer and winter in Lower Canada. Soon that mellow autumnal fortnight of fine weather, which is called ' the Indian summer,' glided by. It came, like the last red beams of the parting sun, to remind us of the glorious climate we had lost, and then the snow-flakes fell noiselessly, unceasingly, till the altered world was white with a covering from three to four feet deep over the plain. Then began the delights of sleigh-driving, and the winter gaieties with which the Canadians while away that long and dreary season. Capital fun we had with our driving-clubs and *in-door* pic-nics, our snow-shoeing parties and ice-mountains, to say nothing of continual dinners and everlasting balls; but my ambition had been excited to hunt and slay the mighty elk in his native forests, extending as they do uninterruptedly from Labrador to within fifty miles of Quebec, and now that balls had lost their charm, I longed ardently to be off and taste the wild delights of a life in the woods with the Indian.

Oh! the hush of those primæval forests, where silence reigns supreme and unbroken, till the very noiselessness seems to smite upon the ear. No hum of insects, no song of birds, not even the sighing of the breeze, breaks the peaceful charm in those deep endless woodlands; and then the wildness of the idea that not a living soul besides your own party, not a hut or cabin, not an acre of cultivated land, exists within hundreds of miles; and that the very spot on which you stand has, in all probability, never before been trodden by mortal foot,—the magic scene on which you gaze has been hitherto veiled to mortal eye; for in these vast solitudes, there are many nooks and corners unknown even to the few Indians who lead their roving hunter's life by lake and forest; and then, over this world of novelty, the ice-queen throws her glittering mantle, with its pure and diamond-sprinkled folds,—the fir-tree, feathered to its stem, bends beneath its load of snow,—the cataract, caught in its leap, hangs suspended in an icy chain, forming column upon column of the brightest crystal, and the broad bosom of the lake spreads away in level beauty, without a spot to soil its glistening surface, save where the track of 'caribboo' or 'moose-deer,' sole denizens of these winter solitudes, betrays the course of our gigantic game, or the impression of his snow-shoe marks the pursuit of the untiring Indian.

A merry, joyful party were we, as we burrowed in the snow, at our anticipated hunting-ground, a hundred miles and more from the out-lying log-house of the very last 'habitant;' nor would we have exchanged our unsheltered bivouac, with its enormous fire, absolutely indispensable in such a climate, and not likely to get low where miles of forests were to be had for the cutting, our sea-biscuit and pease-soup, those most palatable of provisions, and the sparkling ice-cold water, to which health and hard work gave an unspeakable flavour—for turtle and tokay in the saloons of a palace.

Our party consisted of Cartouch, ever foremost in all exploits by flood and field, Dr Squirt, the quaintest, jolliest 'medico' that ever handled lancet, and myself; whilst for our retinue we had obtained the services of an Indian chief, with an unpronounceable name; his son, a handsome stripling of some sixteen summers; a Huron, an Algonquin, and a half-bred Canadian, named 'Thomas,' jester, valet, interpreter, and cook in ordinary to the whole party. We could make ourselves understood by our Indian friends, in a sort of *patois* compounded of French, which they had picked up, and a few of their own words, which we had contrived to learn; but anything in the shape of an explanation invariably came to a stand-still without the assistance of Thomas; and the contrast between his Gallic volubility and the grave imperturbable demeanour of 'the savages' was irresistible. Long and laborious was our march up to the ground in which moose were expected to be plentiful, performed as it was upon snow-shoes,—no seven-leagued boots, even to an experienced practitioner,—and dragging with us on long narrow boards, called 'treborgons,' the few necessaries that 'a life in the woods' requires. A motley crew were we, starting every morning at sunrise from our last night's dormitory, clad in red night-caps, flannel shirts, blanket coats and leggings, of all the colours of the rainbow, artfully-constructed mocassins, and craftily-worn snow-shoes, the Indians dragging after them the treborgons, which constituted our household furniture; the whites every man armed with his rifle over his shoulder, his axe, knife, and tin cup hanging to his belt, and his blanket—a greatcoat by day, a couch and coverlet by night—strapped securely to his back; the chief himself in advance, directing our course, and appearing to find his way through that labyrinth of woods by some intuitive knowledge, some instinct of locality, possessed only by the Indian.

Thus we journeyed on, from sunrise till towards the close of
the afternoon, when approaching dusk warned us to look out for
some suitable spot to form our *cabane*, as the hole was called in
which we passed the night.   A good spring of water was the
primary object, and that found, we set to with a will, and with
one or two shovels and all the available snow-shoes, we soon
scooped out a large oblong hole, a sort of grave, capable of
containing eight persons, taking care to get quite down to the
surface of the earth.   Oh! the disappointment when, as would
sometimes happen, that surface proved to be marshy and unsound:
another place must be selected, and the whole labour begun
again.   This accomplished, a large fire was kindled in the centre
of our 'cabane,' dividing it into two compartments, and Squirt
duly attended to the commissariat, 'the pot was put on to boil.'
Meantime, one was busied in felling trees, for an ample store of
fuel; another in cutting young and tender fir-branches to form
couches for the weary travellers; another, in fetching a copious
supply of fresh spring-water; Thomas and the Doctor were
getting on with the supper, and by the time it was cooked, the
fire had blazed up into a species of furnace, whose effect was
soon visible on the walls of our habitation, crystallising the
snow into every sort of fantastic shape, our fir-branches were
dry, our blankets spread, our appetites whetted sharply as
our knives, and we were completely settled in our temporary
home.

Hunger is the best sauce, and we enjoyed our simple repast
with a zest unknown to aldermen and common-council dignitaries.
Then the delight of a sedative pipe, and the quiet drowsy conversation that preceded an early turn-in, good night, and a roll
in our blankets, were the substitutes for wine-and-water, wax
candles, and dressing-rooms; and deep was the repose that
followed, unbroken, save by an occasional shiver when the fire
got low, and the cold forced some awakened sleeper unwillingly
to rise and throw fresh logs upon the flame.   Such was often my
case, and, as I gazed upwards at the branches of the forest twining
above my head, and standing out in the glare of the fire-light,
and through them at the open sky beyond, glittering with its
myriads of stars, I rejoiced in the wild freedom of a hunter's life

—and a thrill of delight came over me, that convinced me how little removed in his inner nature is the polished denizen of civilisation, from the wild savage who roams houseless o'er the forest or the plain.

Behold us at length arrived where the giant-elk are plentiful, and settled in a home of the same description as our temporary resting-places, but as being a more permanent abode, much improved in its interior arrangements and outward decorations. Here we have screens of fir-branches erected to create a draught that shall carry off the smoke from the wood-fire, so trying to the eyes and irritating to the lungs: '*Lacrimoso non sine fumo,*' sings Horace, in his description of an uncomfortable halting-place; and truly the Epicurean bard, who knew so well how to take care of Number One, must have suffered severely from this annoyance, with his inflamed eyelids and luxurious temperament. But cleared of *boucane*, as the Canadian calls it, and embellished with sundry little fittings up from the creative axe of the Indian, our hunting *cabane* was a perfect palace by comparison; and as we smoked our pipes round the enormous fire on the first night of our arrival, we laid our plans for the morrow, with all that anticipative delight which gives their greatest zest to the sports of the field. Two Indians had been sent forward by forced marches to reconnoitre the ground, and ascertain the locality of the moose, and as they dropped in separately with their reports, Cartouch, who took the management of the party, arranged for us our next day's beat. 'The Algonquin has tracked a good herd nearly to the lake, about two leagues from here,' said he; 'Squirt and I, with the double-barrelled rifles, might, I think, manage the whole of them; but the Huron is full of an enormous moose, whose ravage (the place trodden and bruised where the animal has been browsing) he has discovered on the hill beyond what he calls the Rivière Blanc; only he thinks he disturbed him, for his footmarks are away down the river pointing for the Batiscon. It will be a devilish long stalk, Grand; but you are the lightest weight, a great pull on snow-shoes, and the keenest,' he added, with a half-melancholy smile; 'so perhaps you would like to give an account of this out-and-outer.'

I jumped, of course, at the idea; and it was accordingly

arranged that I should be off by daybreak the following morning, under the auspices of the chief himself—that veteran
having taken a great fancy to his young *protégé*, and being
extremely anxious that I should have a successful *chásse* for my
debút.   I could hardly sleep for thinking of my first shot at an
elk; and as Cartouch said, when I awoke him for the third
time, as I fidgetted from under my blanket to see if daylight
would *ever* come—'You are so very uncomfortable, Grand, one
would suppose you were going to be married instead of being
safe in the woods.'

Dawn arrived at last, as it always does, if you only wait for
it; and the first streaks had hardly 'dappled into day,' before
the Indian chief and I were striding up the wooded hill that
overhung our *cabane;* the savage, as usual, leading, and his
follower husbanding his strength for the work that he knew
was in store.   A little Indian dog, who rejoiced in the name of
Toko, was our only companion, and with the sagacity of his
race, persisted in walking so closely upon my tracks as to catch
the heels of my snow-shoes, and threaten to throw me down at
every step.   On we toiled, silent as the grave, over the top of
the hill, down into a ravine, across a lake, up another mountain
whose crest had been for some time frowning over us, and ere
this the sun was up in the heavens, and throwing his glorious
light over the scenery of a dream.   Never did I see such a view
as burst upon me when I gained the summit of that laborious
ascent.   Far as the eye could reach, an expanse of hill and dale,
mountain, lake, and river, all glittering in the morning beams, as
though sprinkled with an infinity of diamonds: woods, feathered
with their snow-coverings in every sort of fantastic shape, clothed
the land: a broad, unsullied garment of driven snow wrapped the
frozen waters.   Far before me, cleaving the deep blue sky, rose
the clear white peak of the hills beyond the Batiscon—one of
the few rivers in these solitudes that can boast of a name, and
which forms a kind of landmark to the Indians.   It was a vision
of enchantment—a peep into fairyland; and made me doubt
whether Nature might not be more beautiful in these wintry
robes of state, than when clothed with all the luxuriant verdure
of 'leafy June.'

What a curious thing is the association of ideas! I began to think of Zoë, and the bracelet, and the lock of hair, when I was startled from my reverie by the abrupt halt of the chief, who, wheeling rapidly round, confronted me with a startling look of almost fierce triumph.   Not a word had he said, good or bad, since we started—not once had he condescended to look back and ascertain how his panting white friend was getting on ; but now he marked my gaze wandering over the panorama spread out before me ; he felt my admiration, and was flattered by it, and drawing up his spare sinewy frame to its loftiest proportions, he waved his outstretched arm towards the four points of the compass, then smiting his expanded chest, and stamping with his foot once upon the snow, while his eye kindled, and his nostril dilated like that of some roused thorough-bred horse, he exclaimed with a dark flush of pride I shall never forget, '*C'est ma chasse!*' —then turning rapidly away, dived like a hound stooping to the scent into a tangled ravine, where first began to appear signs of the presence of our game.

Enormous footmarks, as though some cloven-footed elephant had been trampling the snow ; branches bent and broken, tender saplings gnawed and bruised, disclosed the ravage of the moose ; but he had been alarmed the previous day, and he was off. Like a very bloodhound, the wily Indian slotted him through the perfect labyrinth of his footmarks, as he had strayed hither and thither over his feeding-ground before he was disturbed, till even as a skein is unravelled, he hit upon the true course by which the scared giant had made away.   Once, and once only, the shrill war-cry of his tribe rang from his lips, and bending with redoubled ardour to the task, he strode on in pursuit at a pace which gave me but little breath for the 'tally-ho!' with which I astonished those venerable woods.   On and on we went ; the chase had commenced in right earnest, and a keen excited Indian on snow-shoes takes a deal of catching.   I was young, I was light, and above all my blood was up, as that mysterious fluid will rise at nineteen only, and I held my own as best I might. Small leisure had I for the wonders through which we passed ; boughs discharged their frozen shower in my face, concealed roots caught the toes of my snow-shoes, and over I went—arms in-

stinctively thrust forward to save, struck shoulder deep into the
treacherous surface, and my face buried itself in the blinding
snow. Up and at it again. The Indian is forward, and the elk
is before the Indian—this is what I have dreamt of for months.
An Englishman must never say die: and panting, weary, and
dishevelled, I toil on in the footsteps of the hurrying chief down
another hill, and on to the firmer surface of the Riviére Blanc.
Here the wind sweeping up the course of the stream has cleared
it of snow for many a long mile; and taking off our snow-shoes,
to our unspeakable relief, we follow the scarcely visible footmarks
at an increased pace. There is little time to spare, but at a
winding of the river my steps are forcibly arrested by a scene of
startling magnificence. A bluff, perpendicular crag rears its
broad front before me, adorned like the façade of some magic
palace, with long glittering columns of the clearest crystal.
The volume of a cataract leaping from its brow has been arrested
in mid-air, as though by some icy charm; and there it hangs
spell-bound, the gigantic icicles forming each a natural shaft that
art might strive to imitate in vain.

But short the pause of wonder and delight, for the chief is
still before me, and the sun is high in the cloudless heavens. I
am getting really beat, and a half-suspicion crosses my mind
that it is possible we may lose our quarry after all. Hark!
infusing new life into my veins, the Indian's war-cry strikes
once more upon my soul, and Toko, with bristles erect and eyes
flashing, bounds to the front. The tracks of the moose have
turned off the wind-swept river into the deep snow, and now we
shall have him—another twenty minutes must see us run into
him, enjoying as we do the advantage of snow-shoes, whilst
every stride he makes buries his long legs up to the knee. The
chief stops to help me on with these auxiliaries, and again we
plunge into the sombre forest. Ha! there is blood on the snow
—our game is distressed—poor beast! he cools his thirsting lips,
and cuts his sensitive muzzle in the frozen element as he labours
on; the pace and the distance are beginning to tell; it cannot
last much longer, and now I hear faithful Toko baying furiously
ahead. Who talks of fatigue? With a rush I come up alongside of the quiet, wary Indian, and passing him recklessly, push

forward in the direction of the sound. Where the trees and underwood grow most impervious, I catch a glimpse of a huge dark object swaying up and down through the tangled branches; at last I am face to face with an elk in its native forest. As I approach him, I become aware of his enormous, and, sooth to say, his ungainly proportions; and rapt in astonishment, I gaze on him, hardly thinking of destruction, till the chief coming up, puts my rifle into my hand, and warns me not to approach too closely. '*Il est malin, le sacré original,*' says he in his mongrel language, *original* being Indian for elk, and I can see by his red, lowering eye, that the unceasing attentions of Toko have raised his ire to the utmost. Often he strikes out at the dog with his long fore-legs, but he is too much blown and exhausted to reach the little aggressor, who remains at a cautious distance.

The caps are not quite firm on the nipples of my rifle, and as I press them carefully down, I keep advancing to within a few feet of the infuriated animal. All this time he has been regaining his wind, and with a desperate rush he makes for me as his most tangible enemy. Luckily the snow is deep, and a friendly tree is near: the next bound would have brought him upon me, but I step aside behind the sheltering trunk, and as he passes within three feet of me, I let drive at him with both barrels: the bullets crash through his heart, and he rolls over on the snow, never to rise again. Game to the last, he dies rearing his head into the air, whilst his frame is stretched quivering in the death-struggle, and, strange concord! an English who-whoop rings mingled with an Indian war-cry through those Canadian solitudes. From hoof to shoulder the giant measures an honest seven feet, and proportionate to his bulk are my triumph and delight.

Never shall I follow the moose through those glorious solitudes again—never more shall I associate with the true, unpolluted, and noble-spirited Indian, savage though he be, the man of unstained faith and indomitable energy, the eagle eye, the ready hand, and the undaunted heart. But often in the trammels which accompany the comforts and luxuries of civilisation, doth my spirit long for the hush of the uninhabited forest, for the wild fresh breeze of the trackless prairies, and fain would I re-enter once again the red man's lodge, fain live once more the free inartificial life of the Children of the Woods.

CHAPTER IV.

THE GUARDS.

OF all sorts of soldiering, from the dashing light dragoon to the scientific sapper and miner—from the staid and steady infantry-man to the 'flying bombardier,' as our distinguished horse artillery are somewhat irreverently nicknamed by their brethren of the sword—of all these accomplished practitioners in the science of manslaughter, commend me to the Guards. Their discipline, though yielding to none in the exactitude with which it is carried out, weighs more lightly on officer and soldier than that of any other corps ; their services it is unnecessary to mention, as it is well known that wherever glory is to be gained, wherever hard knocks are to be taken, and distinction to be won, the privilege of the Guards has ever been to woo honour in the thick of it. Their officers are perfect gentlemen, and thorough *bons camarades ;* their stalwart privates are smart and steady in the field, as, considering the temptations of London, they are well-conducted in barracks ; and their non-commissioned officers, that vital third estate in the well-being of a regiment, are beyond all praise. When we combine with these essentials the advantages of being quartered in the metropolis of the world, in the very centre of civilisation and refinement, we cannot wonder that a commission in the Guards is the grand desideratum to a young man wishing to enter life and service through the same portal—is an object of emulation (not envy) to his brother warriors in the rest of the British army.

But there are two sides to every question. Even a sovereign, unless it be one of those skilful deceptions with which unprincipled jokers toss for the score of a Greenwich dinner—even a sovereign has its reverse; and great as are the advantages of a London life—manifold as are the benefits of what is emphatically called 'good society;' yet on the other hand, pleasure in the metropolis assumes her most alluring garb. Youth is seldom skilled in resistance to temptation. Money melts like snow before the sunbeam; debts accumulate like drifts in the storm; and we all know how soon a man involved becomes reckless —how soon recklessness merges in despair. Ambition, when restrained by principle, is a fine thing—emulation, in all matters of usefulness, is a fine thing. To the constant upward tendency of mankind we owe the multiplying discoveries of science, the increasing prosperity of a nation. But all this may be carried too far. And who that watches with impartial eye the struggle going on around him—who that looks calmly on at his neighbour 'caring too much for these things,' will deny that society, in all its ranks, is irritated with the fevered desire of coping with that which is immediately above it—that the nobleman must imitate the sovereign, the gentry vie with the noble; the tradesman and the farmer ape the gentry; whilst the lower classes, divided by too wide a gulf to be able to compete with what they call 'well-to-do people,' would, many of them, fain pull down to their own level those ranks to whose superior station they cannot themselves hope to rise? Let the reformation begin at the top—let the better educated and more reflective be content to 'do their duty in that state of life in which Providence has placed them,' and we shall hear less of public ruin and private destitution — we shall be spared the anomaly of gentlemen by birth being compelled to support the exigencies of their 'false position' by actions which their chivalrous ancestors would have blushed to own—we shall be told no longer in the clubs, or on 'the Heath,' that the Hon. Mr This is celebrated for his 'very sharp practice;' or the noble Lord That is a 'deuced ticklish fellow to deal with about money-matters.'

But no misgivings had I as I embarked triumphantly on the career before me, and walked down St James's Street in the pleasant consciousness that I was young, well-dressed, and possessed, for my age, of considerable knowledge of the world. Sir Peregrine for once had exerted himself—my wishes were crowned, and I was an ensign and lieutenant in the Guards. Fair heads were bowed and taper fingers kissed to me, as high-conditioned, good-actioned horses whirled landau, brougham, and barouche along the clattering stones; and I lifted my hat in return with unabashed coxcombry, for Lady Overbearing had voted me good-looking, and said I made a capital bow. Well-whiskered, portly *roués* nodded good-humouredly to me from the bay-window of White's, and the murky morning-room at Crockford's; for it was allowed that 'young Grand was a nice gentlemanlike boy;' and that point being established, and his intention of ruining himself and family clearly ascertained, he might have committed all the crimes in the calendar, levanted and robbed the mail, without suffering any diminution in the good opinion of these arbiters of their own world. Already had I been elected a member of Crockford's—already criticised the unpaid dinners, for which, on the principle of indirect taxation, the 'round room' up-stairs compensated so handsomely. Ay, and more than this, I was in the fair road to become one of the *élite* 'over the way.' Two kind friends —a yachting marquis and a dropsical dandy—had persuaded me to face the dread ordeal of 'the ballot:' and had offered their services as 'proposer and seconder'—good offices that, by the way, I have known filled by those who were themselves the very first to blackball the unsuspecting novice.

'Grand, why weren't you at the Opera last night? Rivolte was capital, and looking so pretty.'

'Why, I dined with old St Heliers to meet Grandison, as I was to go on guard with him to-day. What a nice fellow he seems!—but not so fast as his brother, who might be his father, to all appearance.'

'Yes, Grandison is a fresh young-looking fellow of his age; but then he was campaigning when his elder brother was playing the devil; and sitting up all night, and every night, with claret, whist, hot suppers, large cigars, and continual hazard takes it out of a fellow more than all the fighting in Alison's "History" or the Duke's "Despatches." I dare say you had a cheery party there yesterday?'

'Very. And my Lord would not let me go, but kept me to

play whist in what he calls his boudoir. I had a very good night, for there was a light-haired fellow there whose name I did not catch, that was innocent of the game as a new-born babe; and he *would* play so high, that I won a cool hundred of him. St Heliers wanted to have " lansquenet" after that, but the room was so full of cigar-smoke, my unknown friend could not stand it, so I got home by three o'clock.'

' Well, I wish I had had your luck. I swore I would not go to Crocky's, so I dropped in upon that brute Meadows for some supper after the Opera, and lost three hundred. There was a fellow in some line regiment there, who kept backing out, and won enormously. I think Meadows said his name was Levanter.'

' I know him,' said I, as a crowd of recollections came rushing upon me; and Hillingdon not caring to press the subject, the matter here dropped, and the conversation took some other turn. ' The relief is ready, sir,' said a tall soldier-like corporal, as, with military respect, he entered the small dingy apartment at St James's, in which the above discourse was carried on. And I may take the opportunity of Hillingdon's absence in the performance of his duty as lieutenant of the Queen's Guard, to describe the brother officers with whom I was associated in the pleasant task of keeping watch and ward at St James's.

In the first place, then, to begin with the captain of the guard, who, it is hardly necessary to remark, holds the rank of a licutenant-colonel in the army. The Hon. D'Arcy Grandison was the beau-ideal, the very type of a thorough guardsman. Of noble birth and aristocratic bearing, the Colonel was as distinguished for his high unsullied sense of honour in the world, as for his daring gallantry in the field. Respected at the Horse Guards, he was yet beloved by the ensigns, and many a young man owes his preservation from vice and ruin to Grandison's friendly admonitions and bright example. Heir to Lord St Heliers—and verily it must have been a strict entail that could preserve any reversion from that grasping *roué*—Grandison's portion as a younger child had received no addition from his spendthrift brother; and he had risen by his own exertions and military success to the position which he now held. He had made a love-match with a lady of his own rank, but of no larger fortune;

yet, with an increasing family, everything seemed to prosper with
him. It was a noble sight to see that fine soldier-like man, with
his Waterloo medal on his breast, walk into the Colour Court,
accompanied by his lovely wife, and two or three beautiful children, to hear the band of the regiment, of which she was as proud
as the Colonel himself. The officers liked him, the men adored
him; and if there was any person in the world for whom his
selfish brother cared one snap of his fingers, I do believe it was
D'Arcy. Such was the officer to whom I had been introduced the
previous evening at Lord St Heliers' table, and under whose command I carried the Queen's colours into the palace of St James's.

Hillingdon may be described in fewer words. A quiet, good-
tempered, and gentlemanlike man, with abilities far above the
average order, and which might have won him fame had his
circumstances obliged him to cultivate them. As it was, he possessed an easy fortune, which he was doing his best to destroy.
Another victim to the fascination of play, that appeared the only
pursuit which could prick him into excitement—the greatest of
luxuries to an imperturbable disposition like poor Jack Hillingdon's. Alas! his eventful fate may be summed up in those few
words that have told the career and the catastrophe of many a
bright intellect and many a kindly heart : 'He was a good fellow;
but he was ruined by gambling.'

Of the others, D'Egville was young, conceited, and a beautiful
dancer. Lord Maltby, unaffected, good-humoured, and a York-
shireman—bored with ladies, but very happy at mess—rather
uncouth in his manners, but a capital judge of a horse, and a
most undeniable bruiser.

Strictly as the discipline of the Guards is carried on in all
matters of real importance, it is not to be supposed that so essential a department as the commissariat can be neglected, and an
excellent dinner furnished at St James's daily for those officers
whose duty demands their presence there, is an economical substitute with her Majesty's Government for officers' barracks,
allowances of coals, candles, &c., for all of which this very well-
cooked repast is, by a pleasant fiction, supposed to be a complete
equivalent. Eight o'clock strikes as two of the Blues come
clinking up from the Horse Guards to join the mess. There is

one vacant seat at the Colonel's disposal, and it is filled by a guest in plain clothes, of the mildest manners, and most unassuming deportment; and yet that quiet old grey-haired man is a major-general, who led three forlorn hopes in the Peninsula, and whose frame, scarred by sabre-cut and riddled by musket-shot, has withered beneath the burning sun of our Indian peninsula. I face the Colonel, who takes the top of the table; and soon we are all engrossed in that lively and varied conversation so surely engendered by the good-fellowship of a mess. 'Grand! a glass of wine.' 'Maltby, have you been to Jem Burn's lately? They tell me he has got a black fellow that is to come out a wonder.' 'Hillingdon, do you like your box at the opera as well as the one we had last season?' 'How do you go to the Derby? Marygold can't win.' 'By the by, I saw a horse at Tattersall's yesterday that Maltby ought to buy.' 'Would he make a charger?' Such is the recitative going on amongst the younger portion of the company; whilst, at the upper end of the table, the older officers are engaged in lively discussion on the merits of a newly-invented shell, and the general is describing, almost in a whisper, the particulars of an exploit from which he was taken away for dead, and for which he received 'the Bath.'

Presently the evening wears on, till, after a very temperate symposium (for we are on guard), the hoof of Napoleon's favourite charger, Marengo, set in gold, and converted into a gorgeous snuff-box, makes its rounds. Ten o'clock strikes. The general departs; the officers betake themselves to their respective guards; and Colonel Grandison, in cloak and bear-skin cap, proceeds to visit the different sentries.

Apollo does not always keep the bow strung to its utmost tension, nor are the clustering curls of the Guardsman—a crop farmed by Willis with such protective care—constantly concealed beneath the frowning terrors of his bear-skin cap. The routine of military duty is pleasantly varied by the smiles of beauty, and wheeling evolutions in the field are gladly exchanged for the mazy dance. Ay, the lamented hero of a hundred fights, the iron warrior of the age, was himself a ball-goer and a ball-giver; nor was a card for Apsley House the least coveted invitation amongst the gaieties of the season. Such was 'the pasteboard' that greeted my eyes on a well-covered breakfast-table in my comfortable lodgings in Park Street, and for one of those magnificent *fêtes* I attired my person with the utmost care some few evenings afterwards. From the sombre inside of a box upon wheels, from the dusky street and the dirty crowd, the transformation was instantaneous to a blaze of light illumining the splendours of the warrior's palace. It was dazzling, but delightful ; and I felt within me the butterfly nature that experiences a keen sense of pleasure from the mere contemplation of a mob of well-dressed well-born men and beautiful women, met together avowedly for the purpose of appearing to the best advantage—always premising that the butterfly himself is part and parcel of such a pageant. Reflection is not a matter of hours in a dark room with a dry volume. Self-communing may take place in a second of time, surrounded by all that can enchant the eye and excite the feelings. In the short interval that elapsed between leaving my carriage and entering the ball-room, during the putting on of one kid glove, and the translation of my unassuming name from mouth to mouth as 'Mr Grand,' 'Mr Brand,' 'Mr Lang,' until ushered into the presence of our noble host, under the aristocratic title of 'Mr Sam !'—in those few seconds I had time to say to myself, 'Digby, this is the life for you—this is the element in which you can really exist ; for this be contented to sacrifice comfort, competence, friends, fortune, and self-respect.' I had not then applied the chemistry of experience to separate the metal from the alloy—the test of time to recognise the true from the counterfeit. I was satisfied to take things and people as they were, nor trouble myself about that period which, sooner or later, overtakes us all, when we are startled to discover that we have lavished the worship of a life-time upon idols—that we are lonely and helpless at our need—because, forsooth, 'our gods are clay.'

'What a pretty ball, my dear !' says fat Lady Trunnion to shaky Mrs Marabout. 'How well dear Jane is looking—quite lovely, I declare. Has she been dancing much ?' How pleased she is to hear that Jane, who suffers from a lack of partners, poor girl ! has not danced at all ; so there is a better chance for Lady Trunnion's three, one of whom is pretty ; and the other two, flirts. 'How d'ye do, Mr Grand. Mary, Mr Grand, my daughter! I think you know Selina?' But Mr Grand, though a young bird, is not to be caught by chaff, and bows himself away without requesting the honour for the next dance, as was intended by artful mamma.

'Who is he?' whispers Mrs Marabout to her next neighbour, chattering Lady Jay.

'Sir Peregrine Grand's son—the eldest, my dear. *Will* be enormously rich, I fancy. Goodish-looking; but has got into a wild set.'

'I know you are not weak enough to dance, Grand,' says Maltby, lounging up to me—'at least, not without a reason; so come with me. Mrs Man-trap has asked to be introduced to you. A great compliment, by Jove! She is not much in my line; but I want to get away to go to Jem Burn's; so having performed one good action, I shall cut *my* stick with an easy conscience.' With these words, the good-natured peer brought me up to a particularly well-dressed lady, who, at the first glance, I could see was *crépé*, 'flounced,' and 'got up,' in a manner which left no doubt of her aspirations after universal conquest. Notwithstanding a beautifully rounded figure—if it had a fault, somewhat too *embonpoint* for her height,—notwithstanding a merry blue eye, a saucy smile, a skin like alabaster, and a profusion of showery light hair, my first impression of Mrs Man-trap was disappointment at those charms of which I had heard so much; and I whispered to Maltby, as we approached, 'Not half so handsome as I expected, but devilish well-dressed.' Little did I suspect the fascination which she exercised over all that came within range of her artillery. How low, in my ignorance, did I estimate the power of the sorceress. But I was doomed, like many a wiser man, to fall down and worship where I came only to gaze and criticise. Gradually and insensibly the charm stole over me. Lights were glittering and fairy forms were flitting around; beauty and perfume steeped my outward senses in enjoyment; and the brazen *refrain* of some 'waltz of Paradise' wafted ecstasy to my soul: and so I stood as one entranced, leaning over the chair of that witch in muslin, and sustaining my part in a conversation that became every moment

more dangerous. 'She don't care for him, the baby-bride!' said
Mrs Man-trap, speaking of a young couple who then passed us.
'Fresh from the nursery, and in all the first bloom of girlhood,
depend upon it, she can spare no time from the world and its
"engagements" to waste upon her husband. She has not yet
learnt to *feel,* poor child! And if her mamma had told her to
marry a bishop, she would have liked him just as well. A
woman must have suffered, Mr Grand, before she can really
love; and then if her attachment is fixed upon a boy—on one
younger than herself, who is, day by day, making good his footing in that world which is gliding from *her,* she is deserving of
pity indeed;' and the blue eyes looked up into mine, with a
soft, pleading expression that was irresistible, the saucy features
changed for an instant, as a shadow of deep thought stole over
her brow, investing her with that sorrowing, chastened beauty
which the hand of Time reserves for those who are no longer in
the early freshness of youth—rich amends for all the dimples
and roses of laughing girlhood. What wonder that I forgot our
acquaintanceship was but of three-quarters of an hour!—that I
gave myself up to the delirious intoxication of my position! and
shutting my eyes resolutely to all I had heard of the lady herself—a runaway match, a divorced husband, a brother shot in a
duel, and a father who died of a broken heart—that I talked
sentiment deep and devoted as her own; and vowed, in the
despicable hypocrisy of my heart, that 'the love of a silly girl
was unworthy of a man.' I spoke the last words in a somewhat louder tone than that in which our whispered conversation
had previously been carried on, so much so as to cause a lady
who was passing to turn her head towards the impassioned
speaker: with a thrill of shame and remorse amounting to
agony, I recognised the massive black hair, the pale and careworn features of Zoë de Grand-Martigny. Luckily, at that
moment, I felt my arm touched by Colonel Grandison, who had
come across the room to present me to his wife; and in the confusion of an introduction, my emotion escaped notice. I resolved,
however, to seek an interview with Zoë immediately, to ascertain
why she was in England, and express to her my unaltered feelings; for, strange to say, that gentle, sorrowing face exercised

the same power over me here in the midst of London's noblest revel, as beneath the silent moon and cloudless sky that look calmly down upon the turmoil of Niagara.

From room to room I bowed, and glided and edged my way upon the fruitless search. I tore a countess's skirt, and trod upon a duke's toe. I passed Lady Overbearing, without the slightest token of recognition; my heart was with Zoë on the Lake of the Thousand Islands, and I toiled on in vain. Could it have been a vision sent to warn me, or was it my Canadian love thus assisting in the body at a London ball? I had pictured her to myself many thousand miles away; I had been haunted for months by that calm face, with the very same expression that it bore as she passed me a few minutes ago; the same agonised look that had once seemed to bid me an eternal farewell; and now she was in the room, in the house, and I could not find her; it was heart-breaking—it was maddening. The lights danced around me, the gaudy crowds swam before my eyes, while ever and anon a strain of music from the dancing-room arose fitfully, like the wail of a lost spirit, or the mocking laugh of a demon, and combined to drive me well-nigh out of my senses. At length, in despair, I was compelled to seek the cooling atmosphere of the open street; and it was with a beating brain, and a sickness at my heart, that I staggered down those broad and stately steps which I had ascended so triumphantly but two hours before.

'Are you for St James's Street, Grand?' said Hillingdon's well-known voice, as he put his arm within mine, and proffered the soothing refreshment of a cigar to my excited nerves.

'Anywhere,' said I, wildly,—'anywhere for excitement; Jem Burn's, Crocky's, Meadows', or the Devil—it's all the same to me.'

And so it was; all I wanted was to escape reflection, and another minute saw my companion and myself cooling our brows in a Hansom's cab, hastening to the emporium of a retired prize-fighter, where we might see two redoubted champions of our species pommel one another to their hearts' content, and then 'walk round and show themselves' in all the unsavoury triumph of first-rate muscular condition.

'Any orders, gen'lemen,' said a dwarfish waiter of the dirtiest description, as, flourishing his dingy napkin, he dodged about a small square apartment, with an area in the centre, on which, as on a stage, the science and tactics of the ring were being displayed. On three sides of the lists were ranged the goodly company, none of the choicest, but numbering in their equivocal ranks some stalwart frames, and honest, courageous-looking countenances. On the fourth side a wooden bar stretched completely across the room, partitioning off an alcove at its extremity into a species of private box, where the hospitable 'Jem' received his more aristocratic visitors, and to which, as 'Corinthians,' or 'swells,' we were immediately admitted. Here we found Maltby completely in his element, an enormous cigar in his mouth, a comforting glass of brandy-and-water at his elbow, and his elaborate costume of white neckcloth, studs, and ball-going suit of sables, covered by a rough and venerable pea-jacket. He was busily engaged in watching the preliminaries for an amicable set-to between the 'Battersea Snob' and 'Nappy Jim,' or the 'Sprig of Seven Dials,' two dwarfish heroes, who were now exchanging a cordial shake of their gauntleted hands previous to an uncompromising encounter. 'Won't ye do as we do, gentlemen?' said our host, offering a tankard full of champagne and a box of tempting 'weeds.' 'We may as well wet our whistles, while these little chaps give and take a belly-full.' And as we lit our cigars, and prepared for a good view of the proceedings, we saw, by the manner in which pots of beer were set down untasted, and pipes removed from sundry queer-looking countenances, that each stunted Hercules was an object of intense interest and admiration to his own backers in that motley assemblage. I confess to a partiality for a glove-fight—a fine athletic exercise, it develops the muscular vigour, and, to a large extent, the mental resources, of the combatants, without any of the brutality, the butchery, of an actual prize-fight. It exhibits the same amount of activity, the same fine proportions and commanding attitudes, the same presence of mind in difficulties, the same generous forbearance to a fallen foe; nor does it disgust the eye and shock the feelings by the spectacle of a brave man, reduced to helplessness through punishment and exhaustion, struggling gamely on, when over-taxed nature has cried, 'Enough!' It is, in short, a tournament in place of a combat à *l'outrance*; and to those who own to an affection for manly and athletic exercises, a rattling 'set-to' between two proficients cannot fail to be an interesting sight. There is much to be said for and against our national practice of prize-fighting. Its enemies do not hesitate to denominate it 'a brutal exhibition;' its friends and supporters seldom go further than admitting that it is 'a necessary evil;' but without entering upon the oft-repeated arguments, sustained by such expressions as 'Old English pluck,' 'British love of fair play,' 'cowardly recourse to the knife,' 'bull-dog courage,' and 'never hit a man when he's down'—it must be acknowledged that the history of the P. R. records instances of gallantry and heroism that would not have disgraced the romantic chivalry of the middle ages. When the famous Jackson, 'champion' of Eng-land, breaking his leg in the second round of a prize-fight, requested to be allowed to sit down, and offered to finish the battle in a chair, he presented no bad specimen of that spirit which, under other circumstances, and with other opportunities, has made the name of Englishmen a type of all that is resolute, daring, and invincible. We have a high authority in the expres-sion of Napoleon, that 'they never know when they are beaten.' But in the meantime, the 'Sprig of Seven Dials,' after a miraculous display of science, tactics, ingenuity, and activity—after a vast deal of scuffling, struggling, and kicking up the dust—after many a sound thwack and lightning parry, at length finds his head under the griping arm of the 'Battersea Snob,' who rains down on that unprepossessing countenance a shower of blows that but for the muffle which covers his relentless knuckles, would present a ghastly spectacle indeed.

'The Sprig is in chancery,' says mine host,' removing a cigar from his lips; 'walk round and show yourselves;' and the pant-ing combatants, untwining from the close embrace of strife, proceed to regain their breath, as they strut round the arena, displaying to their admirers two very ugly faces, two wiry, muscular, and hardy-looking frames.

'A shower of browns,' the coppers mingled with silver from

our private box, rewards their exertions ; and a call of ' Time '
from our landlord stimulates them to fresh activity, or, as Maltby
says, putting on his hat to accompany us back to St James's
Street, ' They take a suck at the lemon, and at him again.'

We were in the act of leaving the door, when a tremendous
' hullaballoo,' and loud voices in angry altercation, caused us to
return in time to see reduced to practice those principles of
self-defence which had lately been witnessed in theory.   A tall,
savage-looking negro was standing in the bar, and with all the
volubility of his race when excited, was abusing all who came
near him, and, as he dwelt upon some unintelligible grievance,
working himself into a passion that was frightful to behold.   At
length, grinding his ivory teeth, while the whites of his eyes
rolled with rage, he addressed an epithet to our hostess, a most
respectable woman, that roused Maltby's chivalrous ire to the
utmost, and being a large, powerful man, and an accomplished
fighter, he would soon have annihilated the black, had he not
been checked by the stalwart arm of our host.   ' He is not big
enough for you or me, my lord ; we should kill him,' said he,
laying his heavy hand on the chafing nobleman.   ' Here, Buster,
this darky's getting troublesome ; come and put him out.'   I
looked round to see the champion who was to accomplish this
dangerous feat ; and, to my astonishment, recognised the dirty
little waiter, who came tumbling out at the summons in the most
business-like manner imaginable.

The contrast was too ludicrous between the tall well-grown
negro, and the diminutive, quiet little Londoner, and the first
blow aimed by the child of the sun must, I thought, have demo-
lished his adversary.   Not so ; it passed harmless over the waiter's
bushy head, and the little man rattled in his ' one, two,' in return,
with a force and velocity that sent the black down as if he had
been shot.   Once more Sambo made his attack, butting with
his woolly head at the active little combatant ; and once more,
foiled by science and agility, he measured his length upon the
floor, this time in the immediate vicinity of the door, through
which he found himself bundled into the street by the dexterous
Buster, with no inclination to renew the contest, the waiter
returning to his former employment of pot-filling and glass-

wiping, as though such encounters were in the common course of his daily business.

Many a hearty laugh did we enjoy over the incident during our walk along the now silent and almost deserted streets, and we reached the broad steps and frowning portals of Crockford's pandemonium ere we had half done discussing the fighting qualities of the waiter and the speedy emancipation of the black. Good-natured Maltby would not suffer either of us to enter the club, insisting on our accompanying him home to his comfortable little bachelor's abode in Queen Street. 'If Hillingdon once gets you in there,' said he to me, 'you will both begin "punting," sit up till five o'clock, lose three hundred a-piece, and go home disgusted. Much better come with me; I'll give you some supper, the best brew of cold punch in Europe, and then we'll smoke a cigar and have a good long talk about hunting.' We laughed heartily at our friend's devotion to his favourite pursuit, and with the easy readiness of youth to accept the first diversion that offers itself, we strolled on, arm-in-arm, to his abode, and finished the night in the manner he proposed.

CHAPTER V.

THE WORLD WE LIVE IN.

IF ever man existed of whom it might be said 'that he knew the right, and yet the wrong pursued,' that man was Lord St Heliers. With a high position, a large fortune, great abilities, a powerful frame, and an iron constitution, he had opportunities of fame and distinction enjoyed by few, and yet he made all these advantages subservient to the purposes of amusement and self-indulgence ; whilst others of his own standing, far inferior in talents and acquirements, were taking 'the House' by storm with their eloquence, or convincing by the calm arguments of reason the unimpassioned judgments of 'Another Place,' St Heliers was betting at Newmarket or hunting at Melton ; whilst

the associates of his boyhood were winning fame and building
reputations in the varied walks of public life, he was celebrated
but for the cutting sarcasm of his witticisms, or the dissolute recklessness of his orgies.   To the scoffer's requisites for living well,
'a bad heart and a good stomach,' he added a temper that nothing
could ruffle, and nerves that no catastrophe could shake ; perhaps
a more good-natured man than St Heliers never existed, nor one
with a worse heart.   He looked upon the world around him but
to laugh at it, and measured by his own selfish gauge, not only
the conduct, but the very feelings of his neighbours.   Did he
see a kindly action, he set it down to the score of a far-seeing
self-interest ; did he hear a virtuous sentiment, he dubbed it a
well-acted piece of consummate hypocrisy.   'I never give any
man credit for being a fool,'—such was one of his favourite
maxims ; and he considered no piece of folly so glaring as that
of inconveniencing self for the purpose of benefiting another.
And yet was this man the most agreeable companion ; in the
language of the world, 'the best fellow' that was to be met
with in the whole range of London society.   His anecdotes were
so well told, his satire of himself, as well as others—for he never
spared his own failings—so lively and humorous, his dry, quaint
manner so original, that as the ladies smiled at his repartees,
and the clubs rang with his sallies, he was universally voted
the most popular fellow in England.   With his quick insight
into character, and insatiable appetite for amusement, new faces
and young companions were absolutely necessary ; and from my
first introduction to him, he 'took me up,' as people call it, and
bestowed upon me the equivocal advantage of his intimacy.
From my lively disposition and reckless habits he probably
foresaw that I should contribute much to his amusement, so
long as I could 'live the pace' with him ; nor did he care that
when ruin stared me in the face, I must eventually drop into
the rear, beggared and dishonoured through *his friendship.*
What did it matter to him ?   There would be more young ones
coming on.

Such was the man who had invited me to accompany him to a
dinner at Richmond, with a small party as he said, 'not composed entirely of men ;' and as we were to go early, and enjoy

the fine weather on the river during the afternoon, I had scarcely finished a late breakfast, consequent upon Maltby's prolonged hunting-lecture, ere it was time to adjourn to his lordship's house, whence we were to take our departure. A perfect little dwelling-place it was, too, with its front windows enjoying the comparatively fresh breeze from the park, and its hall opening into a quiet street, whose cul-de-sac precluded all the noise of traffic which pervades each busy thoroughfare. The sun shone with a tropical warmth upon the dry white pavement, the crossings alone being knee-deep in mud ; for it appears that in London there can be no medium between the dust of the Sahara desert and the floundering difficulties of a morass. St Heliers had asked me to come early, and smoke a cigar with him before starting ; and on my admittance by his servant, I was immediately ushered into his lordship's snuggery, or 'boudoir,' as he called it, where I found him sedulously engaged in the consumption of tobacco, and assisted by a good-looking, gentleman-like man, whom he introduced to me as Captain Lavish, of some hussar regiment.

Sitting on a well-cushioned ottoman, in the quiet enjoyment of an enormous pipe, his low, square frame enveloped in the folds of a shawl dressing-gown, his broad forehead, short curly hair, and large bushy whiskers, all betokening strength in repose, I could not help thinking what a good Turk St Heliers would make in a picture, if taken in that attitude and costume; nor would the sly humorous twinkle of his eye have been out of character with some sedate Mussulman, grave by profession and rollicking by nature. He received me with some joking allusion to military punctuality, and ran on in his dry, amusing manner into a most laughable account of the battalion to which I belonged retiring in rather unseemly haste from a field-day, when caught in a tremendous shower of rain some days previously ; and as he was quizzing the hurried retreat with an affectation of military language and detail, I interrupted him with ' Right in front, St Heliers ; you civilians can never understand these things—we marched into the barracks right in front.' ' So you did, my dear fellow,' was the instantaneous reply ; ' of course that was the reason that you were *left behind ;*' and he went on with his

description in a manner that brought tears of laughter into the
eyes of his two listeners. Such readiness, such a happy knack
of creating mirth, such a keen sense of the ludicrous, I never
met in any one else. And yet this flow of wit, abundant as it
was, never became obtrusive—never for an instant verged upon
noise and vulgarity.

Nothing could go off better than did our dinner at Richmond.
Lavish drove me down in one of St Heliers' phaetons; he himself,
Mdlle. de Rivolte (a *danseuse* of European celebrity), a much
rouged German Countess, and another dandy completing the
party, and travelling socially in a britzka. I found my companion
and charioteer a very agreeable, careless, good-humoured fellow,
and we struck up a great alliance, much cemented by sundry
potations of champagne-cup, a beverage highly approved of by
the fairer portion of the company. We agreed to dine early, so
as to have the whole evening to enjoy upon the river, when the
heat of the day was past. Jest, repartee, merriment, and broken
English—the popping of corks, the ringing of glasses, half-blown
roses, floods of sunshine, Venetian blinds, and cold currant-tart,
made up a highly inspiriting scene. Mdlle. de Rivolte decl red
her determination to be sculled about upon the river by no one
but *ce cher Grand*, an arrangement which St Heliers did not
seem entirely to approve, but which, with his usual imperturbable
good humour, he immediately acceded to. Lavish got the
others safely afloat in a punt, not without misgivings on the
part of the German, whose unsteadiness was not wholly attributable
to the water; and lighting our cigars, the two freights
floated luxuriantly down the stream, as the last beams of sunset
gilded the fresh green foliage of the merry month of May.

An occasional stroke of my sculls soon bore us far beyond the
more tardy progression of the punt, and as I gazed at my companion, whose eyes sparkled and cheeks flushed with enjoyment
of her holiday (for it was not an opera night), and whose tasteful
dress, classical head and neck, silky dark hair, and long eyelashes, made amends for rather irregular features and a very
inferior complexion, I could not help thinking that she was
really fascinating, and that all this was uncommonly pleasant.
'You like England, Mons. Grand,' she said, in her pretty broken

English, after a long description of the sunny haunts she loved in *la belle France;* 'but you have nevare seen my contrée,' and she warbled out the refrain of some melodious old French roman—

C'est l'espérance, qui fait l'avenir ;
Sans espérance, mieux vaut, mieux vaut mourir.

'*Mieux vaut, mieux vaut mourir,*' she repeated, almost in a whisper, and relapsing into a dreamy reverie, she gazed downwards upon the water, as though its rippling current could bear her thoughts far, far away into the golden regions of the future. And here, thought I, is a woman whose whole education has been for the public; whose appearance nightly on the stage is greeted by the applause of thousands; who cannot step into her carriage without hearing a passer-by exclaim, 'There goes Rivolte!' whose name is in every paper, as her picture is in every print-shop; who has achieved fame, for such she has been taught to consider this notoriety; who has arrived at the pinnacle of her ambition, and yet, in her woman's nature she pines for the domestic pleasure of a peaceful home; she anticipates the time when she shall retire from the public gaze, and hide her weary head beneath a husband's roof—probably when the time does come, it will bore her exceedingly, but that will be the fault of her previous education, not the law of her instinct. Meanwhile, she is melancholy and depressed; she must be consoled; and with this charitable view, I offered her those quiet and respectful attentions ever so much prized by a woman who is not quite certain of her position, and doubly acceptable from their contrast to the obtrusive gallantries of which such women are generally the objects.

If you would make arrangements for a pic-nic, a *fête champêtre* or any out-of-doors excursion in our native land, mind that, in addition to the corkscrew and the salt, you remember to take with you plenty of plaids, umbrellas, and Macintosh cloaks, for the three fine days of an English summer too surely end with their proverbial thunderstorm. We were far ahead of the party in the punt, gliding smoothly over one of those wide reaches which form so delightful a variety in the Thames; the sun had been some hours below the horizon; the moon, after

F

an unsuccessful attempt, had been obscured by clouds; and the weather, sultry all day, became more oppressive as the dusk deepened into darkness. My fair companion and myself were so engrossed with our conversation, that we had scarcely observed the threatening aspect of the night, and we were in the act of turning homewards, with a remark that the others would wonder what had become of us, when a few heavy drops, plashing loudly into the stream, warned us of what was to follow. I put the boat's head round and pulled vigorously for the shore; the only thing I learned at Eton (to my shame be it said), the art of sculling, now stood me in good stead, and we reached the bank just as a heavy peel, thundering above our heads, brought down a deluge of rain, which rendered poor Rivolte's exclamation of '*Eh! la pluie!*' an unnecessary commentary. Despite the danger of such a position, there was nothing for it but to take shelter under a huge elm tree, preferring the remote chance of being struck by lightning to the disagreeable certainty of being drenched from head to foot. It was a bore even for *me* to undergo a complete drenching in light summer costume; but for my tender companion it was a serious matter indeed. Luckily the tree to which we had fled was in full summer foliage, and a roof of green leaves will keep out a certain quantity of wet; so for a time I had only to defend my charge from the chilling night breeze, which struck colder and colder as the rain descended. Divesting myself of as much clothing as decency would permit, I wrapped my neckcloth, coat, and waistcoat round her shivering form, reserving for my own defence a pair of thin white trousers and a linen shirt. What a situation for a *première danseuse* at her Majesty's Theatre and a subaltern of her Majesty's body-guard! There were we, Coralie de Rivolte and Digby Grand, cowering beneath the storm under an old tree on the banks of Father Thames, the one lavishing, the other receiving, those cares and attentions which, under such circumstances, are due from the stronger to the weaker sex. The storm cleared off—would it had lasted twice as long! Coralie had been kept tolerably dry by my solicitude, and a bright moon shone placidly down upon us as I sculled the dancer back to Richmond, bending leisurely to my oars, and ever and anon whispering in her ear no unwelcome syllables of homage and admiration, couched in her own polished languish, so expressly adapted to the voice of gallantry.

'*Oh, que faire? il est parti, milor,*' exclaimed Coralie, in an altered voice, and with a frightened expression of countenance, as, on mooring the boat under the terrace of our hotel, a servant, evidently awaiting our arrival, informed us that our party had taken their departure for town immediately after the storm had cleared off, leaving a message that if we ever returned, we should follow them in St Heliers' brougham, which had come down expressly to take him home at night, but which his lordship, with his usual gallantry, had left for the accommodation of Mdlle. de Rivolte. Surely, thought I, my star is in the ascendant : first of all, to be storm-stayed on the river with the charming French-woman, and then to come in for a *tête-à-tête* drive of ten long miles back to London in the same fascinating society.

'Don't hurry that bay horse,' I said to Lord St Heliers' coachman ; 'I am sorry you have had so long to wait.' And as I crossed his palm whilst making this civil speech, he took me at my word. The brougham horse was a rare trotter, but I think we were quite two hours on the road ; and as we parted at the door of Coralie's neat little villa, where she was received by an anxious elderly lady, we had become such friends as can only be made by a partnership in difficulties, with youth on one side and beauty on the other. How dreary looked the inside of the dark-lined brougham without the white dress of my companion ! How her pretty rapid accents rung in my ears, and the gentle pressure of her little gloved hand still seemed to cling to mine ! The lamps glared reproachfully in upon me as I sat in solitary reverie ; and the accelerated roll of the wheels kept incessantly repeating a monotonous chorus—'Fanny Jones, Fanny Jones,' 'this is worse, this is worse,' till I was set down at the door of my own lodgings, with a beating heart and an excited brain, to dream through the livelong night of the piquante smile which lent such an indescribable charm to Coralie de Rivolte.

Enslaved by the fascination of the dancer, I now frequented the opera with a regularity that the unassisted attractions of music and 'spectacle' could never have brought out. Hillingdon, Lavish, and myself, were fortunate enough to possess the

best box in the house, as we considered it—that which commanded the nearest view of the dresses and features of the performers—enabled us to catch every one of the 'asides' not
intended for the amusement of the public ; and, above all, possessed a communication with that region of chalk, machinery,
and reality, denominated 'behind the scenes.'   Here would we
assemble to pronounce our opinion on tenor, soprano, contralto,
and baritone ; to discuss the efficiency of a chorus, or the harmony of a scene.   I, for one, could never even whistle an air
correctly ; Hillingdon, who, by way of being an amateur, made
fearful havoc of Bellini on the violoncello ; and Jack Lavish, if
unfortunately he arrived before the concluding scene of the opera,
could hardly keep his eyes open, till roused by the attractions of
the ballet.   Such were the trio that sat in judgment on the
gifted composers of the sunny south.

   We usually dined together at Crockford's if not otherwise
engaged ; and after the very best dinner it was possible for
Francatelli to serve, diluted by the most undeniable of liquors,
we rose from our unpaid-for banquet (the great charm of those
little *réunions*), and sped our way to the scene of brilliancy and
enchantment that burst upon our view from the dark interior
of 'Stage Box, No. 1 Ground Tier.'   What a thrill of excitement and pleasure used to come over me, as, drawing aside the
heavy curtain that shrouded us from the public, I adjusted my
double-barrelled glass to take a thorough survey of that varie-
gated assemblage, to note the occupants of those boxes to which
I had the *entrée*, and to mark the new faces or unexpected combinations of old ones, which formed the detail of this worldly
kaleidoscope.   Then, as I carefully set aside the rare bouquet
furnished by Harding for Coralie, Jack Lavish would enter,
with some choice bit of scandal which levelled all our glasses
at a small dark box on the third tier opposite, to take a deliberate survey of a classic and beautiful head, with one white
camelia in the dark massive hair, bending gracefully towards a
white waistcoat, surmounted by a large pair of whiskers and
accurate mustachios ; whilst Jack whispers in my ear an improbable story about Austrian tyranny and a Hungarian countess.

   Swiftly sped the moments on the wings of song, and soon the

preparations for the ballet brought us back from the different
boxes where we had been paying visits and retailing small-talk,
to our own incomparable position for inspecting the 'many-
twinkling feet,' and swallowing the dust and chalk kicked up
by those active members, whose proportions, however, will not
always bear the closest survey. But the band of figurantes opens
out in graceful undulating lines, and bounding forth into light
from the dark background of the stage, like a butterfly released
from its dingy prison, Rivolte bends curtseying to the ground,
in acknowledgment of the tumultuous applause which ever greets
her entrance. 'Rivolte' she is to that admiring crowd; but
'Coralie' to me, as I feel, when her dark eye, glancing round
the house, softens into tenderness as its rests upon my box.
Bouquets are showered upon the favourite dancer, and as mine
goes spinning to her feet amongst the others, it is distinguished
from the rest, and I can see *that* is the one she presses to her
lips whilst bowing her gratitude to the enthusiastic throng;
that is the one which accompanies her through the intricate
evolutions of the *pas de fascination*, and is clasped to her
panting bosom in the impassioned attitude with which that
voluptuous dance concludes. Mine, too, are the congratulations
which greet her most acceptably, as, hurrying behind the scenes,
I await the breathless fair one with cloak and shawl; and tender
are our mutual inquiries and allusions to the Richmond wetting
and its consequences. Coralie's carriage is in waiting, and
having wrapped her up most assiduously, I conduct her carefully
to the stage-door, through all the confusion of men in paper-
caps, moving scenes, dancers in full dress, but whose rouge and
white satin shoes look less brilliant in colour, more brick-dust
and less carmine, more yellow and less snowy, than when illumined by the glare of the foot-lights; actors and actresses,
dressed in plain clothes, going away like other people, and all
the litter, dust, and rubbish inseparable from the getting-up of
a magnificent spectacle.

As I hurried with Coralie down the dark street at the end of
which her brougham lamps were shining, and was making the
most of the very short time allowed us for conversation, she
stopped suddenly in the midst of some playful coquettish remark,

and grasping my arm convulsively, staggered against me as if she would have fallen; at the same instant a swarthy, Spanish-looking individual, coming brusquely between us, and addressing her by her Christian name and in language I could not understand, but whose accents betrayed anger and impatience, seemed to chide her fiercely though familiarly. I returned the push with interest, and interposed my person between the dancer and her unwelcome acquaintance, Coralie begging me, in trembling accents, to be calm, whilst the stranger turned the whole tide of his wrath from the lady upon her companion. Not one word could I understand; but the man appeared so angry as to be dangerous; and I kept my eye steadily fixed upon him, whilst I gradually edged my companion towards her carriage, which we were now approaching. Lucky for me that I did so: infuriated by my perseverance, and probably additionally irritated by receiving no answer to his torrent of abuse, he drew from beneath his waistcoat a long, narrow dagger, with which he made a lunge at my breast, that, had it taken effect, would have been fatal. I saw the cold blade gleaming in the lamp-light, and catching his wrist rapidly with one hand, I dealt him with the other such ' a facer ' between the eyes, as sent him down upon the pavement prostrate, and for a moment insensible. Quickly I placed Coralie in her carriage, amidst her incoherent entreaties that I would not accompany her, and closing the door, I bid the coachman drive rapidly home. But short as was the time that elapsed in these arrangements, when I retraced my steps a few yards to look after my late antagonist, he was gone—not a vestige of the fracas remained; and had it not been that Coralie's voice was ringing in my ears, imploring me to be patient, and assuring me that ' he knew me,' I should have looked upon the events of the last few minutes as the delusions of a dream, so unaccountable was this sudden outrage and its conclusion.

All night long I tossed and turned upon my bed, thinking over this adventure. Now I fancied I had been attacked by some unfortunate lunatic; but the evidence of the man's previous acquaintance with Coralie, and the manner in which he conversed with her, forbade the supposition. Then it occurred to me he might have some claim upon the dancer, which he had a right to establish—a brother, a lover, perhaps a husband. The latter supposition was decidedly uncomfortable, as it involved the probability of a further acquaintance with this swarthy hero, and the likelihood of another fracas, to end, perhaps, in a duel. From this contingency, my thoughts naturally turned to Coralie herself, and the anomalous connection that existed between us. We carried on a vigorous flirtation, which on her side appeared to be fast verging on the sentimental; whilst for my own part, I felt conscious that I liked and admired her as much as it was possible for me to like and admire any one but myself. This was all very well for the present; but how was it to end? I was not by any means satisfied with the terms upon which Coralie stood with Lord St Heliers; she certainly encouraged no danglers about her but my unworthy self; yet to all denials, and 'not at homes,' St Heliers was an invariable exception. His carriages were at her service when her own horses were lame. His servants were continually going and coming from the house in Park Lane to the pretty villa. Yet he never appeared at the latter domicile himself, and seemed to encourage, or at any rate to have no objection to, my frequent visits and constant attendance upon Rivolte. And now if, in addition to all this, a husband should turn up unexpectedly, what a piece of work there would probably be. With this consolatory conviction I fell asleep. Nor were my waking thoughts much clearer when, on being called the following morning, I received a tiny three-cornered note, addressed in Coralie's well-known hand to Mons. le Capitaine Grand, &c., &c., imploring me, in highly figurative French, not upon any account to call upon her, or come near her till I should hear again, and promising to explain all on the Saturday following, after the opera.

Whether my cogitations had any effect upon my actions, I know not; but certain it is, that after bath, breakfast, and matutinal cigar, I strolled leisurely down to a well-known fencing-room, of which I was at that time a member; and with a sort of vague idea that all foreigners were adepts with the small-sword, and that I only wanted a little more practice to become a fencer, I donned the wire mask, the buff jacket, and

gauntlet-glove, and took my accustomed place amongst the pupils
of this courtly science. The *maître d'armes* himself, an old
officer of the Grand Army, with the strength of a Hercules,
and the energetic activity of a Frenchman, was, besides *rusé*—
beyond his compeers in the management of his weapon ; and I
knew that to hold my own with him was to be infinitely superior
to any chance antagonist in Europe. As I entered the room
he was busily engaged with a wiry, active-looking figure, whom
I could not help fancying I had seen before, but whose mask
prevented the possibility of my identifying him. 'Who is
he ?' I whispered to Maltby, who was of course present, devoted
as he was to all athletic exercises, and who was regaining his
breath after having, as he expressed it, ' polished off a corporal
in the Life Guards.' 'I don't know,' he replied ; ' but he is
the best fencer I have seen in England. He hit Fleury three
to one in an assault just now, and we think Fleury one of the
quickest in Paris ; and I doubt if our muscular *maître* himself
will be able to hold his own with him.' And sure enough, as
the stranger disengaged, doubled, lunged, recovered, and returned,
with a new and apparently fatal *riposte*, I could see that the
best fencer in London had enough to do to cover his body
with his blade.

'Now then, Grand, for a breather,' said Maltby ; and ere
long, I found myself fully occupied with carte, tierce, thrust,
and parry, and my whole energies concentrated on the button
of my opponent's foil. There were several other pairs of
fencers in the room, besides an assistant giving lessons ; and
what with the stamping, shuffling, clashing of steel, cries of
Hola ! Hein ! and other vociferous French exclamations, and
the deep voice of the assistant, with his reiterated words of
command—' *Fendez-vous—en garde—double—degagé—battement
—un, deux—fendez-vouz*'—a general action might have been
carried on with less noise. This confusion, and my own engagement with so skilful an adversary as Maltby, prevented my
noting much of what was going on ; but in the midst of a
rapid and furious assault, we were both arrested, as if spell-
bound, by a deep groan of agony, and a heavy fall on the dusty
floor—the stranger was run right through the body by a broken

foil! To describe the consternation and tumult that ensued is impossible; voices in every key and half-a-dozen languages demanding explanations, and proffering advice and assistance. One rushed off for a surgeon, another called loudly for cold water; the more composed bore the form of the ill-fated fencer into the ante-room, and order was at length restored by the *maître*, who was the only person that preserved his coolness and judgment amidst the confusion. A surgeon speedily arrived, and whilst he was examining the wound, and pronouncing it dangerous in the extreme, the *maître d'armes* explained to me the circumstances of the accident.

It appears that the stranger, who gave his name as Mons. de Rivas, but whom my informant thought much more like a Spaniard than a Frenchman, and who that morning made his first appearance in the fencing-room, had taken off his buckskin jacket, and was reposing himself after an assault in which he had displayed wonderful science and dexterity, when Mons. Fleury, his previous antagonist, who had retired to put on his everyday attire, re-entered the fencing-room, and taking up a foil, proceeded to discuss with the stranger the advantages of a certain 'parry' and 'return' which had been put in practice in their late contest. The latter, whose French was not very intelligible, anxious to explain his meaning, placed himself in position to give a practical illustration, and in defiance of the fencing-master's warning, begged Fleury to lunge at him; observing, 'they were equally defenceless in point of costume.' The quickest wrist in Paris took him at his word; but in the *battement* which preceded his lightning lunge, the weapon broke short off beneath the button; and ere Fleury could stay his hand, the foil, now pointed and sharp as a small-sword, had entered beneath the ribs of his antagonist, and going clean through his body, re-appeared at his back. The wound was dangerous in the extreme, if not mortal, and poor Fleury's distress was awful to witness. The kindest-hearted man alive, he seemed quite paralysed at being the unconscious cause of so fatal an injury. As they bore the now insensible form from the scene of the catastrophe, I caught a glimpse of his depending head, and pale, wan features. What was my horror and astonishment, to recognise my antagonist of the night before, and the mysterious acquaintance of Coralie! His livid and sallow features, distorted with pain, looked scarcely more ghastly than when I had seen them some twelve hours before, contracted with rage and jealousy, as they glared upon me in the lamp-light; and to render assurance doubly sure, and prove his identity beyond a doubt, there was a red and swollen mark upon the forehead, that I well knew was the impress of the crushing blow I had been obliged to deal him in self-defence.

CHAPTER VI.

WAYS AND MEANS.

AS may be supposed, the life I was now leading was not very consistent with a small allowance, irregularly paid; and the friendship of Lord St Heliers, the favour of Mrs Man-trap, who was pleased to 'take me up' very fiercely, and the *liaison* with Coralie were, each and all, the means of draining the account at Cox's to the uttermost farthing. Of course, no bills were ever allowed to be 'advanced a stage' by being looked over, and the idea of *paying* was not dreamt of for an instant. My actual income kept me in gloves and perfume, perhaps blacking. And the uninitiated will marvel how I obtained the necessaries, not to say the luxuries of life. But the artificial state of society, which forces the youngest son or the embarrassed heir to 'spend his half-crown upon sixpence a day,' in justice furnishes means and appliances wherewith to solve that problem, for a time at least. The noble invention of counters, forming a fictitious credit, opens to him the resources of the gaming-table, at which an opportune run of luck may enable him to win a fortune he has never staked. Early intelligence, or as it is called 'good information,' on the turf, encourages him to invest large sums upon what may fairly be termed a foregone conclusion. If A beats B in public, giving him three pounds, and C beats A in a trial, giving him seven, it is obvious that when C and B are to meet at even weights, the exclusive possessor of the result of this trial has a great advantage in 'backing his opinion.' Billiards, too, for a skilful performer, may be worth a flourishing retail business, and whist realise a larger income than in these times could be wrung from many a dirty acre.

My proficiency in the two latter sciences, and my habit of never paying ready money, helped me for a time wonderfully; but it was to the turf that I looked as a permanent provision— an ever-yielding mine of wealth. My Derby-book, constructed upon strictly mathematical principles, had won me a few hundreds; but this was a certainty, as I had been 'betting round.' There was, however, another card in the pack, that I fondly hoped was to be 'the best thing out for many a year.' I had it from the very best information, in fact, reduced to a proof there was no gainsaying, that Major Martingale's 'Queen of the May' was to win the Oaks. She could not lose, so they said—the race was over! Queen of the May would come in by herself! Levanter, who was now on half-pay, and a regular turfite, had backed her heavily at Newmarket. I had 'got on,' as the term is, at long odds; and now her stable companion had won the Derby, and we, the select few, knew what an example the mare could make of him. This brought her up in the betting, and still I went on booking bet after bet in her favour. She left off even against the field on the Thursday night, and stood to win me a fortune. I dined with Colonel Grandison, and a party of brother officers, but was absent and impatient till the repast was over. At Crockford's I could hear nothing new with regard to the morrow, and I went to bed earlier than usual to pass a fevered, restless night, and dream of the events of the following day.

I was awoke from a golden vision, in which the chesnut mare, adorned by Martingale's well-known colours, was leading the van at a killing pace, while the shouts of the multitude rent the sky, by my ruthless servant entering the room to inform me that Captain Lavish was waiting breakfast; and making as rapid a toilet as I could, I found my hungry friend, who was to drive me down to Epsom in his drag, with a party of scape-

graces like himself. The day was beautiful—the dust laid by
just sufficient rain—the team tractable and fast—the party all
in high spirits and good humour, mostly backers of Queen of
the May. Lavish was an agreeable companion, with a pleasant,
careless manner, that was extremely fascinating; and what was
more important to his freight, an excellent coachman. Many
a jest and repartee enlivened our drive; but even whilst our
mirth was fastest and most furious, the sight of the pleasant
country—the summer sky, and the fresh-blooming lilacs, so
redolent of spring—brought back to one of the party thoughts
and feelings much at variance with the actual scene. The sweet
influence of Nature in her loveliest aspect stole over my senses,
and I found myself speculating as to whether there was not a
higher destiny for man, even in this world, than to support a
life of pleasure by a career of recklessness; whether the path I
had chosen was, in truth, the happiest; and whether a course
of self-denial and self-sacrifice—a sort of crusade in the cause
of virtue—would not be, in reality, a far more satisfactory lot.
'If Queen of the May wins the Oaks,' I thought, 'I shall
retire from all this, pay my debts, get out of the hands of Mrs
Man-trap, cut Coralie, and devote myself to Zoë, my old and
faithful flame; in short, turn over a new leaf.' Ah, those new
leaves! If half of them were turned over that are talked about,
what a gigantic volume would they form in the life of every one
of us.

But here we are at Epsom, looking so cool and roomy after
the crowd and confusion of the Derby-day. How much pleasanter a meeting is the Oaks; with not half the people, or a
quarter of the noise, it is so much more racing-like, so much
more a matter of business, than the great three-year-old-scramble
that precedes it. Off the drag I jump in a twinkling, and away
to Martingale's stable, where the mare stands, looking as like a
winner as if she had already been painted by Herring in that
character. Every one is full of confidence—from the Major's
whiskers, curling in stupendous magnificence, as though they
already anticipated a triumph, down to the stunted stable-boy,
who believes there is but one racehorse in the world, and that
one is his own especial care; all seem to think the event a cer-

tainty. The trainer begs me to put another fifty on for him, when I go into the ring; and Martingale swears that 'if Queen of the May can't beat them all to-day as far as they can see, he will never keep a racehorse again.'

Flushed with confidence, and greedy still of gain, I elbow my way into the waving mass and Babel-like confusion of the betting-ring. What do I hear? They are laying odds upon the 'Queen,' as they call her; they are betting 6 to 4, 'they name the winner,' what a time to *hedge!* Shall I make a certainty of winning a good stake, and lay against the favourite; or shall I stand the shot, and make a fortune? 'Stand the shot,' whispers the busy fiend at my elbow; and I accommodate a vociferous 'fielder' with 6 to 4 in hundreds as my concluding stake, and close my book with the air of quiet determination with which we may fancy Napoleon shutting up his telescope, after giving his last orders at the critical moment which should decide the fate of an army. Now I am at leisure to talk to the ladies, and pay my accustomed homage to Mrs Man-trap; now I can trifle in half-crown 'lotteries' and glove bets—glad to cover with an affectation of frivolity the gnawing anxiety that is eating at my heart. Hark! the bell rings—the numbers are up—nine come to the post—and jewelled pencils are wielded by fairy fingers to mark the starters on 'Dorling's Correct Card.' The course is cleared; and the only two figures left on the turf are Martingale and his jockey, exchanging a few more last words. One after another the competitors sweep by in their preparatory canters; and, to my eye, the only dangerous-looking forms of the lot are St Agatha and the Hospodar filly. St Agatha made a sorry display at Chester, and we have got the filly's capabilities to a pound; so I feel much relieved by the certainty of victory. Mechanically I light a cigar; and ere the first half-dozen fragrant whiffs have perfumed the atmosphere, they are off!—the pace tremendous; and St Agatha's stable-companion, a ewe-necked, lop-eared weed out of Atropos, making the running!—our mare well up. The hill tells off the leader; and Queen of the May, accompanied by St Agatha and the Hospodar filly, creep to the front. Down the hill and round the corner they come like a hurricane, the terrific pace creating a tail of half a mile; and at the distance, the race

is between the three, whose names are equally vociferated as
winners, according to the fancy or the investments of the shouters.
I am watching Martingale's colours narrowly with my glass.
The Queen is halfway up the distance, nearly a length in advance.
Can I believe my eyes? Hands and heels are at work as the
Hospodar filly draws upon her; and the icy conviction shoots
through me that our mare is beat. And now the three pass the
stand, neck-and-neck. Our animal is game to the last, and it is
just possible that she *may* pull through. No—no—ridden by
Newmarket's finest horseman, nothing can save her. The
Hospodar filly struggles to the front—St Agatha clears the two
with a tremendous rush, and, after one of the finest races on
record, is landed a winner by a neck, the Hospodar filly second,
and Queen of the May a moderate third!

What a facer! £2900,—and where to get the money? for on
Monday next must this unfortunate stake be paid. If anything
could console me—if anything could raise a laugh at such a
moment—it would have been Martingale's crest-fallen appearance
after so unexpected a defeat. The ruby countenance had become
livid, the ambrosial whiskers hung limp and helpless, and the
whole man was completely beaten and undone. I believe I did
laugh and jest like others during the remainder of that eventful
afternoon, but it was with a load at my heart that all the merriment in the world could not have got rid of.

Long and earnest was our consultation that night on the steps
at Crockford's, as Jack Lavish and I formed a committee of ways
and means. I could not have applied to a better person than
Lavish for advice in pecuniary difficulties, as, probably, no man
in England lived so continually in hot water with regard to
money-matters as did that light-hearted dragoon. 'The only
fellow to get you out of this,' said Jack, ' is my old acquaintance
and benefactor, Mr Shadrach. The time is so short that no
regular practitioner in London would be man enough to produce
£3000 by two o'clock on Monday. But Shadrach will do it, I
have no doubt; only you must submit to be robbed enormously.'
And to Shadrach, accordingly, Jack agreed to drive me betimes
the following morning.

It may be a grateful partiality—it may be an amiable weak-

ness; but I confess that the Jews have always appeared to me a
calumniated race. From spendthrift King John downwards, the
Christian has ever pocketed the ducats, and abused the donor.
Very frequently has the worthy Israelite's loan become a gift;
for gentlemen who are compelled to have recourse to such assistance are not always the best payers, even to their fellow-
Christians; and the usurer's profits, like those of a fashionable
tailor, must needs be large to cover the amount of his bad debts.
And directly there is a word said about suffering a Jew to become
a legislator, the ingratitude of his clients knows no bounds.
What, a Jew!—'an Ebrew Jew' to become a lawgiver!—to
pollute with his presence the chaste atmosphere of a British
House of Commons! Forbid it, that religious and high-principled
assemblage! Forbid it, worn-out revellers, who have all their
lives been indebted to that wealthy tribe! Forbid it, fathers,
who have eldest sons on fire to mortgage, and younger one's
athirst to borrow! He has smoothed the paths of pleasure for
our youth; he has mortified the cankering love of gain that
blights the flower of our manhood; he has taught us foresight
and caution, very likely a little practical law, to recreate our old
age. And this is our return!

But here we are at Shadrach's door; and Captain Lavish, who
is evidently well known to the servant, is immediately admitted
with his friend into the sanctum of the usurer. Unlike the dens
of the city, where dirt and capital appear to go hand in hand, in
whose dingy corners the emblematic spider spins unmolested, Mr
Shadrach's gay and lightsome apartment was gorgeously furnished, with a good deal more style than taste, though adorned
by one or two pictures of considerable value; whilst ottomans,
flowers, and nick-nacks brought far more vividly to our minds
the picture of hapless Rebecca than of the miserly Isaac of York.
Our modern Isaac himself was a fresh-coloured, portly, good-
humoured looking man, with little about him to betray his
Hebrew origin, save a pair of dark curling whiskers and a fine
aquiline nose. And his air was courtesy itself, as he requested
us to sit down, and begged to know in what he could be useful.
I stated the case in a very few words, and expressed my willing-
ness to 'make any arrangement'—the term invariably used to

express the hopeless entanglement of one's affairs ; only I insisted that the money must be forthcoming immediately.   After a few pointed inquiries as to my expectations, it was decided that a post-obit bond was the only means of raising the necessary funds ; and after some more unceremonious questions as to Sir Peregrine's age, health, habits, &c., it was finally agreed that I should give my bond, and all other necessary legal securities, for something like treble the amount I was anxious to obtain, with a handsome premium into the bargain to Mr Shadrach ; in consideration of which I was to receive on the following Monday morning, after the deeds were signed, &c., the sum of £3000, being just one hundred over and above my losses on that unfortunate Queen of the May.   This knotty point settled, a glass of rare Amontillado was produced to ratify our treaty—Lavish whispering in my ear that I was fortunate not to be obliged to receive a butt of that straw-coloured vintage in lieu of hard cash, —a species of barter which would assist but little in liquidating my debts at Hyde Park Corner.

Heavy as was the weight thus removed from my mind by Mr Shadrach's assistance, I had still very considerable misgivings as to the course I was now pursuing.   It was evident that paying three for one in my numerous extravagances would ruin the finest fortune in the world ; and, with all my thoughtlessness, I was not quite a fool, and had already perceived that, with Sir Peregrine's habits of carelessness and total disregard to business, his successor would find himself considerably hampered and involved.   These reflections were none of the pleasantest, and I was not sorry to join Lavish, Hillingdon, and a few more, in what they called a quiet Greenwich dinner, where champagne-cup and other exhilarating mixtures should drown dull care, and where fun and frolic, amongst a man-party assembled for the express purpose of enjoying themselves, should reign unchecked. Hillingdon had agreed to drive me down in his cab.   We had been for some time constant associates, and what the world calls ' great friends ;' and as we sauntered leisurely along, inhaling the cool country breeze and enjoying the luxury of ' weather '— the only pleasure that with me has never palled,—my companion, who had a rich vein of poetry and originality in his composition, was most delightful. All Greenwich dinners are the same—flushed faces in a setting sun, old jokes, brown bread and butter, and an enormous bill, in which the white bait, as Maltby calculated, are charged at the rate of half-a-crown a piece. We talked about racing and the Italian Opera, both rather sore subjects to one of the party; voted the beauty of the season had 'no figure;' took away the characters of sundry ladies of our acquaintance; and, finally, when the moon was up, and it was time to be going, prevailed upon Jack Lavish to sing us, 'The gallant young hussar,' a monotonous chant, describing the success in love and war of a mustachioed juvenile, who generously promotes the espousals of a deserving bât-man with his own ladye-love. I had begun dinner in a state of unenviably low spirits; but as bumper after bumper sparkled in my glass, I found my difficulties becoming 'small by degrees, and beautifully less;' and when I lit a two-foot regalia, and took my place in Hillingdon's cab for our homeward drive, I had quite recovered my accustomed elasticity of temperament. Nay, more—I felt that sort of confident presentiment of fortune which, if not the actual cause, is so often the forerunner of success.

Beautiful was the moonlit sky, and refreshing the cool night-breeze that fanned our heated temples, as we drove back to town. Careless, riotous pleasure-seekers as we were, the holy stillness of the hour awoke in us that higher and better nature of man, never wholly extinct even in the worst. We talked of the wonders of astronomy; speculated on the inhabitants of the myriads of stars which glittered overhead; got to Paley's *Evidences*, and discussed our own wild notions of a future state—not with the vague speculation of the free-thinker—for, with all his faults, poor Hillingdon had a strong conviction of the truth, as he had learned it in his happy boyhood at his mother's knee—but rather with a dreamy tinge of romance and poetry, in which such spirits as my friends are apt to indulge. There was something very German about Hillingdon's ideas, more particularly of the immaterial; and he was a devout believer in ghosts—having, as he himself averred, received no less than two warnings from those heralds of another sphere. Poor fellow! could all his talent, wit, and imagination have been exchanged for a

G

few grains of common sense, it would have needed no ghost to
foretell what must be the close of such a career and such a
character as his.

Left fatherless from his boyhood, he had spent the greater
part of his youth in travelling over the Continent. From the
bull-fights of Madrid to the reviews of Peterhoff—from the
salons of Paris to the ruined temples of immortal Greece, he
had seen and done everything before he was eighteen ; and at
that discreet age found himself passionately in love with an
Austrian lady, who had, unfortunately, taken the veil in a convent at Verona. How they manage these things I am unable to
explain, nor was my friend disposed to enlarge upon the subject ;
but despite of bolts and bars—despite of monastic rigour and
precautions, the cage was, one fine morning, found empty, and
the bird had flown to take shelter on the breast of young Hillingdon. Such a connection was not likely to prosper. And
the unfortunate girl, a prey to remorse and superstitious terrors
—to say nothing of a well-grounded apprehension that she might
be retaken and immured alive—being, besides, of a nervous,
weak, and excitable temperament, terminated her existence by
poison, and died in her lover's arms a very few months after the
ill-fated elopement. At twenty, Hillingdon entered the Guards,
in point of feeling and experience, an old man. Nothing but
gambling appeared able to excite him. In all the sports and
pleasures in which his comrades found such delight, he took
part readily and successfully ; but his heart was far away ; and
the only time his characteristic listlessness seemed to be overcome—the only moments in which he seemed to forget the past,
and entered with energy into the present, were when dealing the
cards upon which a fortune depended, or brandishing the dice-box
whose imprisoned cubes should replenish or exhaust his yearly
income.

Nor was it wonderful that such a character should be essen-
tially a gambler. I have already adverted to his firm belief in
ghosts ; and his faith in ' luck' or fortune, as he termed it, was
not inferior to his superstition. Often have I seen him rise
from the ' board of green cloth,' and turning his chair thrice,
from right to left, reseat himself at the play-table, confident that

success would follow this mystical manœuvre. Often have I
known him object to play in the company of certain individuals,
whose faces, forms, or dress he fancied were inimical to his
' destiny,' and patiently would he wait till such birds of ill-omen
should take their flight, and allow him to enter unthwarted
upon his speculations. With regard to his ' spirit-creed,' it
was firm and unassailable. That very evening, as we rattled
through the busy streets of London—so gay and lightsome after
the unillumined country highway—who would have supposed
that the dashing, fashionable-looking dandy, driving that well-
appointed cab from a jovial dinner-party to the glittering halls
of Crockford's, was relating, in tones of awe and emotion, to his
brother-reprobate, the thrilling experiences of what he called his
higher state of being. Yet so it was. ' I give you my sacred
word of honour, Grand,' he said, with an earnestness that impressed me with his own conviction of the truth of that which
he related, ' that since she died in my arms I have seen her
twice—ay, seen her clearly and distinctly as I now see you. She
has spoken with me in words that I dare not and may not repeat,
but with all the warmth and affection of her loving youth. Twice
has she appeared to me, and each time has her visit been one
of warning—each time has it been followed by some heavy and
dreadful calamity. I saw her the night before my mother's
death. I saw her the morning of that fatal duel, when I went
out with Congreve as his second, and poor young De Valmont
was shot dead upon the ground. And I shall see her once, and
only once again. At Rome—at Paris—will the third time be
in London? I cannot tell; I know not how long it may be
before my spirit-bride revisits me once more; but when that time
does come, I shall know full well what it forebodes. I have a
solemn presentiment in my own mind, that within four-and-
twenty hours of the *third warning*, we shall meet never to part
again. And then people talk to me about the absurdity of
believing in ghosts, as they call them, as if all the argument, all
the reason in the world, could make me doubt that which I know
to be a fact, not only by the evidence of my outward senses, but
by the inborn conviction of my soul. However, here we are at
Crockford's, and I only hope my dissertation on the supernatural

will not affect your appetite for supper, or your " sacred thirst
for gain " afterwards.'

Doubtless, if men must play, and in the days of which I
write it certainly appeared to be one of the exigencies of human
nature, Crockford's was the best place at which to indulge that
fatal passion. Now, when so many fine fortunes have melted
away, so many bright spirits been ruined, in the undeviating
pursuit of the science of numbers, illustrated by mechanical
contrivances of dotted ivory, in which certain combinations too
surely produce ' a seven ' when the quotient deserves to be ' a
four,' and *vice versâ*—in these more straitened times, of wheat at
thirty-eight shillings, and an inexorable income-tax, it is perhaps
as well that there should be no palace thrown open to the
noblest and the gayest of the land—no board spread with the
rarest dainties, and flooded with the choicest wines—and all
' free, gratis, for nothing,' in order to encourage more liberally
the spirit of speculation and the practice of arithmetic. I firmly
believe that many men played at Crockford's who would never
have played elsewhere ; and such being the case, it will not
admit of argument that the destruction of that establishment is
one of the improvements of the age ; but nevertheless, it was
very pleasant whilst it lasted ; and to my frame of mind on the
evening in question—harassed by my pecuniary difficulties,
flushed with wine, and thirsting for excitement, no resort could
have been so agreeable as the familiar halls of ' Crocky.'

' Nobody can throw a hand to-night,' said St Heliers, rolling
good-humouredly into the supper-room, where Hillingdon and I
were discussing a pleasing compound of champagne and seltzer-
water. ' Grand, my boy, how goes it ? I am afraid the Derby
winner was not so good a trial-horse as the stable fancied, and
Queen of the May, proved Queen of the May not.'

' Don't talk of her, I beseech you,' I replied. ' I shall offer
Martingale fifty pounds for her, being a pony more than her
value as a hack, to have the satisfaction of riding her to death.'

Whilst we thus conversed upon the topics of the day, the
supper-room became more and more deserted ; and as the occasional rattle of the dice-box in the next room became more distinctly audible, Hillingdon's impatience to go and ' have a shy '

got more and more uncontrollable. I know not why, but although I had quite recovered my spirits, I felt a strange unwillingness to enter the play-room; and after the fatigues and excitement of the day, would far rather have smoked a soothing cigar upon the steps in the moonlight; but the eagerness of my companion induced me at any rate to go and 'see what they were doing;' and I sauntered listlessly behind him into the little screened-off temple sacred to Fortune.

Business was going on rapidly, and apparently most prosperously for the proprietor, whose capital furnished the bank. Every seat at the table was occupied, and a double rank of spectators, and occasional speculators, stood behind those who played. As I came in, a Russian prince was in the act of throwing aside the box in disgust—his eleventh hundred having been quietly disposed of by a deuce-ace. His next neighbour, an English earl, was as instantaneously placed *hors de combat* for the present by the monotonous 'twelve out,' proclaimed by a lynx-eyed official with a rake and a green shade; and his rising in ill-concealed vexation gave me a vacant chair, of which I immediately possessed myself. I was pretty well known as a fortunate player, and a glance went round the table which seemed to intimate that a change might now be looked for in the course of fortune—the bank having enjoyed an unprecedented 'run.'

'I won't back him,' muttered old Lord Growler; 'he's out of luck. They say he lost five thousand pounds on the Oaks.'

Not much reassured by his lordship's remark, I asked modestly for a quiet hundred in counters: and with no vivid anticipation of success, waited till the box should come round to me in due course of the game.

Most of the players again threw out, amongst them Hillingdon and St Heliers, who were sitting opposite, and my turn soon arrived to make my set, and call my main. I had remarked that 'seven'—usually a favourite number amongst hazard players—had got into disgrace early in the evening, and was now seldom called. To this 'main' I accordingly determined to nail my colours, and putting down a fifty as my set, whilst I 'threw away a pony' on 'the nick,' I manfully shouted, 'Seven's the main—Seven!' whilst the croupiers joined chorus with their buzzing

repetition of 'Make your game, gentlemen; the main is Seven.'
The dice rattled, the box fell, and a dotted eleven turned its
welcome surface upward. I need not say this was what is termed
a nick, and as such, won me four 'ponies' for the one I had
risked, as well as fifty pounds on my set. Again I repeated the
auspicious number, and again with like success. In short, I was
in a vein of good fortune; and as the players murmured accordingly as they won or lost—'What a capital caster!' or 'What
infernal luck!' I increased my stakes to the utmost limits allowed
by the table, and pursued my triumphant career. If a four or a
ten came leaping from the box at the first intention, instead of
the seven I had invoked, so surely that four I dribbled over the
baize—so surely that ten dashed thundering on the board once
again, in time to win me, according to the rules of the game,
twice my investment on the chance of its appearance; and, finally,
ere I threw out with my thirteenth main, I had what is termed
'broken the bank,' that is, exhausted the whole sum that they
were prepared to lose on a single night, and had won, to my
own share, upwards of four thousand pounds. How clean and
crisp were the fresh, new notes that I thrust into my waistcoat
pocket; how pleasant the rustle of those tangible witnesses of
my success. What a thrill of delight did I experience, as I felt
that the infernal post-obit might now be dispensed with, and I
was again comparatively free. However, I was too well schooled
in the manners of 'my set' to allow my triumph to become
apparent, and it was with an affectation of extreme carelessness
that I received the congratulations of St Heliers and Hillingdon,
both large winners, and allowed that 'I had been tolerably
lucky, and had won a fairish stake;' much to the disgust of Lord
Growler, who overheard my remark, and who was ready to cry
with vexation, because his unbelief in my good star had induced
him to bet against me, and had been the means of mulcting him
to the amount of fourteen or fifteen pounds, a heavy loss to his
lordship, with no family, and an income of £70,000 a year—the
reason he never ventured more than a sovereign at a time was,
dissatisfied if he won, and miserable if he lost!

I am not usually an early riser, but the following morning saw
me astir with 'the milkmaids and the postman,' representatives

in London of the matutinal lark, and in the saddle, bound for the domicile of that modern Samaritan, good Mr Shadrach. Of course he was out of town, and spending the day at his 'willa,' as his servant called it, several miles from London, whither, without loss of time, it was incumbent on me to follow him. Suffice it to say, that two thorough-bred hacks were reduced to that state of exhaustion which a sporting baronet once described as being 'done as crisp as a biscuit,' ere I returned, having satisfactorily arranged matters with the usurer, and settled, as he prophetically remarked, 'that we should not require to do the post-obit *this time !'*

So eventful a week as that of my signal defeat at the Oaks and unlooked-for triumph at Crocky's might well excuse me for some inattention, during that period of excitement, to the fairer portion of my acquaintance. Of Coralie I had heard nothing. I concluded she was out of town, as I saw by the bills of her Majesty's Theatre that an inferior ballet was advertised in gigantic type, in which divertissement Mesdlles. Entrechat and Gavotte were promoted for the nonce to the principal parts. I did not like to inquire of St Heliers, and had no time to get as far as the villa, so I was compelled to remain in ignorance of the lovely dancer's whereabouts. Not so with Mrs Man-trap; that enterprising lady, who had a passion for everything that was 'fast,' took care to remind me continually of her existence by a series of notes and messages, which at length brought me to her feet, or rather boudoir, into which charming little room only the most favoured among her visitors were admitted. Here, as in duty bound, I underwent a torrent of inquiries as to everything connected with my late proceedings, Mrs Man-trap being one of those ladies who dearly love the last bit of news, whatever may be the subject thereof, and who are never satisfied without learning what they call the 'rights' of it. Dearly I paid for my entrance on the numerous list of her adorers; for of all deaths, the most painful to my mind must assuredly be that of being 'talked to death;' and blue eyes, however languishing—showering curls, however glossy—forms of grace, and skins of alabaster—become wearisome, if accompanied by a tongue that 'onward rolls, and rolls for ever.' I used to drive away from her door at such a pace, when released from these courts of inquiry, that, upon one occasion, the safe and commodious wooden pavement being watered into a perfect glaciarium, whilst the adjoining streets remained parched and dusty as the Great Desert, I lamed my cab-horse so badly as to be reduced to the necessity of throwing him out of work altogether, and replacing him immediately by a new purchase. Of course, there was but one emporium in London where a youth of my pretensions was likely to be able to suit himself, more particularly as the vulgar question of ready money was one with which the gentleman conducting the establishment was always unwilling to trouble a customer; and accordingly, the first time I found Maltby disengaged, I prevailed upon him to accompany me as far as Fitz-Andrews' yard, and give me the benefit of his judgment and experience in ' a deal.'

Time was that the horse-dealer, a race *per se*, was to be distinguished by his dress and appearance from all other trades and professions whatsoever. Slang, not to say vulgar manners, and apparel redolent of the stable, were the characteristics of the cloth; but *nous avons changé tout cela*—the 'dealer,' for we have dropped the substantive prefixed—the 'dealer' of the present day would, we conceive, rather astonish those grandfathers who have spent all our money, and entailed upon us only their love of horse-flesh and its appliances. A quiet suit of stables, a highly-polished exterior, and a choice vocabulary, are quite in keeping with the stall at the opera in London, and the second horse, silver cigar-case, and sandwich-box, which accompany them over the green uplands of Leicestershire. And surely this is a good exchange for the noise and vulgarity which betrayed the 'drunken couper' of the last century. We have now to deal with a man who is a gentleman, if not by birth, at least in manners and actions; and notwithstanding the proverbially sharp practice of those connected with the sale of horses, I will venture to say, that in no other trade will a customer meet with more fairness and liberality than will be shown him by the great dealers of London and 'the Shires.'

But here we are at the clean and dainty passage which leads into Fitz-Andrews' yard, and ringing the counting-house bell, we are ushered into the presence of a good-looking, middle-aged man, extremely courtly in his manners, and particularly well-dressed, to whom we state our business and requirements. Notwithstanding the affliction of an intermittent deafness, he takes our meaning with surprising quickness, and ringing another bell, we are handed over to the care of a most respectable-looking family ostler, if we may use the expression, who, in his turn, having accompanied us across the yard, consigns us safely to the guardianship of Mr Sago, the real mainspring of the establishment, the ostensible proprietor returning to prosecute his business in the counting-house.

'I have brought Mr Grand to look at a cab-horse,' says Lord Maltby. 'Have you anything likely to suit him ?'

To which Mr Sago bows like an ambassador, and looks at Mr Grand.

'Perhaps the Captain will like to walk round the stables, my lord,' says the man in authority ; and forthwith a couple of helpers are summoned, the one to strip, the other to re-clothe the horses submitted for an approval.

Before I can spare a glance for the animals, I inspect Mr Sago, and it strikes me that never, no never, have I seen breeches and boots fit so marvellously well as those which encase his slender, well-turned limbs. Of course, he sleeps in them, and they are cleaned on his person, as such a fit cannot possibly be made 'to take off.' The man himself is moulded to be a horseman, and when mounted can perhaps make more of the animal that carries him, both as to action and appearance, than any other equestrian in London. In the meantime, Maltby has selected a grey, that looks very like what we want, and as, on being stripped, his make and shape are found to be faultless, we have him out into the yard, to ascertain his capabilities when in motion.

' Fine airy goer,' says Mr Sago, as the grey horse fidgets sidling down the yard, in a manner that would give but little room for the vehicle intended to be attached to him ;—*beautiful* action, Captain Grand, and great docility—dray-horse power, sir, with the action of a *sylph !* Like to see him in harness, Captain ?—a child might drive him with a silken thread ;' and, accordingly, the grey is lapped in leather forthwith, and I embark on a voyage of discovery by the side of Mr Sago.

'*Let him go — don't hang at his head*,' says the charioteer, making a virtue of necessity, as the horse, plunging vigorously forward, breaks away from the grasp of the attendant helpers, while Mr Sago goes on talking as if he were sitting at ease in an arm-chair. 'Town very full, sir, just now,' as we graze a landau, to avoid coming in contact with an omnibus. 'Great comfort to drive so handy a horse as this. I'm a *very* poor coachman myself; but I think I could steer him into the City to buy stock or to borrow money, Captain. Will you like to get your hand on him?' he adds, as by dint of consummate skill, and that delicacy of touch which horsemen call 'hand,' he succeeds at length in making the animal go quietly up to his bit; and as my practice in olden time with Cartouch's drag had given me some little insight into driving, I soon find that, with regular work, the grey is likely to make me a pleasant and valuable cab-horse. After a short trial, I make up my mind to have him, and the only remaining point to be settled is as to price. For this I am again referred to the counting-house, where, after a brief interview with the proprietor, whose affliction has again attacked him, giving me some difficulty in making him understand that I do not wish to pay immediately for the horse, it is agreed that, if I like him, I am to give two hundred for him at no very remote period—if on further trial I find he will not suit me, I may return him for twenty-five pounds, which is a fair and liberal arrangement on all sides, and I walk out of the yard with Maltby, congratulated by Mr Sago on my purchase, which he assures me is 'the most eligible cab-horse in London for appearance and knee action; and with *your* "finger" upon him, Captain Grand, to make him bend himself, he will be the cynosure of a thousand eyes!'

CHAPTER VII.

MIMIC WAR.

THERE is a *bon-mot*, attributed, though I believe very un-justly, to F. M. the Duke of Wellington, to the effect that 'if he were to put 40,000 men into Hyde Park, he had not one general officer in the service who could get them out again;' and this military sally has for years delighted the inexperienced civilian, who imagines that large bodies of soldiers are to be moved simply by word of command,—in other words, that it is only necessary to holla at them, without the slightest regard to the technicalities of 'covering,' 'distance,' and 'priority of position;' for with reference to the latter essential, you would commit no greater violation of etiquette by walking Lady A. quietly off to dinner under the very nose of the Duchess of B., with whom, as host, the laws of society exact that you should lead the column, than would be laid to your charge, if in your arrangements for a field-day, you should post your infantry on the right of your artillery, and destine your smartest regiment of light dragoons to occupy the left of the line. I have been led into this digression by the recollection of the important manner with which my servant proffered the order-book to my notice, in the pages whereof it was distinctly enacted in 'brigade orders,' that on the following morning the three regiments of Guards should form 'contiguous columns' in the explosive neighbourhood of Hyde Park powder-magazine, while a regimental ukase announced that we were 'to parade in review order,' and that Captain Grand and a party would be 'furnished' to keep the ground. And in compliance with these distinct commands, the following morning, at nine, saw me adorned with glittering epaulette, sash of gold, and bear-skin cap—no pleasant covering under a sweltering summer's sky —offering my valuable assistance to a troop of Life Guards and a handful of police, in restricting John Bull to a certain portion of the Park's dried-up surface, and prevailing on him to abstain from trusting his unwashed face and opaque figure between the reviewing generals and the troops they were there to inspect.

Certainly the good humour of an English mob is deserving of all
praise; even under circumstances of political excitement they
seldom lose their natural relish for fun and frolic; and when
they are met together for anything in the shape of a sight—the
Lord Mayor's show, the prorogation of Parliament, the Derby, or
a spectacle such as the present—their sense of the ludicrous, and
determination to enjoy themselves, are not to be surpassed. The
temper displayed by our police, who are truly a long-suffering
generation, assists largely in keeping up this feeling of good-
fellowship; and though a stalwart sentry may drop the butt of
his heavy musket on a pair of sensitive toes, or the managed
charger of a Life Guardsman disperse a knot of idlers with his
disciplined gambols and the whisk of his long, heavy tail, roars
of laughter alone greet the sufferers, who in their turn can seldom
refrain from joining in the general mirth. I was much struck
with this on the morning in question, when having stationed
myself at the point of greatest attraction, and consequently
where there was most pressure from the crowd, I found that not
even the size and weight of our athletic guardsmen were always
sufficient to stem the rush of the populace, and I had occasionally to call in the assistance of a black charger and its immovable
rider, the effect of which was instantaneous. But there was one
figure that I had observed two or three times trenching the forbidden line, and being a gentlemanlike military-looking man, he
had perhaps been allowed to creep rather more forward than the
rest unmolested; but at length, on his attempting to separate
himself from the crowd, and take up his position in the space
set apart for officers in uniform and those who had tickets to
witness the review, one of my sentries lost all patience, and
ordering his firelock in most unpleasant proximity to a well-
varnished pair of boots, he at the same time bid the intruder
stand back, and interposed his own massive person in a manner
that left no alternative. I saw an altercation was going on, and
as I approached to request the gentleman civilly to withdraw, I
overheard an angry expostulation between the intruder and the
unmoved private.

'I'm an officer, sentry. I insist upon being allowed to pass.'
'Can't help it, sir—not in uniform.'

'I tell you I'm an officer. I have a right to go through the lines.'

'Can't pass without a ticket.'

'I'll report you, sir; I will, by Heaven! I'm an officer; there's my card. My name's Walker—Major Walker, East India Company's service.'

'Major Walker, is it?' said the stoical guardsman, who was moreover a bit of a wag, in a quiet way—'then if you *be* Major Walker, the best thing as you can do, is to *walk* off!'

I had some difficulty in preserving my gravity as I came up, and was appealed to by the irate field officer. However, having every reason to suppose, from his manners and appearance, that he was what he represented himself, I passed him through on my own authority, and was thanked with a courtesy that showed my civility was not misplaced.

Sundry little episodes of the same kind, varied by the occasional 'break down' of a temporary wooden stand, and comical discomfiture of its occupants, served to pass the time until the troops had taken up the several positions assigned to them; and as my situation was close behind the saluting point, from which favourable locality all the intricate manœuvres of the field-day were to be witnessed, I had an uninterrupted view of one of the most beautiful spectacles to be seen by the public in London, and one for which, unlike all other national exhibitions, 'there is nothing to pay.'

> 'By Heaven! it is a splendid sight to see,
> (For one who hath no friend, no brother there),'

says Byron in his thrilling description of the eve of mortal fray; but in this mimicry of war, the sight is even more splendid: there is no after-thought of pain or pity to mar the enjoyment of the glittering present, while happy is the fair one who recognises, or thinks she recognises, amidst that immovable mass of red and white, the martial form of a brother, a lover, or even a husband, assisting in the much-admired pageant. Wonderful is the infatuation of woman as regards a scarlet coat. In the absence of a veritable dragoon, and the gloomy listlessness of November, even the stained and draggled crimson of the fox-hunter has a charm; but a real uniform of the killing hue, bedizened with gold lace, more especially if surmounted by a pair of mustachios, is irresistible.

Not the least beautiful portion of the day's display was the mass of lovely and well-dressed women who had congregated to see the review; and many an exclamation of wonder and delight rose from that bewitching assemblage, as column after column moved steadily on to the ground, and halted in its proper place with military exactitude and precision.

'Look, papa!' said a gentle voice behind me, in accents of unmistakable enjoyment — 'here come the 17th Lancers, and there is your old corps, the Artillery, as far as you can see, upon our left. And what is that regiment of dark people coming from behind the trees?'

'The rifles, my dear, probably,' was the reply: 'but my eyesight is so bad, I cannot make out anything at that distance.'

'Oh, how I wish somebody would explain to me what they are going to do, I do so love a review!' said the excited girl.

And thinking it a pity so much military enthusiasm should be thrown away, I was in the act of taking advantage of my official position to furnish the young lady with a programme of the proceedings, when, turning round, I recognised, in the old gentleman of fading vision, a Colonel Belmont whom I had once met at my father's house, but of whom I knew very little, except that he was a widower with an only daughter.

'Can I be of any service to you, Colonel?' I said. 'Probably you have forgotten Digby Grand?'

And whilst papa was occupied in shaking hands, cordially expressing his delight at our mutual recognition, and overwhelming me with inquiries about Sir Peregrine, whom he had probably seen long since his undutiful son, I had time to look at the daughter, whose charming voice had first attracted my attention. Heavens! what a beautiful girl she was! Far be it from me, like Olivia, to enter upon an inventory of her charms—'*item*, two lips, indifferent red, &c.'—but she had the good fortune to possess those violet eyes, with long black eyelashes, that, with dark hair and a fair complexion, have made a fool of many a wise man since the days of King Solomon. Ere I was presented to her I had seen at a glance that she was *bien gantée* and *bien chaussée*, those two essentials in a lady's dress; and as she turned her graceful head towards me, and received papa's introduction with her own sweet smile, I thought I should wish no better amusement than to act cicerone to this fascinating Miss Belmont during the whole of the coming performances.

But the dark massive columns have deployed into line, and far as the eye can reach, extends a belt of red and white, flanked by the dusky Rifles and grim batteries of artillery; while the lightsome pennons of the Lancers come wheeling rapidly from the rear. All eyes are directed towards Hyde Park Corner, and the crowd are mute with expectation, for a hoarse and indistinct command, reiterated in the front, is followed by the flash of steel along the whole line, as a thousand bayonets leap into air, and the brigade 'shoulder arms,' preparatory to receiving, with due respect, the time-honoured hero who is to inspect them. A brilliant and glittering staff winds through the iron gates near Aspley House, and sweeping rapidly into the Park, advances almost to where we are standing, as if expressly to give Miss Belmont an uninterrupted view of the Iron Duke, whom she adores with lady-like devotion. The line opens its ranks, and 'presents arms;' the Commander-in-chief returns the salute, and though he bears a venerable head, white with the snows of eighty winters, the frame below is lithe and hardy, almost as in the prime of life, the heart within game and dauntless as ever. The populace cheer, the band plays 'God save the Queen,' and the tears sparkle in Miss Belmont's eyes.

'How well the old Duke is looking,' says every one, with an affectionate emphasis on the adjective. And then the *habitués*, proud of their better information, instruct their country cousins in the identity of the different notabilities. 'That's Prince George; and there's the Duke of Hessians; and here comes Earl Sabre-tache—*how* well he rides; and there goes one of the Plantagenets;—what a nice bay horse! and which is the Marquis's *other* leg?' as the finest horseman in England sways his mutilated figure to every motion of the highly-broke charger he bestrides. And so they run over the whole staff, with a remark for each—delighted beyond measure if a nod of recognition should reach them from any individual of that brilliant *cortège.*

All this time the review is going on, and I have the pleasant task of explaining to Miss Belmont the different manœuvres of the regiments in motion. How they advance in column, covered by skirmishers, as the smart and active riflemen dot the surface of the Park; how they form line with wondrous rapidity ere the smoke created by the artillery has half cleared away. How the cavalry make a brilliant and inexplicable charge, then opening out like some ingenious display of fireworks, retire by wings, and are no more seen. How the infantry in the meantime have betaken themselves to the formation of impregnable squares, and having 'prepared to resist cavalry' by creating living fortresses bristling with bayonets, are peppering away to their hearts' content. The only drawback to this striking manœuvre being the critical position of the 120th Foot, who receive and return the combined fire of her Majesty's three regiments of Guards with a gallantry and steadiness that, if ball-cartridges were substituted for blank, would win them undying fame. However, the spectators do not find it out, so it matters but little. And now there is more smoke than ever, and a little divertissement by a dismounted aide-de-camp, whose loose horse much distracts the attention of the ladies. When we have ascertained he is not killed or even hurt, and have time to look about us a little, the line has re-formed, and after a steady advance, commences a series of 'file-firing,' producing, as Miss Belmont observes, very much the effect of running one's finger rapidly down the keys of a pianoforte, and the precision of which is testified by the attitudes of sundry ragamuffins and boys of the looser sort, who having got within the lines, are now feigning to suffer great loss and slaughter amongst themselves from the efficient aim of the troo s, and are lying about the field in every distorted species of p ntomimic death. 'Fire a volley,' says the senior in authority. 'Fire a volley,' repeat colonels and majors to their respective regiments and battalions. 'Steady, men,' says the sergeant-major; 'lock up! that rear rank' (which does *not* imply that one-half the regiment is to be condemned to solitary confinement), and a thundering volley discharges itself, under cover of which the uncompromising bayonet is levelled, and a combined charge executed by the whole line, which looks as if it would sweep general-officers, staff, police, spectators, ladies, and all into Park Lane. Abstaining, however, from so general 'a scrimmage,' they halt and retire in admirable order, covered by cavalry and artillery, and throwing out clouds of skirmishers, till they have reached the same ground and taken up the same positions with which the review commenced.

'And now, Miss Belmont,' I explain to my attentive companion, 'the points are being placed, and the regiments will march past.'

'Oh, how delightful!' says the fair enthusiast. 'And will *your* company march past, Captain Grand? and shall we hear the band? Papa, now you will see the Guards quite close.'

And quite close the imposing columns came; and many an adjutant's heart leapt for joy as company after company, Guards, Rifles, and Infantry of the line, moved steadily past the saluting point exact as a machine regulated by mechanism, level as a wall of brick. There always appears to me something awful in the uncompromising, unwavering advance of a large body of disciplined men. It is his resolute, unflinching bearing, his steady demeanour, totally uninfluenced by extraneous circumstances—in a word, it is the magic power of discipline that gives the soldier his moral advantage over all the headlong gallantry and numerical superiority of undrilled thousands. And this steadfast reliance on himself, his officers, and his comrades, is only to be acquired by constant mutual practice in the field—practice that must be often repeated on the drill-ground before it can be brought into play under the fire of an enemy. This is the secret of all the marchings and counter-marchings, so often sneered at by the ignorant of military affairs. This is the object of the frequent parades and countless manœuvres that to the unreflecting appear so unnecessarily to harass the soldier. And all this must be brought to a very high state of perfection before such a 'march past' can be witnessed, as delighted the unpractised eyes of pretty Miss Belmont, and called forth an approving sentence from 'the Duke' himself.

And now, much to my annoyance, the movements of the day are come to a conclusion. The line, once more formed, advances

in open order to the music of the three finest bands in the service,
and again 'present arms,' as a sort of farewell to the illustrious
hero.   A few words of approbation addressed by him to the
respective colonels are soon made known to the officers and
privates of the different troops and companies; and I am compelled to bid Miss Belmont farewell, not, however, before I have
discovered her whereabouts in London; and collecting my dispersed party together, I march them back towards the barracks
under the wing of the battalion to which they belong.

CHAPTER VIII.

GOOD RESOLUTIONS.

A S I willingly exchanged the oppressive confinement of a
uniform for the cooler habiliments usually worn in London
during the summer, I found upon my table, amongst a whole
heap of unanswered letters, unpaid bills, gloves, cigars, and all
the miscellaneous litter of a bachelor's abode, a small rose-
tinted note, written in the palest ink, indited by the white hand
of Mrs Man-trap.

'Confound the woman!—what can she mean by all these
dashes?' I thought, as I opened and read the following emphatic
missive :—

'———— STREET, *Saturday.*

'DEAR CAPTAIN GRAND,—If *not* too much *fatigued* by your
MILITARY DUTIES, shall you be at Lady Cockle's *to-day.*   I am
MOST ANXIOUS to *see* you, and shall *go* EARLY.   If you are not
here in *time* for me *to take you down,* I can, at all events, BRING
YOU BACK.   I shall be *enchanted* to hear ALL the particulars of
the *review.*—Yours ever,

'MARGERY MAN-TRAP.'

This was a fair specimen of Mrs Man-trap's usual style of
correspondence; but why she should suppose that she rendered
her sentences more intelligible by underlining every second

word, I am at a loss to conjecture. Of one thing, however, I was certain, that the volley of inquiries concerning our field-day would be unbearable under a hot sun, and I therefore determined to drive my own high-stepping grey cab-horse quietly down to Lady Cockle's, and trust to chance for making my excuses. The fact was, I never felt so tired of Mrs Man-trap as on that morning. Fresh from the society of my new acquaintance, the charming Miss Belmont—the recollection of the *manièrée* woman of the world was thoroughly distasteful; and yet but a few short days ago it was the height of my ambition to be an especial favourite with the latter. There was a degree of *éclat* in certain circles conferred by her preference that was very fascinating to my vain imagination; and in the absence of Zoë, and the uncertainty of my relations with Coralie, I had almost fancied that I was a little in love with a woman old enough to be my mother. And now a newer idol had driven the images of all these from my mind. Even poor Zoë I could scarce bear to think of; and it was with a bitter feeling of shame that I was obliged to confess such a heart as mine was not worth having—'unstable as water,' and fickle as a leaf upon the breeze. But, in the meantime, I dressed as carefully as twenty ever thinks it necessary to adorn itself,—and armed at all points, found myself a well-satisfied item of a fashionable throng, enjoying the bright sunshine of the summer afternoon on Lady Cockle's smoothly-shaven lawn.

There were all the usual ingredients of a ' breakfast ' in the vicinity of London. There were flowers to look at, and shady walks to flirt in; there were glee-singers concealed in a shrubbery, and bloated gold-fish in a pond; there was plenty to eat and drink, and much too few chairs to sit down upon; in fact, good-humoured, gouty Sir Harlequin Hautboy whispered to me, looking ruefully down the while at a pair of tiny white brode-quins which imprisoned his venerable feet, ' that he should go and sit in the carriage till his daughters were ready to come away'—in short, there was all and everything necessary to make the breakfast go off to the satisfaction of every one concerned; and even Mrs Man-trap, whom I soon discovered sitting in a striking attitude and a commanding position, allowed that

it was all very pretty and well done. As I bowed my way up
to that irresistible lady, I could not help being struck with the
contrast which forcibly presented itself between my new flame of
the morning, and the well-known coquetteries of her to whom I
was now to render homage. What a difference between the artless grace and unconscious charms of Miss Belmont, and the
studied attitudes, flounced and furbelowed dress, and *crêped*
ringlets, of Mrs Man-trap ! Beautiful she certainly was, though no
longer young ; but even her most devoted admirers must allow
that she would have looked better had that fair hair been
suffered to droop in natural curls, and not been frizzed out and
tortured into a species of glory round her head. With her
rouge we will not quarrel, as it was but a *soupçon*, and made her
eyes sparkle with a brilliancy all her own ; but why, with a
really well-turned and fully-rounded figure, did she think it
necessary to disguise its proportions in such a voluminous multi-
plicity of starch and draperies, as might have defied the most
experienced dressmaker, and skilful anatomist to boot, to distinguish the actual from the ideal—the real from the illusive ?

'How badly you have behaved, Grand,' she began, stretching
out to me the prettiest little white-gloved hand, surmounted by
a puffed-out cloud of muslin, and adorned with a gold chain and
locket, containing Mr Man-trap's hair, a piece of sentiment the
more creditable, as their separation, *a mensâ et thoro*, had long
since relieved the tedious routine of business in the House of
Lords—'shamefully : you haven't been near me for two whole
days, and I wanted to ask you the rights of this business about
young Swindle and the Jockey Club, and whether you had seen
the carriage St Heliers has ordered for Rivolte ?'

These were two home-thrusts, as in Mr Swindle's business I
had taken a strong part, which was likely to give me a good deal
of trouble ; and when Coralie's name was mentioned, a mingled
feeling of anxiety and regard for the pretty *danseuse*, made me
almost commit the indecency of blushing.

But the worst of Mrs Man-trap was, that she had a cool *naïve*
way of asking impertinent questions, and making remarks upon
the subject nearest one's heart, as if one's private feelings were
of no earthly consideration whatever. I strove to answer her,

nevertheless, with a carelessness equal to her own, and thinking I had really been somewhat inattentive of late, I tried to make amends by doing the agreeable to the best of my abilities. In all affairs of flirtation, I have invariably found that *l'appetit vient en mangeant*, and in that, as in many other situations of life, if not going 'too fast to be pleasant,' we often find ourselves 'going too fast to be safe.' We were soon as good friends as ever, and were rapidly arriving at that indefinite boundary where friendship ceases and a warmer relation begins. As usual, I thought only of the present; and adopting St Heliers' maxim, 'never to look forward beyond dinner-time,' I cut out for myself a very pleasant afternoon of gossip and love-making with Mrs Man-trap, varied by observations and scandal of our neighbours, tea and strawberries and cream for ourselves. What cared I, that ninety-nine out of one hundred most intimate friends were good-naturedly remarking, 'What a fool that boy makes of himself, with a woman twice his age!' or 'I see Mrs Man-trap has got hold of that unfortunate young Grand!' These observations were not addressed to us; on the contrary, people rather refrained from interrupting our *tête-à-tête*, and civilly got out of our way as much as possible. So I plied my fair companion with compliments and flattery, and, what she liked nearly as well, fed her insatiable appetite for news. We arranged a picnic; talked about a joint excursion to Cowes; voted, almost in plain terms, that we were very unhappy when separated, and agreed to ride together regularly every day at five; in short, we were getting on at railroad pace, and Heaven only knows where our journey would have terminated, had I not been suddenly arrested in my most emphatic assurances by the drowsy voice of good Colonel Belmont impressing upon another elderly gentleman, in a buff waistcoat, that 'turnips might be grown the size of his head on light land, or red land, or some other kind of land, by applying a certain compost made of sundry costly articles, but which must pay in the long run, as had been proved by a millionnaire on an experimental farm.' The elderly gentleman, to his shame be it said, was no agriculturist, and looked as if he did not much care whether the turnips paid or not; but a noble duke, who overheard the conversation, and who was heart and

soul interested in the cultivation of the soil, was soon at close
quarters with the Colonel, and walked him off before I had time
to see whether or not he was accompanied by his pretty daughter.
I need not say that I recognised the good Colonel's drawling
tones in an instant, and had some difficulty in concealing from
my companion the anxiety I experienced to ascertain if he had
come (which was very unlikely) to the breakfast on his own
account.

'Do you know Colonel Belmont or his daughter?' said Mrs
Man-trap, with an intuitive perception of what was going on in
my mind.

I stammered out, 'No—yes—that is, I have been introduced
to *her*.'

'He's a dreadful old bore, but she's a nice-looking, unmeaning
sort of girl,' was the careless reply; yet a settled flush on her
cheek-bones, lowering through the rouge, with a contracted smile
about her mouth, showed that the speaker was ill at ease.

I was now, however, so eager to discover Miss Belmont, that I
felt no scruples in leaving Mrs Man-trap to the tender care of a
gouty peer, who was by way of paying her great attention when
he had nothing better to do, and cursing my own stupidity in
not having thought of asking the fair Flora whether she was
going to the breakfast before I parted with her at the review, I
hunted all over the gardens, like a shepherd in French polish who
had lost his love.

What a difference does it make in ball, breakfast, or party
whether we go there simply with the somewhat hopeless intention of being amused, or whether we have 'an object' to which
all the lights, ornaments, music, crowds, champagne, and dancing,
are merely accessories.   Elderly gentlemen, depend upon it, you
have the best of it.   The lot of woman has ever been to fidget,
and when she has done being uncomfortable about herself, there
is but a short interval ere it is time to be uncomfortable about
her daughters; but you, respected head of a fine family!—you,
portly and port-wine drinking patriarch! what have you to do
when, to your astonishment, you find yourself at a *fête*, but to
stick your hands in your pockets, and, hob-nobbing with your old
cronies, enjoy yourself to the utmost?   What care you that

Maria's hair has come out of curl, and Mr Jilt has never so much as asked Jane to dance? You leave these matters in perfect confidence to your energetic lady, whilst you discuss last night's division and the ever-present ministerial crisis. Now look at your son Augustus; 'tis true that his form is graceful and his step is light, his hair is glossy and his whiskers curled. He is the image, so you think, with retrospective flattery, of what you were at his age, and for an instant you sigh to think how long that is ago. But could you peep behind the embroidered shirt-front that covers his manly chest—could you lay bare the secrets of his bosom, you would not envy son Augustus. He came to the ball on purpose to meet Miss Eglantine, and she is waltzing for the second time with Lord Haycock, and has not vouchsafed poor Augustus a word. His ambition (at his time of life) is to be in a good set, and to know all the great people. Alas! Lady Overbearing, whose carriage he calls like a town-crier, and whom, in such difficulties, he attends like a running footman, has even now passed him without a nod. Painfully alive to ridicule, poor lad, Mr Sneersby has just complimented him, ironically, upon his hack; and with all these mingled annoyances, and a variety of outstanding unpaid bills, of which, as yet, you know nothing (but take comfort, *your* time will come upon that point)—can you lay your hand upon your heart and say that you would exchange your half-century of experience, and the comfortable mental repose which it has brought, for the hollow excitement and craving restlessness of incipient manhood?

Here was I, in the first bloom of youth, and the good spirits which accompany that unreflecting age, with health, position, not money, but credit, which did equally well, and everything else to make life enjoyable, and yet I doubt if a more restless discontented spirit ever walked the earth than was mine on that sunny afternoon whilst searching for Miss Belmont; and then when I did find her, and took her into a crush-room to drink weak tea, and then prevailed on her to accompany me down a shady walk to inspect certain camellias, of which I hardly knew the names, did I not, in that very peaceful alley, come face to face with Mrs Man-trap, of all people in the world, who gave me a look that said, as plainly as look could speak,—'Aha, young gentleman!

so I have caught you out at last; but I will put a spoke in your wheel, take my word for it.' And well did she redeem that prophetic pledge in after-days. It must have been an instinctive feeling of well-grounded horror that made Miss Belmont shrink involuntarily from her, and ask me 'who that bold-looking lady was?' 'Tis in vain to recapitulate the feelings crowded into such an afternoon as that. If there is a turning-point in the career of every man, when his good and evil destinies are balanced to a hair, and his future fate is determined by some trifling circumstance, too insignificant to mention, surely that sunny evening that saw me wander through those fragrant shrubberies with Flora Belmont had an influence on my later life—at times almost imperceptible—at times the only redeeming point in a character otherwise steeped in sin.

Need I say that Mrs Man-trap's barouche was innocent of my weight as it rolled back to town. I was in one of those moods when solitude and reflection are our greatest luxuries. A new life was dawning upon me. I found myself shrinking with disgust from the associates and the amusements which yesterday had appeared so delightful. I looked into futurity, and pictured a happy home, blessed by the presence of such a one as her from whom I had so lately parted. I saw myself descending on the stream of time, a wiser and a better man, living in the country, ministering to the wants of the poor, happy and respected. Then a momentary twinge came across me, as I recollected that one of the indispensable attributes of respectability was the payment of one's debts; and here, I must confess, I did not see my way very clearly; but without dwelling too long upon that point, I pursued my day-dream, shutting my eyes to its disagreeables, and was in the midst of a fairy vision of Haverley Hall with a young and beautiful mistress, a weekly soup-kitchen, a Christmas gathering of friends and relations, and a life of calm, rational, domestic enjoyment.

I had got thus far, and had just carried in the affirmative a knotty point I was debating in my own mind, as to whether I should keep a pack of foxhounds, when a dainty umbrella, thrust into my horse's face, arrested our progress, and dissolved my castles in the air at the same instant, while Hillingdon's well-known voice shouted out my name, as he picked his way across Piccadilly into St James's Street.

'Lucky that grey horse is only blind of one eye, Digby, or I should have been a case for the hospitals, to a certainty,' said my friend, whom I had all but run over; and interrupting my vehement defence of my cab-horse's eyesight, an aspersion I was not inclined to give in to, by assuring me I looked savage and hungry, he proposed that we should dine together at Crockford's in half an hour, and, if not too late for the ballet, go from thence to the opera. What could I do?—the gastric juices of a boy who has just done growing are clamorous in the extreme about eight o'clock. I was not engaged to dine anywhere else; I had no home but the clubs,—a home, by the way, much appreciated by sundry middle-aged gentlemen who ought to know better,—and, though I do not excuse myself for the inconsistency, I merely state the simple fact, that the upshot of all my good resolutions and virtuous schemes for the future was my sitting unusually long after dinner with St Heliers, and sundry other choice spirits who joined our party, and losing five hundred 'up-stairs' before I went to bed.

In making these confessions, I may as well state, once for all, that I do not seek to conceal, far less to palliate, the follies and vices into which I, and such as I, unhesitatingly plunged. Conscious of my own defects, I am aware that many young men enter the world under far worse auspices than were mine, and come out of that searching ordeal pure and unscathed; but I greatly fear that these, if not exceptions, are at least only a minority; that mine was by no means an unusual case; and if such be the truth, may I venture to hope that the simple relation of facts and feelings, the plain, unvarnished recital of each step in the downward course, each circumstance in the moral perversion of a man born and bred a gentleman, and entering life through one of her fairest and most promising portals, may serve as a warning and a beacon to those who are themselves aware of their instability when exposed to temptation—their organic incapability of saying 'No!'

How often do we see a youth, and more particularly the younger sons of the nobility, thrust upon the world in the

falsest of all false positions—placed in a station which he has
not the means of keeping up, and moving in a sphere whose
necessary expenses must eventually entail ruin upon him.   He
has probably been educated at Eton or Harrow, with his brother
the marquis, and when he came home for the holidays, either
because he was mamma's pet, or because he was better-looking
or cleverer than the peer presumptive, he found himself in every
respect quite as important a personage as his elder brother.   He
rode as good a pony, and rode him a turn harder; was put into
as 'warm a corner' by the keeper at his grace's lordly battues,
and was in every respect on the same footing.   So far so good;
it would be hard to make a distinction between boys, and it
might, perhaps, be as bad for the elder as it would be wholesome preparatory training for the younger.   But ere long the
jacket is discarded for a tailed-coat, and there is a question of
razors and a dressing-case.   Then comes Oxford or Cambridge,
and still the young one holds his senior a neck-and-neck race;
they are both 'tufts,' and, as far as income goes, very much on
a par, as they each run into debt pretty handsomely, as a matter
of course, which debts the duke, though not as a matter of course,
pays.   And now comes the tug of war,—now the younger lord-
ling enters upon the world, armed indeed, generally speaking,
with a frontlet of brass, but wofully deficient in the more valuable metal he has all his life been learning to squander so freely.
'Lord of his presence and small land beside,' his rank gives him
an entrance into the gayest, the highest—what is called the best
society, which his previous habits teach him to enjoy and appreciate.   Pleasure is for a time a willing handmaid, and the butterfly frolics gaudily in the sun; but, unfortunately, a day of
reckoning must come; the longest-suffering tradesmen like to be
paid once in three years, and a creditor too often put off becomes
at each postponement a more pitiless enemy.   Our scion of
nobility, like the child of toil, must be clothed and fed; but
what would be luxuries to the million are to him the necessaries
of life.   It is as indispensable for him to be well dressed as it
is for a man of middle station to be dressed at all; and although
he may feed at the mahogany, and repose on the mattresses, of
another, yet he and his valet must move from Castle to Hall;

and posting is proverbially only to be effected by means of ready money.

Then, must he give up hunting, to which he has all his life been accustomed, because, forsooth, he cannot keep horses?—brought up with the Racing Calendar and Stud Book at his fingers' ends, must he abjure the bracing heath and the velvet sward, over which he loves to see the favourite skimming like an arrow? Must he be poisoned with rough, loaded port, to whom the clean and silky Chateau-Margaux is as mother's milk? —or must he starve upon roast mutton, whose appetite has been hitherto appeased with *salmi de bécasses?* No; you cannot break through the habits of a lifetime with an effort: you cannot reclaim the eagle whose untamed youth has matured in his lofty eyrie, and lure him to your fist like a sparrow-hawk; neither can you expect that the young patrician, whose boyhood has been undisciplined and uncontrolled, shall suddenly assume with manhood those principles and habits which it costs years of self-denial to acquire. He will go on as he has begun, and when hopelessly involved, and irretrievably ruined, it will be well if he confine himself to preying upon the unoffending tradesman, and do not carry his depredations into the class of society to which he belongs.

We are apt to attach a certain degree of credit to the expression, 'living by one's wits,' and rather respect the individual who so exists as being a very clever fellow; but if we consider for one moment to what especial profession we apply the term, we shall esteem it a less enviable distinction. What is the man who lives by his wits, in fact, but one who trades upon the want of those essentials in another?—who makes use of his own greater dexterity, better information, or more favourable luck, to fill his pockets at the expense of his friends and associates?—who loses no opportunity of getting the better of the very man whose roof shelters him, and whose bread he eats? And is this a worthy occupation for the well-born scion of a long line of chivalrous ancestors?—is this a fitting station for one in whose veins the pure old Norman blood courses unstained? When the mailed grasp of his warlike sire closed but upon the knightly lance, shall his degenerate fingers wield only

the covetous pencil of a betting-book? Shall the noble steed,
the generous auxiliary, the very source of the old champion's
fame, be to his descendant but an unconscious machine of fraud
and disgrace? And yet to such shifts as these may be driven
the noblest of the land, by a bad education and the exigencies of
a false position.

I have only stated the facts of the case as they may have come
under the observation of most of us. Let wiser heads than mine
propose the remedy.

But to return to Flora, as I now found myself calling her
in my day-dreams, the attachment, sprung up amidst the noise
and turmoil of the review, grew and flourished even in the
worldly atmosphere of a London season. I avoided Mrs Man-
trap; I made no further inquiries as to Coralie, and the first
time I saw her again, pirouetting as a sylphide in her vocation,
she studiously avoided looking towards my box, and showed no
inclination to renew our strange acquaintanceship. I went less
to Crockford's, and when there, shunned the little room; and I
dined a good deal at Colonel Belmont's, whose cook would have
completely destroyed the *stomach* of any man whose *heart* was
unaffected. I took to morning-walks in Kensington Gardens,
where, quite incidentally, I used to come across Miss Belmont,
promenading under the guardianship of a particularly grim personage, who, having been her nurse in childhood, now acted as
waiting-maid and local *duenna* to my ladye-love. These were
very pleasant walks, and I often look back to that peaceful time
as a sort of smiling oasis in the waste of my reckless and tem-
pestuous life. People may sneer at the cockney-beauties of
Kensington Gardens, but for my part I love those trim alleys
and long deep glades as well as anything I have met with further
afield; and were it not that the stems of the fine old trees
become so engrained and blackened with soot, you might fancy,
in the heart of that sylvan scenery, that you were hundreds of
miles from London. The sun does not shine now-a-days as it
used to shine upon those early strolls; and then, when the
world's *morning* began about half-past five P.M., we were wont
to meet again; for it was a time-honoured custom with the kind
old Colonel to take his darling out for a ride in the park

regularly as the afternoon came round : and being, partly from
absence of mind, and partly from short-sightedness, a most inefficient guardian, I always received a hearty welcome from papa,
as an additional escort. Need I say the welcome, though not
so loudly expressed, was as warmly murmured from the lips of
the daughter. The rides were nearly as delightful as the walks,
for Flora looked unspeakably lovely in a riding-habit; and being
a somewhat timid equestrian, required all the little attentions
and assistances which it was my delight to lavish. Many men
are wonderfully susceptible to beauty on horseback, and are
completely captivated by the skilful equitation of the woman
they admire; but I confess to a partiality for the less daring fair
one, whose characteristic helplessness and dependence on man are
more agreeably manifested when she leans towards him for support and encouragement, than when she kicks the dirt up in his
face, as she tears along before him, in all the triumph of holding a thorough-bred one that its lord and master is unable to
ride, but that carries her, with her light and gentle hand, quietly
enough.

I have seen women mounted and accoutred at the covertside,
as if they meant *business*, eager and excited as the very huntsman
himself, when the shaking gorse re-echoed to the crash of the
pack. I have seen them, though not many, sitting steadily
down in their saddles, as they got away alongside of the leading
hounds, skim the pastures, and flit over the fences, like birds
upon the wing; and there have been instances of the weaker sex
winning the honour of 'going best' through a run from 'find to
finish,' and 'cutting down,' from sheer nerve and determination,
the bearded sons of Nimrod themselves. But I confess that I
was never prone to be captivated by prowess such as this; and
have even had the bad taste to think that these heroines would
have been infinitely more fascinating sitting at home with their
feet upon the fender and perpetrating worsted work, ay, even
although it should entail the very counting of the stitches themselves.

No Diana of the Ephesians was Flora. She possessed a bay
mare that she thought and believed perfection, for whose prowess
she entertained the greatest respect and admiration, not un-

mingled with fear; and, truth to say, the bay mare was a good-looking animal enough, and with her mistress on her back, completed a very charming pair; and alongside of this bay mare it was my greatest pleasure to saunter, regardless of the good Colonel, who occupied the other flank, and who was sure to pick up some old friend or companion-in-arms, with whom he interchanged a considerable amount of twaddle, whilst Flora and I rode on in that sweet communion of kindred spirits which is even more delightful, when tempered with a degree of doubt and uncertainty, than when the fatal words, once spoken, have given to the relation existing between the twain a decided character and a name.

'There is that horrid woman again,' would Flora say to me, as we paced up and down the crowded 'ride,' and in each oft-repeated turn encountered the rounded form of Mrs Man-trap, on her showy steed. 'What makes her stare so?' would add my gentle companion, as the bold eyes and saucy smile would greet me with a meaning nod. I felt instinctively, I know not why, that I had made an enemy, and ever after, receiving and returning the salute of my *ci-devant* goddess, I felt a creeping sensation of impending evil that was unaccountable as it seemed absurd.

Gradually, as these rides went on, and I became a more and more familiar guest at the house of Colonel Belmont, I found myself relapsing in society into the grade of an 'engaged man,' and consequently of less and less account amongst the ball-giving dames and ball-going damsels of my acquaintance. People began to nod to me with a meaning smile; and one or two intimate friends of my own had already (the profane and confirmed bachelors!) 'hoped it wasn't true,' and begged to know when I was to be 'turned off.' And yet I had never spoken a word that could be construed into a proposal by Miss Belmont, or hinted my intentions to the good old Colonel. However, I had thought a good deal about it myself, and had made up my mind that it was absolutely essential for Flora's happiness as for mine, that we should spend the rest of our lives together as man and wife; this infatuation being the more confirmed by my own restlessness and discomfort, when the illness of a near relative occasioned the temporary absence of the Belmonts from London.

I began seriously to think of rushing into matrimony, and with-drawing myself from all the dissipations and follies of the world; for which I deserved the less credit, as the London season was now rapidly dwindling to its close. I took to leading a rational and manly kind of life, depending upon my brother officers for society, and entering ardently into all those vigorous sports and athletic exercises so popular with the young officers of 'the brigade.'

It was our greatest delight on those fine summer mornings to rush down to the margin of dirty and venerable Father Thames, and, embarking in a four-oar, dash merrily up the river to breakfast, in the time-honoured parlour of the Red House—an edifice now, alas! to be swept away by the unsparing march of modern improvement. No more shall the jovial crew, leaping from their shallop, rush headlong to the charge, and demolish a breakfast, such as those alone dare to face whose appetites are sharpened by the keen, healthy morning air, and digestions for-tified by the vigour of an oarsman's condition. No more shall the cool and unerring shot level his deadly tubes, as he quietly lays five to two upon the gun, and ere the 'blue rock,' swiftest of the children of air, rises three feet from the opening trap, mows him down upon the sward with a rapidity and precision that deserve to win, as win he does, a golden victory. No more shall Messrs Pitcher and Wing shoot off their ties with Captain Rocket and Major Snap, and decide within these echoing lists who shall claim the honour of being the best shot in England. No, the place must go to make room for a new park, that the increasing population of our wonderful metropolis may have a space wherein to breathe themselves when released from toil; and much as we may regret the loss, we cannot cavil at the object. We can only say, 'we could have better spared a better house.' But in the palmy days of that waterman's resort, we made the most of it indeed. Morning after morning might be seen our four-oar, with or against tide, shooting over the muddy waters on its upward voyage through the mimic waves of a pass-ing steamer, that caught the tossing blade of the oar, which, unless dexterously feathered, enforced upon the novice the dis-grace of 'catching a crab.'

'Give way! my lads,' says Maltby, as he bends his stalwart back to the stroke, and times each dip of his oar with the regularity of a pendulum, while the sharp-nosed craft springs forward like a racehorse to the spur—'Give way!' and we dash under Westminster Bridge, with its grim yawning arches, and massive stone buttresses, by which the tide always appears to be rushing so furiously—'Give way!' and we speed past the New Houses of Parliament, seen only to real advantage from the river, and now shining gorgeously beautiful in the warmth of the rising sun—'Give way!' and our lungs respire more freely, as the perspiration starts from our brows, and we swing gallantly along by the dull frowning walls of what the watermen call 'the Plenipotentiary on Millbank.'—'Give way!' the Red House looms in sight, and the bow-oar is discovered turning his head round to look for the promised haven, and reproved accordingly—'Give way!' for a hundred more of these long, vigorous, and welltimed strokes will take us across the river to where breakfast is even now being prepared—'Give way!' for even as the jockey finishes his race with a rush, even as the post-boy *boils up* the gallop he has reserved for 'the avenue,' even so does it behove the well-trained crew to throw the whole vigour of their stalwart shoulders and lithe, athletic forms, into those concluding efforts that are to shoot their quivering bark to the shore, and, as Jack Emery, the best of fellows and most skilled of watermen, calls it, 'bring her in handsome.' Willingly do we bend to the task, and just as we are speeding along at our best, and are thinking, some of us, that lungs and muscle will not last for ever, the welcome 'easy' poises every oar above the surface, as though arrested in mid-stroke by a charm, 'and rowed of all' is followed by the rattling of the thole-pins, and the immediate loosening of every tongue, that has hitherto been too short of breath to speak, as our long taper oars are shipped, and our fairy keel grates against the shingle of the destined port. Out jumps the bow-oar, armed with a boat-hook, and, bold as Captain Cook amongst the savages, and leaving our careful waterman to secure the boat, we rush tumultuously in to breakfast.

With constant practice, under the able tuition of the 'professional' above-mentioned, we formed no despicable crew, for amateurs, at that time. Maltby, who was always present with his regiment during the summer, in order that his leave might commence in November, a month whose saddened hues and leafless copses were far dearer to the enthusiastic fox-hunter than all the luxuriance of glorious June—Maltby took the office of 'stroke,' and acquitted himself as so keen a spirit and stalwart a frame were likely to do in that responsible situation. Hillingdon, with his calm, pale face, his lithe frame, and indomitable pluck, pulled No. 2. My duty was to labour like a galley-slave, with straining sinews and grinning countenance, at No. 3; whilst Tom Tuft, a pocket Hercules in frame, a dismounted Bacchus in habits, wielded the bow-oar and flourished the boat-hook with a vigour and a quaintness all his own.

Such a crew, in such training, were no unworthy foes even for the top-sawyers of the Goosander Club; and as it would have been a sad pity that so much energy and condition should be thrown away, articles were entered into, at my instigation, that we should make a match with a certain chosen four of that aquatic body, to enliven the dull season of an autumn in London, and furnish food for the columns of the weekly sporting journals. My old habits were sufficiently strong within me to induce me to get, by every means in my power, the best information as to the pace of our antagonists, and the 'time' in which they did their several distances; on comparing which with our own, it appeared to me that there was money to be made out of the proceedings, and that if we could only keep Tom Tuft from the decanters and the beer-barrel, we ought to make a pretty good certainty of winning. After a great deal of discussion, called by the vulgar 'chaff,' time, place, and distance were arranged, and our respective crews having decided upon the colours of their Jerseys, and the capabilities of their steerers, went into strong training forthwith. I cannot answer for the diet prescribed to them, or the particular regimen adopted by Messrs Ruffles, Mallerd, Stretcher, and Bowes, our four laborious adversaries, but I can only bear witness to the perseverance with which our own crew discussed raw mutton-chops and porter at each period when exhausted nature required refreshment. I have ever since loathed the taste of beer, and appreciated most heartily the scientific

I

transformations of a skilful cook. Day after day we fed like cannibals, and worked like Helots. Day after day, the skin got clearer, the muscles harder, and the face thinner, till at last we boasted that we were not to be 'blown' by pace or exhausted by labour. Once only Tom Tuft was granted a dispensation from the severity of our rules, and allowed to dine out with an aunt in Eaton Square, whom it would have been impolitic to offend. But the aunt possessed a store of a certain dry old port, and by cross-examination of her butler, an office I took upon myself, I discovered that Master Thomas had drunk thereof two whole bottles to his own cheek during the very short interval that he was left alone in the dining-room, whilst coffee was being prepared up-stairs. We allowed no more dinner engagements till the match was over, and our jovial 'bow' was obliged to console himself for present abstinence by anticipating the glorious jollification with which he was confident of celebrating our coming victory. As the time for the match drew nearer, so did the weather become more and more unpropitious, till the eventful day itself arrived, heralded by a continual downfall of rain that, if St Swithen had anything to do with it, must have truly gladdened the heart of that lachrymose worthy. First of all, we thought it was sure to clear at noon, and when noon came, the rain descended in straighter lines than ever; then we voted, as we shivered in the damp, dull atmosphere, it would be far pleasanter to pull in the cool of the evening, and the weather must improve by that time. Then we had to look at the style of the other crew, as they came down with the tide in a preparatory breather—Maltby thinking it better to reserve his own forces entirely for the struggle. It was the longest and most unsettled day I ever spent, and I felt quite rejoiced when, at seven in the evening, the weather still clouded and drizzling, I found myself seated in my own place in the boat, arranging my stretcher, and preparing for the coming tug of war.

It was seven o'clock ere the preliminaries were fairly arranged, the judge appointed, and the umpires placed. The dulness of the weather prevented our being honoured with a large quantity of spectators, at which we were as well pleased, and the river for once was clearer of craft than usual. Like a racehorse taking his canter, ere he engages in the strife of speed, we shot away for a half-mile 'spurt,' to get thoroughly into our swing, before the real contest should commence ; and when we felt our muscles elastic and our lungs clear, we wheeled the long narrow boat into its appointed place, and, with beating hearts and quivering limbs, sat watching eagerly for the start. The signal shot is fired—and we are off! From that moment, till, with bent and aching back, with numbed arms, and dripping brow, I staggered on to *terra firma*, and knew by the congratulations of my friends that we had won a severely contested race by a length, I have but a vague recollection of the events of the match ; it is all confused and misty as the dim perceptions of a dream. There was the shooting rush of our keel and the ripple of the water in our wake, keeping melodious time to the roll of the oars, as they feathered regularly in their rullocks; sounds echoed indistinctly from the adversary, which, like some phantom-boat, still hovered near,—now alongside, now on our track, now drawing slightly in advance ;—there was the steersman's eager face peering at times over Maltby's shoulder, as he bent to and fro with every jerk of the dancing craft, as though he, too, were helping her along;—there were the swelling muscles of Maltby's back and shoulders, rising and falling, as our stalwart captain bent gallantly to his oar; there was the hot breath of the calm and indomitable Hillingdon fanning my bare neck at regular intervals, as he laid his lengthy frame well forward to the sweeping stroke ;—there was my own blood boiling with labour and excitement, and the indescribable exhilaration of spirits, arising from severe muscular exertion and the unfailing determination to die rather than give in. Once and once only I was able to steal a look at the other boat : it was towards the close of the contest, and we were slightly ahead. There was but one word spoken by any of our crew, and its effect was electrical. 'Now!' said Maltby, as with redoubled vigour he strained to the task;—'Now!' gasped Hillingdon, behind me, in a sepulchral whisper through his grinding teeth—and 'Now!' I repeated, as with desperate energy, I tugged at my resisting oar. The monosyllable did it ! —I know not how or when, but having pulled as I never pulled before, and hope never to pull again, having outlasted by sheer 'condition' the unfair tax upon nature which such efforts demand, I had the satisfaction of knowing that, after a severe and well-contested struggle, we beat our adversaries on the goal by a short boat's-length.

Let me draw a veil over the triumph, and the dinner, composed of both crews, which celebrated it. Tom Tuft took the chair, and however many bottles he owed himself for his abstinence and self-denial, I think he must have paid them all up.

CHAPTER IX.

THE SHOOTING PARTY.

IT was now about the middle of August, and the excitement of our boat-race being over, London began to get insufferably hot, dusty, and stupid; everybody had left town, and the very waiters in the clubs were looking forward to their little excursion to the sea-side. St Heliers had been absent on the Continent for the last six weeks, and was the person I should have least expected to meet, when, to my surprise, one hot and languid afternoon, as I sauntered listlessly down St James's Street, I discovered that the only other individual occupying the pavement of that once-crowded resort was St Heliers himself—*en route*, as he immediately informed me, for the best moor and the most comfortable shooting-lodge in the north of Scotland; 'where, Digby, my boy,' added the good-natured peer, 'if you will come down with me, I shall be happy to give you lots of grouse, an occasional deer, and a good deal of that old claret you so highly approve.' I jumped at the offer, and having with little difficulty obtained sufficient leave from my military duties, that very night saw me, in company with my noble host, occupying a *coupée* of the London and North-Western Railway, and in defiance of directors' bye-laws, and forty-shilling penalties, filling it with the fumes of the choicest and most fragrant of cigars. And now, I think I cannot illustrate St Heliers' views upon men and things, including women, better than by detailing a conversation which took place between us, as we sped along northward at the rate of forty miles an hour, and which he opened by an observation on what he called the 'mistaken notion' of marrying at my time of life. 'What is this I hear, Digby,' said he, between the puffs of his cigar, ' about you and Miss Belmont? Of course you don't mean to marry her?'

' Well,' I replied, 'I certainly did think of it. But why not?'

' Why not!—why should you? Has she a very large fortune?'

' Not a sixpence, I believe, during her father's life,' I answered; ' but, of course, if I married, I should sell out, and go and live very quietly somewhere in the country.'

St Heliers' face, at this proposal, would have been a picture.

' Have you considered how badly such a life would suit you?' he said, with more earnestness than he usually showed in any matters not bearing directly on *himself;* ' have you considered how very much disgusted you would be before two years had elapsed? Of course it is no business of mine, and I never like to bore people by giving them advice, but when I see an agreeable, pleasant fellow making, with his eyes shut, for the brink of a precipice, I cannot, in common charity, refrain from asking him if he knows where he is going.'

' Well,' I interposed, ' but I do not see the irrevocable step quite in that light.'

' That is because you do not in the least know what you are going to undertake. Trust me, I have seen a great deal of life, my dear Digby, and for a fellow like you, marriage on a small income would be worse than transportation. You like to come and dine with me, for instance, because I have a really good cook, and you meet a pleasant party, with whom you have lots of fun. Are you prepared to sit down—*every day* mind you—to a bad dinner, with the same individual, whatever may have occurred to damp the spirits or ruffle the good humour of that constant *tête-à-tête* companion? You hate being bothered about

trifles, and looking into any items of expense—how shall you
like to have to speak to the butcher about the mutton being
too fat, and add up the grocer's book with a ready reckoner, to
find out whether he has overcharged you for your tea ?   I conclude you are fond of what the lower orders call a day's pleasur-
ing, as you are constant even at Hampton, and never miss a
Derby,—but how will it do to exchange Lavish's drag and the
jollity of luncheon on the course, for a drive in an open carriage
in all weathers as far as the turnpike and back, more particularly if Mrs Grant should happen to be nervous, and, what is
no unusual effect, becomes cross when she is frightened ?   I
pass over all the minor annoyances of squalling children (instead
of the opera, at which I happen to know you are a pretty constant attendant), squabbling servants, smoky chimneys, windows
that let the water run through them, and drains that do *not;*
neither will I dwell upon the petty details of what housekeepers
call ' sundries,' such as mops, brooms, toothpicks, soap, soda, and
sand-paper, all of which somebody must look into ; but I will
only ask you calmly and dispassionately to reflect for an instant
on the galling restraint, the intolerable discomfort it would be to
a man of your habits and pursuits, to be obliged to maintain a
respectability of demeanour, and to behave himself with propriety
on all occasions.'

The gravity with which my monitor propounded this last
objection, as if it were indeed a poser, was too much for both
of us, and bursts of laughter prevented the possibility of our
carrying on the conversation with the seriousness the subject
demanded : but as I drew my travelling cap over my brows,
and composed myself to sleep in my corner, I could not help
thinking how thoroughly the man of the world had exposed his
own character, his own intense regard for self, in the matrimonial
lecture with which, in really intended kindness, he treated me.
I saw what he meant : I knew there was a great deal to be given
up,—that if, in my position, I chose to marry, I must forego
luxuries, and do without excitement ; of all this I was aware, and
fully conscious that the sacrifice might cost me many a sigh ; but
still, I thought, there are many pleasures enjoyed by those who
live for others rather than themselves, of which I am as yet

wholly ignorant. Man is not intended to exert all his highest energies for his own gratification—the reflected happiness of another should be the greatest happiness to ourselves, and we increase our sources of enjoyment as we increase our responsibilities. With all his wit, all his plausible arguments and unsparing ridicule, my better nature told me that St Heliers was wrong. And yet—and yet, I pondered and hesitated, marriage was a serious undertaking; I would put it off a little; the present, as usual, was my first object. I had a delightful six weeks of sport to anticipate, and as many a wiser man has done on a far more important subject, I shrunk from coming to a final decision till 'some more convenient season.'

In the meantime, we soon arrived at St Heliers' picturesque lodge in the far north, now, in these days of steam, brought within a comparatively easy distance of London, but once a good fortnight's toil, and wild and rugged with its frowning mountains, its boundless moors, and deep, dark silent loch, as if civilisation had never penetrated into those fastnesses—the haunts of the heath-cock and the mallard, the wary red-deer and the tameless eagle. Never a merrier party met together to enjoy the best of dinners and the most undeniable of wines, after tramping and toiling the livelong day over rugged mountain and heathery corrie, than assembled nightly at St Heliers' hospitable table. Jack Lavish, of course, was there, and the life and soul of our party. Major Martingale, who could shoot in a form that Norfolk itself cannot surpass, and who was ever prepared to back his own prowess with 'the grooves,' the 'smooth bore,' or 'the rod,' for any amount of wager that the incredulous might choose to hazard, was no mean auxiliary on the hill, no lifeless companion over the mahogany; and he, too, was one of the select assemblage. My kindest friend and favourite associate, the talented and romantic Hillingdon, who, with all his love of the picturesque and fondness for travel, had never been in Scotland, was expected at the end of the week; and with such companions, Highland sport, Highland scenery, and, above all, Highland air, what more could mortal man desire? My first day's grouse-shooting, in company with our host himself, will serve as a specimen of the manner in which we passed our mornings: our evenings, alas! were devoted to excitement neither so healthy nor so harmless.

Everything St Heliers did, whether in the way of sport, or in the graver matters of life, was done in the most efficient and, at the same time, in the most comfortable manner. He never began shooting till the 20th of August, instead of eagerly fore-stalling his sport on the 12th; consequently his birds were full-grown and fit to kill, and his annual 'bag' better than his neighbours'. Others, who could not boast half his bodily vigour, would toil and exhaust themselves before half the day was over, and return languid and weary, leaving the best part of their ground untouched. Not so, my lord; he shot, as he said, 'for pleasure;' and a pleasant sight it was to see him mounted on the cleverest of shooting-ponies, whose back he never quitted till luncheon-time, knocking over his birds right and left from the saddle, with a merry smile and jovial remark, whilst ever and anon he refreshed himself from a huge wicker-covered jar of sherry-and-water, the element bearing small proportion to the wine, and carried by his 'gillie-Ganymede,' as he quaintly called a heather-legged retainer, told off for this especial duty, and strictly enjoined upon no account to quit for one moment his master's side. Two couple of highbred pointers, broke to hunt together without a mistake, obeyed the signals of a wary and silent keeper, to the wave of whose arm they instantaneously dropped; two more couple, straining in the leash, held by two active 'gillies,' were ready to relieve their companions; whilst, walking steadily in the rear, two lynx-eyed assistants were devoted solely to the duty of marking game and picking up dead birds. I walked upon St Heliers' left, the position in which he always placed his friend, for as he truly remarked, 'I can shoot him, but he cannot shoot me.' And in this order we mar-shalled our forces, to beat up the quarters of the grouse and the black-cock.

Of course, we could both shoot 'above a bit,' as in these days of improvement in fire-arms who cannot? and woe to the unwary bird that crossed within range of Lancaster's deadly tubes, 'Mark!' I shouted, as a brood, flushed almost at my feet, wheeled down the wind to my companion, leaving the two old

birds flapping their life out on the heather in front of me.
'Bang—bang,' is the reply, and two more fall to his deadly
aim, whilst the well-drilled pony stands like a form of granite,
and the peer reloads with the rapidity of a Cossack. We count
our spoils when luncheon-time arrives, and thirty-two brace bear
witness to our success. The mountain-spring sparkles like a
diamond, and the pure rarefied air wafts the scent of a thousand
wild flowers that peep from out the purple heather; but there
are truffles lurking in the bowels of that cold grouse-pie, which
exact all our attentions, and I fear the gushing spring only serves
to cool an enormous measure of 'Badminton,' that grateful compound of mingled claret, sugar, and soda-water; and then comes
the fragrant cigar, and, soothed by its wreathing fumes, we gaze
with half-shut eye on the glorious landscape spread out before
us—a sea of mountains magnificent to contemplate. An hour's
repose, and it is time again to be up and doing, but the white
mist has come down upon the hill-tops, and as it drives before
the rising gale, the birds become wary and difficult of approach;
now must we change our tactics, and sending off a party of dogs,
and men to sweep the opposite hill, we station ourselves, St
Heliers still glued to the pony, in a certain rocky pass, where,
as he observes, we shall have 'better fun than pheasant-shoot-
ing.' Brood after brood come skimming down before the wind,
high in air above our heads, and swift as the blast that whistles
round us. Brood after brood pay their tribute to our skill; for,
right and left, brace after brace keep tumbling headlong to the
ground from their pride of place. This is, indeed, sport; for
nothing but quickness of hand, accuracy of eye, and judgment
of distance, not to be deceived by space, can succeed in such
shooting as this. The weather moderates, and as we traverse
the lone moor on our homeward way, we keep picking up scattered birds, and flushing undisturbed coveys, till we arrive at the
Lodge, exulting in the slaughter of sixty brace of fine, well-grown,
dark-plumaged moor-fowl. Notwithstanding the labours of the
day, these lonely wilds were disturbed by the voice of revelry
far into the night,—ay, even till the small hours of the morning
lights were sparkling, and laughter was ringing, under the long,
low roof of our mountain home.

Knock, knock, knock, from the impatient knuckles of Hillingdon's London valet, awoke me, some few mornings after my
arrival, from that dreamless slumber which follows a hard day's
walking, and a good deal of claret. Sleepless Mæcenas! for
whom the tennis-ball bounded by day, the wine-cup flowed at
eventide, and the distant fountain murmured at night, that you
might taste repose—and all in vain! I think that even you
would have slept at St Heliers' Lodge, could you have exchanged
the toga for the plaid, the classic buskins for Highland brogues;
and, after a day's walking with Major Martingale on the hill,
and an evening spent in pledging his lordship with bumpers of
'25, have wooed Morpheus in a bed such as that I left so
unwillingly, in reply to the summons of the impatient gentleman's gentleman.

'My master desired me to call you, sir,' said this exotic; 'he
is nearly dressed, and there are several deer in the vicinity of
the house,' he added, with a degree of imagination that did him
credit, as an additional inducement to me to lose no more time.
Hillingdon had arrived the previous day. We had heard of deer
from a rugged Highlander who had taken an especial fancy to
me; and it was agreed that my friend and I should be off at
daybreak, and endeavour to account, if possible, for 'the master-
hart of the herd.' Away we went accordingly, in the gloaming
of early morning, Hillingdon pleased with everything, and, for
him, quite excited. Our only guide was the 'gillie' aforesaid,
and a long and weary tramp he led us, as we explored every
rocky pass, and deep dark corrie, with that extreme caution so
excessively provoking, but so very necessary where red-deer are
concerned. Strange to say, Hillingdon, who had never in his
life been on 'a hill' before, was the first to perceive deer, much
to the admiration of our guide; but he was gifted with extraordinary powers of sight, and had often told me, that when in
the Desert with the Arabs, he could distinguish objects in that
deluding atmosphere more clearly than the hawk-eyed Bedouin
himself. The stoical Highlander was now all excitement, as,
throwing a few heather blossoms into the air to discover how
the wind set, he held a rapid consultation in his own mind as
to how he was to 'staaalk' them, as he called it; and a grim

bloodthirsty smile illumined his countenance, as he hit upon the most likely method. And now we began a series of manœuvres wily as those of an Indian, whilst every posture was put in practice that might dislocate the joints of the human frame. First we ran for a good half-mile stretch over the open, to secure a position to start from, before 'the deers' should move. The ground was deep, the pace terrific, and, as Hillingdon said, 'the boat-race was nothing to it;' then we walked miles in a contrary direction, to get 'their wind,' an operation in which we had some difficulty in preserving our own ; then we crept, bent to an angle of forty-five, up the bed of a mountain-stream, not yet wholly dry, which introduced us to a friendly corrie, where we could stand upright, and rest our aching loins in concealment; and lastly, we 'crawled on our bellies,' like the serpent, over an interminable space of bare stubby heather, which led to some large grey stones, and which the Highlander called 'a face.' At length we reached the shelter of this favourable covering, and when we dared to look up and feast our eyes upon the wanderers we had taken so much pains to circumvent, it was, indeed, a sight worth all the labours of the stalk. Within a hundred yards, point-blank distance, a mighty stag was feeding, 'broadside on' to us, and looking almost as large as a cow. He was apparently unconscious of the vicinity of foes or ambush, and as he unconcernedly now whisked an ear, and now moved a leg, annoyed by some troublesome fly, I had time to scan him attentively, and 'count his points.' 'Royal ! by the shade of Scrope ! Twelve points, as I'm a sinner ; three in a cup at the top of each horn, and the largest brow-antlers I ever saw. We must have that head ! ' I had agreed that Hillingdon was to have the first shot, and I now stole a look at him to see whether he was likely to be deadly. Not he : the excitement was too much, and his flushed cheek and flashing eye told me the wrist would waver, and the finger tremble, when the important moment arrived. The Highlander, as usual, in his eagerness for the sport, was in too great a hurry, and he put a rifle into my companion's hand with a glance that spoke volumes.

In vain I whispered almost under my breath, 'Take lots of time, Hillingdon—no hurry.' The lock of his 'Purdey' clicked with noise enough to startle a whole forest, and the nearest hind lifted her head, and snuffed the breeze as if anticipating danger. 'The monarch of the waste' naturally enough turned half-round to ascertain what had disturbed one of the ladies of his family; and Hillingdon, afraid of losing him altogether, instantly let drive at him, when in the only position that could have made a deer at that distance a difficult shot. I had seen how it was likely to be, and had remained in readiness for a miss on the part of my friend. I calculated, and with reason, that on being disturbed, the herd would take towards the hill, and I marked a sort of pathway, about one hundred and fifty yards from us, that formed the easiest access to the brow over which they would probably disappear. Sure enough they came pitching and lurching along over the very ground I had marked out for them; and apparently in no great hurry, the very last of the parcel, came the still scathless stag. Like everything else on which bets might be laid and won, I had sedulously practised every kind of shooting, and aiming well in front of him, with perfect confidence in my rifle, I stretched him lifeless on the heather with a bullet through his heart. Hillingdon, who had not an atom of jealousy in his composition, and to whom sport was nothing compared with scenery, was as well pleased as if he had slain a hundred stags himself; and we returned to the Lodge in all the triumph that attends the 'downfall of the deer,' when, in the lack of a regular forest, you can only get the occasional chance of a shot at this seductive quadruped.

Would that we had been satisfied with the healthy and legitimate excitement of the moor and the loch—would that the demon of play had never been allowed to enter those mountain solitudes; then would our shooting have been confined to the grouse and the red-deer, and no disgraceful fracas, no bloodthirsty encounter have destroyed the harmony of our morning's pleasure and our evening's glee! However, 'there's a divinity doth shape our ends, rough-hew them how we will;' and grateful must I ever be that a meeting, which, although, as in most cases of the kind, there were faults on both sides, I greatly fear originated in my own intemperate haste, was innocent of that fatal conclusion which might have left me a corpse, or stamped me a murderer on the spot. Thus it fell out that two friends, in the common acceptation of the term, certainly two daily associates, were placed at ten paces distant, with levelled weapons, thirsting for each other's blood.

I had already spent three delightful weeks with St Heliers, and, except that we played high in the evenings, and I had lost largely, had enjoyed them to the uttermost, when on coming down to breakfast one cloudy morning, equipped for fishing, and promising myself from the state of the atmosphere a capital day's sport, two letters were put into my hand, on one of which the superscription of ' Her Majesty's Service ' warned me immediately to read the missive. Alas, the stern requirements of duty exacted my presence in London forthwith, and there was nothing for it but to be off on the morrow. ' Well,' thought I, ' this is a bore, but still it 's a change ;—and now for the other letter.' As I turned to the direction, I recognised the hand of my old friend and Colonel ; and as I sauntered leisurely down to the river I perused the following epistle from Cartouch :—

' CROCKFORD'S, *Sept.* 12, 18—.

' MY DEAR DIGBY,—How surprised you will be to hear that I am in London ; where I had not been very long, as you may believe, before I beat up your quarters, and to my disappointment, only found your address in the Highlands instead of yourself. As you are staying with St Heliers, an old friend of mine, I have no doubt you are in very lively society, but I must write you a stave to tell you the little that is going on in London, and likewise—what I am sure you will be glad to learn—all about myself. To begin with the latter edifying subject, you must know that I am now a " gentleman at large," being for the third time in my military career on half-pay. I could not stand the slowness of the Canadas, nor the sort of young ones the War Office put into the 101st, so I left them to come over and have a season's hunting in England, wherewith to recruit my war-worn frame. I came home through the States, and paid our old friend Sauley a visit. He had a trotting-match coming off, which was a real good thing, and I won an infinity of dollars from a gentleman of Alabama, who paid up like a trump. You

remember Levanter, who was in the regiment. I met him likewise; he has found out a dodge at long bowls, which fixes the
Yankees to a certainty, and I left him at Baltimore winning their
money, chains, watches, and handkerchiefs. He told me one
"rowdy" literally played for his shirt, and Levanter winning it,
on stripping him they found he had only "a collar." As he had
a long way to walk, they left him his boots to go home in. I
understand Levanter was only there for a flying visit, as he is a
regular turfite in England—but he must have made his trip pay.
Sauley asked after you, whom he remembered as being "ever-
lastin' 'cute for a young one"—a great compliment from him,
and a talent which I hope you turn to good account.

'I am buying horses, and have got a few very clever ones
together. You know my sort—well-bred to carry weight. I
find I am quite keen about November, and look forward to it
almost as much as your friend Lord Maltby, of whom I see a
great deal. I was not home in time for Goodwood, but I have
a capital book on the St Leger. I stand to win five thousand
by Tipstaff, and have not a losing horse in the race.

'So much for self. Now for our friends. I hear Grandison
is to leave the Guards for a regiment—you probably know all
about it. This will give Tom Tuft a step. The latter worthy
has been celebrating his boating victory ever since, and gave a
policeman such a licking the other night, that he was within an
ace of getting "a month at the mill"—probably the only "mill"
at which our friend Tom would not find himself at home. However, the magistrate was lenient, and he got off for a fine. De
Rivolte is in Russia with a French marquis, so report says, but
comes back to London in November; this I do not understand,
as she can have no engagement at that season. Talking of
Frenchmen, Carambole is at Cowes with a yacht! He came to
town the other night, and won £2000 here. I saw him coming
away to start again for Cowes by an early train in the most
elaborate "get up" you ever saw, and no greatcoat! He is a
hard fellow, and they tell me is a capital sailor, though a Frenchman, but too reckless. Evergreen has returned from abroad, his
affairs having completely come round—one of the advantages, he
says, of being ruined early enough in life; but he is beginning

to look old. Mrs Man-trap lingers on in town, and I see her now constantly driving about young Lavish, Jack's brother, who was rusticated the other day at Oxford; he is not good-looking, but she says he has excellent principles. She abuses you shamefully, and I had quite a row with her the other night at the Locksleys, standing up for my old pupil. She says you are a *roué*, and a gambler, and thoroughly unprincipled, and not to be depended on in any, and all sorts of things, which I will not repeat. I conclude she is piqued at something you have said or done. I have no more news, as London is at its emptiest. I met a very charming girl the other day at Hastings—a Miss Belmont, whose father is an old friend of mine, and who knew you. If I was young and foolish, I should be in danger, as I think I never saw a nicer girl. However, it would be useless, as she is to be married almost immediately to Sir Angelo Parsons, a man you must have met. How so slow a fellow ever could get hold of such a wife is more than I can tell. They say he is very rich, which I suppose explains it.—Ever, my dear Digby, yours very affectionately,

' Henry Cartouch.'

To describe my feelings as I read the concluding paragraph of this letter, penned in all the cheerful unconsciousness of high spirits and kindly feelings, would be impossible. It never occurred to me to doubt the authenticity of my friend's information, and I felt stunned and stupefied, as I tried to realise the loneliness, the utter misery of my position. And bitterly did I regret the selfishness which had prevented my coming to an understanding with Flora ; how did I curse in my very soul the vain, unstable nature that had wavered and procrastinated till it was too late—the despicable heart that was incapable of sacrificing the most frivolous pleasure for all that it held most dear. And now she was lost to me for ever, and I was alone in the world !

Till I felt that she was gone never to return, I knew not that to me Flora was all in all. Those higher principles, the noblest privilege of man, that enabled the Christians to meet with unblenching front, the worst that this world can show, were to me a sealed book and a mystery; and I had nothing, nothing on earth to look to for support and encouragement. The day-dream had melted into air, the bubble had burst, and, spoilt child that I was, I felt capable of wreaking my spite upon every object, animate or inanimate, that might cross my path. I felt as if it would be a relief to battle with the very wind.

Of all sports, probably that of fishing is the one least congenial to such a frame of mind; nor did unsuccessful efforts and broken tackle serve to raise my spirits or improve my temper. Dismissing the venerable Triton who attended me on these excursions, I wandered listlessly along the margin of the still, calm Highland loch, and gave vent to my misery unobserved. What a contrast was all around me to the heart within. The dark massive mountains, the grey-clouded sky, the broad smooth waters, unruffled by a breath, all spoke of peace and repose; but the angry spirit that was chafing in my breast turned, loathing, from the quiet of the scene. I pined for action, I longed for excitement. I strove to subdue the restless workings of the mind by laborious fatigue of the body. Faster and faster I walked—I ran—hill after hill I surmounted, and prospect after prospect I turned away from in disgust. It was dark ere I returned to the Lodge, fevered and exhausted, but bearing about with me still 'the worm that never dies'—the gnawing canker of remorse that comes too late.

Why did my spirits rise higher and higher; why was my laugh the loudest, the most frantic in its mirth, when I took my seat at St Heliers' luxurious board? Why did bumper after bumper that I poured down my unslaked throat, fail to bring forgetfulness, and only serve to raise my craving for excitement to a maddening pitch? The party were jovial as usual. St Heliers, with his dry, sarcastic humour—Jack Lavish, with his merry, thoughtless laugh—Hillingdon's quiet smile, and Martingale's eternal Newmarket stories, were all as they had ever been; and as, in consideration of my departure on the morrow, an additional *magnum* made its appearance, they voted that I was in shamefully good spirits for one who was so soon to lose their agreeable society. But the excitement of wine alone was insufficient for my boiling blood. Our usual whist-party, although the regular stakes we played nightly would have satisfied most men, was voted 'slow,' and at my instigation the party, who had all drunk deep, were nothing loath to substitute 'chicken-hazard' for 'four by honours and the odd trick.' The stakes were 'set,' the dice rattled, and first notes, then I O U's began to circulate freely round the table. Fortune divided her favours pretty equally among my friends, and I alone lost heavily. For this I cared little; the excitement was the thing; and like the immortal Fox, of playing memory, next to the pleasure of winning was the pleasure of losing. At last the game began to get serious; once or twice had St Heliers good-naturedly attempted to moderate the stakes, but in vain. Cigars and brandy and soda came in, and with these additional incentives, hundreds began to change hands rapidly—and still I lost. I could have borne to be beggared by my friend Hillingdon; to jovial Jack Lavish, or hospitable St Heliers, I could have paid my last farthing unflinchingly, like a gentleman; but at the bottom of my heart there lurked a feeling of dislike towards Major Martingale, and it was galling beyond measure to lose to him those hundreds which were now so rapidly decreasing. At length, nettled by the tone of superiority which he was fond of assuming, especially after dinner, and maddened by my continued reverses, I invariably increased my 'set' heavily as soon as I saw him prepared to 'cover it;' and at last an absurdly large sum depended upon my cast of the dice. The others paused to see the throw, and Martingale, with an insolent sneer, asked if I would like to stand another hundred. 'Two,' I exclaimed, furiously, 'and two more besides that, if you dare;' and notwithstanding St Heliers' remonstrances, the already enormous stake was increased by that amount. I dashed the box down upon the table, and one of the wished-for numbers was triumphantly landed—the other die as it rolled over on its corner struck against my adversary's hand, and I lost! I claimed another throw with vehemence, asserted that Martingale's hand had no right to be on the table, and insinuated it was done on purpose; he retorted (not courteously); and a wrangle ensued, which was referred to the party present, who gave it against me, deciding that it was impossible such a thing could have been done intentionally, but recommending that we should draw the stakes. To this we would neither of us consent, and the affair terminated in my losing all control of my temper, and presenting Martingale with a cheque for the money, whilst I informed him 'that I distinctly begged him to understand I considered it a robbery, but not the less welcome or the more unusual to him on that account!' A dead silence ensued after this most unjustifiable demonstration. I saw his fingers quiver, and his fist clenched for an instant; but he curbed his temper in a manner that ought to have made me thoroughly ashamed of losing mine, and lighting a candle, marched out of the room without saying another syllable.

For two long hours did poor Hillingdon sit with me, endeavouring by every argument in his power to prevail upon me to apologise for this unprovoked insult. But I was too obstinate to listen either to the dictates of my own better feelings or the remonstrances of my friend. No, the excitement I longed for had come at last; in the immediate prospect of a duel my restless spirit found a sort of false repose; and, strange to say, when Hillingdon left my room with a lingering step and clouded brow, to arrange with Lavish an early meeting for the morrow, I felt more composed than at any previous part of that eventful day. I undressed, went to bed, and slept soundly for hours.

Who has not felt the instinctive oppression with which we wake to misery, that our yet half-dormant faculties are unable to realise! Who does not know the steps of gradual torture with which the first dawn of discomfort swells to the full amount of anguish that appears too heavy to be borne! As the faint streaks of early morning found their way into my apartment, I started from that deep slumber of thorough exhaustion, and woke to the realities of my position. Oh, the agony of that hour! ruin and misery stared me in the face—perhaps immediate death; I almost felt as if I could welcome its stroke, and forget all in the grave; but as I dressed, the mental strength which in most men rises with the requirements of the moment, enabled me to look upon my past conduct and present situation with a clearness and fortitude of which the day before I had felt incapable. I knew myself in the wrong as far as Martingale was concerned, and although too proud to confess it, I determined that nothing should induce me to lift my hand against him. I made up my mind to receive his fire, and discharge my own pistol in the air. I felt more comfortable after this resolution, and walked with Hillingdon to the destined scene of combat with a *sang-froid* and carelessness that surprised even myself.

It was strange that, knowing as I did my antagonist to be an unerring shot, I could not realise the danger of my position. I tried to fancy I was on the brink of another world; I tried to think of the future, but in vain; the most trifling objects arrested my attention, and my mind kept wandering through all the levities and frivolities to which I was accustomed. Is this one of the weaknesses incidental to humanity? Can this power-lessness of mental concentration be the cause of that supreme indifference which we hear of even in criminals on the scaffold?

The mist was curling down the mountain-tops as our seconds 'put us up' at the longest ten paces ever measured by mortal stride, but which we owed to the generous length of Jack Lavish's legs. Hillingdon's lip quivered as he put my weapon in my hand. What hours seemed to elapse ere the signal was given. A sharp whiz, and quick, suppressed report found me still unhurt, and lifting the muzzle of my weapon, I discharged it high in air. We shook hands, and walked back to breakfast. *Sic transit, &c.;* but as we neared the house, Hillingdon whispered to me, ' Touch and go, Digby—he put " one " in your sleeve ;' and sure enough the coat and under-garment were perforated by the mischief-meaning messenger. Good heavens !' said St Heliers, as he delightedly welcomed us to breakfast, 'when I asked you fellows to shoot, I had no idea you meant to vary your sports by such a performance as this.'

As I steamed southward towards the Scottish border, I could hardly fancy that the events of the last twenty-four hours were aught but a dream. Alas! I had Cartouch's letter to convince me of their reality ; and as again and again I scanned the bitter paragraph that told of Flora's destiny, deeper and deeper ' the iron entered into my soul.'

CHAPTER X.

THE OLD HOUSE AT HOME.

'There be bright faces in the busy hall ;
Bowls on the board, and banners on the wall.'

AT least we have the authority of Byron for supposing that such was the reception of the Polish chieftain in his ancestral home ; and such was, indeed, the ' order of the day ' at old Haverley, on the auspicious occasion of the heir's completing his twenty-first year.

'The serfs were glad in Lara's wide domain,
And slavery half forgot her feudal chain ; '

in which respect those semi-barbarians of the north seem to have conducted themselves much in the same manner as their more civilised fellows of the Anglo-Saxon race. The gentlemen 'in powder and plush,' who still swarmed at Haverley, giving vent to their rejoicings by an enormous consumption of provender and wassail at the shortest possible intervals; whilst 'so numerous ! so flourishing ! and so influential a tenantry !' as the farmers holding land under Sir Peregrine were invariably denominated in all after-dinner speeches, forgot hard times, hazy weather, and indifferent crops, whilst they poured bumper after bumper down those insatiable and vigorous throats, which still shouted good wishes, health and future prosperity to the ' young 'squire.' All was hilarity, hospitality, and merry-making. A stranger would have supposed that he saw in that dignified landlord, those hearty retainers, and that princely old hall, the very type of English prosperity and comfort. Alas ! alas ! the gilding was but upon the surface ; the house of Grand was rotten at the core. Look down, Sir Hugo le Grand ! fifth baron of the name—look down from the dingy canvas, in the background of which a furious battle is raging, much out of drawing, whereat, trusting in the cumbrous defence of your mail and plate, you are carelessly turning your chivalrous back,—look down, and look your last upon a scene of rejoicing that shall never again take place in your old halls. Could you have foreseen the termination of your line, the fate of your posterity, on that triumphant day when, as veracious chroniclers assert, you broke a lance in knightly courtesy with 'the Montmorency,' High Constable of France, and kings and emperors, peers and paladins, looked on and signed approval of the 'gentle and loving passage of arms,' you would have wished to exchange the Spanish coat of proof for a silken jerkin; you would have prayed that the Constable's honoured weapon, driven home by the arm of that practised warrior, might splinter in your heart. But in the meantime riot and revelry must go on under your very nose; and often are you pointed out, and much is your representation criticised, for you are the great card of our family, and Sir Peregrine is never tired of talking about 'the famous Sir Hugo—one of my ancestors, sir, a man who knew his position, and an ornament to the house of Grand.'

It was my one-and-twentieth birthday, my 'coming of age,' and I had the evening before arrived from London to assist at the rejoicings which heralded this important period. The duel in the Highlands, a nine-days'-wonder, was forgotten by all but Sir Peregrine, who rather liked it, and was much fonder of dwelling upon the particulars, and discussing 'that affair of honour, sir, in which my boy was concerned as a principal,' than was agreeable to 'my boy' himself, who, having behaved badly, had the grace to be ashamed of it. Rapidly as I had journeyed to town from the scene of action, rumour, with her thousand tongues, had preceded me, and had furnished as many versions of the 'rencontre.' Mrs Man-trap actually made advances towards a reconciliation, I am convinced in the hope that I might give her the earliest and fullest account of the whole business; but miserable as I was about Flora, hampered for money, and disgusted with myself, I studiously avoided the society of that gossipping enchantress. Cartouch was not in town when I arrived,—I could hear nothing of the Belmonts,— Sir Angelo Parsons I myself saw coming out of 'Storr and Mortimer's,' a convincing proof that _he_, at any rate, was going to be married; and thoroughly sick at heart, I was glad when a summons arrived from Sir Peregrine to recall me to

Haverley, as the most important item in all his arrangements for festivity.

It was late in the autumn; but a few of those fine days of which summer had hardly given us our share, seemed to linger yet, and as I drove across the park, a glorious sunset was bathing in its golden light the fine old trees, still unconscious of the axe. How well I knew each nook and corner of the domain. The very deer seemed like old familiar friends, and every turn of the avenue appeared to greet me with a silent welcome. Here I had shot my first partridge; there I had jumped my pony over the sunk fence, to the admiration of an Etonian schoolfellow. Yonder, where the corner of the lake gleamed through the low wood, I had landed my first pike; and in those smooth, peaceful waters, Flint, the keeper, had taught me to dive, float, and swim. The next turn opens a view of the house, and stately, in truth, looks the massive grey old hall, of that particular order of architecture which, for want of professional knowledge, I am fain to call the 'composite irregular,' inasmuch as it had been built in the fourteenth century, added to in the sixteenth, much damaged during the civil wars, and very inefficiently repaired at the Restoration, partially burned down in the reign of Queen Anne, and reconstructed upon an enormous scale by the spirited proprietor, who, however, did not live to complete his intentions. Since then rooms had been added and offices built, as suited the exigencies of the moment or the taste of 'the Grands;' and now the very irregularity of the mass gave to the old place a picturesque, even a romantic appearance, at least to my eyes, which I have looked for in vain elsewhere.

As I drove up to the house, my better nature, influenced as usual by the accidental force of circumstances, was in the ascendant, and I felt that I could indeed love my home, that I was capable of any sacrifice for such a place; and how readily at that moment would I have exchanged the false glare and heartless frivolity of 'the world' for a peaceful country life in these long-loved haunts, with farming, field sports, and rural duties to occupy my mornings, and Flora's thrilling smile to welcome my return. But that might never be now, and as I felt in my own heart I was forced back upon a career that in these more rational moments I loathed, I laid the blame upon my destiny, that convenient scapegoat on which a weak spirit places all the misfortunes and miseries brought about by its own incapacity or misconduct. Destiny, indeed! as though Providence had not arranged that every man should be the framer of his own destiny, and that the strong firm mind, the unblenching, fearless heart, should shape its course steady and persevering to the end, though exposed to the storms of obloquy and buffeted by the waves of misfortune.

'Welcome home, Master Digby,' said old Soames, chief butler ever since I could remember, and on whom the course of time seemed powerless to imprint marks of decay. His hair had been white and his face red when I used to run up and down stairs after him in a frock and bare legs, holding on by those broad coat-tails, or petitioning for a ride on that sturdy shoulder; and now, though the countenance had deepened in hue, and the waistcoat increased if possible in volume, he was the same Soames still. 'Welcome home, indeed, sir. This way, if you please, Master Digby. Sir Peregrine have been expecting you since three o'clock.' And he ushered me down the well-known passage leading to my father's snuggery, adding, with paternal affection, enhanced by an early dinner, 'How you have growed, Master Digby,—quite a fine gentleman, and it seems but the other day as I made the bishop for your christening,' alluding to the exhilarating compound dignified by that ecclesiastical title. Ere Soames had concluded his reminiscences and reflections, I was face to face with my father, and my heart smote me to think of my unfilial behaviour and systematic neglect of him, when I saw so visible an alteration in the form and features of the old man. He was much bent and wasted in figure, whilst a drawn look about the eyes, and sharpened expression of the whole countenance, betokened increasing feebleness and decay. Still there was the same proud bearing, the same courtly gestures, above all, the same concise, forcible, and rather satirical manner, which marks the former associates of 'the Prince Regent,' and which is fast dying out with the remains of the 'Carlton House School.' Sir Peregrine was kindness itself, but his affectionate demonstrations were tempered with a degree of reserve and self-respect inseparable from one who was ever conscious of 'his position,' and our greeting was something between that of father and son, monarch and heir-presumptive.   Once, and once only, nature asserted her dominion over the parent, and it was with faltering voice and moistened eye that my father expressed his desire to make some arrangement which, now that I had come of age, should render me to a certain extent independent, 'and which,' he added, with a momentary pang of self-reproach, 'I fear I have too long neglected.   But we will *see about it.*   We must have Mortmain down, my dear Digby; and it is indeed strange,' he continued, relapsing insensibly into the old vice-regal manner, 'if, with our influence and in "our position," we cannot place everything on a footing which shall be satisfactory to the future representative of the family.'

Such were the generalities in which my poor father was wont to indulge, and thus would he delude himself into a vague idea of prosperity which had vanished, and power which had never existed.   As to Sir Peregrine's influence, it was completely swamped, in a political point of view, by a neighbouring earl, whose grandfather, an enterprising manufacturer, had bequeathed to his descendant, besides that knowledge (of business) which is better than 'houses and lands,' a very large proportion of the latter inferior articles, and capital enough to buy every free and independent voter in the county nine times over; and as regarded that position of which from childhood I had heard so much, what was it but a large ill-regulated establishment, a discontented tenantry, and a property mortgaged to its full value?   But this was no time to dwell upon such unimportant matters.   A large party, including the aforesaid earl, were staying in the house, and a host of neighbours invited to dinner.   The following morning, my birthday, was to witness merry-making and rejoicings for every class of the community within miles of Haverley. An ox was to be roasted whole for the poor, who prefer their meat under-done, and digestion to be promoted by sack-racing, pole-climbing, beer-drinking, and other rustic sports.   There was to be a grand dinner to the tenantry, and a ball for their wives and daughters in the evening; whilst the remainder of the week was to be devoted to those guests of higher rank who were staying with us to shoot our pheasants, ride our horses, drink our champagne, and, in all probability, repay our hospitality by voting the son a puppy and the father a bore !

The morning came, and bright and beautiful 'the glorious sun uprist,' promising us one more fine day in October. Breakfast was hardly concluded, and I was struggling to obtain sufficient sustenance for the fatigues of the future, between the ceaseless chatter of Mrs Ramrod (who, in consideration of having known me as a boy, had taken possession of me, body and soul), and the long sunny ringlets of Miss Batt, who was obliged to sit so near me that they were continually interfering with my egg and drooping into my plate—an arrangement I should have less disliked had the keen country air not made me so voracious. Well, breakfast was coming to an end, and I was striking up a great friendship with the damsel of the long locks, when a powerful band, much out of tune, and performing an air commonly known in agricultural districts as that which destroyed one of 'the milky mothers of the herd,' marshalled down the avenue a sturdy throng of ruddy faces and stalwart forms, known as the Odd Fellows' Friendly Society, who, with military precision formed a circle in front of the house, while the oldest and oddest fellow of the lot, whom I recognised as the clerk of an adjoining parish, read from a much-bethumbed paper a congratulatory address in verse, vigorous in conception, and somewhat startling in rhyme, as the concluding stanza sufficiently exemplifies :—

> Then, Captain Grand, accept our heartiest wishes,
> And do not deem your humble friends officious.
> Health, length of days, a fair and blooming bride,
> And bless'd with babes and sucklings too beside.
> Such is our prayers ; before we do adjourn,
> Accept our welcome, as we hope for yourn.

How could humble prose, even the prose of a Demosthenes of a Cicero, reply to such 'winged words' as these? Nevertheless I stood under the old portico, and with bared head and respectful gestures, thanked my well-wishers for their courtesy, preserving a gravity for which I have ever since enjoyed the reward of an approving conscience. The Odd Fellows cheered my speech heartily, for which, as a very young orator, I was much obliged to them, since it requires a long apprenticeship indeed among the practical and experienced ranks of our senate to bear unabashed the chilling silence, or, worse still, the sarcastic applause, with which a brilliant and long-studied peroration is so often received in that assemblage.

This ceremony well over, the slaughtered ox was borne in procession, the aforesaid band performing in divers keys the air of 'Oh, the roast beef of Old England!' and having been about as much roasted as the woodcock which is allowed to see the fire ere introduced to a thorough epicure, was cut up and distributed in no very appetising-looking morsels to the poor of the parish, whilst stentorian voices pledged health and prosperity to the young 'squire, in floods of good strong Haverley ale. After which the shouters recreated themselves with wheel-barrow races, the charioteers being blindfolded, and creating no small confusion from their furious driving; then they climbed a pole, which emblem of ambition was well greased within a few feet of the top, and he who had struggled manfully to within an arm's-length of his aim, found that when almost within his grasp he was doomed to be disappointed, and to go down, as is usual in real life, a good deal faster than he came up. The prize surmounting this perpendicular difficulty, was at length wrested by a cunning chimney sweep, who, taking a pocketful of soot up with him, and refreshing his palms therewith at intervals, got them so completely grimed at last as to render any amount of soap of no effect, and thus succeeded in carrying off the huge leg of mutton that had tempted him so long. Nor were the fair damsels of the district excluded from their share in these rural sports, an under-garment of snowy texture being provided for her whose dainty feet could brush the dew quickest from the lawn. This race, to use a turf expression, brought together 'a capital entry;' and after a severe struggle, and the production of many divers-coloured garters, a nimble dairy-maid bore off the prize.

As the afternoon waned, and the hearty farmers began to feel that their usual dinner hour was long since gone by, many an eye was wistfully directed towards the tent prepared for our great repast, and many a vigorous appetite voted four o'clock the best part of the day, as they seated themselves at the three lengthy tables, of which a cross one at the top, raised upon a sort of dais, formed a nucleus for the great guns of the party, the rector of the parish, the member for the county, the neighbouring earl, two or three adjoining 'squires, Sir Peregrine and myself.

Beef and venison were rapidly consumed, and strong port and sherry, varied by deep draughts of John Barleycorn, as rapidly disappeared; faces waxed red and apoplectic, and tongues, now loosened from the bands of shyness and reserve, chattered in deafening confusion. Toasts of loyalty and patriotism serve to bring in the chief event of the evening, and the steward of the estate, rapping loudly on the table, obtains a dead silence, truly appalling to old Farmer Scales, who, in right of seniority, has taken upon himself the office of proposing the young 'squire's health. The sturdy yeoman has not, as he honestly confesses, ' the gift of the gab;' but when he wants a word he waits for it with a patience and determination that would drive a nervous man frantic. The pauses become longer and longer as the orator gets deeper into his subject, till an extremely abrupt conclusion and an ambiguous compliment, referring to the fatted calf being slain on my return, empties every bumper of ' black strap' like a shot, and vociferous cheering proves that Farmer Scales has completely expressed the feelings of his audience.

Now for the reply. ' Honour—much flattered—early boyhood —familiar faces—agricultural prosperity—yeomanry of old Eng- land—no place like home—kind father—(cheers)—indulgent land- lord—(more cheers)—hope often to be thus surrounded—allusion to the old roof-tree, and a Greek quotation taken at random from Thucydides (the latter as being perfectly unintelligible is received with uproarious applause),' serve to express the heartfelt senti- ments of gratitude with which I beg to drink all their good healths; and down I sit, having ' done it' to a turn. The mirth gets fast and furious; the county member sings a capital song; Sir Peregrine executes an oration, such as might have been made by Leonidas to his doomed band, so pompous, so imposing, so almost funereal is it in its grandeur. We drink the earl's health; we drink the member's health; we drink Dr Driveller's, who weeps tears of port in his reply; we drink the fox-hounds, and

the welkin rings with every cheer and holloa known to the
votaries of Diana; we drink the 'Merry Harriers,' and Mr
Mottles, the sporting manager of that rather 'scratch' establishment, is so overpowered by his feelings as to be obliged to be
taken away senseless, a broad hint, which suggests to us the
propriety of breaking up the present sitting, and adjourning to
the ball-room, where we are followed by all but a few steady old
sexagenarians, whose clay, probably in consideration of there
being no time to be lost, requires a deal of moistening ere it
returns to its parent soil.

There is much beauty amongst the farmers' wives and daughters; and I may fairly hope that my powers of endurance and
activity on that laborious evening won me golden opinions from
them all.   Country dances without end, waltzes, galops, polkas
innumerable, a cotillon with pretty Miss Batt as a great treat,
and a cigar to wind up the night at six in the morning with the
Marquis de Carambole, a good-humoured Frenchman, who had
come all the way from London to 'assist at our festivities,' concluded for me the hardest twenty-four hours I can recollect to
have ever experienced.

The sun was rising ere I sought my pillow, and, looking out
over the expanse of hill and dale, wood and water, growing into
life under his beams, I turned away with a sickening feeling
at my heart as I thought, 'Flora, Flora, what is all this, when
thou art lost to me for ever?   What are wealth, magnificence,
and merry-making without thee?   What care I for the old hall,
the rich and lovely domain?   There is no beauty where thou
art not!'

Mournful thoughts for twenty-one!   Happy is he who hath
not out-lived his boyhood, till ripened Prime brings with it the
conviction that all is vanity; the experience that teaches us to
expect no resting-place here below, to look steadfastly forward to
the future—not the immediate future of our short span of existence, but the real future of eternity.   Some men are boys all
their lives, and as such are envied and enviable for the lightness
of their spirits, their keen enjoyment of life.   But these can
never know the stern, severe training that leads direct to Truth.
Perhaps for them such ordeal may not be necessary, and is mer-

cifully dispensed with. For beneficial as may be the ultimate
effects of disappointment and unhappiness, it cannot but seem
hard that the unfurrowed brow should ache with thought, the
beardless cheek waste and pale with care. Nor can we expect
the youth, however fast he may have spent his boyhood, however
dearly he may have purchased his knowledge, to arrive at once at
that resigned and happy period, when man is enabled to say, in
heartfelt thankfulness and humble confidence, 'It is good for me
that I have been in trouble.'

Who is there that delights in the deadly tubes, levelled with
accuracy and quickness against the flying covey or the dodging
coney? Who is there that loves to range the rich stubbles and
the russet coppice, to start the frightened hare from her form, or
flush the gaudy pheasant from his covert, and doth not welcome
with all his heart the keen, pure air of a bracing morning in
October, when the outlying spinnies are to be beat, and the
scattered partridges, wild, wary, and quick upon the wing, will
prove no unworthy triumph? Haverley was the place of all
others for a varied and enjoyable day's shooting. Without the
masses of game which swarm like locusts upon a Norfolk manor
—without 'bouquets' of pheasants, radiating in all directions
from what is appropriately termed a 'hot corner,'—there was a
fair sprinkling of both winged and ground game, that might
satisfy the keenest sportsman as to the sufficient number of objects whereon to exercise his prowess; whilst the large enclosures,
double hedge-rows, and undulating surface of the land, imposed
upon him that bodily exercise which so much enhances the pleasure of all field sports. Nor was the party marshalled in deadly
array upon the steps of the old Hall, the second morning after
the coming-of-age day, loth to enjoy to the utmost all the amusement our coverts could afford. A motley crew we were, lounging about under the portico or on the lawn, in every variety of
costume yet invented for the slaughter of the beasts of the field,
from old Ramrod's antediluvian velveteen jacket, with skirts to
his heels, and pockets in whose yawning caverns you might
almost stow away a red-deer, to Carambole's smart and fanciful
tunic, picturesque as that of a Robin Hood, with its braid and
facings, and harmonising well with the 'Marquis's' carefully-

trimmed beard, curling moustache, and redundancy of jewellery
—not to mention his white kid gloves, and the enormous cigar
which, ever glowing between his lips, seemed like a Phœnix to
spring from the ashes of its predecessor. Nor was the Church
unrepresented in our sporting assemblage. The Reverend Amos
Batt, the shortest-sighted man that ever squinted over a gun-
barrel, the most dangerous neighbour that ever lined 'a ride,'
was as usual the keenest to begin, in his excessive fondness for
that amusement to which of all others he was least adapted by
nature, and fidgeted about in his dark clerical shooting-dress in
a manner that called down the contemptuous reproof of Mr Flint,
the keeper, who, grouped with his myrmidons and half a dozen
spaniels, stood within ear-shot of the Hall door.

'Never do to begin without Mr Spencer,' said Flint, probably
in consideration of many a golden benefit received and expected,
—'and here he comes,' as my old schoolfellow, Tom Spencer, a
first-rate shot, and the pleasantest undergraduate Oxford could
boast, cantered up to our party, and apologising for the delay,
more especially to Mr Batt—on whose daughter, the damsel of
the long locks, I soon found out my old chum was sweet—
announced his readiness to commence.

Guns were shouldered, dogs strained in their couples, the
'Marquis' began to sing, and we were soon in the thick of it.

'*L'affaire commence,*' said Carambole, as we heard a shot upon
our right, probably from the unerring weapon of Tom Spencer,
who was always placed where the shooting was most difficult,
and had now been detached by Flint on 'particular surface,' to
stop any wandering pheasants that might take a fancy to a prolonged flight into a neighbouring manor.

'*Voyons,*' added the Frenchman, as an over-anxious hare cantered leisurely across the ride, and he tumbled her heels-over-
head into the opposite brushwood.

'Mark!' sung out Ramrod, and a magnificent cock-pheasant
came sailing down the wind on his broad pinions, right above our
heads, and 'rocketer' as he was, I brought him to the ground.

'*Tenez ce n'est pas mal,*' said my talkative companion; and
his observation lost him a double shot at a couple of rabbits that
were stealing warily on towards us.

And now the constant rustle among the dried leaves, and occasional snap of a rotten twig in the cover, show us that the beaters are approaching; and the pheasants, unwilling to rise, are hurrying to and fro in an unenviable state of uncertainty. Carambole and I get outside the fence, and standing well away from the plantation, prepare for action.

They must leave home at last, for the beaters are drawing near, and the hedge prevents their running any further. Up they get by twos and threes, amongst cries of 'mark!' 'hen!' 'rabbit to the right!' 'hare back!' and down they come, before the Marquis and myself—the former, I must confess, shooting like a trump, and smoking away the whole time like a steam-engine. Presently, Flint appears through the thickest part of the hedge, and with strict injunctions to a ragged little urchin, holding on by a stick as long as himself, to 'beat it out,' touches his hat, and inquires into the amount of slaughter. Of course, a good many pheasants 'went back,' to that mysterious bourne from which no game ever returns; and of course, we ought to have had an additional man somewhere else, 'to stop,' for who ever yet knew a keeper satisfied with the list of killed? But our party were flushed with success; and, walking in a line over a few intervening fields to the next covert, we picked up a stray hare, and two or three brace of wild partridges, that did credit to our aim, ere we again entered upon the woodland chasse.

A fabulous report of a woodcock supposed to have been seen by Mr Batt! created much excitement in this locality, not diminished by my 'viewing away' a magnificent old fox, which I had great difficulty in preventing Carambole from shooting. It did me good to see the gallant animal gliding easily along over the ridge and furrow of the adjoining field, his bright rich coat glistening in the sun, and his stealthy form the very impersonation of speed and symmetry. Ere I could give him a second 'view-holloa,' he had disappeared, and I felt half-ashamed of my enthusiasm when I saw 'the Marquis's' look of astonishment at an excitement he could not the least comprehend.

The love of fox-hunting is indeed an inexplicable passion; the man who has once really felt it, never forgets his attachment to the cause. Let him leave off his favourite pursuit for years—

put him to any other sport, business, or excitement you will—
place him in any position, or under any circumstances, which
render it impossible for him to gratify his prevailing taste—but
only mention the word 'fox-hunting,' only lead to some subject
connected with that fascinating sport, and you will bring the
colour to his cheek, and the light to his eye, though age may
have dimmed the one, and sorrow furrowed the other.   But in
the meantime, walking knee-deep in stubble, and straggling
waist-deep through tangled brier and impervious covert, had
made us all excessively hungry.   Nor were we sorry to behold,
on the lee-side of Upper Long-wood, a gipsy fire cheerfully
burning, a pot of comforting soup hanging gracefully thereon ; a
screen cleverly constructed to keep off the wind, and a table laid
out with sundry good things for the refreshment of the inward
man : whilst Soames, who piqued himself much on these impromptu out-door arrangements, trotted about, greatly to his
own satisfaction, with a jorum of a curiously-compounded ' mull,'
grateful beyond measure in the raw air of an October afternoon.

What a merry party we were.   Our sport had been excellent.
Ramrod, a regular old poacher, who always asked to take away
what he killed, had amassed a capital bag, by dint of shooting hares sitting, taking unwary rabbits by surprise, and poking
most perseveringly at game upon the wing.   The rest of the
party had been equally successful in a more legitimate manner.
Even Mr Batt, after the expenditure of a vast deal of powder
and shot, had succeeded in bagging a hen-pheasant and a wood-
pigeon.   Carambole had hardly missed a shot (I should be
afraid to say how many cigars he had smoked), and his mercurial
spirits were now at their highest—he *would* drink '*encore un coup
of ze moll,*' as he called Soames's fragrant mixture—he *would* sing
French bacchanalian songs, in a rich and mellow voice, which
delighted even the austere Flint, who allowed us more time than
usual for our repast ; and, in short, nothing could have gone off
better than the whole thing, had it not been for an untoward
accident, perhaps partly to be attributed to the jollity of our
luncheon, which damped our afternoon's amusement, and which
might have had a very serious termination.

We were shooting the last covert, and twilight was rapidly

approaching, when the Reverend Amos Batt, whom I had placed next to myself, in order, if possible, to moderate his keenness, which always increased as the day drew towards its close, was suddenly seized with a strong inclination for ground game, having discovered that he was most successful in that style of gunning. As long as he was close to me I prevented his shooting back amongst the beaters, loading one barrel with the other at full-cock, and a few like eccentricities, in which it was his habit to indulge ; but on my leaving him to take up a position a few yards further down the ride, what was my horror to behold him deliberately level and fire both barrels in the direction where I knew Flint must have placed a gentleman, or, as he called it, ' a gun.'

A simultaneous roar of agony from old Ramrod, and exclamation of satisfaction from Mr Batt, 'Poor thing, I thought it best to put it out of its pain!' convinced me that the Major's York-tan gaiters must have received a charge of No. 6 from the short-sighted divine ; and on rushing up to the sufferer, who fortunately, from the distance at which he ' stood fire,' though much stung at the moment, was not seriously injured, a general explanation took place, from which it appeared that the yellow gaiters, peeping through a hole in the lower part of the hedge, presented to the clergyman's imperfect vision the image of a fine old hare sitting ! This was an opportunity not to be lost, and taking a deliberate, point-blank aim, the eager sportsman pulled. The writhing of the object attested the accuracy of his eye; and in his merciful intention of putting the animal out of its pain, and anxiety not to lose this addition to his ' bag,' he unhesitatingly gave the sufferer the contents of his other barrel.

No wonder the Major hallooed ; and when he found that the accident had taken place, as he called it, ' on purpose,' his wrath was not to be appeased. We sent him home in the game-cart, swearing horribly ; and as it was by this time quite dark, we here terminated our unlucky day's shooting.

I fear the old warrior's ire would not have been mollified could he have heard Tom Spencer and myself laughing over the catastrophe, as smoking our cigars we walked home together behind the rest of our companions. There is nothing like ' a

L

weed' in the dark to draw on confidential communication
between two long-parted friends ; and, ere the lights of the Hall
twinkled on us through the shades of night, we had touched
upon one subject after another, made reciprocal disclosures in
the strictest confidence, as to our respective studs, and interchanged an abbreviated history of our first loves, till Tom at
last intrusted me, in the openness of his heart, with the important secret that he was over head and ears in love with the
fair Julia Batt ; that he was resolved to marry her as soon as
he had taken orders and got ' a living '—two events that young
men, till undeceived by experience, are apt to consider synony-
mous—but that he had not yet declared his attachment to
his ladye-love ; and he had a shrewd suspicion that, however
agreeable they might be to the daughter, the Reverend Amos,
in his paternal care, highly disapproved of my friend's attentions.

'If I can assist you in any way, my dear Tom, command me,'
said I, as we entered the house, and stumped off to our respective
dressing-rooms.   'To-morrow is our county ball, as you know,
and you will have every opportunity of making play with the
damsel, as I can undertake to keep papa in conversation, as to
the respective merits of heavy and light guns, self-primers,
revolvers, and other deadly weapons, long enough to enable you
to propose, be accepted, ay, and carry her off in a postchaise-and-
four to boot.'

So saying, I opened the door of my comfortable snuggery,
where hot water, dry things, and a blazing fire, presented all the
materials for restoring the outward man to a state of gentlemanlike sleekness and order.

But, alas ! the post—that remorseless emblem of Fate—had
arrived during my absence ; and with a blush of shame and
remorse, with a vague feeling of unaccountable apprehension that
made my heart beat, and my breath come quick, I recognised, in
a foreign letter that lay upon my toilet-table, the well-known
handwriting of Zoë de Grand-Martigny.

When Soames knocked at my door an hour afterwards to say
dinner was on the table, I was still sitting in my arm-chair,
with that open letter in my hand.   Thoughts, thoughts—those

mysterious workings of the soul, which form alternately our blessing and our curse—were inundating my brain in countless succession, like the waves of the sea. In that hour I lived over many a long and happy day of the irrevocable past. Again I saw that glorious girl, in all the pride of her beauty, as I beheld her for the first time. Again I walked with her in the magnificent scenery of Niagara, and heard her gentle voice thrilling to my very soul, despite the roar of the cataract. Again I gazed upon her graceful form, and long black tresses, drooping over the still deep waves of the St Lawrence, as many a time and oft I had seen her, and sat with her by the margin of that mighty river, in the golden summer evenings of the West. Again I saw the glittering jet bracelet unclasped from that snowy arm ; and once more was her gentle sorrowing face turned upon mine, in mute, appealing agony, as she bid me a long and last farewell. And then how maddening to think that I had seen her once since, in the pompous revelry, the noisy frivolity of a London ball ; and that my cursed fate had prevented me from so much as exchanging a syllable with one erst so fondly loved.

But the letter—gentle, feminine, high-principled as herself —explained all this ; and as I sat out the tedious formal dinner, and strove to sustain my part in the forced gaiety, the vain nonsense that wore through a weary evening, I felt indeed unworthy of that generous missive which reposed upon my heart. Not a word of reproach, not a word of repining did it contain ; far above such feelings—far above the weaknesses of her sex, was the pure, high-minded writer. Simply and kindly, with no soreness of injured pride, with no affectation of indifference, did she point out to me the instability of my character, the heartlessness of my conduct. She had long discovered—so she went on to say—she had long discovered by my letters that such a weak and wavering affection as mine was no equivalent for the loving heart which she surrendered so wholly and entirely ; but while no other shared my love, insufficient as it was, she was content. When, however, my letters got fewer and cooler, when she heard not only of follies and vices in my London career, but likewise found my name coupled with those of Sirens celebrated for the

destruction to which they lured their votaries, she resolved, with
a firmness and determination that marked her character, and
made her the resolute though feminine being that she was, to
judge for herself. An opportunity offered for her to come to
England, and of that she took advantage. She was in London
for more than a fortnight, without informing me of her whereabouts ; and 'judge, Captain Grand,' she wrote, ' whether that
was not a struggle. At last came the night of the Apsley House
ball. I need not repeat what I saw and heard there, nor how
evident it was to me that the absent Zoë was at length completely forgotten. I left the ball, and in a week was crossing
the Atlantic on my homeward voyage. I had satisfied myself
of the reality of my worst fears ; and it was evident to me that
a continuance of our engagement would be to you a source of
restraint and annoyance, as of utter misery to myself. It is
better for us both that we should part ; and much as it has cost
me, long as I have pondered, ere I could make up my mind to
write this letter, I feel less unhappy now that it is accomplished.
Perhaps it would have been better had we never met ; but it is
useless to look back into the past, or to speculate upon what
might or might not have been. You have my best wishes, my
heartfelt prayers for your future welfare and success. It will be
better that you should not answer this letter ; and as this is the
last time that I shall ever write to you, forgive me if I venture
to offer a few words of humble advice to one in whom I shall
always feel deeply interested. The fault of your character is
want of purpose. Do not mistake the impulse of the moment
for the true feelings of your heart, and do not throw aside every
pursuit as soon as success dawns upon your efforts. Bend those
talents which I know you to possess to some definite object, and
hesitate no longer to embark on some worthy career. Had I
been a man, I should have been ambitious. Forgive me, my
dear Digby (for the last time I call you so), forgive me for thus
presuming to dictate to one whom I so kindly regard, and
believe me ever your true well-wisher,

'ZOË DE GRAND-MARTIGNY.'

And this was the woman I had thrown over for a Mrs Man-trap; this was the true and noble heart I had disregarded and forgotten. And now, forsooth, I had my reward. I should never see her more. I had lost her love, and was unworthy of her friendship. Ah, Zoë! it would indeed have been better had we never met. I was not worthy of you, even in my thoughtless and unpolluted boyhood; and now, alas! how can I dare to think of purity such as yours! My weak and vacillating character, ever acted upon by the influence of the moment, could never have mated with your high resolve, your noble and unselfish spirit. I am, in truth, a being of an inferior order. Ay, even now, when I am fresh from the perusal of your generous and forgiving letter—when my heart is sore with the thought of your utter sacrifice of all your hopes—a sacrifice which I am incapable of making, but which I can still appreciate —the image of Flora Belmont rises amidst the wreck of your happiness, and outshines in its fresh beauty my earlier idol. Even now, unmanly, ungrateful, heartless as it may appear, despite of pity, despite of shame and remorse, something in my inmost soul whispers triumphantly—I am free! I am free!

Some people are determined believers in the truth of 'presentiments,' others assert that all such fancied foreshadowings of the future are but the nonsensical effect of weak nerves acted upon by an excited brain. Be this how it may, I can only account for my buoyancy of spirits during the day following the receipt of Zoë's letter—a communication which ought to have made me thoroughly unhappy, which did fill me with bitter regrets and burning self-reproach—by some vague prophetic sense of what was awaiting me at one of those solemn performances yclept a county ball, immediately about to take place. This ball, be it understood, was a yearly penance, undergone by the nobility, gentry, and squirearchy of ——shire, with a fortitude and resignation worthy of a better cause. That their presence in the county assembly-rooms—a spacious structure, erected over the gaol, where the votaries of Terpsichore disturbed with their revels the gloomy malefactor in his cell—was a voluntary discipline of the severest order, I gather from the fact that, excepting some of the youngest of the very young ladies, I never heard any one put in a good word for the unfortunate ball. 'It was a bore—it was a nuisance—the rooms were always hot, and the weather always cold—the passages were ill-lighted, and the moon sure to be off duty—all the roads in the vicinity were bad, and as for the music—don't talk of the music?' But notwithstanding all these drawbacks, long consultations as to the propriety of attending were invariably wound up with the annual 'however, I suppose we *must* go ;' and this ideal obligation served to bring a very considerable number of white satin shoes and snowy neckcloths to assist at the festival. We had, of course, talked it over well at Haverley. With the exception of Carambole, who thought it *charmant*, we had severally and collectively expressed our decided intentions of not going. Nevertheless, post-horses were ordered as on all previous occasions, every vehicle and carriage-horse in the stable was put in requisition ; and half-past nine P.M. saw the whole party, all but Sir Peregrine, whose infirmities would have made it imprudent to venture, cloaking and flirting in the hall previous to a dark drive of ten or eleven miles. Julia Batt looked excessively pretty. I thought her eyes were all the brighter for an anticipated waltz with Tom Spencer ; and I could take my oath, by the care with which that worthy was pinning a camellia in his button-hole, that the long-haired damsel had the same morning purloined it from the conservatory. I think I earned her eternal gratitude ; I know Tom Spencer told me I was ' a brick,' when I arranged that they should go together in the chariot, with only sleepy Mrs Ramrod as a chaperon. Her injured lord, with Carambole and another dancing-man, trusted themselves to my guidance in the phaeton. I believe that had old Ramrod known the off-horse was a four-year-old, then in harness for the second time, he would have preferred walking ; however, where ' ignorance is bliss,' people are easily satisfied : and we rattled over the ill-paved streets of the county-town and up to the crowded door, from whence strains of ceaseless music were issuing, in perfect safety, having done the distance handsomely in seven minutes under the hour.

Why is it incumbent on every one to come so late to a ball? Or wherein lies the peculiar disgrace attached to being among the first arrivals? Our party, on entering, found the room but thinly sprinkled, and chiefly with people on whom, as they had not the advantage of our acquaintance, we held ourselves privileged to make impertinent remarks.

'What a gown!' said Tom Spencer to his goddess, as he hovered round her like an unquiet spirit, directing her attention to a young lady hardly out of ear-shot.

'Shocking!' replied the fair Julia; 'and how badly her hair is done!'

'*Mais elle n'est pas mal, cette petite,*' said Carambole, who was always pleased; '*quelle fraîcheur, quelle chevelure.*'

'Middling,' responded the dandy to whom he addressed himself, looking at his boots *en profile;* 'but no action.'

In the meantime the plot thickened, and the room gradually filled. Ample mammas fluttered in with their mincing broods; elderly young ladies, whose mouths, as Lavish would have said, don't bear looking into, smiled behind their fans, and seemed as if they wished somebody would ask them to dance; and while the country damsels blushed and giggled, the London girls stood erect and scornful, under the conscious advantage of having experienced a season in town. Elderly gentlemen toddled comfortably up to the fireplace, and smiled blandly from behind their white waistcoats. I maintain that nobody enjoys a ball so much as a quiet old gentleman. Young would-be dandies stood in the doorway, and the more aspiring clung tenaciously to their hats; and still fresh arrivals kept pouring in, and quadrilles were being formed down the whole length of the room.

I had already executed sundry duty-dances, thereto strictly enjoined by Sir Peregrine previous to my departure, and was in the midst of what has always been to me a favourite amusement —namely, watching the histrionic powers of my fellow-creatures when on their best behaviour and attired in their company manners,—I had even been rewarded by witnessing a beautiful piece of acting on the part of Mrs Grump, who was addressing ' dear Angelina ' in an affectionate whisper that would never have led one to suppose she worried the poor girl's life out at home —when, far off amongst the crowd, turning away from me, I caught the outline of a graceful head, the droop of a glossy ringlet that could belong to none upon earth but Flora Belmont. My head swam—I felt almost sick with excitement; but man-

ning myself by a severe effort, I elbowed my way across the
room. I found myself face to face with Flora. I know not
what I said—I have no recollection of what took place; but a
few minutes later found me standing opposite to her in a quad-
rille, trembling like a girl, but nerving myself to the utmost to
master that emotion which I could see was shared to no small
extent by my partner. Hardly a word did we exchange—hardly
once did our eyes meet during that shortest of quadrilles; yet
something told me that silent, distant as she was, I had not
been forgotten. She looked paler and thinner than when I had
seen her in London; but hers was a loveliness which neither
sorrow nor sickness could destroy—that winning beauty of expression, to which regularity of features is only an outward
auxiliary, the setting of the opal, the becoming garment of the
soul within. Her hand shook as she rested it on my arm at the
conclusion of the dance; and, with a nervousness equal to her
own, I hesitatingly proposed to take her to the tea-room. We
seated ourselves in an alcove somewhat removed from the rest
of the dancers, and in a shaking voice I found courage to ask
her where she was staying, and whether Sir Angelo Parsons
was one of their party? The look with which she replied
served to show me how completely I had been mistaken—how
cruelly I had misjudged her. ‘On that hint I spake.’ The
torrent that had for months been accumulating at my heart
burst its banks at last: I told her of my love, of Cartouch's
letter, of my utter misery and despair. I attributed my reckless
habits, my deep play, all my misdemeanour, to my hopeless
wretchedness when I heard of her rumoured marriage. She, in
her turn, confided to me how heart-broken she had been at the
many reports concerning my conduct and character which Mrs
Man-trap had taken care should reach her ears—how she had
disbelieved for a time, till circumstance after circumstance, each
corroborating the other, and ending with ‘that dreadful duel’
with Major Martingale, had forced conviction upon her—how
her father had warned her that I was a *roué* and a gambler—
and how she was at that moment happier than she had been for
months! It would be sacrilege to relate all that took place
during that important interview; nor are scenes such as we

then enacted for our mutual benefit, of much interest save to the couple immediately concerned. Suffice it to say, that words were spoken which the lapse of years might never teach us to forget; feelings given way to which no hope deferred, no coming trials and disappointments, should have power to efface.

I put Flora into her carriage with all the tender care, all the conscious ownership of an accepted lover; and as I drove the phaeton home, cheered by Carambole's unceasing melodies, a fresh love-song, rich and mellow as his native South, for every glimmering milestone that flitted by, accompanied by the prolonged bass of Ramrod's truly British snores, the stars looked down upon a different world from that which had surrounded me a few short hours ago. Hope, more than hope—a feeling of blessed certainty—thrilled through my inmost heart; and though my joy was still and quiet in proportion to its depth—though I was jeered by the merry Frenchman for being, contrary to my custom, silent and *distrait*—who shall say that, notwithstanding all their noisy hilarity, I was not in truth far, far the happiest of the home-returning party.

CHAPTER XI.

THE RUN OF THE SEASON.

AMONGST all the heathen gods and goddesses to whom we sacrificed so liberally at Haverley, Morpheus was the only one that could with reason complain of systematic neglect. Diana we worshipped most perseveringly during the day— Bacchus could boast a phalanx of unflinching votaries in the evening; for who might resist Sir Peregrine's dry champagne, or pass untasted by the silky 'twenty-five, with a 'magnum' of which Soames, no unworthy representative of the wine-god, appeared punctually every quarter of an hour? Nor was Venus forgotten; when mirth, music, singing, and *ecarté* in the drawing-room, with an occasional impromptu dance as midnight approached, showed how willingly we yielded ourselves to her rosy fetters. But for the god of sleep we professed, one and all, but little regard; the only time at which he seemed to vindicate his power being that too-fleeting twenty minutes which elapsed between the summons of one's vigilant domestic, and the painful effort, so dreaded by the sluggard, termed 'getting out of bed.'

I could have sworn, on the morning after the ball, that my repose had only lasted five minutes—a brilliant five minutes truly, illumined as it was by the image of my affianced Flora—when my uncompromising servant entered the room, under a burden of hot water, clean linen, top-boots and spurs, and snowy appliances thereto belonging, wherein it was my intention to over-ride as much as possible the Hark-Holloa hounds, advertised to 'meet' on that day at Haverley Hall. Oh the delight of that first moment of consciousness, ere I could gather from my scattered faculties *what* it was that made my heart bound so lightly in my bosom!—the first dawning of 'the sober certainty of waking bliss,' worth all the dreams ever yet sent by Proserpine through her 'ivory gate.' Could mortal man be happier than I was on that auspicious morning? Debts, difficulties, and annoyances were all forgotten; if I thought of Zoë, it was but with a twinge of reproach which enhanced the joy succeeding so momentary a pang. Flora was mine! Such a thought alone was sufficient to fill my mental atmosphere with sunshine, nor was it an unpleasing undercurrent of ideas that I was that day to ride a capital horse, with as crack a pack of hounds as England could produce. The original young thoroughbred one, whose tuition first brought about that interview with old Burgonet which obtained for me a commission in Her Majesty's service, was now an experienced, steady, and very capital hunter—

> 'A matchless steed, though somewhat old,
> Prompt in his paces, cool and bold;'

and, in honour of the friendly old general, denominated 'Sir Benjamin.' Such 'a mount' was in itself an anticipation of success; and who that remembers the ideal laurels which 'going well' through 'a fine run' confers upon the brow of imaginative twenty-one, will refuse to sympathise with my feelings of exhilaration and excitement, as I descended the stairs to partake of that merriest of meals, a hunting breakfast!

The party were assembled when I entered the dining-room, and my being five minutes later than the rest called down upon me many a jeering reproof for my 'dissipated London habits.' The ladies were all present, having expressed their intention of seeing as much fun as possible from the carriages, under the guidance of Sir Peregrine, who for the first time was unable to join 'the field' on horseback. Julia Batt was very anxious to have ridden, but the Reverend Amos—who despised all sports but shooting, and thought hunting very dangerous—would not hear of such a performance. Had it not been for these parental objections, Tom Spencer would never have seen as well as he did one of the finest runs that ever took place over that country. How the young lady looked in a hat, I am at a loss to say; but judging from what she was in a certain pink bonnet, I should imagine her riding-costume must have made her fascinating and *piquante* to a degree. Poor Tom Spencer! Sundry neighbours dropped in ere the hounds arrived, to pay their morning salutations to my father, or to talk over the previous evening, and its events past and to come, with that sort of retrospective scandal that makes half the pleasure of a ball in the country. Stained red-coats dotted the steps at the hall-door; and booted gentlemen, whose nerves required a little bracing before encountering our Haverley fences, straggled into the house for a small glass of cherry-brandy, after their gallop to covert. Draggled and panting hacks were being led away, whilst silent sharp-looking grooms were using their own pocket-handkerchiefs to remove every speck or stain that might mar the glossy coats of those powerful high-bred hunters they had brought so carefully to the place of meeting.

'Here they come!—here they come! oh, how pretty!' exclaim the ladies; and 'O you darlings!' chimes in the enthusiastic Miss Batt, as the clean and various-coloured pack are seen trotting on to the lawn; where, grouping themselves round their huntsman, they take up a highly picturesque position in front of the house. No *provincial* establishment is that of the Hark-Holloa hounds. In all its various gradations, from the noble master down to the feeder's assistant, 'pace' is indelibly stamped upon every individual, every article connected with the kennels.

Joy, the huntsman, a snake-headed, wiry, active man, devoted to his profession, and a first-rate horseman, looked as game and undeniable as the two thorough-bred ones provided to carry him through the day. Quickness of thought and action, energy of mind and body, were impersonated in Will Partridge, his first whip, a man whom nature must have framed for the express office he filled so well. No anatomist could venture to doubt that those limbs were made on purpose for the boots and breeches which fitted them so wonderfully; and the general opinion amongst ourselves was that Will must have been born in these sporting appliances. Nimrod was doubtless an adept in all the practices of the chase; but I question if Nimrod, though mounted on Pegasus, the greatest flyer on record—ay, even had Mercury lent him the use of his heels—could have slipped away to the 'down-wind' end of a woodland, and when there bored through the blackest and bitterest thorn-fence that ever staked a hunter, with half the ease or half the rapidity of Tom Prince—whose duty it was, as second whip, to enforce upon the younger members of the pack the propriety of their 'harking forward' and 'getting together,' and the necessity of abstaining entirely from 'hare.'

Woe to the riotous puppy that should indiscreetly proclaim his discovery of the forbidden fruit. Tom's thong was indeed 'swift to smite, and never to spare;' and it was quite unnecessary to request that functionary to 'ride at him and cut him in two,' so rapidly did summary punishment follow the eager culprit's offence. The hounds themselves were level in size, and faultless in frame and symmetry; their condition was perfect, as was shown by their quick earnest movements and the bloom upon their skins; some of the old school might have thought them a little too light, but even such critical veterans must have confessed that they looked 'all over like going.' The horses were well-bred, powerful animals, unusually sound, and with action that promised jumping capabilities to take them over that strongly-enclosed country. All the minor appliances were in keeping with the more important items of the establishment; and though last, not least, the noble master himself, a perfect specimen of his class, the high-bred English gentleman, was every inch a sportsman. Look at him now, as he comes galloping up, a little late; for a seat in Parliament entails its duties as well as its advantages, and letters must be answered, even though a field of eager horsemen may be kept waiting by the delay. Look at him now, with his manly, open bearing, his fine athletic form, the flush of health upon his cheek, and the sparkle of pleasure in his eye, as with frank courtesy and hearty good-humour he exchanges greetings with one and all, from the stately peer to the burly yeoman, ere he rides into the middle of the pack, who, with fawning countenances and waving sterns welcome that well-known voice, and say if Lord Rasperdale is not the *beau idéal* of what a master of hounds should be. Joy touches his cap, glad to see him at last, for now we shall begin. My lord exchanges his hack for his hunter—a powerful, thorough-bred chesnut, that it is not every man who could ride, but who, when handled by a workman, can show ' how fields are *crossed.*' At that signal, there is a general move, and in the midst of fidgeting horses, mutual greeting, and much cigar-smoke, the hounds trot away to draw Haverley Gorse.

'How are you, Digby, my boy?' burst on my ear in well-remembered tones; and turning sharply round, I recognised my old friend Cartouch—the last person I expected to see at that particular moment. Hearty was our mutual greeting, and many were the inquiries as to our doings—past, present, and to come. Cartouch was fond of hunting as ever, and having got together a capital stud, was now commencing the season with all the ardour and enthusiasm of a boy. Save a few additional crows'-feet, and an occasional line of silver in the glossy black hair, the Colonel looked as young as ever; and although he could not then have been very far from the half-century, his fine figure, graceful seat, and daring horsemanship, would have led a stranger to suppose he was still considerably on the sunny side of middle age—whenever that very conventional period may be supposed to begin.

'There's a fox in that gorse, I'll take my oath,' suddenly exclaimed he, in the midst of a long Canadian conversation, in which we had got interested; 'look at those hounds, how keen they are,' he added, as one after another, emerging from a large long strip of open wood, which they had been unsuccessfully drawing, rushed, with ears erect and rising bristles, towards the prickly covert. 'Sir Benjamin' seemed to partake of their excitement, for he fidgeted about, snatched impatiently at his bridle, and trembled under me almost as much as the evergreen branches which were shaking above the backs of the busy hounds. 'Always a fox at Haverley,' said Lord Rasperdale, as he galloped by to call some foot-people off from a highly-commanding position they had taken up, exactly against the spot at which the wily animal was likely to go away. Even while he spoke, a clear sonorous holloa rang through the air, and though I crammed the spurs into 'Sir Benjamin,' and rattled him down the middle ride of the covert at a pace which would have made some racehorses look foolish, I only reached the other end in time to see the hounds pouring like a cataract over a high stake-bound fence, which crested the opposite eminence, accompanied by the faint and unnecessary 'too-too' with which Joy indulged himself on his horn, and the flutter of 'my lord's' coat-tails, as he disappeared on the further side of the fence. 'Now for it,' I thought,—there will be a rare scent over Haverley pastures, and he *must* cross the vale after that; by Jove, we are in for a tickler!' as I caught fast hold of 'Sir Benjamin's' head, and sinking the wind a little, to make up for the badness of my start, put an awkward 'hog-backed' stile and a fairish ox-fence between myself and the crowd, who as usual rushed violently into the gateways, where they herded in inextricable confusion. My manœuvre answered admirably; for ere another field was crossed, the hounds, turning at right angles down the fence, enabled me to get alongside of them; and short as was the distance we had yet come, the pace at which they were going gave me ample room to look about me. They were streaming like a meteor, and running perfectly mute, so that after the row and turmoil created by the trampling crowd from which I had just escaped, all seemed silent as the grave. On the right was Joy, still horn in

hand, skimming the large fences like a swallow on the wing,
whilst, stride for stride, and leap for leap, Cartouch was riding
by his side, sitting down in his saddle, and handling the powerful bay horse under him in the most masterly manner. On the
left, and a little in advance of these, was Lord Rasperdale, going
straight as a line, in his own quiet determined way, swerving
neither to right nor left, for gate or gap, but taking everything
as it came, and, to use a forcible expression, apparently 'glued
to the hounds.' A loud crack from a broken rail made me look
behind, to see Tom Spencer just *save* a fall, as he landed in the
field. He told me afterwards that he was in such a hurry he
he did not like to 'shut off the steam,' as he called it, by collecting his horse for the effort, and the pace carried him through
four strong bars as if they had been paper. A momentary
'hover,' which one could hardly call a check, and another turn
to the left showed me some ten or twelve more men, in red,
black, and green, who, although not quite so forward as ourselves,
were still going gallantly with the hounds; whilst a loose grey
horse, with streaming rein and flapping stirrup-leathers, who
seemed determined to see as much of the fun as he could, now
that he had got rid of his encumbrance, completed the picture of
which I obtained a momentary glimpse. It was but for a moment, as I had soon enough to do again to keep my own place.
Although my horse was fast as the wind, could get over anything
a quadruped might jump, and in condition was fit to run for the
Derby, yet with all these advantages, and no great weight upon
his back, the deep ridge and furrow, the wet holding soil of
Haverley pastures, large enclosures of from 50 to 100 acres, together with thick, blackthorn fences, sometimes adorned with
two ditches, and occasionally fortified by a strong oak rail, gave
him, clipper as he was, quite enough to do at the extra pace
created by that good scenting ground. I fancy none of us regretted the delay, when a ploughed field, just in front of
Waterley Ash-bank, brought hounds and horses to a check, and
afforded a little breathing time, sadly required by the latter.

'What a capital thing,' said Cartouch ;—' such a country.'

'The fastest fifteen minutes I ever saw in my life,' remarked
Lord Rasperdale, pulling out his watch ; to which Tom Spencer

added, as he jumped off for one moment to relieve his panting
steed, 'We have not done yet; I'll bet my future bishopric
he's over the vale, and we shall have "the Squelch" to negotiate,
twenty feet of water and rotten banks!'

Sure enough Joy hit off his fox, in his own masterly manner,
at the further end of the Ash-bank, and we were soon cantering
down the hill at a somewhat reduced rate, and over an easier
country—the hounds, who had proved to us the pace at which
they could *run*, now showing to admiration the closeness with
which they could *hunt;* whilst far in the distance, amidst the
vivid green of the fertile water-meadows, a line of willows disclosed the winding course of the remorseless Squelch. Deep,
silent, and sluggish as the waters of Lethe is that forbidding
stream. Many a gallant hunter has cooled his reeking sides in
its broad wave, and, extricated with difficulty by a team of his
fellow-creatures and a stout cart-rope, has acquired a high-bred
disgust at the pure element, and never cleared a brook again.
Many an aspiring youth, whose vaulting ambition would acknowledge neither difficulty nor danger, has here baptized the unpaid-
for coat, and drenched to wretchedness the vainglorious leathers;
while many a cautious veteran writhes under a twinge of sym-
pathetic lumbago, as he recalls his ill-advised attempt to ford
the treacherous Squelch. Bridles, stirrup-irons, spurs, whips, and
cigar-cases,—how many treasures lurk concealed in those waters
of oblivion; and who can tell over how many more they may
close for ever, ere that gloomy day,—long, long may it be
deferred!—when the last who-whoop shall sound over the decline
of fox-hunting, and merry England—merry then no more—shall
see her sole remaining pack of hounds vanish before the uncompromising approach of an iron age. In the meantime, the pace
is improving; we are all once more in our swing; the old grass
on which we have again got is sound and springy; and the
horses, as may be supposed, completely sobered. There are ten
men with the hounds, and, of these, three are showing unmistakable symptoms of having had 'enough.' Cartouch has got a
dirty coat, although he is unwilling to confess the fall, which no
one seems to have witnessed. Lord Rasperdale is still slightly
in advance of us; and 'Sir Benjamin' is striding away under

me, as only thorough-bred horses can go, when subjected to severe and sustained exertion. Joy is sailing along, never taking his eye off his hounds, and leaving everything but the choice of pace to his horse, who repays such unlimited confidence by doing his best. The scent is so good that a huntsman has to interfere but little, and ours has given us a specimen of his skill at Ash-bank, which proved him an adept in his craft. Thus it was that, notwithstanding all the instinctive cunning of his kind, we were still upon such good terms with our fox as promised to place him in hand ere he could reach the distant forest, now scarce visible in the far horizon. Just one field short of Waterley Ash-bank—a straggling open strip of plantation, that seemed to be annually subjected to the axe—the hounds, with a dash and gallantry inseparable from a really good pack, had so far over-run the scent, that when, with their huntsman's assistance they again took it up, it was in a direction inclining towards the line they had already come. With the rapidity of lightning it seemed to flash across Joy's mind that they were running what is termed 'heel;' that is to say, although actually upon the track of the animal they pursued, in the reverse direction to that in which he was really travelling, and consequently at a disadvantage increasing with every yard. Two blasts of his horn, two cheers with his mellow voice, brought the well-disciplined and sagacious body about his horse's heels; and galloping off in an exactly contrary direction, towards the farther corner of the sheltering ash-bank, he drew his hounds quietly across the line, and taking it up this time the right way, they stooped one and all to the scent, congratulating each other with a merry peal on having lost so little time or distance by the adroit double of their wary victim. On they went, downwards into the vale, and along the level meadows, with an increasing speed, that sorely taxed the powers and, above all, the training of our steeds. And now there is a holloa from a labourer far across the brook which we are so rapidly approaching, and Cartouch, whose eye rivals a hawk's in keenness, declares he sees our fox travelling steadily across yon large grass-field, nearly half-a-mile ahead of us. I take a strong pull at ' Sir Benjamin,' reducing him to a moderate canter, for the hounds unhesitatingly stream down towards the

M

brook, and it is evident that, as Tom Spencer predicted, we must
charge the Squelch. For an instant they disappear, as though
the earth had swallowed them, and the next moment, straining
up the opposite bank, they shake the wet from their draggled
coats, and throw their tongues in joyous concert, as they sweep
on again. Cartouch and Joy are racing for the spot where they
crossed, always, in the absence of other landmarks, to be presumed the narrowest place in a brook; and I hear the ring of
their stirrup-irons as they fly over it together and abreast. On
their left Lord Rasperdale charges it at a fearful pace, thereby
gaining a slight turn upon the hounds, and clearing it with a
tremendous effort, rolls, man and horse, into the field, but on
the *right side*, and without loss of time is in the saddle and away
again. I glance my eye rapidly along the banks to select my
place, as I dare not pull 'Sir Benjamin' out of his stride to
follow any of the others, and spying a sound-looking take-off
under a tree, steer the thorough-bred one towards that uncertain
spot. No need to quicken the old horse's pace as he nears the
difficulty. Many a brook has he got over gallantly, and never
yet has he been in; so as the surface gleaming in a momentary
sunbeam catches his eye, he cocks his small ears, and pulling
savagely at his bridle, rushes like a colt unbroken towards the
cavity, and lands gloriously on the further side, the waters
glancing beneath me like a cataract, and a large piece of the
bank cut away by his hind legs subsiding dully into the stream.
It was touch and go, but he recovered himself at the moment I
thought we must both have gone backwards, and with a snort of
triumph, laid him down again to his work, whilst I said to myself for the twentieth time, 'Can anything be so like flying as
riding a free-goer over a wide place?' All our friends, however,
were not so fortunate. Six or seven more gallant hearts charged
it unflinchingly—two of them on horses so beat that they had no
strength to jump or to refuse, and overhead they went, without
an effort to save themselves. Two got safely over, by dint of
great good luck and a pitiless application of the spurs; and
another, to the best of my belief, is there still. The Squelch
was no child's play after thirty minutes from Haverley Gorse,
and out of a large field, those alone whom I have mentioned

had the hardihood to attempt it. The rest never saw a yard of the run, and 'hold their manhoods cheap,' when this famous day is mentioned, a day never to be forgotten in the annals of the Hark-Holloa hounds. Ten minutes more have elapsed, and what a change has come over the scene. The forest is no longer far off, and we are getting into a wilder and less cultivated country, which, slightly on the ascent, becomes less and less favourable to our horses. The hounds are still streaming away, now two fields ahead of us, and Joy's efforts to get closer produce little result, save a corresponding whisk of his horse's tail. Lord Rasperdale's chesnut, notwithstanding two falls, is still pretty fresh, while the care and judgment with which Cartouch is riding promises to enable him to last some time longer. The ground is deep, the fences wide, tangled, and straggling; patches of rushes stud the ill-drained fields, and here and there a stunted thorn or blighted fir-tree affords a perch to a solitary carrion-crow or jerking magpie. The forest is looming in our front, a long black belt of interminable wood, and for the forest we are pointing straight as a line could be drawn. 'Sir Benjamin' is still pulling, and I willingly deceive myself into the belief that he is yet quite fresh. Now for it! This is the time to shake to the front, and cut down three of the best riders England can produce. I urge my horse forward, and for five delicious minutes I am alone with the hounds! Tom Spencer trying hard to overhaul me, the more experienced hands, Cartouch, Rasperdale, and Joy, economising their speed, a field behind me, with Tom working away a little in their front; one more man, a parson, three fields further off, and not another soul to be seen anywhere—the hounds still running as if nothing would ever stop them. This was indeed a triumph; and notwithstanding 'Sir Benjamin's' pitching on his head over a very moderate fence, and getting up again in a sadly incoherent manner, I would take no warning, and crossed the succeeding enclosure, a black, deep, boggy sort of field, with unreduced haste. That finished him. The fence at the further end was thick and strong, the ditch towards me deep, though narrow; and when I felt the old horse, usually so eager and elastic, make his effort as though he cared but little what became of him, I knew how the event must be. We hung for a

few seconds entangled in the strong, unyielding blackthorn,
struggled in vain with the slippery perpendicular bank, and as
the rider glided off over the shoulder, his horse subsided into
the ditch upon his back, from whence his four iron-shod feet
protruded pitiably towards the heavens in an attitude of helpless
supplication.

'Cast, I see,' said Lord Rasperdale, as he went by me; 'he'll
struggle out when he gets his wind.'

'Can I help you, Digby?' good-naturedly asked Cartouch, at
the same moment, on my other side—not that he waited for an
answer.

Joy, of course, was too intent upon his hounds to take any
notice of aught else under the skies; and although Tom Spencer
and the clergyman, whose horses were both 'done to a turn,'
would have stopped to render me any assistance in their power,
I waved them on again towards the line of the fast-fading chase.
Eight-and-forty minutes by my watch from the find, and see, the
hounds are doubling down yon old hedgerow, two fields from
the forest. 'He is running short for his life; he must be dead
beat; I shall see them kill him?' I stood on the fatal bank
with straining eyes, and viewed the hazy forms of the hounds
fleeting down one hedgerow and up another; whilst Joy, here
urging his unwilling steed at a stile, there blundering him
through a gap, strove in vain to reach his darlings, and share
with them their well-earned triumph. See! he is off his horse
and amongst them; Rasperdale and Cartouch have sprung from
their saddles, and the sighing November breeze wafts a faint
who-whoop to my expectant ear. At the same instant 'Sir
Benjamin,' awaking from his stupor, extricates himself from his
awkward position by a tremendous effort, and a series of those
laughable gymnastics with which a horse usually emerges from
a scrape, and gives himself a hearty shake, as if to ascertain his
own identity—a fact of which, judging by his scared eye and
distended nostril, he seems by no means sure. Mounting him
and jogging quietly on, three or four friendly handgates bring
me up in time to be one of the triumphant six who see this
gallant fox broken up after a run of fifty-five minutes, unprecedented for pace and straightness, nearly eleven miles from point

to point, over the finest country in England, and with but one trifling check, if check it might be called, from find to finish!

•   •   •   •   •   •   •

CHAPTER XII.

FATHERS AND SONS.

TO an unprejudiced observer, few performances would probably appear so thoroughly uncomfortable as that of a long and weary ride, through lanes and by-ways, knee-deep in mud, upon a tired horse, with the small rain that so often accompanies the close of a short November day, drizzling in one's face, and the prospect of the already dubious twilight becoming pitch dark, hours before it can be possible to reach one's home. The hunter, conscious of having done his duty, and knowing by experience how often the length of his homeward journey is most unfairly proportioned to the severity of his previous exertions, jogs on in a deliberate sort of compromise between trotting and walking, relapsing completely into the latter pace whenever a slight ascent or inequality of ground affords an excuse for the delay, and varying the monotony of such a method of travelling by an occasional alarming demonstration of throwing himself into the middle of the road upon his head—a threat that, for the honour of the noble animal, I am bound to confess, I have never yet known fulfilled. After such a day as that which witnessed our run from Haverley Gorse, ever afterwards known as 'the Great Haverley Run,' it may be supposed that Tom Spencer and I enjoyed to perfection all the comforts I have mentioned in our homeward ride; but far were we from being discontented with our lot; I question if, in the whole habitable globe, there existed, on that eventful afternoon, any two individuals so thoroughly satisfied with themselves as myself and my companion. After exchanging congratulations with Cartouch, Lord Rasperdale and Joy—after a brief and glowing account of the run, intermixed with much personal anecdote, to the first detachment of unfor tunates that came up when we had killed our fox, and who were commanded by Will Partridge, that worthy having held himself ready at any time to struggle to the front and render his professional assistance, if required,—after a cordial farewell to our companions in glory, whose road lay differently from our own, Tom and I wended our way homewards in a frame of mind amiable and enviable beyond measure. How we praised each other's horse and each other's riding, a somewhat reflective flattery, as we had been together most of the day; and the compliments paid by the one to the prowess of the other were but an additional tribute of admiration to his own success. Nor were our absent friends forgotten. Rasperdale and Cartouch were voted the two finest riders and best fellows in England; Joy the most talented huntsman in the world; the Hark-Holloa hounds unequalled by any earthly establishment, and their country a perfect paradise to live in and ride over. Tom Spencer began to have great doubts about going into the Church, as it was rapidly dawning upon him that he could not exist without hunting *at least* five days in the week; whilst I completely made up my own mind to give up soldiering altogether, sell out, marry, and devote myself entirely to the worship of Diana. Alas! that the tripartite goddess should combine in two of her characters such antagonistic attributes, and that the exigencies of the fertile Lucina should be so inimical to the pursuits of the vigorous virgin of the woods. But such calculations enter not the teeming brain of twenty-one; and we plodded home in perfect contentment with ourselves, our horses, and our day's amusement. Every turn in the road brought us in contact with some less successful horseman, for whom the oft-told tale, though planting thorns of discontent and disgust in the breast of the auditor, thrilled with untarnished freshness from the lips of the historian. Here we were overtaken by one gentleman 'who had seen everything we did—was never more than a field behind us: and if hounds had only run *straight*, could have been with us at any time.' And a little farther on we met an honester and more disconsolate sportsman, who confessed to having lost us altogether, and added, with desponding energy, that it was 'just his luck.'

Various and amusing were the excuses for their non-appearance, and far-fetched and ingenious the reasons insisted upon, to prove that there was no lack of courage or determination to be laid to the charge of the unwilling absentees. If Major Slasher had not been riding a young one (now in his third season), he could have had a capital start (the Major argued *ab initio*); and when that is the case, no man alive, so he thinks, can beat that gallant officer. Varnish, the dealer, ' had been going in front for the first half-hour,' and appealed to Squire Softly, who had unfortunately gone home, to corroborate the fact.

'Just as I came to the bruk, Captain, with little Golightly pulling "oudacious," for, as *you* know (!) he's a devil at water, my old snaffle-bridle broke off short at the mouth-piece; and I went four times round that identical field before I could stop him. He's a rare little horse, Captain—how he'd fly with your weight! Look at him now, how fresh he is!'

And on casting my eye over the exhausted steed alluded to, sure enough the bridle had come in two near the bit, and the broken pieces, looking very much as if they had been severed with a penknife, were fastened together with a bit of string. Mr Cane had been deceived by a boy scaring crows, and rode to the urchin, under the impression it was a veritable 'holloa.' Whilst young Mylde, who was notorious for 'pottering in the gaps,' had ridden his own line gallantly at starting through a 'hand-gate;' but being unsuccessful in his search for an easy exit from the field he had so incautiously entered, was forced, after making a complete circuit, again to emerge through that inglorious portal. Lord Lately had been floored by a collision in mid-air with Farmer Bull—the peer getting considerably the worst of it. Sir Francis Fakeaway had stopped his horse (since dead) in the first twenty minutes; and young Fearless, after riding over two fallen sportsmen and three gates, had finally deposited his father's favourite hunter in the yielding mire of the bottomless Squelch. George Jealous, old Venom, and Captain Snarl would not allow that the hounds ever went any pace *at any time*, but that *when they did*, there was nobody with them !—and listened to our unwelcome raptures with a sneer of incredulous disgust. Poor Carambole was the only one who had the manli-

ness to confess his misfortunes, without any attempt at concealment or palliation; and him we overtook vainly endeavouring,
by the light of his cigar, to decipher some mysterious hierogly-
phics on a time-worn sign-post, not too distinct at any period,
and perfectly illegible in the dusk of a November evening.
The active Frenchman had raised himself by his arms to a level
with the important inscription, and when we discovered him,
was perched in mid-air, puffing forth volumes of smoke, and
blowing up a tremendous light from a huge Havanna, wherewith
to improve that typographical knowledge on which his dinner so
entirely depended.

'Holloa! Carambole, have you lost your way?' and 'What
have you done with your horse?' were our simultaneous inquiries.

'He very good horse,' was the reply, 'but I shall nevare see
him again. *Il m'a joué un joli tour*—I gallopp, I jomp. *Nous
arrivons ensemble à un*—"stake-him-bound"—you call him "ox-
fence." *J'enforce mon chapeau sur ma tête, je me suis mis la
cravache à la main; je lui dis, Montez, donc, maudite bête! il a
grimpé là-dessus. C'a ne va pas mal.* I lance his side, I come
to thicker "stake-him-bound." I tomble in. He gallopp away,
and shake his tail. *Je dis, "Bon jour, mon ami; je ne te
reverrais jamais." Fortune de la gue-r-r-e; il faut marcher
par exemple! mais on n'est pas défendu de fumer.'*

And the voluble philosopher strode on by our side in perfect
contentment and good-humour, not diminished by the welcome
information that three more miles would put a period to his
labours, and that, in all probability, the missing hunter would
be home before him. On cross-examination and inquiry, it
appeared that Carambole, though perfectly unused to the sport,
and, like most foreigners, more at home in the *manège* than the
field, had gone in the front rank up to our first check, riding
over timber, and charging his 'stake-him-bounds,' as he called
them, with all the gallantry of his nation. The horse on which
Sir Peregrine had mounted him—an old and excellent hunter—
acquitted himself to admiration, although, doubtless, somewhat
surprised at the inconsiderate recklessness with which he found
himself ridden; and Carambole was in the height of his triumph

when a double ditch, or some such unforeseen obstacle, caused the active and well-trained animal to make a second spring when in the air, totally unexpected by his rider, and which had the effect of precipitating him into the adjoining field upon his back; whilst the horse, released from his burden, galloped on for several miles with the hounds, till, finding the pace more severe than was consistent with his ideas of amusement, he turned his head in the direction of Haverley, and trotted quietly home to his own stable, where, on our arrival at the Hall, we found him comfortably established, all anxiety on his account having been transferred to the fate of the Marquis. Unpromising as was Carambole's *debut* in the hunting-field, he took back with him to France a passion for the chase which all the difficulties he has to contend with, all the annoyances to which he must be subjected, in that unsportsmanlike country, seem unable to eradicate.

Ah, well! hunting is good fun, and so is moistening the recapitulation of your morning's exploits with bumpers of Bordeaux; nor did we spare the latter seductive fluid in the evening, after devoting the day so successfully to the former pursuit. But the realities of life entail sterner and more disagreeable duties than riding over a grass country and drinking claret in an arm-chair; and the more I reflected on my present position—the more I considered my existing relations with Flora Belmont, the more I felt that it was only due to her that I should, as speedily as possible, come to some understanding with Sir Peregrine previous to making my proposal in form to her father. I was well aware that there would be many difficulties in our way—that the old Colonel's bad opinion of my principles and conduct would prove a serious obstacle to our union; that 'money,' ever the first consideration in this business-like world, would be wanting on both sides, and I shuddered to think of my debts, and the large sums that I had squandered upon trifles, and worse than trifles. Young as I was, the veil was gradually falling from my eyes; and the career that had once seemed so jovial, careless, and high-spirited, now that I fondly hoped I had some one to think of besides myself—some one to depend entirely upon me for guidance and support—appeared selfish and contemptible in the extreme. Bitterly did I deplore my past follies, and the un-

worthiness of such a character as mine to mate with my gentle
Flora. In shame and sorrow I recalled my feigned adoration of
Mrs Man-trap, and my heart died within me to think that Fate
might have in store for me—alas! but too just a reprisal!—
such a disappointment as I had inflicted upon the high-minded
Zoë. But, above all, I chafed and fretted to reflect that the
filthy lucre which I had heretofore despised — the dross that
I had hitherto considered but as a necessary inconvenience
attendant upon civilisation—might now prove 'the one thing
needful,' the only insuperable obstacle to the triumph of my
better feelings—to my entrance upon a nobler and purer state
of being.

Stung by such thoughts as these, I placed as high a value upon
gold as I had previously depreciated that very necessary com-
modity; and ever in extremes, thought myself capable of any
exertion to attain that which I had often squandered so profusely.
There is less difference than the world is apt to imagine between
the spendthrift and the miser; the same selfish temperament that
makes the youth greedy of pleasure and ungrudging of aught
save his own enjoyment, produces in after-years an insatiable
desire for the means by which such indulgences may be procured;
and as the owner of 'the splendid shilling,' whilst the coin is his,
possesses everything that a shilling can purchase, so the hoarding
capitalist, though he may deny himself all the luxuries and most
of the necessaries of life, has the satisfaction of feeling that he
can at any time command all that his fellow-creatures are
striving so unceasingly to obtain. Thus it is that the same
individual who at twenty risks hundreds on the turn of a die
and thousands on the speed of a horse, nor suffers such excitement to impair his appetite or disturb his repose, shall at forty,
with ten times the knowledge and twenty times the means,
grudge to spend a penny upon the most simple and economical
of amusements; and whilst acres are fertilising to increase his
rents, and consols accumulating to swell his ever-growing capital,
shall remain, in the midst of all his wealth, continually haunted
'by the ghost of a shilling.'

Nevertheless an explanation must be come to, and an interview
with Sir Peregrine, always rather a formidable undertaking, must

be arranged for the purpose. Divers ceremonies required to be gone through on these occasions. In the first place, a footman was despatched for Soames, who was charged with a *vivâ voce* appeal to his master for the honour of an interview, which invariably called forth the same reply, delivered with becoming pomposity by the messenger, 'Sir Peregrine will see you, sir, directly he is at leisure.' I was always at a loss to know the line which my father drew between his hours of what he called his leisure and his employment, for to business he had an unconquerable aversion, and he seldom or never looked into a book. An hour or so of waiting then produced Mr Soames once more, who, throwing the door wide open, as though to announce a duchess, would inform me, as if I was an utter stranger, that 'Sir Peregrine would see me if I would *step this way,*'—and *this way* I accordingly stepped, with a beating heart and much-misgiving mind.

'Soames has informed me you wish to speak with me, Digby,' was the unpromising commencement; 'may I ask the cause of your demanding such an interview? I have five minutes to spare, and must beg of you to come at once to the point.'

This was not a reassuring mode of entering upon what I felt would be a delicate business, but, determined not to be staggered, I at once laid the case in a very few words before my father, stating openly my own engagement to Miss Belmont, and concluding with the somewhat startling demand to know what he would make up his mind to do, in a pecuniary point of view, to support the 'position' (this I thought a hit) of the heir to his name. Never shall I forget the pause of astonishment with which my father, pushing his spectacles up on his brow, gazed at me whilst I delivered my peroration; and willingly do I draw a veil over the scene that followed, in which retort and recrimination, ill-judged censure on the one side, and unpardonable irreverence on the other, created a breach never afterwards to be repaired between those whose interests, even in a worldly point of view, should have been in common, whose reciprocal attachment nothing on earth should have been able to undermine. Amidst the whirlwind of censure with which Sir Peregrine attacked my habits, my pursuits, and even my character, I dis-

covered that the real offence was my having dared to cast my
eyes upon a penniless young lady, and that in his sanguine and
ambitious mind the old man had always looked to my future
marriage with some wealthy heiress to re-establish the prosperity
of our house, and was living on from year to year, sinking deeper
into his difficulties, and becoming more hopelessly involved in
his affairs, cheered by this vague hope which I had now dashed
to the ground. In my indignation and despair I lost all self-
command, and, to my shame be it said, forgot that reverence
which under all circumstances is ever due from a son to his
father. I vowed that I was utterly reckless of what should
happen to me if this marriage was not to come off—that I would
return to my dissolute courses and extravagant career. I scouted
our dignities, and scoffed at 'our position.' I blasphemed the
memory of Sir Hugo, and swore that I cared not what became
of Haverley; that the estates might go to the Jews, and the
family to the devil! and, in short, our interview concluded with
so little prospect of reconciliation, after all that had taken place,
that the next morning saw me posting back to rejoin my regiment in London, having quarrelled irretrievably with my father,
vowing vengeance against Haverley and all belonging to it, and
utterly regardless as to where I should go or what should become
of me—a dangerous state of mind for a young man just turned
one-and-twenty hurrying back to the seductive arms of the
modern Babylon.

CHAPTER XIIL

LIFE IN LONDON.

THERE seems to be a charm in life at the University which,
amongst all temperaments and all dispositions, extends its
influence far into after-years, and the bright recollection of which
smiles as the one green spot in many a cheerless destiny and
disappointing career. Two old campaigners will sufficiently pros*
about their marchings and counter-marchings, their skirmishes

bivouacs, and general engagements. Two rural politicians will disagree for hours together upon the affairs of the nation, and insist volubly enough upon the arguments borrowed at second-hand from their respective morning papers. Farmers, fishermen, and fox-hunters, especially the latter, are extremely tiresome to an uninitiated listener, as they enter voluminously into the mysteries of their several crafts ; nor are the frequenters of Newmarket free from an ill-judged tendency to monopolise the conversation, unawed by the frowns of graver seniors, who deem all money-getting practices but their own a grievous sin, and undeterred by the suppressed yawns and weary glances of the ladies, who cannot be brought to interest themselves in the supposition that Plato is able to give Aristotle three pounds and a beating, or that Bustle's public running proves that singularly-named animal immeasurably inferior to Canezou.

But much as all these eloquent gentlemen love to dwell upon their favourite topics, they are not to be compared with two old University chums, meeting after an interval of a few years, and living over again in memory the wild jollities and rapid escapades of manhood's morning time. At it they go—pell-mell—both together, without a moment's interval or cessation : how Brazen-nose bumped Oriel, and what the Dean said concerning the desecration of Peckwater—what a 'good-plucked' one was Muffles of Trinity, and how he licked the bargeman, and rode over Tom Sebright—why Sapling should have been senior wrangler, and how Muggins took a 'double-first'—and what fun we had after 'hall' in 'my rooms,' and amongst 'our own set of *men*.' All these recollections appear to revive with a freshness that Time is altogether unable to tarnish, and the admiring auditor who has not enjoyed the advantages of a University education, begins to think that his own youth has been most ingloriously wasted.

No man can have had a larger store of these reminiscences than my old schoolfellow, Tom Spencer. With the fear of academical dons before my eyes, and a most exaggerated reverence for the legal powers of the University, I shall not specify the college to which my friend Tom belonged, but shall only mention that whatever opportunities were offered at Oxford for amusement,

excitement, or instruction, he took advantage of them all.   The
sharp intelligent boy at Eton had developed himself into the
sound and cultivated scholar, whilst the winner of the Sculling
Sweepstakes at the Brocas was the staunchest oar of that gallant
crew which struggled annually with the Cambridge eight.   Everything he undertook appeared to crown him with success.   Not a
Regius professor of them all could render a passage of Euripides
into the nervous English that clothed Tom's poetic fancy and rich
imagination; not a dare-devil undergraduate that would follow
him out 'larking,' as he handed an Oxford hack over gate after gate
for sheer amusement. Ever the first with the 'drag-hounds,' and I
fear not seldom the last at the wine-party, he would retire to the
solitude of his own room after a brilliant day with the former,
succeeded by a joyous gathering at the latter, and tying a wet
towel round his head, he would devote the whole night to intense
study, and after a couple of hours' repose towards morning,
appear at chapel, fresh and ready to repeat the day's amusement
and the night's occupation.   More sleep than this he declared he
never required, and, except that he could always snatch half-an-
hour's slumber at any disengaged period of the day, such a disposition of his time seemed to give him quite as much rest as
his nature demanded.   The dons of his college were very proud,
as well they might be, of Tom's proficiency in scholarship, accompanied and, as I believe in their secret hearts they thought,
enhanced as it was by so many lighter accomplishments; and
several of my friend's enormities were winked at, and sundry
breaches of discipline looked over, in consideration of the honour
which he was one day expected to reflect upon the University.
He was always a regular attendant at chapel, and this praiseworthy habit has ever been known to cover a multitude of sins;
but upon one occasion, when he had before him an unusually
long ride to covert, having made arrangements for a day with a
distant pack of hounds, Tom imprudently clad himself in his
much-worn scarlet, as well as his top-boots and breeches, trusting
that his gown would conceal the one as effectually as a pair of
voluminous over-alls, made for the purpose, covered the other.
The service was short, and the morning dark and gloomy.   Tom,
who had previously breakfasted, was, I fear, too deeply engrossed

in his meditation as to whether his first eighteen miles, if done under the hour, was or was not too much for the hack, who would then be relieved by a fellow-sufferer sent on for the purpose, to attend as he ought to have done under the sacred roof ; but even he, impatient as he was, could not complain of any undue delay or unnecessary degree of formality in the chaplain who officiated. The gown had done its duty well, and the forbidden garment lurked beneath it unknown and unsuspected ; but in his anxiety to be in time, as he was hurrying out of chapel he unfortunately took out his watch, and the act of doing so unavoidably disclosed a stained and crimson chest, before the very eyes of the astonished Dean, who at that moment, unknown to Tom, was close beside him. An immediate invitation to accompany the magnate towards his rooms was the consequence ; and thither, with another wistful glance at his timepiece, was the crestfallen culprit compelled to follow. But ere the frowning portals closed upon them, the Dean, with a good-natured sympathy for the manifest impatience of his companion, addressed him with his usual gentlemanlike courtesy of manner.

' I will not detain you long, Mr Spencer ; but I merely wish to inquire upon what principle you have presumed to enter chapel in a garment of that unbecoming colour and character ? '

' This, sir ? ' inquired the unabashed undergraduate, pointing to the crimson so stained by wet and mire as to be a near approach to black ! ' this is an old " Montem " coat that I had at Eton, and sent to be dyed, for economy ; they could make nothing of it but a " mulberry," which I agree with you, sir, is highly unbecoming to a fair man. I should have wished it a shade nearer black, but *nimium ne crede colori.*'

The joke, the trite quotation, and the effrontery of the whole thing saved him, and the ' unbecoming mulberry ' was again that day in the front rank, as usual. But Tom might thank his habitual obedience to regulations, and the general good character which he had maintained since his matriculation, for bearing him harmless in a scrape which to others might have been fraught with serious consequences.

Many a merry laugh rung across our snug breakfast-table in my comfortable lodgings, over such University anecdotes as these; and even the Dean himself, in all his pomp and power and 'pride of place,' might have been gratified could he have heard with what energy and goodwill he was voted 'a downright trump' by my visitor and myself; for Tom Spencer was relaxing his mind and improving his worldly knowledge, after his Oxford labours, by spending the winter vacation with me in London. It had been a long-promised visit when we were together at Haverley; and after my ill-advised disagreement with Sir Peregrine, it was a great comfort to me to have so old a friend with whom to talk over all my difficulties and disappointments, whose presence would counteract the depressing influence of a winter morning in the metropolis, so keenly felt by the solitary individual for whom the other hours of the twenty-four teem with false and frivolous excitement, whilst to the visitor full of spirits, youth, and health, a month or six weeks spent within the Bills of Mortality was a realisation of all that he considered most delightful.

A well-matched pair we were, in thoughts, feelings, and habits, as after a *very* late breakfast we devoted our customary hour to smoking and gossip, for which the previous evening's amusements or pursuits furnished an inexhaustible theme. Perhaps a brother-officer or occasional visitor would drop in, with a good-humoured jest at our being still in our dressing-gowns and slippers, the only costume for lounging in real comfort, and sitting down to join in our fumigatory conclave, would add his quota to the scandal of the hour. People in London are much more sociable in the winter, as they are in better spirits and more readily amused; there is not that constant bustle, that restless anxiety to 'go and do something else,' that destroys the whole comfort of society in the season; and many a woman that you would vote 'fine' or 'stupid' in July, many a man that in the dog-days you inconsiderately set down as 'a puppy' or 'a bore,' warms into kindliness with the blazing hearth of merry Christmas, and in the gloomy hours of dark December vindicates his or her character to the right of being designated a 'very charming person,' or a 'devilish good fellow.'

When the pantomimes have fairly set in with the frost, when there is skating on the Serpentine, and the streets are dry and

clean, when Melton and other hunting localities have sent up
their different detachments of pleasure-seeking bachelors, when
your own particular friends are sure to be 'at home' to your
'morning,' or rather 'afternoon' call, and you are not supposed
to know that any of those 'disagreeables' are in town, on whom,
at midsummer, you lavish pasteboard as a matter of duty; then
it is that London, to my mind, combines all that is delightful in
civilised life. You brace your nerves and promote your appetite
by a brisk walk in the keen pure air of Kensington Gardens,
where, if not a skater yourself, you watch with interest and
wonder the gyrations and evolutions of those whose 'winged
heels' bear them swiftly and smoothly as the swallow on her
noiseless pinions, and you determine that *next* winter, if there
should be a lasting frost, you will really buy a pair of skates and
begin. The performers seem so thoroughly to enjoy their occupation—the bystanders, with sparkling eyes and eager countenances, seem to take so much interest in the sport—every one
looks so good-humoured and amused, that you can hardly believe
these are the same Kensington Gardens, this is the same English
people, that surrounded you last May in an east wind, when
weary glances, listless gestures, and suppressed yawns were
paying their tribute of feigned admiration to the band of Her
Majesty's 1st or 2d regiment of Life Guards, kindly lent by
the Sovereign for the delectation of her lieges. The early twilight approaches with a crimson hue that promises a long continuance of the cold weather; and if oats are at thirty shillings
a quarter, and you have no horses, you congratulate yourself
internally on your prudence, as you step briskly homewards by
the margin of the frozen waters, and contrast the merry stream
of pedestrians that now throng the ring with the endless string
of carriages 'dragging its slow length along,' that endangered
your hack and covered yourself with dust the day before you
started for Goodwood Races. Then the very dandies looked
haggard, worn, and fagged; the ladies pale, listless, and dejected; whilst one and all complained of heat, and glare, and
fatigue. Now the little face that peeps from out that mass of
fur is rosy as the morning sky; what though the chiselled
Grecian nose may be tipped with a faint tinge of pink, con-

N

trary to the established rules of colouring, those sparkling eyes
and that elastic step may well make amends for any such trifling
liberty on the part of John Frost; and as she moves briskly
onwards by the side of her whiskered companion, twice the
man he was in June, you catch a glimpse of the taper ankle and
arched instep that bear her so jauntily along, and ponder deeply
in your own mind whether any costume yet invented by the
daughters of Eve can be so becoming as a winter toilette.
Such a stroll by the Serpentine, such a lounge in Kensington
Gardens, was the constant afternoon occupation of Tom Spencer
and myself, though our morning engagements sometimes made
it nearly dark ere we sallied forth for our daily walk. Tom
was, like myself, a patron of all athletic sports and exercises,
nor was the accomplished Oxonian any mean proficient with
'the gloves.' 'Mr Spencer is a very hard hitter,' said our
instructor, the 'Chelsea Champion,' after a severe bout in my
rooms, of which the breathless professional had decidedly the
worst. 'What a pity he should have been born a gentleman!
He might have made a *very honest* livelihood in the Ring,'—
and as the morning in question afforded a fair specimen of our
usual mode of life, I may be allowed to describe the scene, as
an illustration of the way in which the earlier part of his day is
spent by a young gentleman loose in London. The first-floor of
a moderately-sized house, not very far from Hyde Park—that
being, in consideration of his military duties, the most convenient
neighbourhood for a guardsman—offered me ample accommodation in a suite of four comfortable rooms, one of which was now
devoted to the service of my visitor. Folding-doors shut out
the dormitories, and gave an air of snug privacy to the two
sitting-rooms in which our mornings were spent. The one, tolerably cleared of furniture, afforded a space wherein were often
waged such trials of strength and skill as those in which the
'Chelsea Champion' had now been worsted; whilst in the other,
every description of appliance for ease and luxury was crowded
in lavish profusion. A print of 'Bolton Abbey in the Olden
Time,' that composition of all others most suggestive of feudal
habits and the ancient field-sports of merry England, occupied
the place of honour over my chimney-piece. Two more of

Landseer's exquisite designs, — the stag challenging his approaching foe in the frosty moonlight, and the calm peaceful 'Sanctuary,' at which the exhausted hart has just arrived, with tottering limbs and dripping sides, flanked the more majestic print of the chivalrous-looking abbot and his welcome visitors. A spirited sketch of '*Rivolte*,' by a French artist, held an equally prominent position with a portrait by Herring of the winner of last year's Derby, and a series of 'moving accidents by flood and field' greeted the sportsman's eye, with Alken's inimitable touches. 'The Dying Gladiator,' dying again in burnished bronze, as still he lives and dies in Byron's immortal lines, was the most valued of all the works of art I possessed ; and on the pedestal that supported his godlike figure, relaxing, drooping, failing, but all unconquered still, were inscribed those glorious stanzas that will survive even the mighty creation of the sculptor's art. In a niche above him stood a cast of Joan of Arc, clasping her cross-handled sword to her bosom, and looking intently forward, with a holy fervour beaming on that calm virgin-face. Stags' heads and horns, curious skins, and strange, fantastic weapons, filled the intervening spaces on my motley walls ; whilst couch, footstool, and ottoman, 'chaise longue,' 'prie-dieu,' and American rocking-chair, crowded the room itself, with every possible temptation to sit down and talk. Three unpaid bills, a pair of white gloves, a cigar-case, and an opera-glass, shared the writing-table with a broken foil, some new music, and a portfolio of caricatures, scattered in every direction ; whilst a watch unwound, coiled in its serpent-like chain, reposed upon the chimney-piece. The room was, in short, what ladies call 'untidy,' which every bachelor knows to mean the essence of comfort ; and on a low table with snowy cloth, a beautiful service of china, and richly-chased teapot, cream-jug, &c., did no dishonour to the remains of a capital breakfast, which appeared, judging by the *débris* of the action, to have been thoroughly appreciated. The proprietor of the caravanserai (for such, as regarded the free-and-easy manner in which its visitors came and went, it might justly be called) was lying on a sofa, attired in morning-gown and slippers, inhaling composure from Cavendish tobacco, through a cherry-stick nearly six feet long, and en

couraging with voice and action the struggles going on in the
adjoining apartment, where Tom Spencer, stripped to his shirt,
and a pair of extremely gaudy and Turkish-looking inexpres-
sibles, was pounding away for his life at the 'Chelsea Champion,' a short, square, ill-favoured individual, who looked as if
nothing could ever knock him down.   Tom was the larger and
longer man, and as he hit out with the rapidity of lightning,
and moved from place to place with the graceful activity of a
young Apollo, it was evident that he gave the professor quite
enough to do to hold his own with so energetic an amateur.
The champion glared, and puffed, and gasped, and dodged, now
here, now there, putting in play all the different manœuvres of
the Ring, which the initiated call 'moves,' and occasionally
getting in a sounding thwack on Tom's ribs, generally returned
by the young one with electric quickness on the champion's unprepossessing physiognomy ; a more noisy rally than usual being
invariably followed by a vigorous application to a certain pewter-
pot, which seemed to afford the combatants much consolation
and refreshment.   Hillingdon, with his hat on and his usual
quiet smile impressed on those more than usually haggard
features, was busily employed in sketching my Joan of Arc in
chalks, a pursuit of which he was enthusiastically fond ; and
as he sat there, with his pale, handsome face looking upward
towards the sweet, sad countenance of the Maid of Orleans, I
could not help being struck with the resemblance between the
copyist and the cast he was studying—the unearthly expression that threw a shade as of coming evil over my friend's
brow, and the air of lofty resignation which seemed to anticipate
the destiny of the ill-fated heroine.   Jack Lavish, on whose well-
curled head care had never presumed to sit, who through good
and ill-fortune, losses, reverses, and annoyances of every description, still showed his white teeth, with his own good-humoured
smile,—still twirled his dark mustaches, and curled his ambrosial
whiskers, as though whilst these treasures were left him, fate
might do her wickedest—Jack, of whom his bitterest foe had
never yet found aught to say worse than that, like *Poins*, he
was ' a second brother and a proper fellow of his hands,' whom
all the ladies voted so ' good-looking,' and of whom the severest

of that cynical sex only added, ' it was a pity he should be such
a goose,' a mode of praise the gentle creatures sometimes adopt,
even when discussing their greatest favourites—Jack completed
our party, and between the puffs of his cigar, imparted to us the
important intelligence that he was going to be married, and disclosed the series of manœuvres and the highly successful strategy
by which he had secured the hand of the wealthy heiress to whom
he was now affianced.

'One must stop somewhere,' said Jack, ' and I was getting
tired of Melton and the shires, localities in which the glorious
system of credit, the main-stay of our commercial country, has
in my case been stretched a little too far ; so having won a
fairish stake at Goodwood, and being thrown over by St Heliers
in a yachting cruise, I determined upon a course I have so often
heard recommended to each other by the little boys in the street,
and made up my mind to "go to Bath." Ever been at Bath,
Digby ?'

' Not I,' was the reply ; ' and never wish to go.'

'No place like it for getting into condition,' said Jack. 'I
mean to stay there for a week every year before I go to the
Highlands. It is exactly like living on a flight of steps. I can
hardly walk along Pall Mall now—I tire so dreadfully over the
flat. However, it was severe at first, but like the treadmill, and
everything else of the kind, one soon gets used to it. Well, to
Bath I went, with a thoroughbred hack of my brother's, and
three horses from Tilbury ; and the very first morning I arrived
there I saw a flaming paragraph in the *Bath Patriarch* and *Somer-
setshire Flying Express,* to the effect that " the numerous and
valuable stud of the Hon. Captain Lavish has reached our *now*
sporting locality. This distinguished and popular *millionaire!*"
(think of that, you fellows without a rap !) " is expected shortly
to follow, as the *avant courier* of a host of fashionables about to
winter in our genial and health-restoring climate." Well, I
thought, if three screws and a pony are a valuable stud, and I,
Jack Lavish, am a *millionaire*, there may be hopes for me yet ;
and, accordingly, I got myself up with more than usual care ;
and as I swaggered down Milsom Street in gorgeous apparel, I
laid out the plan of my future campaign. This was only towards

the close of October; and lo! in two short months my enterprising venture and spirited outlay has been crowned with success.
In the first place, rather than not have two hunters out every day,
I determined to limit my hunting to twice a week; and a second
horse being an unheard-of luxury in these benighted regions, I
was respected accordingly. The next step was to hire a sober-
looking dark-green drag, picked out with blue, and *very* heavy,
which always looks wealthy. Into this I put the three Tilburies
when not otherwise engaged, and my brother's hack, who did not
relish the amusement at all. I made my valet attire himself in
boots and breeches, and a dark-grey frock—an arrangement at
which he kicked considerably when it was first suggested to him;
but the reflection that I took him as a boy out of a racing-stable,
and the recollection of how unmercifully I used to *whop* him when
first he came to me, served to overcome his scruples, and I had
thus a very creditable team, with two respectable-looking servants
attached to it. I never could follow out the train of reasoning
that leads to such a conclusion; but I have always remarked,
that when a man drives four-in-hand he is immediately considered
to possess ten thousand a year; and I had hardly worn out one
silk whip-lash before I found myself caressed and *fêted* amongst
all the best society in Bath. Rich, unmarried, and *so* good-
looking (you may laugh, but I give you my honour, I *was very*
good-looking for Bath), Captain Lavish was a trump-card wherever he went, and I had my choice of several unhealthy widows
with comfortable fortunes, and a tough old maid or two with a
small independence of her own. You know the old adage, that
what will hook a trout will hook a salmon—though I fear good
Izaak Walton would hardly bear out the theory—and on that
principle I resolved to enter for the great race, and see whether
I could not carry off Miss Goldthred, the rich heiress, from a
host of competitors. I soon became acquainted with Alderman
Goldthred, her uncle and guardian, likewise a *most respectable*
man, which means in the city a person of undoubted wealth;
and I cemented my acquaintance with him by a capital dinner, to
which I invited him at the York House. We were *tête-à-tête*,
and with turtle from Bristol, and champagne from Crockford's
sent down on purpose, you may suppose that I did what I could

to make him comfortable. I like to drink a fair share of claret after dinner, as you know—I think it promotes digestion, and, in short, it suits my arrangements. I have found few men who, as the evening waned, became so thirsty in proportion to the approach of midnight, a peculiarity which I have remarked in my own organisation, and which I shared with the worthy Alderman. Bottle after bottle came and went, and still the civic dignitary sat, and conducted himself with becoming stateliness and " propriety." Claret was evidently of no use, but what its gentle influence had begun, some curious Maraschino and one of my long regalia cigars, a *blackish* one, finished. The Alderman tottered, his eye wandered, and he moved uneasily on his chair. One more glass of the liqueur, one more thick full-flavoured weed, and I saw my respectable guest home, and deposited him on his own couch with a caution and tenderness that entailed his everlasting gratitude. From that day Alderman Goldthred voted me the best fellow of his acquaintance, and, contrasting the charitable care which I took of him, as in duty bound after promoting his downfall, with the treatment he had once before experienced from some convivial companions of stronger brains, who had amused themselves considerably at his expense when under the influence of stimulants, and finished by shaving his honest head, decided that I had conferred upon him a favour of the greatest magnitude.

'After this I dined with him three times a week, and had every opportunity of ingratiating myself with Clementina, his niece and ward, a lady of great personal property and attractions, to whom I am now going to be married; there was one difficulty, however, which for a time appeared to me insuperable, and this was that Clemmy, though a nice girl, generally well-dressed, and not bad-looking, was undoubtedly blue, and to my horror I constantly heard her remark that she adored *talent* (that was the word) beyond everything, and vow that stupidity in a man was the only thing with which she had no patience.'

'Rather a " facer " for you, Jack,' said I, ' as you never were much of a bookworm, though you might have called upon several Israelites and other moneyed men to prove that you can write your own name.'

'Besides,' added Hillingdon, looking up from his Joan of Arc, now rapidly growing into beauty, 'bar spelling, nobody writes a better letter than Jack; witness the invitations he constantly sends me to dine at mess.'

'That was exactly the difficulty,' said our good-humoured friend, not the least affronted at our strictures upon his capabilities. 'If I had had the advantage of a good education, like that young bruiser in the next room; if I could play whist and billiards like Digby; or sketch gothic arches, and string rhymes to a grasshopper, like yourself, Hillingdon, I should not be afraid of any amount of learning in a lady—no, not even if she was to write a book! But these are not my accomplishments, and except that I cut out all the patterns for my own coats, and know how to put four horses together, I think, in other respects, I can hardly call myself exactly *clever*. Well, I soon found that Miss Goldthred admired my mustaches, did not object to my society, and rather preferred dancing with me to being whisked about by any of her other danglers—by the way, the Bath swells are wretchedly bad goers—but still we never got any further; it was evident that she had not made up her mind as to whether I was clever, and if I could but establish that point, I saw my way clearly. There was nothing for it but to take up some particular line, and the less she knew about the subject in which I was to appear a proficient, the better my chance of success. I thought of botany, conchology, moral philosophy—the latter, I believe, very easily acquired; but unfortunately Clemmy had a smattering of all these sciences, till in a lucky moment I hit upon politics, and that was the very thing—ladies never understand politics—and I became forthwith an embryo statesman. Like all fellows who live much in society, I know most of the leading men pretty intimately; and it is astonishing what an effect the familiar mention of such men's names, and an anecdote or two of their private lives and personal histories, will have with people who are not behind the scenes. Many of such little bits of gossip I had of course at my fingers' ends; whilst on all the great questions I preserved a discreet and ominous silence. If I was induced to give an opinion, it was delivered oracularly, and invariably wound up with the expression of my conviction that we were "on the eve of a great crisis." When a man is so prophetically solemn as that, it would appear almost profane to cross-examine him, and "the great crisis" bore me triumphantly through many a tough and tangled argument. It succeeded admirably. Clemmy, once under the impression that I was fit to be prime minister of England, became sufficiently attached to me to give herself, her hand, and all her worldly goods, to the penniless younger brother, whose only fortune was his future position in the senate; whilst the Alderman swears by me, as a man of sense and discretion, with great mental powers, veiled under a placid exterior.

' " A far-seeing young man, that Captain Lavish," he has been heard to say,—" of a deep-thinking and reflective turn of mind; none of your talkers, sir, but a man who listens to reason; not brilliant, but sound and safe, and entirely to be depended upon."' And with this satisfactory conclusion to his recital, Jack threw away the end of his cigar, arranged his hat and neckcloth in the glass, and took himself off for what he called afternoon parade, to attend upon his ladye-love.

' Poor Jack!' said Hillingdon, as the door closed upon our good-humoured Benedict. ' Now, do you not consider, Digby, that he has sold himself? It is quite impossible that a man who has lived, as he has, among the highest-born and fairest of the land, can care for this vulgar city heiress to whom he is to be tied for life, in one short fortnight from this time?

' Probably not,' said I. ' But what would you have him do? Lavish has nothing in this world but ten thousand pounds of debt, and had he not married a woman with money, a very few weeks would have seen our friend outlawed, insolvent, and in all probability imprisoned.'

' And what of that?' rejoined Hillingdon, with glowing cheek, and sparkling eye. ' What if he were? A thousand times better to linger out one's life even in the constraint and wretchedness of a debtor's cell, than to endure the galling misery, the eternal slavery of a marriage for money. Day after day, year after year, never to be free from the oppressive presence of the loathed object—and loathe her I should, however undeservedly, had I married her on such terms, and for such a cause. Like

the dead corpse chained to the living man, so would her presence
blunt my energies, and dull my faculties, conscious but of the
load which unceasingly oppressed them. And suppose he should
love another,' added the enthusiast, whilst his eye dilated with
an expression which in these moments of excitement had often
given me painful forebodings. 'Supposing *two* spirits should be
doomed to misery by this accursed craving for luxury and wealth,
because the one—the man—that should be the most vigorous
and self-denying of the two, cannot resist the temptation of
wearing out a few more short years in the career of frivolity to
which he has accustomed himself, till the silken fetters have
grown strong and heavy as an iron chain. What an unnatural
state has this world arrived at, when such unholy alliances are
made every day, and called, forsooth, marriages of necessity—
when half the men we know are driven, by their previous
habits and the false position in which they find themselves
placed, to close what I must of necessity call a career of dishonesty, by such a crowning disgrace as the deliberate prostitution
of the heart. You know my conviction of the eternity of
marriages. You know my belief in the communion we are
sometimes permitted to hold with the other world, and it will
not surprise you, Digby, to hear me declare, that rather than be
guilty of the baseness which Lavish is about to commit, and of
which he and the men amongst whom we live think so lightly,
I would beg my bread barefoot from door to door. Rather than
be faithless in word or deed to my spirit-love, I would seek her
in those regions to which my own death alone could give me
access.'

As Hillingdon ceased, his wasted features glowing with the
energy of his feelings, and his form dilating as he touched upon
the subject of death—a subject which to him always appeared
fraught with interest and excitement, not unmingled with
triumph, I could not help acknowledging to myself the truth of
the well-known line,

'Great wits to madness often are allied,'

as I reflected that the sentiments thus expressed by my gifted
friend, would, by the mass of his fellow-creatures, the every-day

denizens of this practical world, be considered but as the workings of an over-excited imagination, the vagaries of a diseased mind.

Like Hamlet, poor Hillingdon was one whose nobility of sentiment, and acuteness of feelings, ill fitted him to mingle with beings formed of grosser clay. The ideal was to him what the real is to the rest of mankind; and such a temperament, undirected by the mild and steady light of true religion, unschooled in the harsh but wholesome training of necessity, was but too prone to lose itself in the dreamy phantasies and vague conceptions of mysticism and superstition.

With varied talents of no common order, with a memory enriched with all of good and great that history has emblazoned on her undying page for the guidance and the emulation of unborn ages, with a gallant heart that danger or difficulty might strive in vain to daunt or overcome, and nerves which, though cased in no iron frame, were yet not to be shaken by the direst catastrophe, I could not help thinking, when Hillingdon left my rooms that morning, what materials for a hero were in him, spoilt and wasted by the accidental preponderance of a too susceptible imagination. Poor Hillingdon! how few amongst the associates who were charmed by his manners and delighted with his wit, to whom he was but the pleasant acquisition, the jovial companion—how few knew aught of his character, beyond his everyday power of making himself agreeable, or troubled themselves to look below that polished surface, and calm self-possessed exterior! I believe none knew him as well as I did: to none had he opened his heart so freely, or disclosed his sentiments so entirely, as to myself; and none, despite the difference of our characters, the directly opposite views that we entertained upon many important subjects, could admire him or love him half so well; and yet, although not generally given to forebodings of evil, I always felt conscious that I valued his society as a thing of which I should too soon be deprived. There was a melancholy charm in our intimacy, enhanced by the presentiment that it would not last long, although I was in mercy spared the anticipation of its too horrible conclusion.

CHAPTER XIV

THE FORTUNES OF A DANSEUSE.

THE short days of December were now drawing to so early a close, that it was usually twilight before I found myself dressed for the morning, and sallying forth for a breath of fresh air in the park, or an hour's gossip at the clubs. One afternoon, as I was wending my way leisurely down to the latter rendezvous of the 'great unemployed,' I was startled by the peculiar carriage and graceful springy step of a muffled-up female figure a few yards in advance of me, whose gait and manner, as she came into the light of one lamp after another (for the gas was already on duty), appeared more and more familiar to my recollection. Can it be? no—'tis impossible at this time of year. Besides, she is in Russia. But there never was anything so like Coralie. And quickening my pace, merely to ascertain, by looking under the close little bonnet, that it was *not* the dancer, I found myself seized by both hands, with a most cordial and affectionate greeting, which I could hardly return with sufficient warmth, in my surprise at Mdlle. de Rivolte's unexpected appearance in London during December.

'You will come with me to my hotel—I shall present you to *mon cousin*—you will dine with us, *mon cher* Digby—I go away in two days,' exclaimed the voluble lady, whose delight at again seeing me was, however, sufficiently gratifying to induce me to accept her invitation, and send an excuse to old Burgonet, with whom I was engaged to dine, on the plea that I was on duty; nor had I cause to regret my duplicity in thus throwing over the venerable General, for at a pleasanter party than discussed a perfect little dinner at Coralie's hotel, I have seldom had the luck to be present. There was no one but the fair dancer, her cousin, and myself. But the way we discussed bygone jests, new scandal, and *old* times (of last season), would have furnished mirth and matter for a dozen of the regular dull banquets which single men attend so perseveringly for their sins. Coralie had an off-hand way of taking up and dropping her adorers, just as it suited her own convenience and caprice, and without the slightest reference to their inclination, which was as amusing as it was unaccountable, and I now found myself on the footing of an old and valued friend, but *nothing more;* this, under existing circumstances, jumped with my humour far better than affecting a regard I did not feel, and put me completely at my ease in the society of my *ci-devant* flame.

Mon cousin was a delightful fellow, and whatever might have been his real relationship, acted the part of *chaperon* and collateral to admiration. He was connected in some way with the opera at St Petersburg, and his anecdotes of that highly-favoured institution, and its illustrious patron, were, as may be supposed, neither tame nor uninteresting. He was a thorough Frenchman, and entered into everything with a spirit and *jouissance* only possessed by that mercurial nation. We dined, we talked, we laughed, we made the most of the present, for my two companions were to return almost immediately to Russia, and London, usually voted so *triste,* was delightful in comparison as being so much nearer Paris. We sent for a box at the French play; we criticised the audience, and quizzed the performers. We returned to the hotel to supper, where we again ate, drank, laughed, and talked as though dinner was completely forgotten; and towards two o'clock in the morning, after Coralie had retired, *mon cousin,* whether or not instructed to that effect I cannot tell, disclosed to me over a cigar the eventful career and singular history of the famous dancer. Coralie's mother, it appears, was a Spaniard by birth, married to an English officer, of whom she was frantically jealous. Having reason to suppose that her husband was more attentive than he should be to a younger sister of her own—for hers was a family in which beauty was as hereditary as the strong passions which made it a curse—she concealed herself near the spot where they were accustomed to meet, and without waiting for ocular demonstration of her suspicions, rushed upon the astonished pair, and stabbed the ill-fated girl to the heart. Report adds that nothing but the husband's superior strength saved him from the same fate. In any other country but the wild district of Catalonia, in which this tragedy took place, justice must have overtaken the murderess; but the unsettled state of the frontier, and the exertions of her friends, enabled her to escape into France, accompanied by her little girl, the child of that husband whom she was never to see more. What added to the horror of the story, my informant went on to state, was the fact that the husband was passionately attached to his wife, whose jealousy was totally unfounded, and caused by the friendly interest taken by the Englishman in a love affair, concerning which his unprotected sister-in-law sought his advice and assistance. My informant, however, knew but little more of the fierce donna's antecedents, and his acquaintance with her person and character only dated from her second marriage with Monsieur De Rivolte, a relation, as he said, of his own. Friendless and unprotected in the French capital, never expecting to hear more of her outraged and indignant husband, bearing along with her the heavy curse of Cain at her heart, the Spaniard was too glad to avail herself of a legitimate protector, under whose roof she might shelter her own head and that of her friendless little girl. De Rivolte took a great fancy to the child, who went by his own name, and whose fascinating manners and infantine beauty were not lost upon her old step-father, as being a Frenchman, he was, of course, a man of taste.

It was fortunate for little Coralie that she thus wound herself round his heart, for a very short period deprived her of a mother, amongst whose faults, many and great as they were, want of affection could not be numbered. After the death of his Spanish wife, old De Rivolte appeared more than ever wrapped up in her daughter, and all the advantages of masters and education which Paris could boast were lavished upon the graceful and charming little girl. As she grew up, the faultless symmetry of her form, the wondrous ease and smoothness of her motions, made it apparent that she had but to go upon the stage to become the first dancer in the first dancing city in the world. De Rivolte, however, who had himself been concerned in theatrical pursuits, would not hear of such an arrangement, and had he lived, and his affairs remained prosperous, Coralie might have gained a comfortable and respectable establishment in exchange for a brilliant though not unspotted fame, whilst the opera would have lost a sylphide airy as the creation of a poet's dream—

number of its insect admirers. Coralie was but a woman, after all—a gallant and high-spirited woman certainly—but still, like the rest of her sex, 'to be wooed,' and, consequently, 'to be won.' There was a handsome young French officer to whom she became attached, and to whom report, more charitable than its wont, affirms she was married. The gallant *militaire*, however, had served in Algeria, and perhaps borrowed from his Moslem foes some of their more liberal ideas with regard to a plurality of helpmates. However that might be, he had one wife at least living when Coralie bestowed her hand upon him, and the discovery of his perfidy created a total change in the character and conduct of the high-minded and deluded girl. Hitherto she had been pure and irreproachable, now she became reckless and imprudent. She left him immediately, but, alas! it was with another, and from that time, though generally more 'sinned against than sinning,' the uncharitable construction which the world placed upon her actions was not wholly without foundation.

A perfectly irreproachable character, however, though doubtless a most desirable addition, is not absolutely essential to theatrical reputation, and in most of the European capitals the name of 'De Rivolte' was as familiar as that of the reigning sovereign. In Paris, I have already said, she created an absolute delirium of admiration. At Vienna, the phlegmatic Austrians simmered up into enthusiasm when the very airs were played to which she was accustomed to harmonise her graceful gestures. At Berlin, preparations were made to receive her that suggested the idea of some ancient Roman conqueror returning from the subjugation of an empire, rather than the arrival of a good-looking young woman, whose chief merit lay in the twinkling rapidity of her footsteps. And at St Petersburg, not only did a deluge of gold pour itself unceasingly into the lap of this modern Danaë, but the Northern thunderer sent her his own autocratic portrait, valuable from its accurate representation of his handsome and colossal person, and not deteriorated by a costly setting of diamonds, each sparkling gem of which might have bought the ransom of a thousand serfs. In London, we rather flatter ourselves, we are not behind our neighbours in adoration for anything which they have already stamped with their Continental taste; and the harvest reaped by Coralie in our murky atmosphere was, as usual, enormous, in proportion to her being what we call 'the fashion,' an idol to whom we bow even more obsequiously than to Mammon,—nay, to whom on occasion we hesitate not to sacrifice altogether the latter divinity. Pit, boxes, stalls, and gallery, all were crowded to overflowing on a 'De Rivolte night;' and the occupants of all and each seemed, like Briareus, to have a hundred hands a-piece with which to prolong their welcome. The glove-trade in Paris received an unheard-of stimulus, and Houbigant realised a fortune by the unwonted wear and tear of white kid, consequent upon such rapturous applause. Ladies stayed out the ballet, and declared her dancing was perfectly quiet and decorous, though 'how any one could call her pretty, they could not understand;' whilst dandies of all ages, peers, commoners, soldiers, statesmen, and idlers, voted her 'perfection.' St Heliers himself, the man for whom nothing had ever yet been good enough, who sneered independently at the idols set up by his fellow-creatures, and disposed of a character for talent by a single *bon-mot*—St Heliers was at her feet; and such was the position of Coralie De Rivolte when I first met her in that eventful thunder-shower at Richmond, which ripened our acquaintance into an intimacy delightful as dangerous; and such was the history given by her cousin of the career of this European celebrity; but it was only in an interview with the lady the following morning that I learned how this flattered, courted, and distinguished paragon was herself a victim to unfortunate circumstances, a prey to constant anxiety and terror, from causes arising in her own inconsiderate misconduct. She sent for me before she again departed for Russia, and it was evident to me that, with the inconsistency of her sex, she was now anxious to resume those relations between us which the day before she had given me to understand by her manner were no longer to exist. I was not, however, disposed to gratify this craving for admiration, and we parted with perhaps hardly so much cordiality as we had met, although not until she had explained to me the mystery, which I had never yet unravelled, of the attack made upon my person by the dark-looking stranger at the door of the opera-house, when handing her to her carriage.

I will give her account, as nearly as possible, in her own words, only omitting the broken English, and numerous French expletives in which her tale was clothed.

'You have a right, my dear Digby,' she began, in those well-known captivating tones—'you have a right to an explanation of a matter which nearly cost you your life, and which has been to me an unceasing source of anxiety and regret. You must know, then, that when a foolish girl, in fact, not very long after my first appearance on the stage, I was induced to marry a French officer, whom, in my ignorance, I loved with all the freshness and devotion of eighteen. Rejecting each splendid offer made by nobler and wealthier admirers, I bestowed upon the young soldier all I had to give, my talents, my fame, and, above all, my true and untainted heart. Conceive my feelings when I discovered I was deceived and ruined. The infamous traitor had another wife living, and this was my reward for all I had sacrificed on his behalf. My Spanish blood was roused, and revenge was the feeling uppermost in my breast. I could have stabbed him as he lay sleeping by my side, but I bethought me of a course that would wound him more keenly than could any bodily injury, and I forthwith bent all my energies to the task I had proposed myself. He shall love me, thought I, love me to distraction, and when his whole soul and being are wrapped up in me, I will leave him! leave him for another, and force him to drink the bitter cup that he has so treacherously caused me to drain. This *was* revenge—and for weeks and months, by alternate kindness and coquetry, now working upon his affections, now exciting his jealousy, I succeeded in making that man my slave. A mischievous lesson which I have never since forgotten. Yes, Digby, I had my foot upon his neck; he haunted me like my shadow; he grew thin, haggard, and restless; neglected, nay, ill-treated his previous and lawful wife, and became day by day more infatuated in his adoration for myself. At times I could hardly bear it—at times I longed to love him as before, and, oh, what a happiness that had been! but when did a betrayed woman ever forego her revenge? At last, he proposed to me a scheme

by which he was to invalidate his previous marriage, and make
me all his own. My time was come. I listened in affected
raptures, I put my arms round his neck, and whispered words of
love into his ear, such as he had never yet heard from my lips.
He parted from me in a state of intoxicated, almost delirious,
happiness. That night I left him, with the only man in Europe
for whom he entertained a feeling of jealousy—a friend and companion, who, in all the sports and trifles of youth, was ever his
rival, and by whom, I had heard him say a thousand times, that
he could not bear to be surpassed. I never saw him again.
They tell me he is shut up in a madhouse near Paris, that his
beautiful hair is shaved, and he is confined with fetters of iron.
I think my revenge is complete. But mark the punishment
which followed. In an evil hour, wrought upon by his arguments, and confused by his sophistry, I consented to go through
the forms of wedlock with Sarmento—for that was the name of
him whom I had rendered the weapon of my hate—I consented
to marry the man whom in the world I most loathed, only stipulating that I should continue to bear my own name on the stage,
and follow the profession in which I was acquiring wealth and
reputation. Sarmento was totally unprincipled, and a gambler;
the latter request he cordially agreed to, as a means of furnish-
ing him with money for the gaming-table, nor could he well
deny me the former—and I pursued my lucrative career still
known to the world as Mdlle. De Rivolte. But my impatient
spirit could not long bear the constraint of Sarmento's presence,
his jealous supervision and rough ungovernable temper. I procured an engagement at Berlin, of which he knew nothing, and
left him, making arrangements to pay him a certain annuity as
long as I should be relieved from the annoyance of his presence.
This for a time answered admirably, and for more than a twelvemonth I heard nothing of my detested husband; but a long
course of ill-luck at the gaming-table drove him to apply to me
for fresh funds, and when these applications became so constant
that I could not satisfy them, he threatened to live with me continually, to dog my movements, and to claim all the privileges of
a husband. He is likewise tortured by a jealousy, that, until
his unprovoked attack upon yourself, I had always considered

was affected, and he follows me from place to place, and breaks in upon me at times and seasons the most inconvenient and unbearable. Even now I have travelled night and day the whole distance from St Petersburg to obtain an interview with my detested husband, and come, if possible, to some final arrangement for a total separation. To obtain such a release no sacrifice would be too great, and I have offered a settlement, which, although it will impoverish my own resources to a great extent, is so large that I trust it will prevail upon his cupidity sufficiently to induce him to consent never to see me more. I shall know my fate before this time to-morrow, when I start for the north, and should we never chance to meet again, think of me, my dear Digby, as one who, with every earnest desire to do right, has through life been driven, by the force of circumstances, into a course of feelings and actions which those alone who have *resisted* temptations like mine, have a right to condemn.'

Such, as nearly as possible, was the account given me by Coralie of her ill-fated marriage, and such was the explanation of the ominous-looking ruffian by whom I had been attacked, and whom I had afterwards seen run through in the fencing-school. Nor could I help wondering that such a being as the bright and graceful Coralie could ever be prevailed on to link her fate with that dark, forbidding man, whose appearance alone argued him capable of committing any crime, and whose depraved and reckless habits were concealed beneath no comely form, no smooth and polished exterior. The heart of woman is indeed a wondrous mystery, a labyrinth, the clue to which the wisest of mankind have sought in vain, and of which we may truly say, that—

Fools rush in where angels fear to tread.

For do we not see, every day, the wise, the high-minded, the virtuous, and the brave, supplanted by gaudy fools or profligate coxcombs in the graces of that incomprehensible sex? How easy is it to moralise upon general principles, or individual cases! how difficult to apply either the one or the other to our own conduct, or our own character!

Coralie went back to Russia, and I remained in London, to

pursue, under accumulating difficulties, the ever-fleeting pursuit after Pleasure, which like the summer butterfly, that lures the eager urchin from lawn to lawn, and field to field, is still just beyond the grasp, still in that immediate Future which never becomes the Present.

CHAPTER XV.

RAISING THE WIND.

AS may easily be supposed, such a life as I was now leading in London entailed expenses of which the allowance I received from Sir Peregrine (still continued, notwithstanding our differences), could liquidate but a very few items. To say nothing of the absolute necessaries of life—such as dinners at the Clarendon and boxes at the French play, posting down to the Vale of Aylesbury to hunt when the weather was open, and to half the country houses in England for shooting when it froze; to say nothing of these essentials, all requiring an immediate outlay of current coin of the realm, there were likewise regimental entertainments, of which, as a matter of course, I bore my share; benefits for the encouragement of pugilism, and douceurs for information of every kind, on none of which could the confiding system of credit be brought to bear. I say nothing of tailors', saddlers', and coachmakers' bills; of the swingeing livery accounts run up by four capital hunters standing at Tring, nor the actual outlay on the purchase of those valuable animals, as these were matters of expenditure not requiring immediate payment, and therefore considered of no moment; but in the mere everyday disbursements of my life, I found that my personal income was about sufficient to find me in gloves, blacking, and cigars. How, then, to obtain sufficient funds to carry on the war? The problem had long since been solved, and I was no wiser than others of my station and pursuits. By deep and reckless play when in luck; by bills, post-obits, and every species of 'kite-flying' known to spendthrifts and money-lenders, when fortune frowned.

Post-obits I had already done to a fearful amount, nor was it a satisfactory feeling to know that, under such an arrangement, every hundred laid out upon a fancy or a wager must be paid eventually in the enormous proportion of three to one. 'Money.' proverbially, 'may be bought too dear;' and it was obvious that such a resource as this would eventually swamp the finest fortune that was ever inherited by man. I leaned, accordingly, to the less startling, though equally insidious, method of doing bills at three months, which, with liberal interest, an immediate premium, and a friend's name at the back, I found an easy and commodious device for raising the wind. Occasionally a large sum of ready money was wanted immediately, and, as is usual in such cases, the demands of the capitalist, who 'knew a party that might be prevailed upon to advance a part of the sum,' were in proportion to the urgency of the necessity, as I found to my cost on occasions such as the following, when a debt, as it is termed, 'of honour,' required immediate liquidation. I had been dining with St Heliers, whom the frost had driven into London from his accustomed quarters at Melton, and after our usual *séance* at high whist, which invariably followed a capital dinner and a large quantity of claret, my evil star induced me to make one of a party at 'lansquenet,'—that game of all others which may be termed jesting at Fortune, so recklessly does it throw the reins on the neck of the blind goddess.

I had won a large stake at whist, having held good cards, and 'played them up' scientifically to a scientific partner; and thinking that I was in a vein of 'luck,' I determined to make the most of it that night, at least. There were only four of us who remained to court success at that game of utter chance—St Heliers, a Russian prince, a young banker, and myself; nor did my inferiority in capital prevent my setting the stakes of these wealthy antagonists to an enormous amount. At one time, I had lost more than it appeared possible I should ever be able to pay, and I went on in sheer desperation, feeling for the first time in my life that I was *a swindler at heart.* The Russian, secure in his emperor's favour and his thousands of serfs, played on with a stoical disregard to winnings or losses that I have remarked only in the vassals of the Northern autocrat. The banker was fidgety and restless; perhaps he, too, had exceeded his 'unap-propriated dividends,' and then he was only a junior partner in the firm. St Heliers was full of mirth and jollity, as usual, but much as he played, he was never known to venture what could be called a high stake for a man of his wealth; and I, although my brain was beating, and the cold perspiration standing on my brow—although I was sickening at heart to think that I was playing the highest stakes of all, waging my *honour* against the dross which these men need only write their names to obtain, I could perceive at a glance their different feelings and foibles, and with a perspicuity only afforded us during moments of intense excitement, I was enabled to watch their every movement, and felt as if I could see into their very souls. At one time, my losses were so enormous that I determined to abide but one more deal, and then depart; nor did I dare to think of the morrow, and the means that might enable me to face my night's *amuse-ment.* There was a vague idea present to my mind, that men had been known to fly from the consequence of follies such as this, even into the arms of death; but this was all a misty speculative sort of dream; nor was anything in the future clearer to my mental vision. If Reason ever totters upon her throne without sustaining an actual downfall, then was my overstrung brain as near madness as desperation and excitement can drive that organ, short of the bounds of veritable insanity. But when things come to the worst, they mend; the tide turned; my courage rose with the first gleam of success, and I played on as though the Bank of England were at my back. After an un-heard-of run of luck—after the longest deal St Heliers ever recollected to have seen, and one which made even the immove-able Russian open his insensate eyes, I walked home, rejoicing in my loss of *only* six hundred to that hyperborean nobleman more than ever yet neophyte exulted in the crisp bank-notes dividing the starched pocket of his clean white waistcoat, as wending his homeward way from Crockford's, in the faint flush of a summer's morning, he has congratulated himself on having found out to him 'a new way to pay old debts.' And this is what men call pleasure—to watch the turning of a card with an anxiety hardly less than that of a criminal when the jury re-enter their box—to endure by anticipation all the agonies of remorse—to screw your nerves up to a pitch of excitement more racking than the keenest bodily pain, and then to walk away, having endured an amount of misery that makes the actual inconvenience of a moderate loss a positive pleasure by comparison.   Anything for excitement. *Audax omnia perpeti—Gens humana ruit per vetitum et nefas.* But, *fas* or *nefas*, the money must be paid, and that immediately. I had but small acquaintance with the Russian prince ; he was going back to Melton, where he kept a stud of horses, and rode like a demon, the instant the frost should break up ; and there was nothing for it but to have recourse again to Mr Shadrach, whither Tom Spencer accompanied me, for the purpose, to use his own unconsciously prophetic words, ' of backing me up, and seeing me through the business.'

I have already expressed my opinions of that class of men who smooth all the difficulties of youth, and strew its path with roses, when gold is no longer a ' drug,' and future *wealth* must be anticipated to obtain immediate *cash*.   The Jew is now-a-days your only Samaritan ; and he, indeed, is charity itself as long as there remains an acre unmortgaged, an expectation likely to become a bequest.   Nor was Mr Shadrach any exception to the general rule ; he received me as usual, politely, but familiarly ; for our acquaintance was ripening by repeated interviews, and as my visits were more frequent, so were my future prospects less imposing, and the bow became a nod, the courtly inquiry a brief ' How goes it ?' and the deferential salutation a free-and-easy shake of the hand.   Nevertheless, I often went to see old Shadrach, nor had I ever yet found him fail at the pinch.   ' No difficulty whatever, Captain,' was the well-known reply to my demand for an immediate £600 paid down then and there—' no difficulty, except as to time,—could lend it you myself by the 25th, or I could get it you in a week—but really—this afternoon—such very short notice.   However, if you *must* have it, why, of course, it must be done.   Let me see,' and he referred to a quantity of well-thumbed documents tied up with what had once been red tape—' Swindle—long annuities—Morekill and Blight Insurance Office—hum !   Smash and Speedycut Junction —twelve per cent.—young Soluble's bond.   Well, Captain, I

suppose I must risk it, with another name, merely as a matter of
form, for security, and on our usual terms.' In short, after a
little discussion, the money was obtained at an exorbitant rate
of interest ; and Tom Spencer, like a generous, open-hearted
fellow as he was, put his name to my bill, 'merely as a matter
of form.'

Had any one told me, whilst my old schoolfellow was writing
his signature, that I was taking advantage of his feelings of
friendship ; that I was abusing the most sacred ties of school-day
intimacy and ' auld lang syne ;' that I was tempting him for my
own convenience to a step which would ruin his character, and
blast his prospects, I should have scouted the idea with a burst
of indignation. I never intended for an instant that my friend
should sustain the slightest inconvenience from his readiness to
oblige me. I never anticipated that the signature, which I considered a mere matter of form, would ever entail upon him one
moment's uneasiness. I meant, as surely as I stood there, to take
upon my own shoulders the whole weight of this debt contracted
by my own folly—but woe be to him who trusts to the firmest
intentions of a spendthrift, who reposes faith in the strongest
resolutions of a gambler !

Tom and I parted, with our usual hilarity and good spirits—
he to return to Oxford ; I to spend a month with St Heliers at
Melton, little anticipating under what different auspices we two
should meet again.

The prejudice has long faded into oblivion which looked upon
all devoted to the sport of fox-hunting as so many Squire
Westerns of the old school ; nor can luxury and refinement
boast more ardent worshippers, in any locality, than at Melton
Mowbray, or Melton, as that stronghold of the chase is called by
its frequenters. As the Duke of Wellington used to say, that
his greatest dandies were usually his best officers, so it would
appear that he whose daring is most determined in the hunting-
field, whose figure is ever seen gliding foremost with the hounds,
whose nerve is unshaken by all the obstacles to be met with in
crossing a stiff country, as his stalwart frame rises uninjured
from a rattling fall, is still the most polished in the drawing-
room, the most courteous in his manners throughout all the

occasions of life. Nor must it be supposed that he who devotes
his leisure to this most fascinating pursuit is, on that account,
incapable of bearing an important part in the graver business
of the world, or that the ardent and manly disposition, whose
enthusiasm flags not to hunt six days a week when opportunity
offers, is unable, or unwilling, to pursue its weightier avocations in the court, the camp, or the senate, with equal energy
and success.

Many a famous warrior, many an astute politician and distinguished statesman, has disported himself in the merry pastures of undulating Leicestershire ; and the voice that has rung
above the din of battle, the accents that have thrilled through
the hearts of our senators, pleading for a world's welfare, have
not despised to cheer the echoing hound in the depths of Barkby
Holt, to swell the gladdening halloa that cheers away a fine
old fox from his impervious lair in the thickest corner of
Glen Gorse.

The court of St Petersburg has never been supposed entirely
deficient in intrigue ; to represent that court as a minister in
England would argue no slight share of diplomatic dexterity, and
no small tax upon the time and talents of the individual holding
that responsible situation. But what shall we say of a statesman whose office it was to reside in this country as a check upon
the Russian minister, to watch the workings of that machinery,
the wheels within wheels of which carry on the negotiations of
the world, and to report to an irresponsible and absolute master
every shadow of change that might arise, every breath that might
ruffle the treacherous surface over which it was his duty to keep
so vigilant an eye ? Such an one can have had but small leisure
to spare upon his amusements ; such an one would be the last
man in the world whom you would expect to see day after day
enjoying with enthusiasm the delights of the chase, night after
night entering with careless merriment into the conviviality of
the dinner-table. Yet so it was—the Russian diplomatist would
steal those hours from sleep that he was compelled to devote to
his professional duties, and after riding all day in the front rank,
dining at eve amongst spirits jovial and light-hearted as himself,
playing a sociable game at whist till far into the night, would sit

up till the grey dawn of morning inditing (a somewhat ticklish lucubration) a state paper to his emperor.   Peace be to his ashes! Melton has known and appreciated many a talented sportsman, many an agreeable comrade, but none so clever, none so popular as he!   One anecdote that St Heliers told me of his good-humour and *sang froid* so completely illustrates the character of the man, that I cannot resist repeating it.   He had been but a short time in England, and, good linguists as all Russians are, had not then acquired his later proficiency in our difficult language.   He was mounted on a horse hired of Mr Tilbury, and had nearly got to the end of a good run, but at the expense of his hunter, who was completely exhausted.   Riding his own line gallantly, he came by himself to a large stone fence into a lane, which he charged without a moment's hesitation; but his horse, being frightfully blown, declined to make any exertion, and hung his head upon his rider's hand in a state of pitiful help-lessness.   Most men would have given up in despair, or vented their annoyance with whip and spur upon the poor animal. Not so the unmoved Russian—turning him quietly round to give him another run at the forbidding obstacle, he addressed him in soothing accents, and a language he imagined the brute could best comprehend—'We sall try again, my goot friend —we sall try again!' and this time tumbled neck and crop with him into the lane.   There was no affectation in this stoicism, as he had no reason to suppose there was a soul within ear-shot, and it was the accidental circumstance of his being overheard by some one in the lane that brought to light this anecdote, so illustrative of the coolness and good-humour for which its hero was famous.

Everything that St Heliers undertook was done in the best possible manner, and, as may be supposed, his little hunting establishment at Melton was wanting in none of those accessories which would have been considered indispensable in his house in town.   Nothing could be more charming than the domicile to which I found myself invited for a month of excitement and pleasure.   Large enough for luxury, small enough for comfort, there was everything you could possibly want in the exact place in which you were likely to want it.   The dressing-rooms boasted more baths, the drawing-rooms more easy-chairs, the library more writing-tables, and the cellar more claret, than any other house I was in the habit of frequenting. The apartments were low and warm, the walls hung round with portraits by Fernely of 'my lord's' favourite hunters, interspersed with sketches from the same prolific brush, of imaginary runs, and scurries over an unmistakable Leicestershire country, with the same dark December sky, the same open, indistinct, hunting-like background. The adventures of the equestrians represented were diversified as they were humorous. Here you had a short-tailed horse falling neck and crop over a flight of rails, whilst a thoroughbred one, who ought to be *advancing*, was kicking viciously at the leap his rider intended him to face. There, three or four gentlemen, in high collars and pinched-up hats, were labouring along upon horses reduced to the last extremity of distress, whilst the white hounds, relieved by a lowering sky, were toiling on before them, as though the end must be near at hand. In another graphic representation, a wide and deep brook is creating rout and consternation amongst a numerous and well-mounted field of cavalry. A heavy man is charging it as though he must get in, one horse is clearing it gallantly, whilst another is refusing with equal determination, and a sportsman immersed, all but the tiny hat before mentioned, peeps from the Lethæan wave ; *one* hound running *one* fox is the object to which the whole attention of the equestrians is directed, whilst with a dash of sly satire worthy of Hogarth, the body of the pack are represented streaming away in a directly contrary direction, unfollowed or unnoticed by a single soul. All these vigorous sketches were likenesses as well of the riders as of their steeds, and many a good anecdote had St Heliers to tell of such candidates for pictorial immortality. Our sport was but moderate, nor must the less ambitious Nimrod, whose fate it is to follow hounds over what his Meltonian brother calls a 'provincial country,' suppose that the latter is exempt from the same disappointments as to bad scent, bad weather, and bad foxes, which render his own achievements so gloriously uncertain. Bursts we had, of twenty minutes at a time, into which short space, by dint of reckless horsemanship and jealous riding, we crowded the events and catastrophes of a long and severe run ;

whilst every now and then a large brook, or nearly insurmountable obstacle, gave an opportunity of distinguishing themselves to those who aspired to the title of 'customers.' But whatever might be the failure of our morning's amusement, we were certain that when seven o'clock arrived, an agreeable party and a good dinner would console us for previous disappointments, whilst 'whist,' that resource without which society must speedily come to a 'standstill'—whist proffered her attractions, and dealt her honours upon no ungrateful or inconstant votaries. I had not been long at Melton, before I saw that this scientific game, played as it was there regularly every night, and always by the same individuals, average good performers, but *nothing more*, must, if persevered in, prove a mine of gold to one, who, like myself, was a player of the first-class, and who knew exactly his own strength. Alas, thus early in life had I learned the predatory lesson of turning to advantage the weaknesses of my companions, of adhering to the 'sharp practice,' which holds for its chief maxim, 'never throw a chance away.' Here was I living with an open-hearted, jovial, hospitable set of fellows, whose horses I rode (for my own four were of course insufficient for six days a week), whose dinners I ate daily, and whose claret night after night moistened my ungrateful throat, and yet it was from these very benefactors that I hesitated not to win as large sums as they could be induced to stake, at a game in which my own superiority made a certainty in my favour. Yet, had I not done so, had I not hit upon ways and means such as these to replenish my exhaustive coffers, I could not have lived among these very people, who seemed on their part to recognise the right, which a 'young fellow,' as they called me, of fast habits and no capital, had to lay them under contribution. Accordingly, regularly as tea and coffee made their appearance in the drawing-room, so regularly did I adjourn to the lucrative task, where shaded lights and a green-covered table were prepared for the thoughtful pastime ; so regularly did care, science, and memory reap that golden harvest which, in the long run, they never fail to secure.

But the returns arising from successful whist are at best but slow, though tolerably sure, and the practice of playing invariably the same stakes, while it guarantees the loser from any startling deficiency, equally precludes the winner from netting any very large amount. Whist can be merely considered an accessory, and not a provision; other means must be sought for of permanently raising the wind, and such was the opinion of St Heliers, no bad judge of worldly prosperity, as, after a better day's sport than usual, we jogged our tired horses homeward in company, and the peer, contrary to his wont, gave me the benefit of his advice and experience.

' I wonder, Digby,' he began, lighting a cigar, and allowing his weary steed—the second he had exhausted that day—to relapse into a walk, ' I wonder you don't make up to some woman with money, cut the Guards, and have a house in London, with a hunting-box down here; that is the sort of life that would suit you—depend upon it, soldiering is all nonsense.'

' And so I would,' was my reply, ' but I don't see any of these heiresses about; besides, I thought you, St Heliers, were a sworn enemy to marrying and giving in marriage.'

' *Cela dépend*,' said the bachelor peer, ' it would not suit me; but I think it is your only chance. Mind, I don't want you to marry anything but a girl with a large fortune. As I told you once before, I don't think you are at all a fellow for a roast-mutton *ménage*. But now there is that Miss Spinnithorne, who was out with us to-day, she will have seven thousand a year the instant she comes of age; to be sure, she rides like the devil, and that we know has not a softening effect on person or manner: but the pill is well gilded, and she is really a good-looking girl. If I were you I should make a face and swallow it.'

' She wouldn't have me,' was my modest reply; ' she don't like good-looking men. She was riding all to-day with that Russian, whose name I cannot pronounce, and whose appearance would frighten a child into convulsions.'

'Not a bit of it,' said my Mentor; ' like Sir Andrew Ague-cheek, board her, woo her, assail her; you may undertake her in this company; no fellow here can cut you out if you only like to try; and if you will take my advice, you'll begin to-morrow.'

' But,' said I, ' granted that I could come over the young

lady, for girls are seldom overburdened with sense, there is that
red-faced father of hers, who understands fat cattle, and considers himself a thorough country gentleman, I should never go
down with him. I know nothing of farming, and my civilised
habits and refined ideas would equally excite his anger and
contempt.'

'You might learn as much agriculture in a week,' replied St
Heliers, 'as would make you a match for any gentleman farmer.
And you may depend upon it, that such a man as old Squire
Spinnithorne, or any other who boasts himself "one of the
rough sort," esteems no character so highly as that which he
affects to run down, by calling its owner "a fine gentleman," the
more so as it is one to which he can never by possibility aspire.
No, no, Digby, "faint heart," you know——. Enter for the
stakes, and you will come in a winner, as sure as poor old Gallo-
pade will take the next turn, which she knows right well leads
to her own welcome stable, and I shall have the satisfaction of
feeling that for once in my life I have given good advice, and
more wonderful still, that my friend has taken it.'

With these words we parted, and long and deeply did I cogi-
tate upon the future thus shadowed out by the suggestions of St
Heliers, and well did I balance the *pros* and *cons*, the respective
advantages of wedlock, well-gilt, and made to fit as easily as
possible, and of my present unfettered, though precarious position, 'the hollow tree of liberty,' which wanted only the certainty
of the latter being a permanent blessing to make me decide in
favour and the *vie de garçon*. But let it not be supposed that
for one instant I had forgotten my beloved Flora, that my heart
was ever touched by the ruder beauties of this Leicestershire
Diana, or my allegiance shaken to her whom alone, amongst all
the follies and passing phantasies of youth, I had truly loved.
Not so; could I have seen any possibility of marrying Flora, I
would have given up that world, the frivolities of which constituted my whole existence. I would have given up position,
profession, friends, all and everything, without a murmur, for
her. But this was a mere day dream—thus did I argue with
my dishonest heart—my father would never consent to my marriage with Miss Belmont. Should I carry her off in defiance of

the opposition of our respective families, how were we to live? I could not bear to see that gentle girl subjected to the inconveniences and annoyances, if not the actual hardships of poverty; I could not stand a 'boy in buttons' waiting as her only servant on my aristocratic darling. Setting aside my own fastidiousness and false ideas of comfort, it would have annoyed me dreadfully to see my wife trailing about in all weathers, with muddy feet and draggled gown, because I could not keep her a carriage; to see her wearing dark gloves and faded bonnets; to know that she was forced by necessity to deny herself those little luxuries which to a high-bred woman may be considered almost the essentials of life. All this would have been to me a source of real grief; and even as I thought over the possibility of such a marriage, these imaginary evils rankled by anticipation in my heart. I only mention this to show how much of real happiness may be, nay, often is, destroyed by the false ideas of refinement which are acquired by too many of us in early youth, and which are never afterwards to be wholly got rid of. Besides, I reasoned, surely it is my duty to abstain from drawing her I love into such discomfort, merely for my own selfish delight in her society. Far better would it be for her to remain single, or even to marry another who could support her in that station to which she has always been accustomed. Such is the sacrifice that honour and right feeling imperatively demand of me, and such is the sacrifice that I will not hesitate to make. And if I am never to possess Flora, if the force of circumstances compels me to forego the greatest blessing which life has to offer, is that any reason why I should likewise be deprived of a fair proportion of real comfort, and the many advantages which would arise to me from a wealthy connection? Surely not; under similar circumstances I would advise the friend who came to me for counsel, as St Heliers has advised me. I would urge him to make up to the rich heiress, to secure for himself a position in the world, and a luxurious home—to grasp the positive good that hung within his reach, nor distress himself with vain longings after that superlative happiness which was unattainable; and if this is the course which I should recommend another to pursue, common sense points it out as the one which I should myself follow, and

which is alike demanded of me for Flora's sake as for my own.
Such was the vain sophistry with which I strove to delude my
better nature into the mercenary creed of the many, with which
I would fain excuse the treachery of which I was guilty to my
own heart, the meditated injury to my affianced love, which I
ought to have scouted and despised. And so I embarked like
others in the venture—I, too, started in the race with the worshippers of Mammon. I paid devoted attention to Miss Spinnithorne, nor did I neglect the ruddy squire, her parent. I rode
at the lady's bridle-rein, and talked to her papa concerning
mangel-wurzel, when the chase was not too fascinating to make
me neglect my interests for its absorbing pleasures. As we rode
from covert to covert, or watched the wondrous instinct of the
hound tracking his distant quarry by those symptoms which
were becoming every moment more faint and fleeting—an exhibition of sagacity extremely pleasing to old Spinnithorne—as I
have remarked it ever is to those on whom time and good living
have impressed their seal of 'slow,' and who become more and
more delighted with what they term *hunting*, in proportion as
their nerves get too relaxed for the enjoyment of what they con-
temptuously dub *mere riding;* as we trotted slowly along within
hearing of the bustling pack, whose movements in a cold scent
gave us ample leisure for conversation, I had plenty of opportunities for pressing my suit, and ere many days had elapsed, thought
I had fair reason to congratulate myself on my success. But however good might be the opinion Miss Spinnithorne entertained
of her devoted knight, I am bound to confess that it was not
without many a secret pang, without many an unfavourable
comparison, that I carried on this by no means spontaneous
attachment. How often did my heart sicken within me as I contrasted my gentle, high-bred, lovely Flora with the boisterous
hoydenish girl at whose side I rode so assiduously, and in whom
good looks and good humour were the only qualities that could
pretend in the slightest degree to charm or captivate? For the
only time in my life I kept a journal, originally intended as a
mere hunting diary, but which became gradually an analysis of
thoughts and feelings, as well as a catalogue of hounds and
horses. A few extracts from its pages may perhaps serve better

than a simple narrative to give an idea of my state of mind at this eventful period; and as such I give some verbatim :—

March 2.—The Quorn at Belton. Good fox—over a fine country with a bad scent. Rode all day with Miss Spinnithorne, who tore her habit sadly in an ox-fence. Good foot and ankle concealed by trousers, boots, and spurs. Query—Have ladies any business out hunting?

March 3.—The Cottesmore, at Woodwell Head. Miss S. out again. What can she be made of? Looked tired and complained of sleeplessness. I believe she was thinking of a certain person—jumped a gate and found she had followed me over it. St Heliers laughed, and I looked foolish. Got well abused for over-riding the hounds. Miss Spinnithorne voted the master a very disagreeable man. I think that girl is hooked.

March 4.—The Belvoir, at Piper's Hole. A wet morning, and, thank Heaven! no ladies out. An hour without a check, and killed. Rode two of St Heliers' horses, and 'pumped' them both out, but went first from end to end. Delightful day.

March 5.—The Quorn at Barkby. Miss Spinnithorne out again—call her 'Nelly' now. Papa asked me what I thought of the new turnip-cutter; posed him by asking him to explain its mechanical principles. Rode with them all day. Nelly adores London, but would be happy anywhere with a person she *liked*—making frightful running!

March 6.—The Cottesmore at Roecart. Miss S. got an ugly fall in Owston Wood; picked her up and consoled her—leaned on me, feeling so faint. Lost a capital thing towards Somerby, and got rather compromised. Flora! Flora! one look of thine would save me, even now!

March 7.—The Quorn at Widmerpool. No sport; rode with Nelly all day. Her father praising her heavily whenever she rode before us. This looks like business. The girl is evidently smitten, but I cannot help drawing comparisons between her and Flora; the latter so gentle, so beautiful, so bewitching, with her large melancholy eyes and thoughtful brow,—the former so boisterous, so prosperous-looking, so noisy. I believe I shall always hate fine teeth, fresh complexions, and sunny ringlets. Besides, nothing frightens her. She was riding a violent five-year-old horse, and sat him as if he was a shooting pony—complimented her on her prowess, and she looked *so* pleased. *It* must come off sooner or later, and I shall lose Flora for ever. Such is fate! Dined with Salamander, and drank oceans of claret—fellows all very noisy. Won £37 at whist.

March 8, Sunday.—Lay in bed till one P.M. Fearful dreams. Flora on a runaway horse—stopped her, and found she was suddenly transformed into old Mr Spinnithorne—who gave me his daughter and his blessing. Breakfasted, and made up my whistbook. Shocking bad week—only won £42 on the six nights. Shall have to marry the heiress, after all. Put it off till after Croxton Park.

CHAPTER XVI.

CROXTON PARK.

MANY and great as may be the failings of our English aristocracy, and in these days, truly, the more exalted a man's position the more surely are his peccadilloes brought to light, effeminacy and want of daring can never be charged against them by their greatest enemies. Without going into the invidious question, as to whether they are not more moral, better educated, and more intelligent than their Continental neighbours, there is no doubt that their sports and pursuits have a less enervating tendency, their frames are more athletic, and their habits more manly, than those of a corresponding class in any other civilised nation. The sports of the field, and the training of the gymnasium, will ever have a beneficial effect on the moral tone, as well as the corporeal health of those who assiduously follow them, and who 'live laborious days,' which bring their own reward; and there is a nearer connection than one might at first sight suppose between the bodily vigour which resists physical labour, and rises superior to fatigue, and the mental energy which overcomes moral difficulties, and battles strenuously against evil. I do not go so far as the absurdity of saying that the man of muscle is necessarily the man of virtue, but I only suggest, that in more cases than we are generally aware of, the 'sound body' is the most powerful auxiliary to the 'sound mind.' May we not, then, congratulate ourselves that in this country, and, I believe, only in this country, we see the young aristocracy unflinchingly take their share of all the buffetings inseparable from our rough and athletic amusements with a manly good humour not to be surpassed by the brawny clown, who, sooth to say, is of no more stalwart frame than his lordly competitor;—that we see the hereditary legislator labouring at the oar, with a pluck and endurance worthy of a toiling athlete training for the Olympic wreath, or standing up to the blows of a professed pugilist, which, muffled though they be, are still no unworthy imitations of the kick of a horse, with an unruffled countenance, that shows how self-reliance, accompanied by a quick eye and ready hand, can turn the rude struggle into a triumph of science and agility?

Who is the foremost horseman in yon reckless crowd, all maddening for a start, in the enthusiasm of the chase? Who is the daring rider guiding that impetuous and untrained animal, with many a hairbreadth escape, over the intricacies of a strongly-enclosed country, and as he obtained it, still by sheer nerve and determination, keeping the lead? Not the professional rough-rider, paid, as he deserves to be, at the rate of a field officer in the army; not the keen and skilful huntsman, with horse of his master's and spurs of his own, albeit he is somewhere very close upon his heels; no, it is none of these, but some scion of nobility, some gentleman of name, brought up in all the habits of the highest refinement, nurtured in wealth, and cradled in luxury, but neither softened in frame nor dulled in courage by the enervating effects of idleness and vice. The same spirit pervades all classes of English society, a chain that links together the highest and the lowest of the land, that, promoting field-sports, cricket, quoits, games, and gatherings, unites in one manly bond the peer and the peasant, the merchant and the mechanic, gentle and simple, rich and poor. Long may it last! and so long shall our glorious country vindicate her right to the endearing appellation

of Merry England. Amongst no other nation under the sun, I
think we may safely say, could such a race-meeting as that of
Croxton Park, avowedly held for the purpose of enabling gentlemen to figure in the character of jockeys, have received the
support and encouragement which has ever been accorded to it.
And although the higher classes certainly do not excel their
inferiors in this particular description of horsemanship, still the
very attempt speaks volumes in favour of the fearless and manly
spirit of its promoters. Nor have some of our most distinguished
men in arms, politics, and literature, disdained to don the many
coloured jacket and silken cap, that should become the loadstone
of attraction to a thousand eyes, as they sped their giddy course
around that ample domain. I have seen on these plains a white-
haired general, whose name the Sikh warrior blanches to pronounce, bestride an impetuous filly, whose youthful ardour was
to be counteracted by the cool determination of that daring old
man ; I have seen one on whom the poet's mantle has since
descended, and whose name will be remembered while French
Algeria holds a bivouac—whilst the unconquered spirit of the
heroic Abdel-Kader pervades the sons of the desert—rehearsing
in reality, whilst his gorgeous vesture fluttered in the breeze,
those stirring gallops that he has since described so thrillingly in
winged verse. I have seen the graceful representative of one of
England's most chivalrous houses gliding without effort past the
stand, and heard him hailed by a thousand voices the artistic
winner by a length, whilst the cordial congratulations he received
on all sides proved the popularity of the equestrian ; and I have
rejoiced to see that, let utilitarians cavil as they will, the spirit
of their forefathers is not yet dormant in the gentlemen of
England, ' who sit at home at ease.' Besides such reflections as
these, can anything be more delightful than a fine day in early
spring, on a bracing eminence, commanding a rich and well-
wooded country, and surrounded by one's friends and acquaintances, male and female, in such numbers as to enable one to
select the pleasantest as one's associates without risk of affront-
ing the less gifted by neglect? Or should wooing be the order
of the day, and the fair object a lady wrapt heart and soul in
horses, horsemanship, and the mysteries of the saddle, could any

position be so advantageous for the prosecution of one's suit as a place at her ear in the corner of the grand stand during the races at Croxton Park?

Such was my position as regarded Miss Spinnithorne, with whom I was now upon the best of terms, and who, I thought, in my vanity, was only waiting for the important words that should bind me to her for life. These words I had quite made up my mind to speak, and was now only putting off from day to day the irretrievable loss of my liberty, and my eternal separation from Flora Belmont. I had determined my fate should be decided at the Croxton Park meeting; this was the first day of that festival; to-morrow must see me 'booked.' Such was the idea uppermost in my brain, as I sat by Nelly's side, and listened to her artless remarks upon the pageant going on before her eyes.

'Do tell me which horse will win, Captain Grand,' she said, leaning half her body over the balcony, to witness the operation of saddling a refractory chesnut. 'I like "Fakeaway," only he has bad hocks; and "Polly Popples" has better action for getting through dirt.'

'Right again, Nelly,' said a voice at her elbow; which, on turning round, I perceived to come from her cousin Tom, and who, being a cousin, I was forced to tolerate as such. 'Polly's the card for you to stick to, ain't she, Grand? I am to ride her; you see if I don't get hold of her cocoa-nut and fight her along!'

'A nice fellow this for one's wife's cousin,' I ejaculated internally during this refined colloquy; the said Tom being my especial aversion—a sort of half-gentleman, half-yeoman—who would have been a 'buckeen' had he been an Irishman, but who in Leicestershire was only that worst of all varieties, a 'sporting snob.'

'Well, Tom,' said my good-humoured 'future,' 'I'll bet you two to one against your mount.'

'Done in gloves,' said my aversion, 'done, along with you, little Nell! (I should have liked to choke him;) and if she don't win, I'll send you the spiciest pair of real French that Grantham can produce.' And with this refined promise he went down to weigh, previous to mounting the animal aforesaid, which I sincerely hoped might break his neck.

'Is that man a friend of yours?' said Lady Overbearing, who had been listening to Cousin Tom with her glass up, and an expression of intense amusement on her haughty features.

'No—yes,' I stammered out, 'that is a sort of cousin of Miss Spinnithorne—that lady in the pink bonnet.'

'Oh!' said the fine lady, turning away with a look of contemptuous *méchanceté* that annoyed me, I am ashamed to say, more than the occasion deserved.

But the bell rings for saddling; gentlemen riders are seen hurrying to and fro, with long great-coats concealing their professional attire, and magnificent silver-mounted jockey-whips in their hands. Prosperous-looking yeomen are crowding round the strong symmetrical race-horses, on whom five and six summers have bestowed the muscular proportions and rounded beauty of form, denied to their earlier appearance before the public as three-year-old competitors for Derby and St Leger, and propounding pithy questions to the short business-like grooms, whose responses are delivered with a positive ambiguity worthy of an ancient oracle.

'Plantagenet ought to win, Mr Wisp?' says a good-looking young farmer, in an interrogative tone, glancing down at the same time towards the boots and breeches in which he is afterwards to ride for the 'Coplow Stakes,' as though his attire gave him a right to the best information on the subject.

'He *did* ought if the mare don't beat him,' replies a short, pimply-faced man, with miraculously-fitting gaiters, who is leading by a snaffle bridle a quiet, good-looking bay horse, swathed in body-clothes from his little pointed ears to the end of his long square tail. 'Nor she didn't ought to have much the best of him, if you look at their "running," Mr Squiers;' and having vouchsafed thus much information for Mr Squiers to make the best of, which that worthy's total ignorance of the previous performances of either animal renders him utterly incapable of doing, the short man, yawning audibly, expresses his opinion that it will be dark before they begin, and that 'he's bless'd if he thinks the gentlemen ever *will* get weighed.' Nor is the groom's

Impatience unreasonable ; for inside the weighing enclosure there is much crowding and confusion, consequent upon the uncertainty of the aristocratic jockeys as to their specific gravity, all preconceived calculations based upon yesterday's discipline having been upset by a large dinner-party last night, at the Old Club. Seven-pound saddles must accordingly be substituted for the more roomy seat on which gentlemen are wont to accommodate their lengthier proportions ; and in one instance not even that hand's breadth of pig's-skin, which weighs exactly five pounds, and on which it is physically impossible he can sit down, will make amends for the evening's indulgence to yon vigorous competitor. However, there is no great hurry, people who do things for pleasure ought not to be tied to time ; and after many a hasty message and whispered conclave, the turmoil seems to right itself, and one after another the whole troop are at length mounted, and displaying their preparatory canters for the edification of the ladies.

And now do bright eyes scan the cards, and taper fingers point to the 'names, weights, and colours of the riders,' as each fair one reviews with favouring eye the man and horse that approach nearest to her own peculiar ideas of excellence. 'Plantagenet' gallops thrice past the stand, his bright bay coat and glossy tail glistening in the sun, whilst his own beauty and the graceful ease with which Mr Wilson yields so pliantly to every motion of his long, lashing stride, find him peculiar favour in the eyes of the softer sex. Gloves shall be won about Plantagenet ere yon setting sun shall gild the western windows of Belvoir's stately pile. But 'Polly Popples,' steered by my cousin that is to be, likewise finds admirers amongst the connoisseurs, and there is no denying that short square man can ride. 'Nelly' backs her largely for gloves, much to my annoyance. Hie! hie! hie! 'Fakeaway' comes tearing up the course, pulling hard and savagely, with lowered head and snorting nostril that breathes rebellion and defiance. In vain! as well strive to break away from a bar of iron with springs of steel, as from those strong sinewy wrists, that give and take with restraining skill on either side of the lengthy, freeplaying shoulder. 'If "Fakeaway" could live the distance,' Nelly remarks to me, 'he ought to win, with

Captain Black for his jockey.' And Nelly's judgment in all
matters connected with horses is seldom at fault. Three more
gallant steeds, three more riders known to fame, come swinging
past for our observation and criticism. Fine horsemen are they
all, but to an accustomed eye there is something in the seat and
style of each of them which savours more of the pliant strength
of the fox-hunter, than the motionless ease of the jockey. There
is some little delay ere they are settled into their places, and
divers threatened indications of a false start; but they are got
away with less trouble than might have been expected, and a
suppressed murmur in the Stand announces that ' they are off.'
The course is deeper than usual, and the gentlemen riders much
inclined to ' wait upon ' each other; so, for the first half mile,
there is considerable disapprobation expressed by the fair speculators at their ' going so wretchedly slow;' but Fakeaway is
pulling so unpleasantly, and exhausting so much of his energies
in struggling with his jockey, that Captain Black judiciously lets
him out for a few strides, and shoots forward some five or six
lengths in front of his companions, not unmarked, however, by
the practised eye of Mr Wilson, who, having himself ridden
Fakeaway, has been for some time prepared for a demonstration
of this kind, and is ready with Plantagenet to regain his place at
the leader's quarters. This improves the pace of the whole six,
and coming down the hill it is obvious that such speed must, ere
long, tell upon some of them. At the turn of the course, the
two favourites, Plantagenet and Fakeaway, are the last horses in
the race, and Polly Popples comes round the corner in front,
looking very like a winner, but Nelly's cousin cannot hope to
compete with such artistical horsemen as are watching him from
behind, knowing far better than himself the speed at which he
is going, and the powers of his animal. ' He is in too great a
hurry to get home,' and disposes of the little mare accordingly,
who is passed by the favourites as though she were standing still,
Plantagenet having come up with a tremendous rush when opposite the distance-post, closely waited on by the no longer impetuous Fakeaway. Fifty yards from home Captain Black gets at
the latter with whip and spurs, nor could a Centaur urge his
equine half to its utmost speed with more perfect sympathy and

unison of motion than that which exists between Fakeaway and the jockey who is coercing him.   In vain; he reaches Plantagenet's quarters—his girths—his shoulder—but *no further.* Mr Wilson never appears to move a muscle, so equably and pliantly does he adapt himself to every effort of his horse.   His nice judgment of pace tells him that he must win; and calmly, as if cantering in the park, his body slightly bent forward, his hands low upon his horse's withers, a quiet smile upon his countenance, he glides by the goal, a winner by a neck, whilst amongst the plaudits which greet his triumph may be heard such expressions as the following: ' Capital race !' — ' Beautiful finish !'—' Perfection of riding !'—' I win a hundred pounds.'

Although, contrary to my wont, I was neglecting the important business of money-making in the ring, let it not be supposed that I was by any means idle during this and the succeeding races.   Far from it; with a provident eye to future well-being, I was exerting myself to the utmost in making the agreeable to the wealthy heiress, and bringing to bear all my previous experience and fancied knowledge of the sex on the unsophisticated Nelly.   Strange it is, that the man whose heart is in reality untouched by her charms, should ever have the greatest facility in winning his way to a woman's good graces, while he whose whole soul is bound up in her, finds the very intensity of his devotion the greatest obstacle in his path.   How the latter ponders upon every word he might, could, would, or should say, and every construction it can bear, till, in sheer indecision, he finds himself confined to the most constrained commonplaces, or the most irksome silence !   whilst his careless rival, liking or admiring no one half as much as himself, rattles gaily on through all the gradations of lively, agreeable, confidential, and affectionate, till he slips into a declaration of love with half the trouble it costs the sincere worshipper to ask his goddess to ' drink a glass of wine.'   So was it with me; the progress I made, when I paused to reflect upon it, was positively alarming.   As I hied me home to Melton for dinner, and reviewed the morning I had just spent, I determined that the following day should witness my honourable capitulation, and that twenty-four hours more should see Digby Grand in the fetters of an 'engagement'—the accepted suitor of the sporting heiress.

'You must have won a hatful of money to-day, Grand, for I never saw you in such spirits,' remarked Maltby to me, as we wended our homeward way in company, after an uproarious evening of mirth, wine, and jollity; nor could the straightforward Yorkshire peer conceive any other cause for wild hilarity than contentment of mind produced by successful speculation. Little did he know the feelings of a man who, involved in difficulties, and at enmity with himself, is fain to snatch at the excitement of the passing moment as a means of temporary forgetfulness, and whose laughter, even at its merriest, rings all the louder for its accompanying strain of secret woe; and when I wished him good-night, and offered to lay him the long odds against a horse he had to run on the morrow, my old friend turned away with a smile, and gave me credit for being one of the most prosperous and happy dogs of his acquaintance. The hours of sleep brought oblivion and repose as surely as morning brought the daylight and the post. How little do we know the influence that the very next minute may have on our whole future lives! how we do plot, and calculate, and plan, and then just as we have arranged everything to a nicety, and are congratulating ourselves on our energy, prudence, and foresight, the mail train brings down an express, or the daily post produces a letter, that upsets all our preconceived conclusions, and sweeping away the whole foundations upon which we have built, bids us start anew, under circumstances we have never before contemplated, and in a course of which we are totally ignorant.

As I tied my neckcloth before the glass, in the dazzling rays of the morning sun, I felt not more sure of my own existence, than that the well-known face I saw opposite me was the legitimate property of Miss Spinnithorne, about to purchase that valuable with sundry goods and personalities, comprising farms, tenements, and money in the funds. I sat down to breakfast impressed with the idea that I was now about to become a family man, and as such must endeavour to maintain a gravity and steadiness to which I had hitherto been a stranger; and I poured out my first cup of tea, thinking, that were it not for the impossibility of

Flora ever performing that office on my behalf, I had every
reason to be satisfied with the position I that day intended to
assume. Ere that cup of tea was cool, 'a change had come o'er
the spirit of my dream,' consequent upon two letters which I
received during my meal. The first, short, pithy, and to the
purpose, whose superscription, 'On her Majesty's service,' showed
that it admitted of no compromise, was merely to the effect that
'the Adjutant was instructed by the Commanding Officer te
order my attendance, without delay, at head-quarters,' and as
such entailed an immediate departure for London, and postponement of all explanations with my rustic heiress; but the second,
a voluminous missive from Hillingdon, was far more interesting
in its nature, as it was more important in its ulterior consequences. My friend wrote to me in a strain that, even for him,
was high-flown and imaginative to a degree, while it was evident
that his letter, eloquent and affectionate as it was, must have
been dictated by feelings of no common excitement. He had
seen Lavish in London, and from him had heard an exaggerated
account of my positive engagement to Miss Spinnithorne, as well
as a caricatured description of her person and family, with a
fabulous detail of her wealth, and he now wrote to me, adjuring
me, by everything I regarded as most sacred, to pause before
irretrievably taking that step which he held in such aversion—
to wit, marrying for money. Generous and open-hearted as he
was, he offered to do anything in his power that one brother
might for another to save me from this union. He proposed an
immediate loan, which I well knew would swallow up the whole
of his disposable capital, and offered to become security for my
liabilities to an amount that would have endangered all his
remaining property. There was no sacrifice which he was not
prepared to make to save his only friend, as he called me, from
so degrading a fate, and then he argued nobly and chivalrously
upon the duties owed by a gentleman to society and to himself.
'If you are in difficulties,' he wrote, 'stand up to them like a
man, look them boldly in the face, and whatever may be the
consequences, fight them out to the last. For worldly wealth I
have, as you know, the utmost contempt; therefore, to tell you
that you shall command the last farthing I possess, is no more

than you have a right to expect; but I should indeed be ashamed
if I were not ready to sacrifice far more than mere money in the
cause of my friend. You will have to return to town immediately for our Court-martial, and let me entreat of you to come
to no conclusion with this Miss Spinnithorne till you have seen
me. If you are already committed, draw back, do anything but
marry her. Better to behave badly now than for a lifetime;
and whatever may be the girl's present feelings to find herself
undeceived, think how trifling must be her sorrow now compared to the anguish with which she would one day discover, in
this world or the next, that she had been a victim for years to
the imposture of him to whom she had given the purest, freshest
affections of her heart.' Hillingdon went on to say—and this,
perhaps, more than any other part of his letter had an effect
upon my determination—that he had seen Miss Belmont in
London, that she was evidently ignorant of this reported marriage, and that she still spoke of me with a regard and affection
she strove in vain to conceal. He concluded with the kindest
expressions of interest in my welfare, and a repetition of his
generous and munificent offer, urging me to come and see him
immediately on my arrival in town, and declaring he should not
be comfortable till some arrangements had been made to extricate
me from my pecuniary annoyances and embarrassments. Painful,
too painful was it for me to feel, as I perused his warm-hearted
letter, that breathing, as it did, the sincerest friendship, the
noblest sentiments, there was yet running through the whole of it
a strain of exaggerated sensibility, a morbid tone of over-excited
feeling, which brought to my mind, though not for the first time,
a startling doubt, upon which I had never before allowed myself
to dwell, as to Hillingdon's sanity. It was too dreadful to contemplate. The noble, the generous, the true-hearted, and brave
—that he, of all others, should be the monster's victim!—his
glorious intellect even now tainted with that spot, which should
waste and corrode as it spread, till the reasoning creature, the
image of God upon earth, should become an insensate maniac.
Horrible!—Gracious Heaven, how horrible! And yet, drive it
from my mind as I would, ever and anon the dread suspicion
flashed across me, and sent the life-blood back, thick and chilly,

to my heart. I determined to see him as soon as my military engagements would allow; and in return for his brotherly affection, I resolved to watch over him with a brother's care. In the meantime, I wrote an excuse to Squire Spinnithorne, with whom I had engaged myself to spend a few days at his place in Charnwood Forest, with a polite message to his daughter, to the effect, that nothing but regimental duty would have prevented my attending her that day upon the race-course, and took my departure for London, with many good wishes from St Heliers' confidential servant, who stayed away from the races on purpose to administer the stirrup-cup, in the shape of a large bumper of curaçoa, and to receive, with due acknowledgments, the lucrative compliment I tendered him in consideration of being his master's guest.

This worthy, far different from our old family butler, Soames, was an example of a class who have now-a-days completely superseded the white-haired corpulent personage who, in some few antediluvian establishments, still appears in black shorts and gold knee-buckles, to announce, with becoming tardiness and pomposity, that 'dinner is served.' Rapid, energetic, and decided — with absolute dominion below-stairs over everything, except Truffles the cook—Mr Price was qualified by talent and education for any office, however arduous, in which honesty was not indispensable. Tall, slight, and of middle age, he had that quiet and self-reliant air peculiar to his own class and sundry subordinate officials who hang about the House of Lords. The peerage seemed to be his peculiar element; and if his smooth, distinct, and respectful tones were addressed to a commoner, an occasional 'My lord' would drop insensibly from his tongue, as though his communings were usually held with personages of that exalted rank. Where he had picked up his store of miscellaneous information it would be impossible to guess; but, in common with his order, he appeared to possess an intuitive knowledge, which was never at fault, as to railway trains, posting distances, weights of letters, names of hotels, and other obscure and uncertain subjects. He got the earliest and safest intelligence as to all racing transactions, and seldom failed to win a small sum upon the chief public events; whilst on political matters his information was as accurate as his master, with all his confidential correspondence, could receive, and was probably obtained through the self-same channels. As St Heliers said, ' he was the best servant in London, and all the better for being such a confounded rascal.' And I must do him the justice to say, that his attention to his master could not have been greater than that which he showed to his master's guests. However early might be his departure, there was an early breakfast prepared for the wayfarer; and there was Mr Price, composed and respectful as usual, in waiting to preside over his arrangements, and minister to his wants. Nor was this matutinal vigil consequent upon his retirement betimes, and long night's rest, as I have myself had occasion to witness. For once, when staying with a large party for some extraordinary shooting at St Heliers' old family place, I was interrupted in my dinner toilette by Mr Price's knock, with a hospitable invitation to HIS party after ' my lord's' had concluded. ' There will be a little dancing this evening in the steward's room, sir,' he began, with as matter-of-fact an air as if he were announcing my carriage—' and as there will not be much whist upstairs, and you will probably object to retiring so early, we should feel highly honoured if you would do us the favour of looking in for a few minutes. You must not expect much, sir, but take us *quite in the rough,* as this is entirely an impromptu affair!' I accepted, of course, with many acknowledgments, and ' galloped,' ' waltzed,' and ' polkaed ' with ladies'-maids and other functionaries, in low gowns and satin shoes, till five in the morning; whilst ' the rough ' of this impromptu festivity I found to consist of the best supper Truffles could dish up (which accounted for the dinner that day having been less meritorious than usual), washed down by ' sweet ' and ' dry,' such as my lord's gnostic guests upstairs had oft pronounced to be the very perfection of champagne. So much for Mr Price, who shut me into my post-chaise with the most deferential attention, and looked at his watch, while he bade the postboy drive on, as though I were not out of his care till safely at the termination of my journey.

Much food had I for reflection, and into many a reverie did I drop, on my way to the metropolis. Flora Belmont and Hillingdon were the subjects uppermost in my mind; and doubts, scruples, and anxieties chased each other like clouds across my mental atmosphere, as to the course I should pursue with regard to Miss Spinnithorne. What a deal of trouble it would have saved me had I known that in one short month from that time the little jilt would marry her boorish cousin—that she was even then eating sandwiches out of the same box, and talking with the presuming snob about Polly Popples and 'Dandy Grand!'

CHAPTER XVII.

DEEPER AND DEEPER STILL.

I ARRIVED at my lodgings as the day was closing in, with a raw chilly spring rain slopping the pavement, and bringing down the 'blacks,' those aborigines of the metropolis, so inimical to one fresh from the country, in a stream of liquid soot. I was not expected; my fire was unlit, my books shut up, my pictures covered, and my things not yet unpacked. On the table were a host of letters, bills, &c., amongst which I recognised Hillingdon's well-known hand. Alas! he had been obliged to leave London on duty that very afternoon. My regimental order-book, open on the table, appeared the only thing that had anticipated my coming; and on its rather illegible page I read the unwelcome intelligence that I, too, was for duty the following day. Everything appeared thoroughly uncomfortable, and, for the first time in my life, I loathed the selfish *vie de garçon*, and pined for the endearments of a home. Whilst my servant was getting out my things, I proceeded to open my letters, the contents of which filled me with dismay. Tradesmen were clamorous for payment; and bills, amongst others that to which Tom Spencer had put his name, were coming due. A few lines from Newmarket told me that 'Tumbledown Dick' was lame, and would probably not start for the Derby. Pleasant! I had backed him for one hundred pounds when at thirty to one, not a farthing of which had I hedged. A lawyer's letter greeted me from one impatient creditor; and an intimation from the most liberal of bankers that I had considerably overdrawn my account, enhanced the inconvenience of the hostile missive. As penitent an epistle as I could bring myself to write, and which some time previously had been forwarded to Sir Peregrine, was returned to me unopened; and altogether I confessed myself completely overcome and paralysed by my multifarious difficulties. What was to be done? The present, at any rate, must be cared for, let the future bring what it will; and in life's most stormy moments we must dine. I sent my servant down to Crockford's to order my repast while I was dressing, whither I jingled after him in an ill-conditioned cab, full of wet straw and damp cushions; my own well-appointed vehicle being safely locked up in its livery coachhouse, and its attendant functionary in all probability escorting some fair acquaintance to the play.

What a mercurial thing is youth! I never sat down to dinner in such low spirits as those which now preyed upon me, yet was I not insensible to the cheering influence of the comfortable soft-carpeted room, with its blazing fire, so acceptable in spring, and its snug tables and well-arranged screens. A bumper of oily-brown sherry poured balm into my afflicted soul, and a cutlet such as few 'professors' could effect, washed down by a pint of iced champagne, endowed me with a philosophy totally unattainable by the process of reflection on an empty stomach. Claret I discarded as a potation only suitable to a mind at peace with itself; but a bottle of dry old port, somewhat of the strongest, gave a warmer colouring to my view of things in general; and as I filled my third bumper, in these days of small quarts and large glasses, not very far from the end of the bottle, I muttered to myself almost audibly the encouraging remark, that 'I might fight through yet.'

'Put my coffee down at Captain Grand's table, and get some curaçoa,' said a voice at my elbow, whose tones I recognised as having been once familiar to my ear; and, in another moment, I was cordially shaking hands with my old brother-officer Levanter, and comparing notes with him as to our respective movements since we had last met. He was still the same good-

looking, well-dressed man ; if anything more *prononcé* in his
attire than formerly ; but the restless eager expression of his
countenance was now sharper than ever, and this it was, with a
certain forward air, as of one who rather assumes than maintains
his position in society, which prevented his ever appearing
thoroughly like a gentleman.   He had left the army for some
time, and was now fully occupied in following out the business
of the turf—for, truth to say, book-making is indeed a business
of the most laborious kind ; and whatever amount of capital he
might possess was chiefly invested in such speculations.   He
had lately been admitted a member of Crockford's, a proof that
the original exclusiveness of the club was fast relaxing in its
vigilance ; for there was no denying that Levanter was 'bad
style,' and this equivocal offence knows no forgiveness in the
suffrages of society.   After recapitulating our 'tandem' catastrophe, and other freaks of early life, when in the 101st Foot,
we became gradually more and more confidential as to our present resources and pursuits ; and whilst I detailed runs in
Leicestershire, successes at hazard, and triumphs at billiards,
my companion opened to my astonished view golden ways and
means, royal roads to wealth and fortune, of which, with all
my fancied knowledge of the world, I had hitherto been totally
ignorant.

'I made two thousand last week, in the funds,' said he, with
the careless air of a man who tells you how many brace of
partridges he shot on the 1st ; 'and realised fifteen hundred
more by the sale of some shares in the Great Unnecessary, and,
as I have got a ten thousand pound book on the Derby, these
little windfalls may be useful ; but next year I hope to begin on
a larger scale, and make a really "good thing."'

'You must have a good deal of capital to work upon,' said I,
somewhat astounded at the new-born magnificence of my friend's
ideas.

'Not much of that,' he replied, 'but I never throw a chance
away : as in speculating, so in betting, I trust entirely to figures
—the only horses that always run honest—and, barring bad
debts, in which I have been tolerably lucky, I never ought to
lose.   Could anything induce me to depart from my rule, and

back an animal on account of its merits, I should this year be
tempted to do so.   There is a horse engaged in the Derby, now
at twenty to one, that, as far as pace and powers go, is as sure
of winning the race as I am of finishing this cup of coffee.   His
name is Oriel; and I can tell you, as a friend, of course in the
strictest confidence, that he was tried with 'Flat-fish,' and beat
him as far as he could see.   But what are you going to do
to-night, Grand?   I remember, of old, you never were given to
early hours.   I am going to Mrs Man-trap's for some whist, and
a chance pool at *écarté*.   Have you a mind to come?   She mentioned your name, amongst others, whom I was to ask if I
happened to meet them.'

So, thought I, either my friend here has got on wonderfully in
the world, or Mrs Man-trap must be going down-hill very fast,
if such a second-rater as this has the management of her invitations.   There was a time when I might walk into her house at
all hours, welcome and unasked; however, I should like to see
how my old flame wears.   I'll go.   Accordingly, I promised to
accompany Levanter, only stipulating that, as there was sure to
be some card-playing, I should run upstairs for ten minutes, to
get a little small change.

Twelve o'clock had struck, the Temple of Chance was open,
and, in a shorter period than I have named, I was by Levanter's
side, in his quiet dark-coloured brougham, with a fifty-pound
note in my waistcoat pocket, the product of three timely
'sevens,' that, unlike Glendower's spirits, *came* 'when I did call
for them.'

'My dear Grand, I am so charmed to see you!' exclaimed our
hostess, as I went up to make my bow, on my arrival, accosting
me with as much easy good-humoured indifference as though we
had 'never met and never parted.'   'I thought you were at
Melton; how good of Levanter to bring you!   He always
comes to my Thursday-nights, and so must you.'   I bowed my
acknowledgments, and turned round to take a view of the
company, and obtain some slight insight into Mrs Man-trap's
Thursday-nights.   The well-known rooms were brilliant with
lamp-light, and gorgeous with flowers; the faint tinge of the
light-coloured walls, with the rich, dark carpet, served admirably

to set off rose-tinted draperies and motley furniture, dotted here
and there with red. There were more fanciful ornaments, more
Sèvres china, than ever; whilst from the distant conservatory,
forming another well-lighted retreat, came the subdued sounds
of a self-playing pianoforte, just sufficiently distinct to encourage
conversation, not too loud to interrupt whist. But the company
was of a different grade from that which I had been used to
meet, in former days, in these brilliant apartments. The ladies
were more dressed, more rouged; laughed louder, and looked
bolder, than is customary in English society, and, in truth, there
were several foreigners amongst that talkative throng; whilst
the men—German barons, French counts, and disreputable adventurers of our own nation—were engaged at the different
games they played with an affectation of extreme carelessness,
which savours of that dexterity over which fortune has no control. Not a man or woman of them all but had some 'history,'
not entirely redounding to the individual's credit, attached to
him or her; and could the life of the hostess have been written
by herself, it would not have been the least extraordinary
amongst the assemblage. I turned to look at her, as she moved
from one circle to another, with a smile and jest for each, and
was shocked to observe the ravages that time and anxiety had
made upon the once handsome Mrs Man-trap. That is the worst
of your good-looking woman of a certain age, who seem to preserve their beauty beyond its natural term only that it may go
all at once. With them one season does all the mischief that it
has taken ten years' pains to avert; and the less gradual the
process of decay, the more startling are its unwelcome effects.
Mrs Man-trap was now a haggard old woman; at a distance, she
still preserved something of that captivating air which, with all
her dashing style, had once been her most dangerous weapon,
but upon a nearer approach the charm was completely dispelled:
the cheeks were sunken, the eyes hollowed, the features sharpened
and careworn, and the sunny hair grown poor and thin. Dress
might still conceal the altered outlines of her form, but the pro-
jecting collar-bone, the shrunk and wasted hands, told a different
tale. Still she seemed in buoyant spirits, which, if forced, were
admirably assumed for the occasion; nor was it until I saw her

wholly absorbed in the excitement of a game at *écarté*, on which
she had staked a considerable sum, that I could perceive, in
undisguised reality, the haggard change that had overtaken her
person and features.   I had not, however, much time for observation, as I soon found myself set down to a party at whist,
consisting of my friend Carambole, whom I was somewhat surprised to see here, a French countess, and an Irish major, one of
the most scientific players it has ever been my fortune to meet.
Carambole and I were partners, and, as is usually the case
between English and French players of high calibre, misunder-
stood each other's game, and were, consequently, unable to make
any head against the good cards which fortune lavished so liberally upon the hands of our adversaries, more especially when it
chanced to be the Countess's deal.   The Major, having won two
rubbers, thought proper to retire, as I learnt from Carambole
was his invariable custom; and I found myself, though sorely
against my will, obliged to sit down and play *écarté* against
the clever Frenchwoman.   She certainly was pretty and
piquante, though no longer in the freshness of youth; and
I submitted, with as good a grace as I could assume, to be
despoiled by the lively gambler, inwardly resolving to take
my departure as soon as my fifty pounds, considerably lessened
already, should be entirely swallowed up.   It chanced that
my fair antagonist was possessed of a beautiful hand, whose
taper fingers she scorned to set off by the adventitious aid
of jewellery; and, whenever she dealt, I found my eyes
so fascinated by the charms of this unadorned member, that I
could not withdraw my admiring gaze from its pliant movements.
It was some time before I perceived that such mute homage on
my part was extremely embarrassing to its object: she coughed,
she blushed even through her rouge, she changed her position,
and seemed ill at ease, whilst the game proceeded with no re-
markable vicissitude; but, either from better luck or superior
skill, with a decided tendency in my favour.   This was a state
of things unaccountable as it was unlooked-for; but, as it was
not my part to complain of the smiles of fortune, I went on
playing unsuspiciously enough.   Presently, a French gentleman,
with whom I had not the honour of being acquainted, came and

stood behind my chair, expressing his admiration at my science, and requesting permission to observe my play. Of course, I acquiesced most politely; but, though young in years and appearance, I was not quite such a fool as I looked, and this last manœuvre put my attention on the *qui vive*. I had heard of fingers being placed to foreheads, and looks and glances interchanged with affected carelessness, to telegraph from some interested on-looker to the proposing player the most judicious number to be demanded; and I determined that my anxious Countess should have no such assistance as this without remark. I accordingly called to Carambole, who was lounging about the room, and begged him to hand me a glass of iced water, at the same time, by a rapid sign, drawing his attention to the sharper looking over my shoulder. The quick-witted Frenchman took my meaning instantaneously; and placing himself behind the Countess, begged permission to look over her hand, and bet upon the game. The lady declared it made her nervous to have any-one studying her cards; and Carambole then placed himself on one side of the table, still fixing his eyes upon his countryman, so as to watch his every motion. The Countess was now getting almost hysterical: the pretty hand shook, and the thin lips were compressed with anger and vexation. It was evident, the confederates were completely checkmated; my unwitting admiration of the pliant fingers had given their conscious owner reason to suspect that she was watched, and had effectually prevented that accustomed sleight-of-hand by which the practised dealer commands the timely assistance of a king; whilst Carambole's ready aid had counteracted the stratagems of her ally, and disappointed her of the golden harvest generally yielded by the game of *écarté* to her dexterous arrangements. Pleading a headache, she rose from the table, paying my winnings, after all of inconsiderable amount, with a very bad grace; and, retiring to the room where supper was laid out, consoled herself, like a genuine Frenchwoman, with cold chicken and champagne. I made my bow to Mrs Man-trap, perfectly satisfied with what I had seen of her 'Thursday-nights,' and strolled off with Carambole, talking, as we perfumed the midnight air with our cigars, of the scene we had just quitted, the equivocal position of our hostess, and the disreputable set of people she seemed to have congregated about her.

'Shall we look in at Meadows's?' said my companion, as we passed the lamp-lit portals of that establishment. 'I have lost at weest,' as he called the noble game, sacred to Hoyle and Major A. 'I always lose at Mrs Man-trap's Thursday-nights.'

'Agreed,' said I; 'my fortune must be in the ascendant, to have escaped unhurt from the little Countess and her lynx-eyed friend. Carambole, my jolly punter! I feel as if I should throw in.' With these words we passed the folding-doors, that swung smooth and invitingly on their noiseless hinges, and fearlessly approached the iron barrier, from which, through a narrow and pigmy hole, one vigilant eye was watching our approach. Alas! well known were we as any policeman on the beat, and far more welcome. The iron barrier opens, as if of its own accord; and the sleepless warder greets us with a deferential bow, as old and valued customers. A flight of broad, well-carpeted steps brings us into a large supper-room, whose long table is crowded with delicacies, and glittering with plate; Mr Meadows himself, bland, middle-aged and gentlemanlike, presses upon us the various good things so handsomely provided; and, touching cautiously upon the general topics of the day, refrains from any ill-timed allusions to the business of the evening. In the next room, the box is rattling; and, unlike Crockford's, the odour of cigar-smoke reaches us even at the supper-table. Meadows ushers us politely into his temple, and furnishes the sinews of war, with the same stately courtesy with which he proffers materials for writing the necessary cheque. I take my seat between a cornet in the Blues and a brother-guardsman, Carambole being accommodated with a chair opposite to me. The proprietor, still careful of our comforts, supplies us with cigars and huge tumblers of brandy and soda-water. An Indian officer, tanned by a tropical sun, and rejoicing in huge black mustaches, with a Mahratta sabre-cut upon his brow, has just thrown out with a continuance of that bad luck which has dogged him since he arrived at Southampton. Poor fellow! he will have to return to those scorching climes long before his well-earned leave has expired. A rich young Jew, aping the fast man about town, but betraying his Hebrew origin in his tawdry attire and profuse jewellery as unmistakably as in his prominent features and peculiar carriage, rolls the box to me, disgusted at the futile 'deuce-ace' which stands revealed to mulct him of his ten-pound set; and, drawing my gloves on tight, with a presentiment of triumph, I call a fortunate number, and begin. All games at hazard are alike in detail, however different they may be in their effects; and, after a night of morbid excitement, repressed agitation, and false merriment, spent in a stifling atmosphere, Carambole and I walked into the fresh morning dawn, now gilding the chimney-pots of Albemarle Street, under the congratulations and good wishes of the urbane Mr Meadows, from whom we had won, between us, nearly eleven hundred pounds.

A few such nights as this, a few more turns of that extraordinary luck which, despite of daily proof and experience, the worshipper of fortune persists in considering as his own peculiar property, and I should have been again placed above all pecuniary care and anxiety. But who ever heard of a gambler's prosperity outliving the eight-and-forty hours in which it blossoms, blooms, and withers? Like the 'mirage' of the desert, which tempts the thirsty traveller to struggle on and die, so are these fitful gleams of success vouchsafed by the demon of play to lure his victim farther and farther into the toils, till there is no retreat, and come what may, the wretch is irretrievably his own. The next night I returned to Meadows's—and lost; the following night I played desperately at Crockford's—and lost. And so night after night, sometimes more, sometimes less, till the hope of success, as it grew more faint in reality, haunted me more and more in fancy, till I found myself thinking when awake, and dreaming when asleep, of the chances and changes of the hazard-table only. In vain Hillingdon—himself, alas! too deeply enthralled by its fascinations—warned me against this absorbing love of play. In vain my brother-officers argued, and Colonel Grandison admonished. I was deaf to entreaty, and scorned advice. My difficulties soon arrived at such a pitch, that my only hope of extricating myself was by making an enormous *coup* some night, at Crockford's, and breaking the bank. With this fallacious trust I struggled on, getting deeper

and deeper into the mire, every ill-omened defeat only adding to
the embarrassments created by its predecessors, and still the
hour of victory never arrived. I began to shun the society of
my regiment—always a sign that there is ' something wrong,'—
and to live entirely with Levanter and his set, men of desperate
fortunes, no character, and habits like my own. I discontinued
all my former amusements and pursuits, systematically avoided
the company of ladies, and spent my mornings at the Red House,
shooting pigeons, my afternoons over the billiard-table, and my
nights at Crockford's—or, worse still, the minor gambling-houses.
Even whist lost its charms ; the return was far too slow for a
man living at the railroad pace which threatened so soon to finish
my career, and the tedious process of dealing, sorting, and playing the cards, appeared a sad waste of time to one who spent
every day as if there was no to-morrow. By dint of constant
excitement, I continued to shut my eyes to the perils which
hourly environed me, and, taking no note of the flight of time,
stupified myself into forgetfulness of engagements daily becoming due, and liabilities which would admit of no compromise.
Amongst the many bills which were at that time what is technically termed ' out,' and which, adorned by my name, cumbered
the money-market, that one alone for which Tom Spencer had
so generously made himself liable gave me certain qualms of
conscience, as the period of its redemption drew near. I continued, however, for a time, to stave off so disagreeable a reflection till forcibly reminded that the day was already past, by a
hasty note which I received one evening, when dressing for
dinner, from my omniscient friend, Mr Price. How the valet
got his intelligence it would be impossible to ascertain ; but
that it seemed to be of a nature on which he himself placed
implicit reliance appeared from the following note, written
with a steel pen, and sealed, evidently in haste, with the fox's
head :—

' HONOURED SIR,—I take the liberty of informing you, as you
have been looked after these two days past. A party has been
inquiring your address at my Lord's, and likewise in St James's
Street, but, at five o'clock this afternoon, had failed of discover-

ing it.   I was only informed of it this day, or should have taken the liberty of letting you know.   Honoured Sir,—It is concerning a bill of Mr Shadrach's ; and young Mr Spencer, he is likewise in trouble, as I understand.   If I might venture to advise, sir, I should recommend leaving town for a few days, as occurred to Capt. Lavish, last spring.—I remain, honoured Sir, your obedient servant,   WILLIAM PRICE.'

Keeping a sharp look out up and down the street as I jumped into my cab, I drove hurriedly down to Crockford's, where I had appointed to dine with Levanter, and, stating the whole case to him, as a man experienced in such difficulties, consulted him as to the best course to be pursued.   By his advice, I wrote a note to his own lawyer, a gentleman versed in dilemmas of this nature, and begged him to endeavour to make such arrangements as would enable me to appear again in a day or two without fear of arrest, and then despatched a line to Colonel Grandison, requesting a few days' leave, on 'urgent private affairs.'   'Having made that all right,' said Levanter, 'send your servant home to pack up your things, and let him bring them *here* immediately ; order your cab to be in waiting opposite White's from eleven till twelve o'clock.   You and I will dine here, and whilst the harpies are watching for you "over the way," slip quietly off to Limmer's in my brougham—sleep there, and start to-morrow morning by the first train for Downlands, where I am going at any rate on some racing business.   There is a farmhouse on the Down, where I put up when I am in the neighbourhood, as it is near the training stables, and where you will be very comfortable for a day or two—the country air will do you good, and you will get capital butter and cream, besides seeing "Oriel" go by your window twice a week, in his long gallops.'   'So be it,' said I ; 'I put myself into your hands, Levanter ; only I do hope and trust you and your lawyer will make my term of exile as short as possible, for this is not exactly the season of the year to be doing the rural in an east wind on a chalky soil.'   Our plan of escape was carried out as successfully as it had been craftily devised.   Whether or not the stratagem of placing my cabriolet at the door of White's was required in consequence of the enemy's vigilance, I have never been able to ascertain; but we reached our quarters for the night without delay or interruption, and having got over the difficulty of a start at daybreak the following morning, we found ourselves at noon, with a fearful appetite for breakfast, safely domiciled in in the farm-house before mentioned, consuming poached eggs, broiled ham, and home-made bread faster than all the zeal and energy of a cherry-cheeked serving-maiden could supply us. Levanter was to return to town by that night's train, and accordingly, after our huge repast, we repaired without delay to the stables in which he was so much interested. It was a real spring day, not the raw changeable apology for that delightful season with which, in the absence of its reality, we are often fain to content ourselves in this sea-girt isle; but a glorious, soft, balmy afternoon, enriched by sunshine and mellowed by clouds, with its south wind, fragrant as though it had, indeed, been 'stealing over a bed of violets,' and its whole atmosphere redolent of perfume, filled with warmth, and moisture and growth. As we strolled leisurely along, the usual cigar of course between our lips, we looked over an expanse of hill and dale, wood, water, and meadow-land, such as in no other country than our own could have greeted our admiring gaze. In the vale, the perfection of cultivation had but added to the natural beauties of the picturesque and well-wooded landscape, whilst the wild and open downs, relieved by stately clumps of fir-trees, and dotted by distant sheep, stretched far into the horizon, till their hazy outline melted away in the sunny atmosphere. It was a day and a scene to elevate the mind far above the petty strife, the unworthy ambition, the childish anxieties, and uncalled-for cares constituting that existence which we dignify by the title of Life—to remind us by its occasional presence that we have something in common with a nobler and purer race of Beings than the toiling drudges of this nether world. From the pure and fragrant atmosphere, from the dancing sunlight, and the freshening breeze, we stepped into Mr Nobbler's well-filled and well-arranged training stables, and the change of thought and feeling was as instantaneous as that of the very air we breathed. Without, we could almost fancy that we belonged to a higher state of existence—that, in common with the angels, we were privileged to enjoy the gladdening smiles of heaven ; within, we were brought down at once to the consciousness that, jostling and struggling with our fellow-worms in their grovelling pursuits, we were of the earth earthy.

'Your servant, sir,' said Mr Nobbler, acknowledging with an air of respectful assurance my introduction to him by my knowing friend. 'Would you like to take a little refreshment after your journey, before seeing the horses?' and, on our declining his hospitable offer, he proceeded to show us through his long range of stabling, answering our questions and supplying us with information in a manner so affable and communicative as to fill me with astonishment. Talk of the secrets of a racing-stable, and the mysteries of the turf ; everything here was as open as the day. Animals of priceless value were stripped for my inspection, whom I had heretofore only seen concealed in hoods and swathed in clothing on a public race-course, or flying towards the goal at a speed that made it difficult to establish the identity of the favourite as he shot past. Legs, whose infirmity if ascertained a few short months ago would have been worth a mine of gold, were now proferred freely to my sight and touch, if, after an assurance that he was 'perfectly quiet,' not over-satisfactorily confirmed by the precautionary muzzle and defensive stick with which the boy who looked after him armed himself before venturing to the docile creature's head, I chose to go up to him in his stall. Engagements were anticipated, performances recapitulated, and capabilities discussed, with a candour and openness that left nothing to be asked or surmised; though when I came to arrange in my own mind, and to reflect upon the stores of miscellaneous information I had gathered from Mr Nobbler, I could not charge my memory with his having supplied me with a single fact by which I could put a shilling into my pocket on the race-course or in the ring. Levanter's business was soon concluded, nor did I think it my province to inquire as to its tendency ; and after we had gone through the whole range of buildings, and reviewed in succession promising two-year-olds, racing-looking colts, and likely fillies, with here and there a maturer flyer, that our oracular guide pronounced to be 'more than smart,' we stopped at the door of a box, into which I was not admitted till after a whisper had been interchanged between Mr Nobbler and 'the captain,' as he called Levanter, the former merely remarking in an off-hand kind of manner, 'That's Oriel, by Eastnor, engaged in the Derby; would you like to see him stripped?'

The name struck me in a moment, and from sheer curiosity I proceeded to examine this dark three-year-old with more attention than I had bestowed on any of his predecessors. He was a long, narrow, and extremely deep horse, with a short neck, plain head, and lop ears, by no means a beauty; but with extraordinary points for speed, as was testified by his fine oblique shoulder, and peculiar length of quarters, though spoiled to the eye by their singularly drooping outline, and the low setting-on of his tail. His legs were of iron, and, like his feet, calculated to stand any severity of training; whilst his round body, and apparently sluggish disposition, made it probable that such preparation would be required.

All this I saw at a glance, and yet, somehow, I did not fancy him; and my first impression was one of disappointment that this should be the 'Oriel' of whom Levanter had so high an opinion.

Nor did my companions seek to enhance my admiration by any comments of their own, as, beyond a dry remark of Mr Nobbler's, to the effect that 'he was doing good work,' received by Levanter in solemn silence, not another syllable was said about this mysterious steed; and no wretched 'plater,' doomed to drag out his leg-weary existence in running eternal heats at one country meeting after another, could have been shut up, and left to the enjoyment of his setting-muzzle, with greater coolness than was this dangerous 'outsider.' Mr Nobbler provided us with a most sumptuous luncheon in his comfortable dwelling, where silver forks and old sherry in the dining-room, with books of beauty and gilt-edged albums in Mrs Nobbler's drawing-room, bore witness to the general success of the owner's speculations.

Levanter started for London by the evening train, and I was left undisturbed to my reflections, in the old farmhouse in which

I was to spend this the first night of my exile. The two rooms which Levanter had selected and retained as his own peculiar retreat, were comfortably furnished, and abounded with such literature as might be supposed most in accordance with the taste of the occupier. Sporting magazines and general stud-books loaded his shelves, whilst consecutive copies of the *Racing Calendar* littered his table. Sundry works on training and veterinary treatment were scattered here and there, as if on constant duty for reference and consultation; nor was the science of computation neglected amongst his studies, for I came upon a very curious little treatise on Algebra, professing to simplify its abstruse rules, and to apply them to the everyday purposes of calculation. Levanter has since told me that this little volume was of unspeakable service to him in his complicated betting transactions. A backgammon-board and dice-box completed the furniture of the apartment; but, alas! these were not available as a pastime without the assistance of at least one more individual; nor was the literature, though doubtless extremely useful, and in itself intrinsically valuable, of a kind that could exactly be called light reading.

Bored I confess I was, most completely, and, doing as I believe every one does under similar circumstances, I ordered some tea, and went to bed. A whole dreary week did I remain in my hiding-place, my chief amusements consisting in taking fatiguing walks over all the surrounding country, cultivating an intimacy with Mr Nobbler, and seeing 'Oriel' striding away in his long severe gallops, every day convincing me more and more that I had never beheld such a horse; and that if 'make and shape,' and what is technically termed 'form,' were to go for anything, he was as sure of winning the Derby as if the race were already over.

CHAPTER XVIII.

STANDING TO WIN.

WEARISOME and never-ending as the week appeared, its monotony was at length broken in upon, disagreeably enough, by a letter which I received from Levanter's lawyer, and by which, although it put a period to my exile, I was horror-struck to learn that Tom Spencer had been arrested at Oxford for the fatal bill to which he had so inconsiderately put his name. Although, as my correspondent remarked, with business-like *sang froid,* 'this would much facilitate arrangements for my speedy return to town, there being no doubt that Mr Spencer or his friends would immediately liquidate the liability,' it made me miserable to think of the consequences to Tom's success at the University, and future prospects in life, with which this ill-timed arrest would be fraught. I determined, at all hazards, to return to London, even before the period assigned by my legal adviser, and to do anything and everything that was possible, at any sacrifice, to avert from my generous friend the misfortunes which I had brought upon his head. But I could not possibly start before the following day, as the next morning was to witness an event on which I fondly hoped my future prosperity, and my very ability to make some amends to Tom Spencer, were to depend.

A private trial was to come off at daybreak, between 'Oriel' and the 'King of Diamonds,' a recent purchase for this express purpose ; and, from the certainty already arrived at as to the 'King's' powers when opposed to other horses, now favourites for the race, 'Oriel's' chance of winning the coming Derby might be tested to a nicety. The time I had spent, and the pains I had taken, in ingratiating myself with Mr Nobbler, had not been thrown away ; flattered by my attentions, and pleased with my loudly-expressed admiration of his 'flyer,' he had taken me entirely into his confidence, stating openly his own opinion, that 'Oriel' was the fastest horse he had ever trained, inviting me to be present at the forthcoming trial, which should decide positively on his presumed merits, and advising me strongly, should the contest end as we anticipated, to lose no time in 'getting *on*' at the 'long odds,' before the capital invested by himself and his party on their favourite should bring him up in the betting.

Little need had I of being called at dawn on the eventful morning, for hardly a wink of sleep did I enjoy during the night as I lay planning and revolving my future proceedings in my own mind. I was up and dressed by candle-light, and ere the earliest cock had proclaimed to the denizens of the farm that it was daybreak, I was already upon the Down. The weather was thick and hazy, with a drizzling rain, and, at that early period of the day, the silence seemed almost supernatural. Not a soul did I meet, as I toiled up the gradual ascent that led to the trial-ground, save one old gentleman in green spectacles, habited as a clergyman of the Established Church, and, as I surmised, probably some valetudinarian, to whom walking exercise in the morning air had been prescribed. I took but little notice of him, and, on mentioning the circumstance to Mr Nobbler, who soon arrived with his myrmidons, was amused at the anxiety depicted in his jolly countenance, as he expressed a wish that ' the old cove mightn't be a tout after all.' However, the fog being by this time dispersed, and the clerical interloper nowhere to be seen, we proceeded to the business in hand, of which it is sufficient to say, that 'Oriel' fully answered the expectations we had of him, and that having given the 'King of Diamonds' the advantage of seven pounds in weight, he likewise accommodated him with a beating of nearly one hundred yards; old 'True Blue,' who was put in as a third performer, to insure the accuracy of the running, coming in, exactly as we anticipated, three lengths behind the trial-horse.

This was conclusive. I jumped on a thorough-bred hack of the trainer's, was at the station in the nick of time to catch the 'morning express,' and found myself in London at one P.M., charged with a budget of intelligence for Levanter, and determined to go down that afternoon to Tattersall's, and make or mar my fortunes by backing 'Oriel,' till my book was full. As I got out of the train at the Metropolitan terminus, I was sur-

R

prised to recognise in one of my fellow-passengers, the identical
clergyman in green spectacles whom I had met that very morning on the Down; but my astonishment was still greater when
the carriages were opened, and I beheld the reverend valetudinarian run familiarly up to an individual in the full professional
attire of a butcher, and walk away with him arm-in-arm. The
seeming inconsistency explained itself ere I was many hours
older; for on making my appearance at Tattersall's that same
afternoon, and putting forth a 'feeler' or two as to the state of
the market, by offers to back 'Oriel' in small sums, I was disgusted to find that I had been forestalled, and that six and
seven to one was the most that could be got about him. So,
seeing I could do no better, I booked two very large bets
at those odds. And this proceeding having the natural effect
of driving him up still further, I left the subscription-room to
consult with Levanter as to the course to be pursued. It was
evident that other eyes than mine must have witnessed that
morning's trial; and I was now satisfied that my elderly and
respectable friend who evinced such a partiality for exercise at
peep-of-day, must have been the emissary of some crafty speculator, catering for his employer in a disguise the least of all
likely to excite suspicion. Many and deep were the councils
held by Levanter and myself as to the best means of hoodwinking
the public on the merits of our horse.

I say 'ours,' as I believe Levanter was a part proprietor, but
the actual ownership always remained a mystery. It was needless to bewail our want of caution on the important morning,
nor is it in the power of any human being to ensure privacy on
an open down, in a matter which requires its secrets to be kept
by at least half-a-dozen people, although the information sometimes at the disposal of gentlemen has occasionally forestalled
even the rapid movements and catlike vigilance of a professional
'tout.'

To instance the wheels within wheels by which turf affairs
are regulated, I will merely mention a case I know to be a fact,
in which the generalship of a well-known sporting *militaire*,
himself the soul of honour, but with an intellect and acumen
that craft might in vain endeavour to baffle or elude, completely

forestalled the whole arrangements of his unconscious adversary.
His trainer, then in the north of Yorkshire, received a letter from
his employer, desiring him to postpone a trial for the following
reasons, which show the minuteness of the intelligence his
arrangements enabled him to receive, and his implicit reliance
on their accuracy : ' An individual will leave London,' so said
his letter, ' by the six o'clock train to-morrow morning, and will
arrive at your station about dusk. He will be dressed in a white
mackintosh cloak, a hat with crape round it, and a red comforter
round his neck, and is a short, thin man, marked with the small-
pox. He will put up at the Queen's Head, and will be on the
moor to-morrow morning, looking attentively at the different
strings of horses. His object is to see " Backslider " tried against
" Nonsuch." Let the horses both go out and gallop, but on no
account try them till the following morning, when the coast will
be clear, as the individual mentioned must be back at Newmarket
by the middle of that day.' This is pretty minute information,
not only as to the dress and appearance of an enemy's scout, but
likewise as to his object, his habits, and his intended movements;
nor, had we possessed the campaigning skill of the gentleman
who wrote the above letter, should we have allowed the seeming
churchman thus to steal a march upon us. However, it was too
late to repine, and the only thing now to be done was, if possible,
to counteract the damage we had already sustained by the premature publication of 'Oriel's' extraordinary qualities. Many were
the plans suggested, and various the stratagems proposed ; some,
I am ashamed to say, involving a total sacrifice of all principles
of honour and honesty, and one after another was cast aside as
ill-judged or impossible, when accident bestowed upon us that
which all our endeavours were striving in vain to effect. After
an unusually severe and protracted gallop, 'Oriel' pulled up lame
—dead lame ! there was no doubt or compromise about it—the
horse could hardly put his foot to the ground. Levanter and I
started for our old quarters the following morning, and after a
visit of inspection to the sufferer, returned to town, having
decided upon the course to be pursued. The injury was trifling,
though its effects at the time had an alarming appearance ; a
slight concussion of the hoof, owing to an inefficient shoe, was

the whole extent of the damage; and the chances were that a week would see him as well as ever—it wanted three of the race —his actual chance would not suffer the slightest diminution, except in public opinion, and now was the time to strike while the iron was hot.

Levanter was far too well versed in his craft to allow the matter to ooze out except by the most imperceptible degrees. On the contrary, the lameness was kept a profound secret, and, like all other such mysteries, was known to at least a hundred people.   Down went 'Oriel' in the betting as rapidly as he had come up; his principal backer making one affected attempt to stop his decline by investing on him, in small sums, at ten to one.   The Ring, in its astuteness, thought this was nothing but a manœuvre to throw dust in their eyes, and keep the horse at moderate odds, until his friends could get out elsewhere; and, like a river dammed up only to burst over the insufficient restraint with greater fury, the tide of his unpopularity set in with redoubled force after this seeming check, so well timed for the ulterior object in view.   Twelve to one—fifteen to one—twenty to one offered about 'Oriel,' and no takers—they laid against him as if he was dead.   At length one giant speculator opened his mouth in earnest, and offered to stake thirty to one against the colt by Eastnor winning the Derby.   This was the moment for the tide to be 'taken at the flood.'   My time was come, and pulling out my book, I 'shot' him at once in hundreds.   'Do it again, Captain,' said a little man at my elbow, and his name likewise stood on the dexter side of my ledger.   Levanter was busy at the further end of the room, and one or two shrewd old hands took the hint and followed suit.   Over-eager adversaries began to look as if they thought they had been in too great a hurry—it was evident there would soon be a panic the other way. I 'got on' everything I could, and ere I closed my book was glad to take six to one about the mysterious animal.   Not for a moment did I dream of hedging.   I had resolved to stand or fall with 'Oriel,' and I backed him for all, and more than all, that I was worth in the world.

Uninitiated perusers of the morning journals were somewhat puzzled next day when, in the sporting columns of their respective

oracles, they saw a paragraph to the effect 'that in consequence
of rumours about "Oriel," he gradually dropped from six and
seven to one, till twenty and thirty went a-begging. At these
odds, however, he appeared to find friends, and his rise was, if
possible, more sudden than his downfall; since such was the
opinion apparently entertained of him by his backers, that he
left off at five, and even four to one taken freely, and became,
in consequence, "first favourite" for the great event.' Elderly
gentlemen, versed in the fluctuations of the funds and the intricacies of the money-market, pored in vain over the problem, for
which they could find no readier solution than that 'it was some
rascality connected with these racing people;' whilst young
would-be turfites explained to their horrified mammas the various
ups and downs connected with the betting-ring, and the way in
which money was to be made by a judicious use of its constant
changes, a method of gain which nothing could convince the
unsophisticated old ladies was 'anything but cheating, after all.'
The important day drew near, and our horse, now completely
sound, rapidly recovered his previous condition. We were sanguine, and justly so, as to his success, nor were care and caution
wanting on our part to insure his triumph. Vigilant policemen
and trustworthy servants prevented the possibility of any tricks
being played with him. Levanter slept in his stable, and compelled the lad who gave the horse his water himself to drink off
a quart of the uninviting fluid, ere he proffered it to the brute he
served, lest 'there should be poison in the bowl.' A 'brilliant
and numerous staff' attended him on his transit to Epsom, and
a stable, secured like a jeweller's shop, was provided for his
occupation. I was continually on the move, paying him flying
visits, and when not thus occupied, received daily notes from
Levanter, to set my mind at ease. The only thing that annoyed
me was the impossibility of my witnessing in person the triumph
I so surely calculated on. Alas! I was to be on duty the day of
the Derby. An unfortunate combination of circumstances prevented the possibility of my getting a brother-officer to take my
guard; and when the eventful morning arrived, instead of whirling merrily down to Epsom, I was compelled, sorely against the
grain, to swell the pageantry of mimic war in the smoky purlieus

of St James's Palace. What a day of suspense it was! all the
best fellows in the regiment were of course gone to the Derby,
and the 'slowest set,' those of whom I knew least, were my comrades for the day. How wearily the hours seemed to pass! Two
o'clock came—three :—'The race must be over. In another hour
I ought to know my fate.' 'What a time that lad is galloping
from Epsom! and yet he has two thorough-bred hacks to do the
sixteen miles. To be sure, if "Oriel" has won, he is safe to be
getting drunk somewhere.' Such were my broken and disturbed
reflections, till, at twenty minutes past four, the agitation became
too painful to be much longer endured, and my character for
philosophy must have been eternally compromised, had not a
note, addressed in Levanter's well-known characters, been at that
moment placed in my hand. The tramp of the hurried bearer,
galloping off to some other expectant locality, smote pleasantly
on my ear as I read the following short and pithy despatch, evidently indited on the spare leaf of a betting-book :—

> 'EPSOM, *half-past Two.*
>
> 'DEAR GRAND,—Oriel by a neck; Rossini second; very close
> race; what a coup!
>   'Yours,
>   'R. LEVANTER.'

The remainder of that guard passed away as a pleasant dream,
and for the next four-and-twenty hours I felt like a man who
has been relieved from an oppressive and inordinate weight
which has loaded him for years. Settling-day arrived, and at
its conclusion, notwithstanding losses on the Oaks and another
bad night at Crockford's, I found myself the possessor of several
thousand pounds. Spencer's bill was, as may be supposed, the
very first engagement from which I freed my conscience. Alas!
the mischief was already done, and my friend's rustication from
the University, and the difficulties which such a disgrace would
throw in his way on taking orders, had blasted his prospects in
life.

Never did I so bitterly regret any one of my follies and crimes
as that accursed bill, and the manly, kind, forgiving letter which

I received from Tom only served to add poignancy to my regret for the injury I had inflicted on so good a fellow. My own affairs, however, now required most serious attention; for no sooner had I made up my mind to look into them, and endeavour to discharge all the most pressing debts, than bill after bill came pouring in upon me; and difficulty after difficulty, which I had so recklessly contracted, rose in such overwhelming numbers that I saw the whole of my winnings, large as they were, would be insufficient to set me straight with the world. Had I consulted our old family-lawyer, Mr Mortmain, he could possibly have put me in the way of making terms with my creditors, and relieving myself at least of all my heaviest responsibilities; but a feeling of shame that so old a friend should know the whole extent of my involvements, particularly as regarded the post-obits, prevented my seeking his advice and assistance. Instead of this, I consulted several lawyers of a lower class, and acting upon no decided system, and by no really good advice, I soon found that, although the whole of my winnings had melted away like snow in the sunshine, I was still considerably in debt, and harassed for money almost as much as before the successful race. Levanter was too busy with his Ascot speculations to be able to afford me much of his time or council; Hillingdon was out of town in bad health; and Maltby, though an excellent straightforward fellow, and of sound common sense, was a bad man of business. One thing is clear, I must leave the Guards. To struggle on through another season in town would be totally impossible; whereas, by an exchange into some other regiment, I should, at all events, gain a little breathing time, and when out of the way, either abroad or in Ireland, I might possibly effect some compromise with the most pressing of my creditors. Had I commenced the work of reform vigorously at the root; had I made up my mind to enter an infantry regiment, and live, as many a gallant and distinguished fellow has done before me, on less than a hundred a year, I might, in the course of time, have retrieved my fortunes, and saved my character; but I could not bear the idea of 'Dandy Grand' subsiding into 'a Liner.' I shrank from the prospect of 'outpost duty' on the frontier in Canada, or the undisturbed command of a detachment 'up the country,' in Van Diemen's

Land. No; I could *not* stand that. There were some very good
fellows in the ninetieth Lancers, and they had a capital mess
in the seventieth Hussars; but then the habits of these regiments
were little less expensive than the Guards, and I might as well
be ruined in London as at Hounslow; so, much as I should
have liked their service, that was out of the question. I determined, accordingly, to adopt a middle course, and try whether
a troop in a heavy dragoon regiment might not combine the sort
of life to which I had accustomed myself with a temporary postponement of my utter and irremediable ruin. Creatures of the
moment as we all are, and in our most important resolutions
acted on by the veriest trifles, will it be believed, that the simple
fact of my being, for the third time, black-balled for White's
exclusive club, considerably weakened my repugnance to this
measure? For a long time it had been my ambition to occupy
that privileged bay-window 'over the way,' where day after day,
during the season, are to be seen well-preserved dandies, and
elderly *petits maîtres*, framed and glazed in portly magnificence,
as large as life. At Crockford's I had long been considered
' quite an authority;' at Tattersall's I was as well known as the
fox in the yard; my position in general society was sufficiently
established to allow of my being rude to the fine ladies with
impunity, a conclusive proof of being in high favour with that
inexplicable 'set;' and all I wanted to complete my success was
to pass in triumph through the trying ordeal of an evening
ballot at White's. Twice had I failed, and twice, despite of the
exertions of friends and the punctuality of a *packed jury*, had
the three hateful black-balls, which constitute a rejection, announced that ' Grand was pilled.' Once more had I determined
to tempt my fate; and with St Heliers to propose, and old
Burgonet, the best-natured man in England, to second me, I
flattered myself victory was at length ensured. Little did I
know the secrets of that conclave by which my destinies were to
be determined—little did I guess that besides all the natural
difficulties it would be my lot to encounter from uninterested
strangers, whose overtaxed digestions might prompt them to
relieve their bile by doing an ill-natured thing for its own sake,
and favouring the unknown innocent with a gratuitous black-

ball; besides the secret grudges owed by acquaintances whom I had 'cut down' in horsemanship, and friends whom I had abused 'in confidence,' all of which might be securely paid off in the ballot-box; besides such chances of rejection which might fairly be calculated on, I might likewise be thrown over by the faithless opposition of the very man who fathered me in my efforts to attain the long-sought-for distinction. 'What sort of a fellow is this Captain Grand, St Heliers? I see you propose him,' inquired Lord Superfine, in a conversation which eventually reached my ears. 'Decidedly an ass!' was the good-natured reply; 'the club is getting much too common, and I don't think we ought to let him in.' Lord Superfine appeared that night in the drawing-room at five minutes before eleven; and there is no doubt as to what his tacit vote must have been with regard to my entrance, more particularly as his own nephew was the next candidate on the list. Venom, who was present for the purpose, of which he made no secret, treated me as he had already done forty-seven aspirants that season at the different 'friendly societies' to which he belonged. This accounted for two black balls out of three; but the remaining one, solemnly disowned to me in private by every other man in the room, with the exception of my proposer and seconder, I am still at a loss to account for, unless I place it to the credit of my 'particular friend' St Heliers, or conclude that old Burgonet did it by mistake.

Having decided in my own mind that my career in the metropolis was now over, I lost little time in making such arrangements as should obtain me the desired exchange into a Dragoon regiment. I had sufficient interest to overcome the usual opposition to a step of this kind on the part of the Colonel and other officers of my own corps, an opposition founded on the plausible principle that such exchanges stop the course of promotion, and that it is better that one comrade in difficulties should be driven out of the profession and ruined altogether, than that the different lieutenancies, captaincies, and colonelcies should be temptingly withheld from his impatient brother-officers; and nothing was now left for me to do but to find my man, and come to terms with him on our mutual agreement. In London, nothing can be done between the two persons most interested in

any proceeding without the intervention of a third party, for
whose especial benefit this distant communication on the part of
the principals would appear to be arranged ; and the system is
so fully carried out in army-exchanges as to give entire employment to one or two agents, whose only business it is to bring
such contracting parties together, and who seem to make a very
comfortable livelihood by the fees charged upon their discontented employers. To one of these go-betweens I accordingly
betook myself, and many an anxious hour did I spend in his
little business-like parlour, near Pall Mall, fitted up as though it
were a miniature war-office, with army-lists, memoranda of services, stations of troops, and all the literature most interesting
to those thirsters after promotion for whom it was provided.
Long were the conclaves held by Mr Ryder and myself on the
different means by which advancement in the army, combined
with agreeable quarters, was most likely to be acquired ; and
voluminous was the correspondence held through his means with
sundry old captains and brevet-majors, who, although open to
any and all offers that might redound to their individual advantage, had still a hankering after the fancied repose and comfort
of a guardsman's life. It is curious enough that amongst his
brethren in the line a very general idea should prevail, to the
effect that the whole and sole duty of an officer in the favoured
brigade is to attend regularly the different performances at Her
Majesty's theatre, and to furnish a circumstantial report of
all the state-balls, fancy fairs, concerts, breakfasts, and other
fashionable arrangements which constitute the campaign of a
London season—that the early drill, the tedious guard-mounting,
the monotonous barrack-duty, are unknown to this luxurious
warrior, and that leave, interminable leave, the grand desideratum
of all recipients of full-pay, permits him to be absent from the
metropolis whenever he chooses to apply for it. Wofully do these
gentlemen find themselves deceived, when, after a large outlay
of capital, and an exercise of interest that might have obtained
a staff appointment, they behold themselves doing the same
duty in London that they have daily cursed at Gibraltar, varied,
if at all, by more frequent repetition, and discipline fully as
strict ; whilst, unkindest cut of all ! the long-desired exchange,

which they had confidently hoped was to prove an immediate passport into the most exclusive circles of London society, leaves them in exactly the same position that their previous station and acquirements have enabled them to assume. These facts, however, are only learnt by experience; and I had no difficulty, under the auspices of Mr Ryder, in finding a host of applicants eager to substitute my lieutenancy in the Guards for their own troops, companies, &c., in Rifles, Highlanders, Lancers, Fusiliers, Hussars, Light Infantry, Horse, Foot, and Dragoons. The first difficulty was in selection; and after the particular description of service had been decided on in favour of the cavalry, there was a considerable degree of bargaining and arrangement, all carried on through the indefatigable agent, as to the terms, pecuniary and otherwise, of the proposed exchange. Captain Shabrack wished his two chargers to stand as part of the negotiation, but a difference of opinion as regarded the actual soundness and problematical value of these warlike animals prevented the possibility of our coming to terms; and the aspiring captain has since sold out, and keeps a pack of harriers. Sir Launcelot Overalls, who was five feet two, and in the receipt of fifteen thousand a year, would treat only upon the understanding that his old uniforms, considerably the worse for wear, should be taken by his successor at two-thirds of their original price; and Mr Ryder, who had seen Sir Launcelot *en grande tenue*, seemed to think this an extortionate demand, considering the antiquity of the vestments. One wavering cavalier, who was liberality itself as to money matters, changed his mind at the last moment, whilst another found it impossible to gave any definite answer until the state of his personal property had been decided by the event of the coming St Leger; and it was only after a vast deal of diplomatic intercourse and cautious communication, that an arrangement was at length effected, by which the King of Oude's Dragoon's, or North Staffordshire Slashers, obtained the services of Captain Digby Grand, late of the 4th Foot-Guards, in the room of ' Brevet-Major Swankey, who exchanges;' the *Gazette* adding, with that praiseworthy regard for truth and typical correctness for which such documents are so distinguished, ' The

Christian names of Brevet-Major Swankey, appointed to the 4th Foot-Guards, are Leopold Herod Augustus Fitz-Plantagenet, and not Leopold Fitz-Plantagenet Herod Augustus, as stated in our report of yesterday.'

It was a melancholy duty to arrange everything for my departure from the corps I loved so well, to look over the uniforms once donned so proudly, and to think that never more should I have a right to wear that distinguished garb, that the veriest civilian now belonged as much to the regiment as myself. It made me sad at heart to walk down, in plain clothes, and look on at that guard-mounting which I had so often voted an annoyance and a bore, but in which I might never again bear a part; to take off my hat to that colour which I had carried as an ensign, and which in my hearty boyish days I had often hoped I might some time follow to victory and distinction. The tears sprang to my eyes as I returned the salute of the men, once acknowledged so mechanically; and when the pay-sergeant of my company respectfully bade me farewell, and wished me every success, on the part of himself and his comrades, in my new regiment, I could have wept outright. How I wished my appointment could be cancelled, my dear old corps ordered off on immediate service, and that, flinging my debts and difficulties to the winds, I could once more make the bivouac my home— once more feel that 'the service' was before me, that its prospects were my all-in-all.

Let me pass over the leave-takings with my most intimate friends, the hearty good-wishes I experienced from the whole of my brother-officers, the kind and fatherly advice of Colonel Grandison (oh! that I had but followed it), and the misery of poor Hillingdon in bidding farewell to his dearest, as he said, his *only* friend. Let me pass over the remorse and self-reproach with which I looked back on the past course of folly and reck-lessness that had entailed upon me the necessity of this most painful step; but let me *not* pass over that feeling of cordial affection for the corps I was leaving, that devoted interest in its welfare, which, on the morning when I bade farewell to the battalion, swelled not more strongly within my breast than it does to-day ; which, through the lapse of years and the selfish cares of life, shall still warm my heart and stir my blood when memory brings before me the time-honoured image of the gallant, the stainless, the victorious Brigade of Guards.

CHAPTER XIX.

THE BOLD DRAGOON.

FAR be it from me to venture on any remark derogatory to that branch of the service which is appropriately termed the left arm of the British forces, or to deny that the very word 'cavalry' at once brings before us associations connected with all that is dashing in appearance, and daring in action. Brilliant in the ball-room as he is bold in the field, the dragoon doubtless enjoys the golden opinions of his fellow-citizens of both sexes, slightly tinged, it may be, in the one, with envy at the uncon-cealed adoration so freely bestowed upon him by the other ; and what with man's approval and woman's smile, there is no career so fascinating to the generality of youth, as that which promises the constant privilege 'horse to ride and weapon wear,' and moreover confers the enviable distinction, not even discarded when belt and 'sabretasche' must be laid aside, of cultivating on martial lip the honours of an incipient mustache. But with all these *agrémens,* I cannot conceal from myself, that to enter *con amore* upon the career of a cavalry officer in these piping times (long may they last !) youth is a *sine quâ non* for the thorough enjoyment of its supposed delights and positive advan-tages. Alas ! that there should come a time, and too surely doth it come, though with some men far later in life than with others, when the shape of his overalls, and the length of his spurs, nay, even the very action and appearance of his charger, cease to be objects on which the aspirant is satisfied to exert all his energies, and rivet his whole attention—when the admiration

of the other sex, though it never fails to excite a certain degree
of pleasurable sensation, is no longer all-in-all; and then it is
that a doubt first arises in his mind as to the opportunities for
distinction offered by barrack-yard lounge and riding-school drill,
as to the path of glory which ambition shall be able to carve out
of his marches and countermarches 'from Ealing to Acton, and
from Acton to Ealing;' and the warrior, whose heart would swell
and whose spirit would rise in the bivouac or the charge, sinks
into a very lukewarm and somewhat discontented assistant at the
mess-table or the parade.

Far otherwise is it with the young—those joyous Epicureans
with whom the present is life, who neither know nor care for
anything beyond to-day, and whose thoughts for the morrow are
limited to an earnest hope that its requirements may not entail
upon them the necessity of rising early for duty, no contemptible
penance to those who sit up late for pleasure. Of these, and
such as these, the gallant North Staffordshire Dragoons boasted
their full complement; and had it been my lot to have commenced soldiering in their jovial ranks, doubtless I should have
been as merry a 'devil-may-care' cornet as any one of them;
but I began too late—the High Street at Canterbury was a sorry
exchange for St James's and Pall Mall; the jollities of a mess-
table a poor substitute for dinners with St Heliers, and nights at
Crockford's; nor, when I had learnt my duty, no difficult task,
got through the riding-school, and broken in my chargers, did I
see what earthly thing there was for me to do, or any possible
mode of escaping the *ennui* of that which, contrasted with the
constant excitement I was accustomed to, was a life of intolerable idleness. In every storm there is an occasional lull; and
although my difficulties as to money were as hopeless as ever, I
enjoyed a temporary respite from lawyers' letters and creditors'
threats; so I had not even the doubtful amusement of being
persecuted and annoyed. I began to get sleepy after dinner, and
to put on weight; and must, I verily believe, have become, ere
long, a steady respectable member of society, in sheer despair,
had not the revolving circle of time brought round with it a
course of events, destined to mar my self-indulgence and embitter my repose.

It was a time-honoured custom amongst the officers of the King of Oude's Dragoons, to seek refreshment after the fatigue of 'attending stables' (a laborious duty, comprised in smoking cigars whilst the men cleaned their horses), by partaking of a sociable and substantial luncheon, placed on the mess-table at half-past one precisely, and highly acceptable to the famished appetite which had fasted since a heavy breakfast at eleven. At this *réunion*, in which large moustaches and gorgeously-mounted riding-whips predominated, good-humour and cordiality reigned paramount. A better-looking or a better set of fellows than the old K. O. never started into activity at the trumpet-call sounding 'boots and saddles;' and from the stalwart colonel, a living representation of one of the men-at-arms of olden time, down to the last-joined cornet, a fair, curly-headed boy of sixteen, called by his comrades 'Little Nell,' and the wildest scapegrace that ever left Eton, all pulled well together, all were heart and soul devoted to the corps. At this midday gathering, the entire 'plain clothes' business of the regiment was arranged. Was there a race to be concocted, or a steeple-chase planned, luncheon-time saw the entries made, and the forfeits declared. Were the not ungateful fair of the surrounding district to be propitiated, fête, ball, and picnic here received their original impetus and their final arrangements. Here dinners were organised, and invitations discussed; and here, 'Little Nell,' the life and soul of us all, was in his glory. 'An invite to a "breakfast," Dandy,' was his irreverent address to myself, the captain of his troop; 'what a let-off for the old dragon! Hot salad and cold soup, no champagne, and Lady Burgonet in red velvet. We'll go in the drag, and *I'll* drive!' laughed the urchin, as, amidst sundry protestations against so unsafe an arrangement, he threw into my plate a solemn-looking missive, sealed with an enormous coat-of-arms, presenting 'the compliments of Sir Benjamin and Lady Burgonet to Colonel Bold and the officers of the K. O. Dragoons, and requesting the honour of their company at a "breakfast," on Wednesday next, the —th,' &c., &c.; and, as may be supposed, in the absence of any other amusement or occupation, the invitation was cordially accepted without a dissentient voice; and a couple of teams (no difficult matter where every officer had three horses at least) were put into commission forthwith, that we might travel, as heretofore, by those very convenient vehicles yclept 'regimental drags.'

We had a fine day, an atmospherical phenomenon less unusual in Kent than in any other part of England; and as we bowled merrily along upon our journey I amused myself by anticipating kind old Sir Benjamin's surprise at meeting me in the ranks of the K. O., for I was convinced he was unacquainted with my exchange, and speculating upon the sort of person Lady Burgonet was likely to be, wondering at the same time why I had always fancied the old general unmarried, and inclined to picture his wife to myself as a quiet cosy old body, in a poke bonnet and black mittens, notwithstanding ' Little Nell's ' vision of the red velvet gown, which I decided must be totally apocryphal.

The sun shines brightly, the birds sing merrily, and the hedges are clad in the brilliant colours of early summer, as the smoking teams are pulled up at the porch of Sir Benjamin's handsome residence. That ubiquitous body, the regimental band, are in attendance, and as our cargoes of well-dressed, well-bearded, and effective-looking officers discharge themselves at the front door, the K. O. Dragoons, we rather flatter ourselves, form no mean addition to the groups of gay people that already throng the lawn. Most of our party are well-known to their host, and as Colonel Bold, with military politeness, is about to present me to Sir Benjamin, the jolly old General quite startles him by the cordial greeting and the sounding slap on the back with which he accosts the ' Digby, my boy,' of other days. ' What ! you 've got a guardsman now, Colonel ?' says he, still resting his hand on my shoulder. ' Idle dogs ! idle dogs ! But I 've known this fellow from a boy, and he never was good for anything.' And with many inquiries after my father, and good-humoured remonstrances at my having kept him in ignorance of my being so near a neighbour, he hurries me off to present me to his wife; and, as I run my eye over the General's increased corpulence of figure, and mark his vigorous joviality and tottering gait, too suggestive of the gout, visions of the quiet little old woman come upon me stronger than ever, and seeing no one in red velvet, I look about in vain for my venerable ideal of Lady Burgonet.

Talking the whole time, and occasionally stopping short and fronting full upon me, to give additional weight to the somewhat ponderous jokes in which he delighted, the General walked me on through his assembled guests, with whose private history and little peccadilloes he seemed marvellously well acquainted, until we reached a group somewhat apart from the rest, amongst whom the figure of a lady with her back to us appeared familiar to my eye ; and whilst I carelessly ran over in my own mind which of my London acquaintances it could be that boasted those graceful and well-dressed proportions, the lady turned suddenly round on hearing my companion's voice; and, as the jolly General presented me in due form to Lady Burgonet, my astonished eyes were greeted with the well-known features, the old familiar smile of my boyhood's idol, the adored of the army, the pride of the garrisons, the *ci-devant* Fanny Jones ! Brummel used to say that a gentleman might be amused, but he should never be astonished ; and the coincidence is striking between the principles of *manner*, as laid down by the cultivated offspring of an artificial civilisation, and the practice of good breeding inculcated by the child of nature in the savage freedom of the Far West—the sneering apathy of the fop of St James's Street, and the stoical indifference of the forest Indian. But *roué* or redman, Dandy or Delaware, might have been excused for the stare of astonishment with which I regarded her who I once fondly hoped should have been Mrs Grand, who, to my certain knowledge, had become Mrs Dubbs. Not so Lady Burgonet ; with a cordial welcome and a kindly smile, she extended that well-shaped hand, whiter and fatter now than of yore, and, turning to her husband, explained to him that ' Captain Grand was an old acquaintance, though it was a long time since they had met : so long,' she added, with a well-pleased look of conscious attractiveness, ' as to make me quite an old woman.'

' All right, Fanny,' said Sir Benjamin ; ' then take the best care you can of him. We'll have luncheon in half an hour, Digby ; till then I must go and flirt with the young ladies ;'

and away toddled the mercurial old warrior, leaving me in that enviable state of stupefaction which is but faintly typified by the expression 'thunderstruck.' What to do or say next, I confess was beyond me; and, after I had hazarded a vague remark upon the beauty of her gardens, and the fineness of the weather, our interview must have become highly embarrassing, and even painful, had it not been for the readiness with which Lady Burgonet relieved me of my share in the conversation, and the volubility with which she discoursed upon indifferent topics, as though we had been casual acquaintances of fifty years' standing, during which period we had met once a week, and cared as little for each other as any two people that do so meet, in the uncomfortable medley which we mock with the name of society. Whilst I was bowing and stammering, and wondering what had become of Dubbs (the most reasonable supposition being that he had drunk himself to death), and recalling the golden days of spring, when she had nursed me in my illness—*she*, the calm, self-possessed, fashionable woman, now standing before me in her blonde and her flounces, and her clothing of immovable hypocrisy,—and the dreadful morning that blasted my hopes (romantic young fool that I was!) when, an unwilling witness, I saw her weeping her heart out on Levanter's shoulder: whilst all these thoughts and recollections were boiling through my brain, and making me feel as painfully awkward as, with all my acquired swagger and London assurance, I doubtless looked, Lady Burgonet walked me through her conservatory, chatted with me about military promotions and appointments, gave me a geranium, and introduced me to an awful woman in velvet, with as much nonchalance as if she had been my grandmother. And what were my feelings as I contemplated, in bachelor security, the lady for whom I had once been prepared to sacrifice so much? Was I grateful for my escape? Was I philosophically amused with the bursting of the bubble, the fading of the illusion? Did I thank my stars that I was well out of it, and shrug up my shoulders with the mental ejaculation of 'Poor Sir Benjamin?' Alas! no: in my heart of hearts, notwithstanding the lessons of experience, in defiance of the dictates of common sense, there was a pang of bitter regret—as I dwelt on my impulsive boyhood, with all its folly and all its charms, there was a feeling of humiliation and self-reproach, as I thought I was now *incapable* of the absurdities which then constituted the rapture of my existence, and for the indulgence of which I would fain have exchanged all my worldly wisdom and boasted experience, fain have bartered the sceptic's knowledge and the cynic's smile for the unsophisticated faith, the pure fresh confidence of a trustful, loving heart.

Fruit, flowers, iced champagne, white soup, elongated tables, a great demand for clean plates, and rather a scarcity of chairs, brought on the general rush and confusion which betokens a 'breakfast,' as we rationally term an entertainment commencing at four P.M. Those who could obtain seats wedged themselves in, and fed across each other's sleeves and draperies; those who were obliged to stand reached over the heads of their more fortunate neighbours; and, as regarded unobserved flirtations and mutual good offices, the standers-up had rather the best of it. My brother officers, with the foresight and attention which ever distinguished the dragoon, had each paired off with some fortunate damsel, who appeared to congratulate herself upon having even temporarily appropriated a pair of mustaches; and I was left a silent and half-saddened observer of the laughing, chattering, eating and drinking throng, when, somewhat to my surprise, and greatly to my delight, I felt my arm seized by a cordial grasp, and, on turning round, recognised the still handsome face of my old commander and ubiquitous friend, Cartouch.

'Mooning, I see, my dear Digby,' said the Colonel, as he drew his arm within mine. 'We'll have some luncheon presently; in the meantime, come and take a stroll with me through the gardens; I have a great deal to say to you.'

'What are *you* doing here?' I replied; 'the man for whom London is dull and Newmarket slow, what can have brought you into this wild and barbarous country? *You* are not obliged to eat dirt in a riding-school and inspect manure in a troop-stable; *you* may go to Epsom for business and Ascot for pleasure; *you* can show your face in St James's Street, nor shudder when any individual of Jewish extraction meets you on the pavement; and yet I find you wasting all your sweetness on a bevy of rural Kentish damsels, and dancing attendance upon a gouty old general!'

'Business must be attended to,' was the Colonel's reply. 'Our old chief, you have surely heard, has been appointed to a command in India, and, with an appreciation of my conversational qualities, and partiality for my society, which betoken a discriminating mind, has made me his military secretary, and general manager of all affairs, public, private, and dubious, in which he may be concerned. I have been in India, and know what it is, so I can assure you nothing but "the pressure from without," and my regard for "Old Ben," would have induced me to accept the appointment; but I am now in for it, and, were it not for the peculiar temper and constant interference of "my Lady," we should do very fairly. You know who she was?'

Too well, I thought to myself; but, even to Cartouch, I could not bear to confess the whole of my boyhood's folly, so I only replied, 'A Miss Jones, was she not? or some name of that sort.'

'Fanny Jones,' said the Colonel. 'I remember her years ago, in Dublin, a flirting, dancing, clever sort of girl, engaged to young Green, of the Lancers. She used to ride with him every day, and the poor lad was frightfully in love with her. Luckily, his uncle heard of it in time, and put him on his own staff, in the West Indies; and Green soon after married a Creole,—a *black woman*, Lady Burgonet calls her. Since then, lots of fellows have been smitten with her charms, and I have seen little *cadeaux*, "given me by that pretty Miss Jones," in every out-of-the-way quarter of the globe that rejoices in the martial presence of a subaltern's guard.

'For two or three years she disappeared altogether; some said she had gone into a convent, others that she was in a decline, whilst the more uncharitable averred she was no longer a proper person to associate with "regimental ladies," and had retired permanently from the world—when, to my surprise, up she started again as Lady Burgonet, though when, where, or how she was married is an impenetrable mystery. I conclude, however, that it is all right, as she is received everywhere, and talks of going to the Drawing-room, at which, I will answer for it, no greater lady in her own estimation will be present. She winds Sir Benjamin round her little finger, and must have a word in all his arrangements, professional as well as private. Luckily she does not *go out* with him, but is to follow next spring.

'What a curious thing it is, Digby, that old Burgonet, who was always the most impervious man in England to the charms of the other sex, should be captivated at seventy by a faded garrison-flirt, with neither the freshness of a girl, the sobriety of a matron, nor, between you and me, the manners of a lady!'

Without quite agreeing in Cartouch's derogatory opinion of my former love, I confess that I could not help being struck with the peculiar unsuitableness of the General's helpmate, although, to do her justice, the way she managed the old warrior reflected considerable credit on her tact and discernment. All the delicate *petits soins*, all the little attentions which so seldom outlive the honeymoon, were received and responded to with a liveliness and coquetry that kept the General's gallantry constantly at high pressure. I saw him give her a rare plant from the hothouse, which she pressed to her lips, and placed in her bosom with a tenderness that made the old man's eyes glisten, whilst Minerva might have taken a lesson in dignity from the cold severity with which she repelled even the commonest attentions from the younger and better-looking portion of her visitors. Could she be acting a part, or was she really weary of the continual conquest-hunting in which the flower of her youth had been spent—of the forced gaiety, the aching smile, with which, like an actress on the stage, she had been labouring in her profession, striving to win eventual independence and freedom? Perhaps a little of both; perhaps the habits of her youth had now become a second nature, which it required some self-command to restrain; perhaps the position which she had attained was in her opinion far too exalted, the advantages she now enjoyed far too valuable, to be risked for the passing amusement of an hour—the gaudy sacrifices offered by that empty homage of which she, of all people, knew too well the real value. Be it how it may, Lady Burgonet certainly maintained a reserve and decorum which contrasted marvellously with the former hilarity, the indulgent *abandon* of the volatile Fanny Jones.

But when were festivities held in the neighbourhood of a cavalry regiment, and in the presence of their band, ever yet known to conclude without a dance? Cold chickens are soon discussed, and lobster-salad, however inconvenient may be its ulterior effects, is very easily packed at the time. The old Scotch proverb says, that 'a spur in the head is worth two on the heel;' and although the General's warlike guests were in plain clothes, and consequently unadorned with the latter appendages, his champagne had provided the former stimulus in exactly that judicious proportion at which waltzing becomes a dream of paradise, and the wave of a muslin fold, the touch of a soft white glove, infuse that moral intoxication, the effects of which are only to be dispelled by a severe course of unavoidable matrimony. Ere the last remnants of the feast had disappeared, a flourish of trumpets, bursting from a thick screen of laurels, brought on a strain of fitful melody, such as angels whisper to the German composer in his dreams, and finally settled down into one of those beautiful waltzes which, as a very pretty girl near me observed, 'it was *a sin* to sit still and listen to.' The greater portion of the company seemed to be of the same opinion; and although Lady Burgonet declined with a matronly air every invitation to join the dancers, one or two adventurous couples, spinning like teetotums amongst the crowd, soon formed a circle, round the edges of which blonde and mustaches began to whirl in revolving confusion. There is nothing like example, and that of dancing is perhaps the most contagious of all. Ere long there was not a pretty face to be seen disengaged; and no sooner did a panting couple stop to court a brief interval of repose, than another furious brace started off at score to complete the giddy round. Every species of measure was practised by its peculiar votaries, for though all were dancing, all could not exactly lay claim to the title of waltzers. Here a runaway pair bumped in a manner more ludicrous than graceful against two slower coaches, whose studies in the Terpsichorean art had not yet initiated them into the mysteries of *deux temps;* there a phalanx of adventurers entangled themselves in an inextricable heap, leading to much dishevelment of *coiffures* and destruction of flounces; but one and all, from our dandy Major and Miss Dashwell, gliding gracefully along, as became the hero and heroine of a hundred ballrooms, to the stout pale man in creased gloves, who, riveting his eyes upon the heavens, kept turning his dowdy little partner continually round his own orbit, were industriously bent upon the business of the moment, were enjoying to the utmost those thrilling sounds which raised our bandmaster to the seventh heaven of musical delight.

Melodious was the strain, and joyous the scene, and yet I refrained from participating in the seductive exercise. There had been a time when the very act of dancing leavened my blood, and raised my spirits to a pitch that many a damsel of eighteen enjoying her first ball might have envied—but all that was past and gone. I now belonged to a school who deemed it expedient, not to say meritorious, to attend all such mirthful gatherings as the present with an outward demeanour that appeared expressly adapted for the purpose of damping the whole proceeding, and repressing the slightest indication of enjoyment with an apathetic sneer, really formidable to that numerous class of weak minds who are afraid of being laughed at. In London we went regularly to balls, but we stood in the doorway; we were rigorous in our attendance at the opera, but we talked the whole time. We spared no expense, we grudged no labour or inconvenience in the pursuit of amusements which, when attained, we stigmatised as 'slow,' and voted 'a bore.' That chivalrous devotion to the other sex, of which the last generation preserved at least the outward semblance, had been completely laid aside, and a studied carelessness adopted in its stead, which was anything but flattering to their understanding or their charms. The 'fine ladies,' as we termed them, had perhaps themselves to thank for this subversion of all the acknowledged principles of politeness, for it is a curious instinct of their order, and one well worthy of the study of an observer of human nature, which regulates their own urbanity to an associate in an inverse proportion to the neglect he is at no pains to conceal; and any one who has witnessed the nonchalance with which a fine gentleman of the present day turns his back upon a countess in her own house, as if she were of no more importance than her drawing-room fire, will allow that St Heliers was not far wrong when he said to me, in allusion to a fair ball-giver of my first London season, 'If you want her to take you *up*, depend upon it, you must begin by taking her *down*.' Versed in the habits of my class, and thinking, no doubt, that I showed my superior breeding by my utter disregard of the many pretty faces which surrounded me—a pitch of refinement to which, for the credit of the corps, I am bound to say my brother officers of the K. O. Dragoons did not aspire—I had no deserted partner, no appealing damsel to distract my attention from the conclave to which I was summoned by my friend Cartouch, and consisting of that worthy, Sir Benjamin, and myself. With a kind concern for my welfare, and a fatherly consideration of my interests, the old General, to whom his military secretary had confided all he knew of my peculiar position, frankly offered to take me out with him to the East as his aide-de-camp, an offer which, seeing at last an opportunity of extricating myself from my difficulties, I eagerly and unhesitatingly accepted.

Three short turns on the General's shaven lawn—half-a-dozen sentences interchanged with the kind old commandant—a cordial grasp of the hand from Cartouch—and a stately bow of congratulation, accompanied, though, with a sunny glance, that reminded me of other days, from Lady Burgonet, opened out to me prospects that were undreamed of when I rose that morning, pointed out to me a path that I should never have even thought of, had it not been for the accidental circumstance of my accompanying a coach-load of dragoons to an afternoon breakfast-party.

These matters are easily arranged at the Horse Guards when they encounter no opposition from the heads of departments, and from Colonel Bold and my brother officers I met with every facility in taking a step so evidently to my future advantage. In one short week everything was arranged for my departure. For obvious reasons, it would have been the height of imprudence on my part to publish to the world my proposed migration to another hemisphere. If the jungle-fever were to carry off Digby Grand, Mr Shadrach's post-obits might, indeed, form highly instructive documents to elucidate the moderation of his terms, but in a pecuniary point of view would be of no more value than the paper on which they were drawn. The Israelite would be safe to oppose my departure; but few of those with whom I consulted were totally inexperienced in such difficulties, and it was arranged that my appointment should not be officially made out and gazetted, until I myself was safely disposed on board the *Hyderabad*, an enormous teak-built Indiaman, then lying at Portsmouth, in waiting for 'His Excellency Sir Benjamin Burgonet and suite.'

Once in the Channel, I should be free as a sea-bird on the wing; and all arrangements bearing on my appointment, such as the sale of my chargers, the liquidation of my *small* debts, and such negotiations, imperative on those who 'go foreign,' were to be conducted by my brother officers after my departure. Such was the state of affairs when, on the very last evening I was to spend with the corps, as I was dressing for our late mess-dinner, 'Little Nell,' a youth precocious in the ways of the world, and 'wide awake' beyond his years, rushed into my room, with alarm and dismay depicted on his girlish features.

'Look sharp, Dandy,' exclaimed the breathless boy, waxing more and more slangy in his vocabulary as his agitation increased; 'cram on a wrap-rascal and a shawl "choaker." Never mind the gold-laced overalls and spurs. I have got "Jenny Jumps" (a famous pony, the most treasured of 'Little Nell's' possessions) ready saddled, waiting for you at the hospital-door. She'll do the trick, if you give her her head. You must cut and run for it, old boy, or you'll be nabbed, as sure as eggs make little chickens!"

And whilst he ran on in this manner, and crammed into my unresisting hands the different articles of disguise which he deemed necessary, with a hunting-flask full of brandy, and an enormous case choked with cigars, it was not without difficulty that I gathered from the good-hearted Cornet the clever dispositions that had been made by the enemy, and the great probability there was of my Indian campaign coming to a premature conclusion.

'I was smoking a weed just now, and walking promiscuously about, pretty near "Tom Tucker's" stable, for I thought I heard him cough, and you know he's in the Garrison Hurdle Race next week,' said the knowing urchin, 'when I saw two queer-looking coves lounging about the yard, and I heard one of 'em ask the sentry "which was Captain Grand's stables?" The sentry, like a fool, was going to tell him, when I stepped up, and, making my best bow, volunteered all the information in my power. I saw a bailiff once, before I left Eton, and I was down upon these birds in half no time; so I took them to the doctor's loose box, where he keeps "Sawbones," and showed them that Roman-nosed screw as Cap-Grand's famous steeplechase horse "Sanspareil;" and whilst old "Sawbones," who wont let any one go near him but his own bât-man, was dodging them about the box, and had got hold of the fattest one, who tried to make a caption, as the beggars call it, by the arm, I slipped off to your groom, and sent away your two chargers and the hack in some of my clothing up to the Major's training stables, so they are safe for the present. In the meantime —— By Gad! Dandy, we're done! I told that fool of a sentry not to let any civilian into the officers' quarters, and if that's not the two "bums" walking upstairs, I'm a Scotchman,' broke off 'Little Nell,' as an ominous tramp was heard ascending the wooden staircase; and I became conscious that in a few moments more the writ would be served, and I should be no longer a free agent. What was to be done? The Cornet's genius stood me in good stead. Rushing out of my room, he ran down one flight of steps to the passage, of which one bailiff had already possessed himself, and knocking loudly at the Major's door, adjured him, by the name of 'Grand,' to come out and speak to him on most important business. The Major, rapidly catching at the idea, kept his door bolted, and appeared to be parleying from within; and whilst the myrmidon of the law had his attention arrested by their conversation, I made a dash for the stairs, clad as I was in a heterogeneous costume of pilot-coat, wide-awake hat, and military trousers, rushed down the steps half-a-dozen at a time, and gained the door leading towards the hospital gate, just as the man of law, awaking suddenly to the deception practised upon him, started off in chase. I had the heels of him, encumbered though I was by a long pair of brass spurs; but in avoiding Scylla I well nigh met shipwreck on Charybdis, for the wily officer had planted his assistant at the door of the officers' quarters leading towards the mess-room, at which he thought it probable I should break covert; and as I bounded across the barrack-yard at topspeed, the aide-de-camp joined in the hue and cry. It was nearly dark, but I could see 'Jenny Jumps' waiting for me, held by a huge mustached dragoon in stable attire, and straining every nerve to reach the pony, I leapt into the saddle some ten yards in front of my disappointed pursuers. As I gave the little mare her head —and she sprang forward like an arrow from the bow—the last sounds I heard were the cheers of 'Little Nell,' as he halloo'd to me from an upper window :—

'Ride for your life, Dandy, through the garden gate, and across the common; never mind the sunk fence, she jumps it with me every morning!'

A couple of minutes more saw me well over the obstacle, emerging from the common into the lane beyond; and as 'Jenny Jumps' settled down from the furious gallop at which she had started into the easy swing of a thoroughbred one's stride, I was enabled to collect my ideas, sadly scattered by the hurry-scurry of the last ten minutes—for it had taken little more than that brief space of time to bring about the siege, the *coup-de-main*, and the escape—and to arrange in my own mind the wisest course to pursue under the somewhat novel circumstances in which I found myself.

'Jenny Jumps' carried me gallantly. The nearest cross-country railway-station was my point, and thanks to the enduring mettle of the 'little wonder' I bestrode, I reached that haven of safety just as a shrill scream and short irritable puff betokened that those two great red eyes glaring through the darkness were on the very eve of departure. A couple of sovereigns to the official who relieved me of 'Jenny Jumps,' as a security for her careful treatment and safe return—a ticket at the office window, given with sundry glances of surprise at my incongruous habiliments—a respectful greeting from the porter, an official who always sympathises with a gentleman in a hurry, *if* he has no luggage—a banging of doors, a ringing of bells, and I am safely established in the corner of a first-class carriage, speeding for Portsmouth at the rate of forty miles an hour.

CHAPTER XX.

THE BEGINNING OF THE END.

IT was a raw, cold, comfortless morning, as I got out of the train at the Portsmouth terminus, and inquired my way to the nearest point at which I could embark on the dull, leaden-coloured water. Day was breaking, with a drizzling rain that gave promise of small pleasure in any boating excursion, and was but little tempting to a man who expected for the next three months to have enough of the element to last him his lifetime. I could not help shuddering as I caught a glimpse of the ill-defined horizon, and thought of the long, long weeks during which, in all probability, my range of vision would be limited to the monotonous expanse of the great deep; and it required the whole consciousness of my late escape, the full conviction that my only hope of liberty lay beyond the wave, to suppress that instinctive aversion with which the unenterprising biped man, more particularly when chilled and dispirited by a sleepless night and long journey, regards the maritime sphere of his amphibious existence. For me, however, the only chance was to take the water. Hitherto all had gone well. Thanks to my Cornet and his pony, I had reached the railway safe and intact; thanks to the railway, I had arrived, *via* cross-lines and junctions, at Portsmouth seaport; and now, when another hour would place me in security on board the *Hyderabad*, should I forego that immediate sanctuary, and run additional risk of discovery and capture, merely to enjoy a thoroughly good breakfast at the George Hotel, and revel in the last comfortable meal I was likely to partake of for many a long day? The temptation was great, but I withstood it, and lighting a huge cigar to dull the importunate cravings of a healthy appetite (the brandy-flask, alas! had been long emptied), I betook myself to the waterside; and finding no difficulty, even at that early hour, in chartering a boat for my voyage, I confided my person (for of luggage I was totally destitute) to a crazy-looking craft, denominated 'a dingy,' and plumped down into her stern, opposite a venerable hump-backed

Triton, whose unassisted efforts were to propel us to our destination, in the undignified manner with which a landsman usually accomplishes the feat.

'Things is gone aboord, sir, I expect?' said the Triton, in allusion to my unencumbered condition, as we opened the harbour and dipped over the short disagreeable swell of the Channel. 'Going foreign in the *Hyderabad,* as I conclude?' added the old man, plying his oars vigorously, and refreshing himself with a copious expectoration. I answered in the affirmative, and made a natural inquiry as to the position of my future prison, which was immediately pointed out to me, beyond a whole forest of masts, through which, to my inexperienced eye, it appeared we must necessarily thread our way. Not so, however; swinging round suddenly, and catching a sea that drenched me to the skin, we 'took the flood,' as my Charon expressed it, and after passing close under the stern of a seventy-four, and shaving the bows of a tender thereto belonging, we stretched boldly away, as it seemed to me, for the Bay of Biscay, to accomplish the two or three miles of ruffled water that foamed between us and the *Hyderabad.* As the Triton warmed to his work, he became vastly communicative, and although he declined the assistance which I felt bound to offer, I could see that my proposal of taking one of the oars raised me considerably in his estimation. 'Comfortable ship, sir, the *Hyderabad,*' growled the veteran, 'and well-found, too, d'ye see! Taking her water aboard now; let alone stores and such like. She won't sail for two or three days yet, may be; howsomever, that's neither here nor there.'

'She seems a fine ship,' said I, as we neared her enormous hull, and gained some idea of her bulk; 'better off a wind than on one, I dare say.'

'Right again, father,' said the veteran. 'Sail, can she?—like a haystack. I knows her. I come home from Madras in that identical ship twenty years ago, pretty nigh, and she ain't no smarter now than she was then. We made a precious run of it, I don't think; one hundred and seventy-five days, from first to last, and fair weather the whole voyage. Why, the *Duck Lion*—(query, *Deucalion?*)—the *Duck Lion,* Captain Baffler,

spoke us off the Cape, and she came home, and cleared out, and
was half-way to Bombay again afore we made the Needles.
Hows'ever, as I said afore, she's a *wholesome* old barky, and I
wish I might have never worse luck—'Vast heaving, there, you
gallows lubber! — where be *you* a-comin'?' thundered out the
narrator, as the thread of what promised to be rather a long
story was prematurely cut short by a crashing of timber behind
him, and the startling apparition of a boat's sharp nose running
right over our bows, and threatening to force us down into the
forbidding depths of the angry Channel, whilst a gruff voice
exclaimed in a tone of triumph, 'Boarded them, by Jingo! it's
all right; this here is the gent as we're a-looking for! Your
servant, Captain Grand! Sorry to interfere with a pleasure trip,
but business is business; whilst the persuasive accents of a voice
that could only belong to a lawyer's clerk softened the infuriated
boatman with reiterated assurances that 'all repairs should be
made good and damages accounted for by Mr Shadrach, or
parties acting by his instructions,'—a promise in which the
sturdy old seaman seemed to put little faith; in fact, I gathered
from his looks, that very small encouragement on my part would
have induced him to show fight—and had we been concerned
with only the two boarders, the probability is we should have
thrown them both into the Channel. Fortunately, however, for
these myrmidons of the law, the boat which had wafted them to
their prey, and was now ranged alongside of our crazy little
dinzy, contained, in addition to a Portsmouth constable, four
stout fellows at the oars, a glance at whose determined weather-
beaten faces and stalwart forms convinced me that resistance
would be hopeless, and that the wisest course under the circumstances would be to bow to the storm, and give myself up peace-
ably to those gentlemen, who evidently possessed the power, as
they had the will, of bringing me bodily into captivity. In less
time than it takes to relate it, I had been presented with just
such a slip of paper as I had sped from Canterbury to avoid,
and found myself sitting quietly down between two bailiffs, in
the stern of a four-oared gig, for the first time in my life a
prisoner to the law.

The feeling, I confess, was by no means a pleasant one,

although its keenness was to a certain degree abated by the fact that I had often of late contemplated the possibility of such a catastrophe, which, like most other afflictions, loses much of its horror when divested of the exaggerating effect of distance. The first consideration was, 'What must immediately be done?' It was no use to sit in an open boat, wet to the skin, and repine at the unfortunate chance which had seized on the captive when so near his haven—at the bad look-out kept by myself and faithful Charon, owing in a great measure to the fondness for narrative indulged in by the latter—or at the accurate information and keen-scented vigilance which had enabled Mr Shadrach to place in operation two effective forces simultaneously, the one to besiege the barracks at Canterbury, the other to effect a spirited *coup-de-main* in the British Channel. No; the first thing to be done, doubtless, was breakfast, after which some arrangement must be entered upon to restore liberty to the captive, at whatever sacrifice. With a coolness which I owe more to education than to natural strength of mind, I civilly requested my captors to allow me a few minutes to communicate with a friend ere I returned to *terra firma*, and on the blank leaf of a pocket-book I scribbled a few lines to Cartouch, begging him immediately to come ashore, and present himself without delay at 'The George,' where he would find me in durance vile. This missive, devoutly hoping that the Colonel might have already entered upon his duties on board the *Hyderabad*, I intrusted to my hump-backed boatman to deliver without fail, and as the request was not unaccompanied by a *douceur* that would pay handsomely for the damage done to his craft, I had a lively faith that it would be punctually attended to; and the old sailor, evidently sympa-thising with a gentleman in difficulties, readily volunteered to fulfil my commission, and as he rowed off in an opposite direction, and ever and anon dropping his oar for a moment, waved his unoccupied hand, as though in encouragement, I felt, foolish as it may appear, almost as if I had lost my last remain-ing friend.

I flatter myself that I rather did create a sensation in the George Hotel, Portsmouth, as I walked into that most comfort-able caravanserai, in the peculiar costume recorded above, the

startling effect of my attire much enhanced by travelling all
night and substituting a breezy sail on the Channel for the
usual morning toilette of a gentleman; and I thought the
buxom landlady and the 'quality'-loving waiter cast glances of
unmistakable sympathy on my dishevelled person and incongruous attire, as the peculiar demeanour of my companions
betrayed their profession; and the latter observant functionary
whispered in the ear of his pitying mistress, 'Poor young gent!
(breakfast for three directly—mutton chops!) bailiffs, as I'm a
sinner!'

One of Theodore Hook's inimitable characters, the bachelor,
Mr Batley, in expressing his disapproval of all 'joint-stock' concerns, sums up with the following pithy conclusion:—'I never
had a wife, I never had a partner, and hang me if I think I ever
had a friend!' nor to a man well to do in the world, immersed
in business, and wholly wrapped up in his own concerns, is the
last-mentioned article either necessary or always convenient;
but had Mr Batley been a gentleman in difficulties, finding
himself for the first time curtailed of his liberty, in a strange
town, surrounded by unfamiliar faces, and destitute of luggage
or change of raiment, I think he would have been as rejoiced
as I was to see such a trusty ally as responded immediately to
my summons, in the person of Cartouch, who made his appearance at 'The George' ere I had finished my long-expected
breakfast, or my gentle captors had discussed the brandy-and-
water with which they thought it expedient to while away the
time.

'Knowing fellow, Shadrach,' was the Colonel's comment upon
that worthy's *coup-de-main;* 'very cleverly managed. Now,
Digby, we must get this matter put right. Sir Benjamin does
not sail for two more days, and I can run up to London with
you, where we will meet the principals, and see what is to be
done.' 'Useless, I am afraid,' was my reply; 'I am in for a
"screamer," and the bill for which I am arrested is only a ruse
to prevent my leaving England. I fear I must give up this
appointment, and come to terms with the Jew.' 'In the meantime we will be off by the next train,' said the Colonel; 'your
things were to come on board to-day, so they must have arrived

in Portsmouth. I will send to the station for them, and you can shave, dress, and start like a gentleman.' The Colonel's measures were as promptly executed as they were judiciously conceived; and ere twenty-four hours had elapsed, a conclave, consisting of ourselves, Mr Shadrach, and Levanter, to whom, for want of a better friend, I had sent on my arrival in London, were assembled in the Israelite's parlour, to discuss ways and means, and come to terms that should, at all events, set me at liberty for the present. Business details are proverbially uninteresting; it is, therefore, sufficient to say that, upon a close investigation of the state of my affairs, they were found to be so hopelessly involved as to entail an immediate sale of the commission I held in the Dragoons, a total breaking up of my establishment, and the abandonment of my Indian appointment. Nor would all these sacrifices have been sufficient to satisfy Mr Shadrach's demand, had it not been for the liberal use of his name with which Levanter favoured me, and for which, by an understood agreement, I was to return him all the advantages which my own signature might be supposed to confer. 'I'll back your bill if you'll back mine!' What a number of ruined speculators, distressed dependents, and distracted families may trace their misfortunes to this plausible and apparently simple arrangement!

Contrary to the advice of Cartouch, and against my own better sense, I entered into one of these reciprocal arrangements with Levanter, who was now concerned in a bubble scheme, of which the shares were to be unheard-of fortunes, and the public the dupes; but, in the meantime, Mr Shadrach was content to take, for the bills of mine which he held, all the ready money I could muster in the world, in addition to such security as I had to offer; and I walked out of the gaudy little drawing-room in which I had first made the Israelite's acquaintance, a free man certainly, as far as corporal emancipation was concerned, but to all intents and purposes a beggar. Cartouch was obliged to return to Portsmouth, so I had not even his assistance in the final arrangement of my affairs; and when I had written to Colonel Bold, requesting leave ' to retire from the service by the sale of my commission,' and had arranged with Tattersall for the disposal of the few horses and carriages I possessed, I felt quite at a loss as to my future proceedings, and could not for a time realise my forlorn position—the effect of my having no profession, no occupation, no one on whom I could depend, and, above all, not a farthing in the world.

True, I was a beggar; yet I did not find much difference in my daily life, nor any want of those little luxuries which become necessaries to the exotic offspring of civilisation. I ate as good a dinner every day as formerly, and with the same people; though I was obliged to substitute a hack cab for the high-stepping grey horse and the well-hung vehicle on which I once so piqued myself. I went to the same parties that in my palmy days I had voted so great a bore, but that now, when I was living as though every day were my last, acquired a charm they had never before possessed. My wardrobe was well replenished with fashionable garments, that lost none of their gloss by the fact of their being unpaid for, and amid the sale of all my other personalities there was always a certain quantity of 'small-change' available for my daily expenses; so that any one to have seen me swaggering down St James's Street, well dressed and carefully booted, bowing to my Lady this, and offering an arm to my Lord that, while a dinner with one or a whist-party with the other was arranged and discussed, would have been somewhat staggered to be informed that the fashionable-looking gentleman, whose exterior betokened all that was affluent and expensive, who looked as if he lived on the fat of the land amongst her proudest and noblest, was destitute of any tangible property save his whiskers, and had no certain guarantee that, ere a week should elapse, he might not be compelled to occupy airy lodgings under the dry arches of Westminster Bridge, even if such accommodation should not eventually lead to the bed of the river itself. London was emptying fast—fortunately, as I then thought, for I still clung tenaciously to the shadow of that fashionable reputation for which I had sacrificed so much; and day by day those greetings became fewer which I could not help thinking, with the sensitiveness peculiar to poverty, lacked much of their original warmth and cordiality. Besides, garments must eventually become threadbare, and gloves, particularly the

lavender ones especially affected by dandyism, will not long
withstand the effects of a London atmosphere. Shops into which
I had once swaggered as the *arbiter elegantiarum*, and in which
I had been greeted with obsequious politeness, now refused to
pursue any further that confiding system of credit which had
been, to quote the words of my perfumer, ' in Captain Grand's
case so wilfully abused.' Even 'Strides,' the long-suffering
Strides, that creator of manly beauty, who 'builds' your coat
on the model of an Apollo, and to whose wonderfully-fitting
'continuations,' 'pants' he calls them, the 'Anaxyridians' themselves are but as a Dutchman's drawers—even Strides would
stand it no longer; and I never thoroughly appreciated the
degradation of my position till I met with the following rebuff
in what he was pleased to term 'the warehouse,' in which I was
used to be welcomed as ' our best customer,' ' the tastiest dresser
at the West End.' It was a sunny afternoon in early autumn,
and more from habit than anything else, partly perhaps sick of
seeing my own name posted up as in ' arrears of subscription '
in every club I entered, I lounged into Strides' shop for the
purpose of killing half an hour by ordering some new clothes.
A short square figure, surmounted by a shock head of hair, was
undergoing measurement in the centre of the apartment; and
whilst an assistant in his shirt-sleeves rapidly noted down proportions and memoranda, as they glided from the lips of the
busy foreman, I had leisure to puzzle my brains as to the eventual appearance of the mysterious garment which he thus
described :—' Thirty-two '—' fourteen '—' scarlet hunting-coat '
—' superfine '—' Gambroon!'—opossum pockets '—' spoon cuffs '
—'that will do, sir.'—'thank you, sir '—' quite sufficient, sir.'
The square figure thus released was a Nimrod from the city,
and, to judge by appearances, a ready-money customer. Alas !
how different from the successor who now occupied his place.
Instead of the ready dexterity, the glib intelligence I had
heretofore met with, the foreman's tape remained suspended
between finger and thumb, and a grave 'Step this way, sir,'
ushered me into the sanctum of the proprietor himself, whose
usually urbane countenance was now gathered into a frown
betokening uncompromising firmness and defiance. ' Very sorry,

Captain,' said Mr Strides, becoming, like all men of weak nerves, more agitated as he got deeper into his subject—'very sorry, sir; but quite contrary to our rules to supply any further articles, with such a large outstanding account—money very scarce—good many gents leaving town—bill delivered—lawyer's letter totally unattended to—scandalous usage—legal measures,' &c., &c., &c. What I replied I know not, but a scene of abuse and recrimination ensued, to which I ought never to have subjected myself; and, as I walked out of the shop, I confess that, for the first time in my life, I did feel wofully, thoroughly, despicably small! And to this I had arrived!—I, the descendant of a chivalrous family, the heir of an ancient name, never yet sullied by the breath of dishonour—with opportunities enjoyed by few, with a good education, a glorious profession, and a fair start in life! To what had I come at last? —My commission was gone—the doors of my father's house were shut in my face—and I was actually a prisoner at large, enjoying my freedom only on sufferance, dependent for my very right of breathing the open air on the liberality of a tradesman, the forbearance of a Jew! The world might sneer and laugh, dandies in possession might vote I had mismanaged my affairs, whilst dandies in expectation might consider my present strait as the normal condition of man, a lot which sooner or later must overtake themselves, but which they devoutly hope may be long and indefinitely postponed. St Heliers doubtless would say something 'better' than usual anent my discomfiture, as he settled himself comfortably in the *great* arm-chair, in the *great* bow-window, and dispensed the pearls and rubies of his conversation amongst a listless throng, who could scarce condescend to laugh even at his witticisms whom they had raised to the exalted position of their jester in ordinary. Jack Lavish, whose constitutional good-nature not all the training of all the clubs in the world could alloy, would pity me; but he too would smile, for Jack has beautiful teeth, and likes to show them to advantage; but what would be the opinion entertained of me by those whom I really valued and respected? —what would my old comrades think of the broken-down spendthrift, who had once held an honoured place in their ranks as an officer and a gentleman?—what would Colonel Grandison say?—what would Maltby, what would Hillingdon?—and as I thought of my true, my early, my real friend, the tears sprang unbidden to my eyes! Hillingdon would assist me with his advice, and console me with his society—Hillingdon would put me in the way of at least *earning* a respectable livelihood—Hillingdon was the only man in the world to whom my proud spirit could bear to rest under obligation, and to Hillingdon I determined to betake myself whilst I was yet at liberty to guide my own steps. But even this cost me a severe struggle. Even to Hillingdon I could not bear to appear as a suppliant; the idea was too galling that he who in former days had known me the proudest of the proud, the gayest of the gay, should now find me seeking his presence as a petitioner, dependent upon charity for the very bread I was to eat—and yet there was nothing else for it. At least from him I should meet with no gratuitous censure, no unfeeling rebuff. His generous mind would never condescend to alloy the sympathy he was sure to afford with those retrospective strictures which add another drop of bitterness to the cup already filled to the brim; and whatever assistance Hillingdon would offer, he was sure to offer in his own frank, manly, and considerate spirit. Revolving such thoughts as these, I strolled leisurely on towards my friend's lodgings, and as I turned down the well-known street, brighter hopes seemed to dance before me, whilst I anticipated the welcome I should receive, and could almost fancy I heard his enthusiastic enunciation of that sentiment, a favourite one on his lips, which has ere now consoled many a gallant heart, the *tout est perdu sauve l'honneur* of France's chivalrous monarch.

There is truth in presentiments, though it is not for us mortals to explain their nature, as how can we explain the commonest incidents of our every-day life? Yet as there is an unearthly stillness immediately preceding the furious rush of the hurricane—as a momentary palsy, frightful from its indistinctness, appears to pervade nature on the eve of an earthquake, so may the shadow of his uplifted arm be seen athwart the sky ere the Avenger has dealt the blow which is to prostrate us in the dust. An icy chill crept over me, a dull foreboding of evil

came upon me, as I walked up the steps of Hillingdon's well-
known residence, long before I discovered that the shutters were
closed, and that the house bore that solemn mysterious air which,
we cannot tell why, is inseparable from the abode of death.   A
glance at the pale face of the servant who answered the door, a
hasty inquiry for Captain Hillingdon's own man, and I staggered
into a chair in the hall with the whole truth indelibly and
unerringly impressed on my brain.   It was needless to explain.
I required no hesitating sympathiser to break to me, forsooth,
the ghastly reality—I knew it before I was told—Hillingdon
had shot himself that very morning!   Strange as it may appear,
it was more difficult to realise the truth of the awful tidings,
when the old and faithful servant, himself bowed down and
prostrate with horror and consternation, stammered out the
particulars into my ear, than in that first moment of consciousness, when, without the aid of any outward voice, I knew the
frightful truth.   There, in his own sitting-room, his hat and
gloves on the table, the very cigar-case I had given him lying
ready for use—it seemed impossible—impossible!   Everything
betokened life, and life's enjoyments ; the colours were scarcely
dry upon his easel ; and those very flowers which he had himself
disposed in their vase, with his womanly appreciation of everything that was lovely, those flowers were blooming fragrant as
ever, and could he, the master, be lying upstairs with a cloth
over his head, a mutilated corpse!   And such an ending!   To
die by his own hand.   I dared not pursue the train of my
thoughts any further, and it was almost a relief to sit and listen
to the poor old domestic's broken narrative of the events which
had led to the fatal conclusion we could even now scarcely bring
ourselves to believe.   One thing I remarked, and one thing only,
which might lead me to suppose that a change had come over
the habits of my friend.   Occupying a prominent situation in
his sitting-room, hung a portrait, which, ever since I had known
him, was carefully veiled by a black curtain.   Not one of his
friends had ever seen the painting, and the supposition that it
was a likeness of the unfortunate Austrian lady, to whom in early
life he had been attached, was sufficient to check all curious
remarks or ill-timed allusions, as regarded a subject on which he

himself preserved an unbroken silence. The curtain was now removed, and as I sat opposite the picture, listening to the dreadful details of her lover's death, I could not keep my eyes from dwelling on the gentle features of her who had exercised such a baneful influence on my poor friend. She was portrayed as a fair high-born-looking girl, of some nineteen summers ; but what was most striking in the countenance was that eager, high-souled, and yet suffering expression, which gave such interest to poor Hillingdon's own features—that unearthly look which those who are doomed to an early death seem to bear on their foreheads, as the premonitory seal of the Destroyer—a spirit-beauty which the spirit claims to wear in consideration of its premature release : and this was as manifest on the lovely portrait of his youthful bride as I knew it to be on that glorious countenance which was lying upstairs fixed and cold in death.

Let me draw a veil over the scene that followed, over the servant's lamentations, and my own unbearable grief. I saw him—I saw the well-beloved face, the admired form—and I shudder to think of the state in which I saw them. Days elapsed ere I could bring myself to make the necessary arrangements which, as his intimate friend, devolved upon myself, and into the details of which it was loathsome to see how Mammon crept, even into the chamber of death. It is sufficient to say, that from the accounts of his servants, and the examination of his papers, which became necessary, I gathered clearly that my poor friend had been decidedly and undoubtedly insane for some time previous to the fatal act, and this was all the consolation, since consolation unquestionably it was, for the loss of the brightest, truest, kindliest spirit that ever chafed within its tenement of clay.

And it was Play that had brought the enthusiast to his self-selected grave. Play ; first the seductive pastime, then the invincible habit, lastly, the despotic infatuation, from which there is no escape. Deeper and deeper had Hillingdon been drawn into the whirlpool, and this was the result. A pursuit first adopted to deaden the stings of conscience and hush the importunate wailings of remorse, had at length become the one object of existence, the whole being of the man. Lose of course he did,

and largely. Nor were the chances of the gaming-table sufficient
to allay that craving for excitement which indeed too surely
'grows with what it feeds on.' Stock-jobbing, railway shares,
mining investments, all and everything that promised hazardous
ventures and disproportionate returns, were embarked in with an
eagerness too much in character with that imaginative disposition which made him at once an artist, a poet, and a speculator.
For a time Hillingdon's speculations had met with tolerable
success, enough indeed to encourage him to push his ventures up
to the verge of all his available fortune, and his master's spirits,
as the old servant described them, were higher than he had ever
known (for I think I have already mentioned the singular impas-
siveness of my friend's outward demeanour), but even during
this period of temporary sunshine his eccentric habit was never
broken through of sitting undisturbed for a portion of each day,
gazing on that portrait, which appeared to comprise all he
valued and loved upon earth. This was an unalterable rule,
and day after day his cheek was paler and his eye more haggard
after the communion, which he strove to think he thus held
with his spirit-love. Then came reverses and failures. Those
in whom he confided abused his trust. Shares went down to
nothing. An enterprise in which Levanter, whom he always
disliked, had persuaded him to join, failed utterly, and Hillingdon, as the only tangible person concerned, suffered severely.
Whole nights spent dice-box in hand were not likely to restore
matters, and 'the beginning of the end' became too apparent.
All this time his outward bearing remained totally unchanged,
the same calm demeanour, the same mild voice and placid brow,
and, above all, the same sweetness of temper, that won him the
affection of all with whom he came in contact. 'Late or early,
good or evil,' said his old servant, the tears running down his
withered cheeks, 'I never had a sharp word or an unkind look
from my beloved master. O Captain Grand! you know what
he was, I need not tell *you!*' and an uncontrollable burst of
grief checked the poor old man's melancholy recital. At length
it became obvious that his whole remaining property would only
suffice to clear him of his liabilities, and as soon as he discovered
this to be the fact, he made no secret of his involvements. By

one desperate effort he did try to retrieve himself.   Alas! it was a gambler's struggle, and he lost.   With a jealousy of military honour, which may be appreciated, though scarcely understood, he had made up his mind to stop short of a sum which would entail upon him the sale of his commission, and he seemed to have determined that, come what might, he would at least die with 'harness on his back.'   A like reserve was made for leaving handsome legacies to a few old servants and dependents, after which his whole remaining property was devoted to clearing himself of his liabilities.   Thus much I learned from his servant and the lawyers with whom he had been concerned.   The rest of his history, alas! comprising but a few days, I gathered from the papers which he left in his desk, addressed to myself, and accompanied by a few trifling memorials of his affection and esteem.   What his original intentions were I am unable to declare ; but it appears probable, that looking upon the loss of his personal possessions with an indifference peculiar to himself, he had shaped the idea of following out the service as a profession, and winning eventual distinction and independence in a military career.   Of advice he seems to have had plenty, and beloved as he was, he might, contrary to the usual practice in such offers, have had assistance nearly in the same proportion ; but it was one of his peculiarities to be indebted to no man, and his was a spirit to chafe above all at the well-meant counsels of a worldly and calculating friend.   But the philosophy which could smile calmly at the ruin of a worldly fortune should not have been accompanied by the sensitive and imaginative temperament that firmly believed in its power of holding converse with beings of another sphere ; and the excitement of poor Hillingdon's latter career had, in breaking his health and shattering his nerves, sapped the foundations of that mysterious barrier which separates the shores of reason from the illimitable ocean of insanity. Step by step, as I read on, I traced the downfall of my poor friend's reason ; step by step, I beheld the catastrophe approaching, of which I knew too well the terrible result.   For years he had believed in the actual apparition of his Austrian love ; twice, as he often assured me, he had seen her distinctly in the flesh, and the conviction was indelibly impressed upon his mind that a

third appearance would be immediately followed by his own
decease. With the peculiar reasoning of insanity, this belief
appeared now to have assumed the shape of a stringent obligation, a point of honour, and, as he himself expressed it, 'he
should be bound to follow when she beckoned him away.' Once
more the phantom stood by his side, and from that moment the
curtain was withdrawn from the fatal portrait. Twelve hours
afterwards he had ceased to exist ; and the beauteous form, the
gallant chivalrous spirit, the kindly loving heart, were as though
they had never been.

We buried him in hallowed ground. Grateful at least for this.
The sun shone, the streets looked gay and crowded. Business
knit the brows, or pleasure brightened the cheeks of the heedless
passengers as they moved to and fro upon their amusements or
their occupations. Did that death-stroke upon the minute-bell
thrill to the heart of one child of Mammon? Did that mournful
procession, as ever and anon it stopped, and wound on again in
mysterious gravity, speak its solemn warning to one individual
in that busy throng? 'We are bearing one of ourselves to his
real home. Yesterday was he such as ye are, to-morrow shall ye
be like him. His place shall be your place, and where he is
going ye shall go.' I fear me not. We have indeed authority to
believe that where all else hath failed, not even the voice of one
from the dead shall prevail.

We buried him. Shall I ever forget the dull dead sound of
the damp earth as it smote upon his coffin? Ashes to ashes—
dust to dust! Was this the end of all? My friend! my
brother!

As I turned from the churchyard they were bearing in another
funeral—so soon! I felt that he was already forgotten. What
mattered it to me? I was alone in the world!

CHAPTER XXI.

WINDING UP.

IT was high noon when I turned my back on the churchyard which now contained my last friend. I was, indeed, in a mood least of all fitted to encounter the noise and bustle of the crowded metropolis; and as I thought of the vulgar curiosity, the impertinent inquiries of the many busybodies in the haunts of fashion, who would have small scruple in wringing my heart to satisfy their own craving for news, I shrank from the clubs and other places of resort, where I felt conscious that even now the fate of my poor friend was the topic of the gossip's eloquence and the idler's sneer. Little heeding my steps as I walked on immersed in grief, I found myself insensibly drawing near the outskirts of London, and ere long the rapidity of my motion (singular how the chafing mind insensibly communicates its impatience to the frame!) brought me into the open country, smiling and glowing in all the luxuriance of an afternoon sun. That day has ever since appeared to me like a dream. I was then, as it were, on the verge which separates two distinct and opposite states of existence. Shame and ruin alone stared me in the face; but of this I was comparatively careless; the black cloud that overhung the present appeared to benumb my faculties, and my soul, weary and worn out with grief, had arrived at the state of exhausted torpidity which the unobservant mistake for repose. Have you ever marked the expression of dismay which blanks the countenance of some rosy urchin, whose soap-bubble has vanished from his incredulous sight? Long and eagerly has he watched the prismatic colours of the rainbow mantling in that gorgeous globe, his own creation, and just at its brightest, lo! it is not. You smile at the astonished disappointment of the child, but you, grown man as you are, enriched by experience and fortified by self-command, are you not conscious that there was a time when you, too, saw your world fading from before your sight?—when all that made life precious vanished like the beauteous illusions of a dream, and you rubbed your eyes and looked about you, and could scarce believe that the outward world was still the same, so entire, so complete was the change that had taken place within. That day, as I lay upon a sun-dried bank, and gazed upon the blue sky, and the fleecy clouds, and the warm haze, which melted the distance into a halo of beauty—that day was my day of disenchantment. Till then, through all my troubles, through all my difficulties, there had been a tinge of romance, a gleam of hope, which made the future a mine of untold wealth. Without any rational cause for such anticipations, without any substantial basis for my castles in the air, I had always indulged myself with a sort of vague belief that all would eventually be well, and the image of Flora Belmont, to whom, despite of my reckless courses, I was still sincerely attached, shed a ray of comfort over many an hour of annoyance and uncertainty. But the untimely death of poor Hillingdon had awakened me from all such infatuated and unfounded self-delusions. The reality was too forcibly thrust upon my view to admit of my deceiving myself any longer as to my own present position and probable fate. The romance of life was over, the charm of youth dispelled, and the stern training of manhood, the ordeal ever forbidding, often severe, through which all must pass, had commenced. Hours stole unheeded by, as I revolved these bitter thoughts in my mind—alternately indulging in bursts of irrepressible grief as I thought of him whom I had that morning consigned to the grave, and chafing to the verge of madness at my own follies and imprudences, which had reduced me to such a state as made me envy my friend his undisturbed resting-place. The lamps were lit and the night advanced as I retraced my steps into busy London, and, fatigued with the conflict of my feelings, sought repose in the retirement of my own lodgings. But for me there was to be no rest. As I turned into the street, from the corner of which I could see my own house-door, I glanced around me with a caution and weariness that had never deserted me since the well-remembered arrest in the Channel, with the eager vigilance that I had learned as an Eton boy, when prying round corners for the dreaded form of a master, in the forbidden precincts of ' up town,' but which I never thought to be obliged to put in practice in after-life. Many a time since have I seen a gallant fox headed from the point at which he hoped to find a safe and impregnable refuge, whilst the cry of his pursuers swelled louder and louder on the breeze. Many a time since have I marked a well-dressed and fashionable-looking gentleman step forth 'point device' from his residence, and after one hasty glance at his shining boots—ever the first care of a dandy 'got up' for the day—look anxiously around him, up the street and down the street, under the porticoes and over the way, and finally bolt hurriedly back into his own 'sanctum' from whence he cannot again emerge with any certain security until the seventh day of the week. But never have I watched the discomfiture of either predatory animal without a fellow-feeling for his embarrassment —a vivid recollection of my own forlorn condition on that evening when I found the very portals, so to speak, of my own citadel in possession of the enemy !

The scout was doubtless vigilant, but I was the better 'stalker' of the two, saw him first, and thus, by a hasty retreat, was enabled to baffle his arrangements, and elude his grasp.

But now, indeed, I had arrived at the *ne plus ultra* of embarrassment. Weary and worn out, exhausted with grief, and stung by remorse, I had literally not a place wherein to lay my head. The clubs to which I belonged I felt ashamed to enter ; nor, indeed, according to the wholesome rules that regulate such establishments, was I, properly speaking, a member of those associations, which repudiate the society of an individual whose subscriptions remain hopelessly in arrear. Should I present myself at St Heliers' door, or that of any other fashionable friend, why, in my present dusty and travel-worn habiliments, the very porter would refuse me admittance ; nor, did the master know how typical was the outward guise of the dilapidated state of affairs within, would he condemn his servant's zeal in thrusting such a shabby gentleman from the door. Hunger I had none, and my stock of cigars was not yet totally exhausted; but a burning thirst was raging in my throat, and I quenched it—I, the *ci-devant* dandy, to whom Amphytrions once appealed as to the purity of their claret, the flavour of their 'sillery'—at the stable-pump of a mews, where my horses had stood for many a long day—animals whose very shoes were worth more than all I now possessed in the world. This was literally the case, for my whole stock of ready-money was reduced to a few shillings ; all my property consisted of the clothes I had on my back ; my apartments were in possession of the enemy ; and my home, like many another desolate creature in the wide metropolis—my home was in the cold unpitying streets. I thanked God that I was a man ; at least, I was spared the perils that environ woman in her distress, and the corporeal sufferings of hunger and exposure were all I had to dread ; whilst she, the weak of frame, the gentle-natured and the soft of heart, sees ruin, vice, and misery staring her in the face.

How forbidding looked the long perspective of the empty streets, the closed doors, that interposed but an inch of woodwork between starvation and luxury — the child of misery and the minion of abundance ! I shrank along the dark side of Pall Mall, fearful of being recognised by any one of those loungers on their club steps with whom I had so often stood, on a night like this, smoking, chatting, and laughing, as we discussed the past banquet, or planned the future revel ; and my heart smote me to think how often I had omitted to relieve the wants of my fellow-creatures whilst I had the means ; and how, in my present distress, the recollection of every deed of kindliness or charity (alas ! how few they were !) helped to deaden apprehension for the future and remorse for the past.

Further eastward I strolled on, scarcely conscious of where I was going, but with an instinctive inclination to leave behind me that part of London in which I was likely to be recognised. Crowds of foreigners were around me as I lounged through Leicester Square, conspicuous even in that indistinct light for their capacious trousers, into the pockets of which, for want of better lining, hands and arms were thrust up to their elbows, their small hats jauntily set on one side of the close-cropped raven head, and the bushy beard catching the wreaths of cigar-smoke which streamed perpetually from their lips. The night wore on : the foreigners smoked and disappeared : the shabbiest of them had a garret somewhere that he could call a home ; but to me there was but one door open in all that enormous city—

but one roof under the shelter of which I should be welcome, as long as the few shillings I could call my own were forthcoming—I mean a silver hell. Not content with preying upon the highest and noblest of the land—not content with ever and anon the sacrifice of such a victim as the gallant spirit whose funeral I had that day attended—the demon of play hunts unglutted through the lower walks of life, seeking whom he may devour. If the student of human nature would see the passions working in their most frightful intensity upon his fellow-man, let him visit some of these lower haunts of infamy which are nightly open to lure the fool to his destruction.

Amongst the aristocracy, gambling is indeed a vice much to be reprobated; and great are the calamities which it entails upon its votaries; but still their losses, so to speak, are only those of superfluities—the death-struggle for existence is to them unknown; and even were it not so, the discipline of refinement, which, in that rank, has become a second nature, would curb those outward demonstrations of violence and despair which in a silver hell rage unchecked. Here the starving mechanic, the outlawed refugee, the exposed sharper, crowd and jostle each other in the contest for the actual means of existence. It is as though the prodigal were scrambling for the husks upon his knees amongst the swine. Here the trembling hand may be seen clutching those paltry winnings on which, it may be, the suffering wife and children are dependent for their long-desired meal, or staking the last earnings of toil, in the vain hope that Fortune *must* smile upon such a cast. Here the impious execration may be heard rising furious from the blasphemer's lips, as he sees swept away from before him the means of stifling that conscience which to-night shall dog him, sleeping or waking, like a fiend, to whom the wretch has sold himself body and soul. Here may be traced the gradual ruin of the once respectable domestic servant, which, commencing with the habit of speculation for which the ' betting lists' that throng every corner of our streets afford a disgraceful facility, tends steadily on in its downward course, till recklessness merges into dishonesty, and that high character which was at once his pride and his livelihood, is blasted by the infamy of a police report, and lost in the degradation of the hulks.

Well may these dens be called 'hells;' and 'who enters here, may indeed leave hope behind.' Lest the foul lust for gain should not of itself be sufficient to ensure the destruction of its votaries, alcohol lends its powerful assistance to the cause. On a rough deal table are laid out (alas! but in humble imitation of more luxurious haunts) the huge coarse joints that shall inspire an artificial thirst, to be quenched by potations, inflaming and maddening the humbler gamester to the necessary pitch of desperation; and the convulsed hideousness of passion is varied by the palsied stare of drunken imbecility.

Winding up a dark wooden staircase, I pushed my way through a shabby green baize door, and past a ponderous ruffian, whose huge unsightly frame was intended to form a living barrier should the party be disturbed, as was sometimes the case, by an invasion of the police into this temple of Fortune, frequented by the vilest of the vile; and as I did so, I could not help being struck by the resemblance, in some of its most striking points, which, although so different in detail, the scene now before me bore to many other haunts in higher life, devoted, with all their outward refinement, to the same degrading purpose. The game was identical, and the well-known terms peculiar to hazard smote familiarly on my ear. Flaring tallow candles shed a glare upon a much-stained green table-cloth, upon which the dice were descending with as much energy as I had ever seen exhibited when hundreds were at stake. To those eager unwashed faces the chances of the game were indeed of frightful importance, and hungry eyes glared upon the coins (for who would trust counters here?) as, few in number and small in value, they changed rapidly from one rugged hand to another. A savage altercation between an unfortunate-looking wretch, in close-buttoned coat and high threadbare stock, which looked ominous of the total absence of shirt, and the ruffianly groom-porter who took charge of the table, had brought the master of the establishment into the fray, and, just as I entered, the dispute was on the eve of being summarily settled by hustling out of doors the unfortunate, who had probably been robbed of his little all — a measure not accomplished without much turmoil, and the venting of sundry frightful execrations. As I took my place at the table, a quiet military-looking man, with all the appearance of a gentleman, made way for me by his side, and, with a politeness I certainly did not expect to find here, handed me the box, which I hoped was to earn me, at least, a breakfast and a bed.

Often before had I ' cut the light pack, and called the rattling main,' but never as now, with starvation depending on the result. My last half-crown was on the table. I felt I had never played for so high a stake before. Shall I confess that there was a thrill of something approaching to pleasure in the thought! Wonderfully is the human mind constituted ; and not the least of its wonders is that indescribable delight which it takes to balance in uncertainty.

' It must come this time,' said my military friend. ' I should double the stake, sir, if I were you.'

I began to think my military friend was ' a bonnet '—one of those harpies employed by gambling-house keepers to enhance temptation by the influence of example, and generally selected for their respectable and innocent appearance. Come it certainly did, but not exactly as I wanted, and the last two shillings and sixpence I was likely to see for some time disappeared from before my eyes. My military friend was ready with his condolences, and soon suggested that I was not yet what he called ' completely cleaned out.' Young as I was in the experience of poverty, I had forgotten that a valuable watch might easily be disposed of, and that studs and wrist-buttons were at all times convertible into coin in such society as I was at present—always premising that the seller was disposed to make terms easy in proportion to the prompt liberality of the purchaser. Over a slice of reeking beef and a glass of brandy, I disposed of my watch to the proprietor of the establishment for the sum of three pounds ten shillings, about a twentieth of its original value ; and as I did so, I could not help thinking I recognised the countenance of my generous customer. To be sure, it was Sarmento ! Despite the bushy beard, the huge spectacles, the voluminous neck-handkerchief, and the Mosaic jewellery, I was sure I could not be mistaken in the well-remembered features of the stranger at the opera-house door, who seemed to possess such mysterious influence over the fascinating Coralie; and a crowd of recollections teemed in my brain as I remarked, not yet completely obliterated, the scar dealt by my own right hand. Well, it was his turn now! Had he recognised me, of which I was totally uncertain, and known my present circumstances, he might have held himself thoroughly avenged, even without waiting to see the produce of the watch find its way into his own possession, and the studs and shirt-buttons leave their owner without a farthing or the means of raising one. My military friend having, doubtless, completed his tour of duty for the night, wished me a polite 'good evening,' remarking that I 'had been confoundedly unlucky, but should probably pull up again before the end of the week.' The end of the week, indeed! I shuddered to think what was to become of me by the end of the day which had even now begun. Absorbed in the stern realities of what is mockingly called 'play,' the hours had gone by unheeded, and a bright summer sun was calling the world into life and light as I slunk, a penniless vagabond, out of the silver hell. The end had come at last! Leaning my head against the iron railings in Leicester Square, I groaned aloud, and was ordered by the policeman on duty to move on.

Half mechanically I strolled into Covent Garden, to mock my wretchedness with the sight of that earthly paradise of flowers, blooming and blushing in the gorgeous freshnesss of early morning. How their fragrance seemed to reproach me, as it recalled to my memory scenes long past, never to return! My childhood at Haverley, and the roses of its lawns and parterres, filling my romping infancy with delight and wonder. The glorious midsummer holidays, when Latin and Greek held no existence, and all the world was fruit and flowers! the latter days of youth, how short a time ago! when I used to come to this very market, and select the choicest bouquets for my gentle Flora. And now! Had it not been for the pride of manhood, I could have wept loud! The very market woman knew me, shabby as I was, and with her old curtsey, pointed out her freshest posies 'for the captain.' I could not stand this, and turned away from these haunts of Pomona with, I fear, a curse upon my lips. On I wandered through street and square, and, had I been in any silver hell. As I approached him, he raised his head with a wild stare and an expression of unutterable misery, so intense that I could not refrain, even in my own helpless state, from attempting to administer some sort of consolation. 'Are you ill,' said I, 'my good fellow? Can I do anything for you?' 'No, sir,' was his reply to my commonplace offer of assistance; 'leave me alone, sir, if you please; let me stay here and die, or drag myself down to that bank, and finish in the Serpentine; and then what will become of Flora!' And again he gave way to a burst of uncontrollable grief. That name was in itself enough to rouse my interest; but had it not been so, the despair of my companion would have forced sympathy from the most unfeeling, and by degrees I got him sufficiently calm to unbosom himself to one who, equally destitute, was only able to offer him that slender consolation. He had been a man of good education, and I shall tell his short and melancholy history in his own words :—

'I began life, sir,' he said, whilst the colour rose on his wasted cheek, and the tear stood in his dim eye, as he thought of the past—'I began life as a small tradesman, and once did a steady, excellent business, that ought to have been a provision for a family. I occupied a good house in Green Street, and was then a respectable man. I lost my wife, sir, some three years ago— a good wife she was to me; and after that I never prospered. I was always fond of a bit of sport, horse-racing, and such like, but she kept me from harm's way; and if she had lived it might have been different. Well, sir, I should have won a deal of money when "Skirmisher" won the Derby, and when I went to ask for my own, the shutters were up, and the betting-list proprietors bankrupt. I lost what was to me a heavy sum, and was never paid a farthing. After that I got drinking, and speculated more and more. My business fell off, and at last I was sold up, and left the trade. Still I had a bit of money to go on with, and I turned it as I best could to keep myself and my little girl, my little Flora. I went into partnership with a beerhouse-keeper, but things went bad, and I lost most of what was left. After that I got reckless, and in an evil hour I went into the place where you saw me last night. Day after day have I thought, and pondered, and calculated on the game ; and night after night have I tried to make my calculations answer as they should do if there is any truth in figures. Last night I left my little girl supperless, and pawned the only remaining coat I had, for a final chance. The dice were loaded, sir. I'll take my oath that scoundrel knew my plan, and loaded them to foil me. I have been walking about ever since, till you found me here. I cannot go home ; I cannot face little Flora, asking for bread—for bread! and the child had no dinner yesterday. What shall I do? oh! what shall I do?' And the poor fellow's whole frame quivered as he pictured a scene of misery that filled my eyes to overflowing.

Now I felt how destitute I was. I had not even a sixpence to give the parent for his starving child. To think that there should be all this misery in the world, and that it should never have been brought before me till I was unable to alleviate it; that I should have been giving pounds for cigars, and hundreds for horses, and never in my life had the opportunity of saving a fellow-creature from starvation till now! and in vain I ransacked my pockets, and racked my brain to discover a solitary coin or the means of getting one. Poor Hillingdon! you were indeed my good genius—your farewell gift, the last time I saw you alive, was offered on the altar of charity, and, valuing it as I did, I have never regretted the mode in which it was parted with. A small silver tinder-box, for the purpose of lighting cigars, beautiful in design and costly from its workmanship, had been presented to me as a keepsake by my poor friend the last time we were together, and his sad fate had since enhanced a hundredfold the value of the gift. When I lost my watch and ornaments, in the vain hope of winning a small sum for my present necessities, this little memorial remained, as may be supposed, sacred from disposal, and was now the sole occupant of a pocket never skilled in retaining for any length of time its necessary furniture. I knew that any pawnbroker in London would be glad to advance a few shillings upon so elaborate an ornament, and I thrust it into the distracted father's hand, and bid him go home and get bread for his child.

' I have been " cleaned out," like yourself,' said I, ' but I have

no one at home dependent upon me; that is all I have left in
the world—you are welcome to it—take it, and make the
most of it—and, as you hope for heaven, never go into a hell
again.'

The poor fellow's face of gratitude was worth a mine of gold;
and I was forced to bid him a very abrupt farewell to get rid
of his protestations and thanksgivings. 'He may have been
an impostor!' says that worldly prudence which appears to
ignore entirely the existence of actual distress. Even if he
were, I ought to have been very much obliged to him for
affording me the only pleasure I had experienced for many a
long day.

I was too weary to ponder on the much-vexed question of
relief by almsgiving, and in five minutes after the disappearance
of my fellow insolvent, was fast asleep under one of the wide-
spreading elms that shade the powder-magazine, in the deep
repose of physical exhaustion, from which I did not awake till
the sun was high in the heavens. The drill was over; the
nurse-maids and their charges were weary of Kensington Gardens,
with its attractions of hoops and skipping-ropes for the children,
and fascinating Life-Guardsmen for their duennas; and all the
world, at least, all those who had any to go to, were gone home
to breakfast. Neither of the latter conveniences were mine:
and in the sheer listlessness of despair I leaned over the rails by
the Serpentine, and having no future to look forward to, I was
soon lost in the labyrinth of the past. My reverie—no, not my
reverie, for that, if it means anything, means a state of pleasing
unconsciousness, and is, besides, deservedly unpopular as a
mongrel half-foreign word—but rather, my noon-tide nightmare,
was peopled with many quaint fancies and strange recollections.
Often had I leant over those very rails in the full tide of afternoon resort, when Young England passes in review before him
the beauties of the season, and titled and high-born though
they be, makes his remarks, often more impertinent than just,
on their conduct and their charms, as chariot, landau, and
barouche roll by under their freight of grace and beauty, whilst
here and there an unpretending brougham contains one, not the
least fair of these 'unblushing flowers,' not the least sparkling of

'these gems,' which we can hardly call 'serene,' though a jewel intrinsic in value, and set in the purest taste, albeit, alas! not always a diamond without a flaw. *Rusticus expectat*, says the Roman satirist; nor need I finish a quotation which is nightly offered to the admiration of Great Britain's collective wisdom, a body undoubtedly partial to classic lore, but whose reading, strangely enough, seems entirely restricted to that author, who, when he penned the lines alluded to above, must have had in his mind's eye the spectacle of some 'country cousin' waiting hopelessly to cross the interminable stream of carriages which, in the season, 'drags its slow length along' within the magic ring, and which, to his rustic discomfiture, appears indeed to 'ceaseless roll, and roll for ever.' Now I shared the solitude of the Park, with a single equestrian, evidently a horse-dealer, and a man with a dog, dripping from its late immersion in the Serpentine. But still my thoughts were crowding in the past; and, as if to enhance the allusion, see! a neat dark brougham, a fine bay horse, a white glove eagerly snatching at the check-string, the driver's elbows squared above his ears, the bay horse pulled upon his haunches, and, as the carriage stops close to the rails upon which I am leaning, the pretty face of Coralie de Rivolte peers from the dark recesses of the interior, and I am greeted with so cordial a salutation from the kind-hearted dancer, as, addressed to such a disreputable-looking dandy, must have rather astonished the dignified conductor of the smart 'turn-out' already described.

'Digby, *mon cher* Digby!' she exclaimed, in her broken language, as she seized me by both hands, 'how long since I saw you! *Mais qu'est ce qu'il y a donc?* What a figure! You have been up all night. Ah, *petit méchant, toujours le même rôle!* Jump in, and I will take you home! Do you still live in —— Street?'

And, regardless of my excuses and apologies, the good-natured Frenchwoman insisted on my entering the carriage; and when, in answer to her inquiries, I told her I had now no home to go to, she could scarcely be dissuaded from driving me straight off to the hotel where she and '*mon cousin*' were again domesticated upon their eternal private and mysterious business. When,

however, the whole truth came out, and I unbosomed myself to
one who, with all her faults, had indeed a warm and generous
heart, the brilliant metal, touched by the talisman of misfortune,
came out, untinged with alloy, and the 'public dancer,' the
woman of notoriety, 'the brazen creature,' as I have heard them
called, who blushed not to received nightly the homage of an
admiring public, offered to place at my disposal a sum of money
that would have liquidated my debts, taken me abroad, and
given me a fair start in any line of life I might choose to select.
No one but a woman could have made so readily so magnificent
an offer, and no one but a woman could have veiled her generosity so gracefully as did Coralie, under the assumption that it
was merely a loan, to be repaid with interest on my accession to
the Haverley estates.

I am thankful to say I refused it—refused it, though I had
not a penny in the world. Why, I know not. Perhaps, in
honest truth, my generosity was not equal to hers. Perhaps
some spark of what the world calls gentlemanlike feeling forbade
me to become dependent on the bounty of an actress! But my
heart smote me, my reason accused me of pride and unkindness,
when I saw her dark eyes filled with tears at my repeated
refusals of her assistance; and once I had almost given way.
But no! come what might, I would be, at least, answerable only
to myself for my misfortunes—come what might, Flora Belmont
should never hear my name coupled with another, under any
pretence; and I resolved, if the worst came to the worst, to die
like the wolf, untamed and uncomplaining.

'At least,' said Coralie, as I persisted in bidding her farewell,
'at least accept this souvenir, in case we should never meet
again.' And she put into my hand a pretty little ivory memo-
randum-case, with the leaves of which she had been playing for
the last few minutes; and pressing my hand as I left the carriage, whispered, 'Adieu, *mon ami;* think of me sometimes, and
every blessing attend you!'

The brougham rolled on, the white glove waved from its
window as it turned down Piccadilly, and I was left standing
on the pavement near Apsley House, like a man in a dream!

Poor Coralie! she had not been gone five minutes when I

discovered that the little keepsake she had so earnestly pressed upon me contained, probably, all the money she had with her at the time, which, in the shape of a five-pound note, she had slipped between its leaves, and which was indeed acceptable to my starving condition. After the magnificent offers she had made me, I confess I felt no qualms in becoming thus far a recipient of her charity. I kissed the little 'souvenir' again and again, as I took out the welcome note, which would enable me, at least, to rub on for a few days, 'till something could be done,' —that something which is still, doubtless, at the bottom of Pandora's box, but which is ever inseparable from the to-morrow of the unfortunate. In the meantime, the first consideration was breakfast; and after a shave in a smart shop, for which I paid a shilling (had I been a little older in poverty I might have saved elevenpence) I walked into the first coffee-house I could see, and ordered a substantial repast, then the newspaper, and—another extravagance—a cigar!

Ladies always look first at that column of their favourite journal which records 'Births, Deaths, and Marriages,' and so do I. Amongst the latter, what is this announcement that meets my startled gaze?

'At the church of St Genevieve, Quebec, by the Rev. M. Victor, curé of St Genevieve, and afterwards at the Royal Military Chapel, by the Rev. John Strong, William Broadbelt, merchant of that city, to Zoë, eldest daughter of the late Seigneur Gaspard de Grand-Martigny.'

Zoë! Zoë! shall I confess that my first sensation was one of unmitigated astonishment at the very slight effect produced upon my sensibility by the fact of your having become Mrs Broadbelt. Alas! that we should so soon outlive the freshest feelings of our youthful hearts—feelings that the young deem eternal— the old scarcely allow to be existent. But lower down my eye lights upon another paragraph, which, indeed, takes away my breath :

'Died, at his residence, Haverley Hall, on the — ult., Sir Peregrine Grand, of Haverley and Norton-le-Willows, deeply and universally regretted, in the 72nd year of his age.'

CHAPTER XXII.

THE OLD HOUSE AT HOME.

HAVERLEY HALL was indeed a house of mourning, when I entered the fine old avenue, chilled and wearied with my journey down from London, this time effected in a third-class railway carriage. From the dreary looks of the old woman at the lodge, to the woebegone countenance of poor Soames at the house-door, everything betokened the presence of some great and unlooked-for affliction — the sombre over-shadowing of some mighty calamity.

'O Master Digby!' said the old butler, 'if you had but come when I wrote to you, you might have seen master before he did depart.'

'Good heavens! Soames,' I exclaimed, 'I never got your letter; when did you write, and where did you address to?'

'Mr Mortmain will explain all,' said poor Soames; 'he is in the library now; will you please to step this way?'

And as the old man used his accustomed phrase, with shaking voice and quivering eyelid, I felt a solemn satisfaction in knowing that my poor father was at least regretted by one faithful domestic, who had eaten his bread for forty years.

In the library I found Mr Mortmain, our own family man of business; usually a rosy, merry, kind-hearted, and jovial bachelor; now, in the hour of need, a true and steadfast friend. From him I learned the suddenness of my parent's disease, and the impossibility, even if I had received Soames' incoherent scrawl, of my having reached Haverley in time to find Sir Peregrine conscious, if alive.

Sad and gloomy was the present—sadder and gloomier the prospects of the future. For a few days the multitude of arrangements which necessarily devolved upon myself served to shut out from my view, in the exigencies of the hour, the dark horizon that was gathering around. Vain pomp and senseless pageantry followed him to the grave, who had in life been ever too much wedded to the outward semblances of greatness—too other frame of mind, might have admired the fresh beauties of even a London Aurora. Amongst all the denizens of our great metropolis, how few there are conversant with her charms at the only period in the twenty-four hours when she is divested of her usual dusky mantle of smoke. The children of pleasure have just gone to bed; the sons of toil are not yet up and doing; and the early breakfast-stall-keeper, the sooty chimney-sweep, with here and there a particular thrifty milk-woman, or an extra fast youth, looking very yellow, and very much ashamed of his white neckcloth, as he steals home to his virtuous couch—are the sole admirers of the architectural beauties and the vivid colouring displayed by sunrise in London. I could see the whole length of Oxford Street as I paced leisurely along, the sole occupant of that usually crowded thoroughfare; and the cool breeze sweeping unpolluted from the Park, fanned my heated temples and invigorated my languid frame, now sinking from the combined effects of excitement, abstinence, and want of sleep.

Hark! the cheering music of drums and fifes rouses the slumbering silence of morning, and a battalion of the Guards, with their clean white jackets and glancing firelocks, are seen defiling from the barracks in Portman Street to their early drill in the Park. How I envied the stalwart, fresh, healthy-looking men, as they passed by me, and I shrank to their reverse flank to avoid the recognition of an officer. Long I gazed at the figure of the adjutant, whom I knew well, as he paced his quiet charger slowly behind the drums; and, mechanically, footsore and sick at heart as I was, I followed the retiring music till I found myself skulking under the stately elms in Hyde Park, watching, at a distance, the manœuvres and evolutions, in which, however tedious I may have once thought them, I would now have given many a year of life to bear a part. I thought I was the most miserable being in the universe, but infinite, indeed, are the degrees of woe. Stretched upon its face before me, its head buried in the tall grass, and its frame only betokening life by an occasional convulsive sob, lay a figure, that even in that attitude I had no difficulty in recognising as the unlucky player whom I had lately seen so unceremoniously ejected from the careless of its real duties and responsibilities. Arms and escutcheons, empty carriages, and hired mourners, trailed their mimic grief down the stately avenue, the pride of so many possessors, over whose inanimate remains it had waved its gigantic branches, gorgeous in the hues of but a temporary decay, or blossoming in the promise of an oft-recurring spring. Doctor Driveller, ten years older than his deceased patron, read the funeral service with a steady voice and an unmoved bearing, as calm as though his time must not be very near, ay, ' even at the door.' The vault was opened, the ceremony concluded; chief mourners took off their scarfs and unpinned their hat-bands, and those at a distance hastened home to be in time for dinner. Black horses snorted and shook their plumes,—mutes smiled and whispered, as though thankful for relief from their enforced silence,—the bird carolled on the bough,—the bee hummed in the sunshine,—and Sir Peregrine was laid with the Grands.

Old customs, feudal hospitality, and the position of the family, demanded a certain amount of decorous feasting and subdued merry-making, which reminded me, with a mockery hardly to be borne, of my own coming of age in those very halls. But this, too, was at length over, and the stern realities of business left me small leisure to listen to the reproaches of conscience, or yield to the unavailing yearnings of regret. Hour after hour Mortmain and I were closeted in the library; and as we went deeper and deeper into the details of senile ostentation and youthful recklessness, so it became more and more obvious that the ruin was as irretrievable as the wilful blindness which led to it was unaccountable.

'It is evident to me, Sir Digby,' said Mortmain, addressing me for the first time by my new title, the only bequest which it appeared I was to inherit, ' that in addition to the difficulties which your poor father has entailed upon you, and of which it is only due to myself to say I have till now been kept in total ignorance, your own liabilities, as far as you have informed me, will swallow up all our available resources, even should we be compelled, as I greatly fear we shall be, to sell the estate!'

'I was prepared for as much,' I replied. 'I have seen this

coming for long, though I have never had courage to look it in
the face.   But if there is any means of avoiding the sacrifice I
am prepared to live on bread and water, and work like a slave,
to save old Haverley.'

'It cannot be done,' said Mortmain.   'Listen to me, my young
friend.   You are a man of strong mind, or I should not have
spoken to you so abruptly as I have done this morning.   *Everything* must be sold—the property, the house, the furniture, pictures, wine, horses—in short, everything ; and you must begin
life again.   It is hard, cruelly hard, but there is no use disguising
the fact—there it is !'

'So be it,' was my reply ; and from that moment the house of
my ancestors ceased to be my home.

Then came the sickening details, the inquisitive condolence of
neighbours, the cold regrets of the 'county families,' no better
in their generation than their fellows in town ; the making out
of catalogues, the slang of appraisers, the impertinences of
'parties on view.'   How the furniture seemed to increase and
multiply as the dear old hall was desecrated by having its most
hallowed associations turned into 'lots ;' carpets rolled up, and
hangings taken down ; gorgeous mirrors numbered with chalk,
and marble busts standing forward in cold unsightly prominence.
My mother's boudoir, the revered retreat of that mother whom
I had never seen, hitherto preserved sacred almost in the state
in which she left it, trodden by hobnailed shoes, and polluted
with the unwashed hands of vulgar curiosity ; my father's guns
numbered and ticketed ; every article of convenience and luxury
in his own chamber made the theme of rude jest or ignorant
criticism ; pictures of value selling for nothing, from want of
competition ; rare old wines bought with depreciating comments
by neighbouring 'connoisseurs,' who had been good enough to
laud it highly when, in former days, in that very room, their
flowing bumpers pledged health and long life to him who was
now no more ; lamps dethroned from their pedestals, curious
nicknacks scattered about in all kinds of incongruous places ;
straw littered everywhere, and the ancestral home of the Grands
become a fleeting possession, passing from lip to lip as the

fervour of competition overcame the scruples of prudence; and the dignity of centuries, the associations of history, hung trembling upon the word of an auctioneer!

But one article was saved from the general wreck, and I shall be ever grateful for the kindness and consideration with which that memento of the past was rescued. Old Doctor Driveller, with the avowed determination of presenting it to his descendant whenever that unfortunate should have a house to put it in, purchased the old family picture of 'Sir Hugo le Grand;' and the representation of that chivalrous warrior, which my poor father valued, I believe, more than any other earthly possession, was spared the degradation of a tradesman's parlour or a dealer's showroom.

The sale continued for days. From the neighbouring earl to the humble mechanic, every rank sent its representative to the auction at Haverley. Old oak chairs, quaint and curiously-carved chests and wardrobes, are still to be picked up by the virtuoso, in the humble cottages and retired farmhouses for many a mile round what was once known as the Hall. How the eagles gathered to the slaughter! Vulgar, flashily-dressed men in black attire, relieved by a profusion of electro-plated jewellery, traversed the passages with pencils in their mouths, and seemed immersed in calculations of incomprehensible magnitude.

Ere many days had elapsed, a post-chaise drove up to the door containing (strange alliance!) the persons of Mr Shadrach and my former friend Levanter. The latter appeared somewhat confused at my meeting him in the society of such a companion, but swaggered off his embarrassment with his usual assurance.

'Sad thing this, my dear Grand,' said the turfite; 'I trust only a passing cloud. I have come down to look at the yearlings, and got a cast from this gentleman,' pointing to the Jew, who was staring about him with a rueful air, that seemed compounded partly of anxiety as to his own profits, and partly, to do him justice, of commiseration for the pillage going on around.

With a blush of conscious humiliation, I was forced to present

the money-lender to Mr Mortmain; and it might have amused
an uninterested observer to mark the cold reserve with which
the shrewd upright man of business, 'the regular' of the profession, saluted one of its foraging *condottieri*, to whose despoil-
ing talents he could not but yield his meed of approval, whilst
for his practice he betrayed, as he entertained, a high-minded
contempt.

Whilst I took Levanter to the paddocks and stables, as containing those articles of barter with which I was most conversant, Mortmain, in whom I had placed unreserved confidence,
and to whose guidance I had completely committed my affairs,
invited the Jew to a conference in the library, where he hoped to
be able to make some terms with the usurer short of his actual
and exorbitant demands. As we lounged here and there through
the park and grounds, and criticised the make and shape of this
yearling, or the pedigree and probable performances of that foal,
I observed in my companion's manner a degree of restlessness,
and want of self-possession, which I had never before remarked
to the same extent in one who was proverbially known as a
'cool hand.' True, he had never, even in former days, that
unassuming ease which marks the high-bred gentleman; but
now the abruptness of his manner, veiled as it was by occasional
bursts of enforced levity, was positively startling. So was it now
with Levanter; and long as we had known each other, old
brother officers and cronies as we were, our conversation was
restricted to a few of the merest commonplaces; and we both felt
it a relief when a passing shower drove us back into the now
dismantled hall. Mortmain and Shadrach were still hard at it;
and the result of the interview was, I am bound to confess,
creditable to the liberality of the Jew.

'Sir Digby,' said Mr Shadrach, 'was not to be dealt hardly
with. He himself would be happy to accept a compromise—
always wished to be liberal and give satisfaction. Mr Mortmain's terms were *uncommon* hard; but still, as far as *he* was
concerned, he thought things might be arranged. But there
were other parties equally interested in the post-obits; a gentleman in the city, a foreign gentleman, was to a certain extent a
holder of those engagements. The gentleman was not at home

at present—might be abroad—was a very uncertain gentleman, and this must be a ready-money transaction. Sir Digby's word was now quite as good as his bond. With regard to the remaining £5000, it would be indispensable to consult Mr Sarmento'—and here the Jew suddenly stopped. With the instinctive cunning of his profession, he had caught my eager glance of curiosity as he pronounced the 'foreign gentleman's' name, and he was not to be lured any farther in committing his ally. As for me, I saw immediately into what sort of hands I had fallen, and in private communicated to Mortmain the style of people we had to deal with. The good old man entered heart and soul into the struggle, and certainly, for keen intelligence and thorough legal knowledge, had greatly the advantage of his opponent. The upshot of it all was, that Mr Shadrach covenanted, in consideration of certain monies to be paid immediately into his own hands (that was a *sine quâ non*), to deliver over forthwith, and resign any further interest in, all post-obits, bonds, and other promissory documents, bearing the signature of Captain, now Sir Digby Grand, with the exception of that unfortunate parchment in which, as he expressed it, 'other parties had a vested interest' (the real fact being that Sarmento had bought it of him as a bad debt, for probably as many shillings as it numbered pounds), and would likewise use his influence with 'those parties' to induce them to come to a speedy and liberal arrangement, which should be 'satisfactory to all parties.' With which peroration Mr Shadrach, having offered each of us a cigar the size of a rolling-pin, shook Mortmain cordially by the hand, much to the disgust of my old friend, and mounted into his post-chaise—to which, by his orders, a pair of leaders had been added—with the air of an emperor, utterly confounding old Soames, whose experience did not afford him the slightest clue as to the *genus* of this gaudy but unwashed *magnifico*, who travelled with four horses, but wore a shirt that would have disgraced a chimney-sweep.

Levanter was likewise to go back to town, nor could I understand why he was not to return, as he had come, with the luxurious Israelite. He himself explained his movements by a friendly desire that I should accompany him to his lodgings at Fulham.

'A little way out of town, Grand, for the sake of the air, where I shall be happy to give you a bed, till you can make your arrangements pretty square.'

'My dear Levanter,' said I, 'I *have* no arrangements, and I think it only fair to tell you that I am completely and irretrievably *floored!*'

'Never say die,' was his answer. 'Our shares are getting up like smoke, so you will have plenty of capital in the meantime; besides, Fulham is not London, and nobody will know you.'

No more eligible plan seemed to offer itself, and after a consultation with Mortmain, who was himself not above the general weakness of mankind, in placing a belief, as implicit as it is unaccountable, in the vague superstition that 'something will turn up,' I resolved upon accepting Levanter's invitation, and taking my place in the great metropolis amongst those suppliant ranks who beg almost on their knees that they may obtain a share in the curse of our first parents, and earn their bread in 'the sweat of their brow.'

Little, truly, was there for me to regret when I turned my back upon those grey old towers. Was I leaving home as I shrank into the corner of the post-chaise that took Levanter and myself to the nearest railway-station? What did I leave behind me? A dead father, alas! unreconciled; oh, how bitter that thought! —how hopeless the conviction that we can *never* make reparation! —that the past can *never* be undone! A desolate hearth, from which the few poor old retainers who had all their lives been taught to consider it as a home, must now be driven forth into the world, at an age when they ought to be reaping repose and comfort as the reward of years spent in faithful toil. A beautiful domain to lie waste and neglected till some future possessor should be found ready with the axe to the avenue, and the architect to the mansion, and dear old Haverley should be clipped and 'opened out' into an unsightly desert, and plastered and stuccoed into a prim representation of an ill-built almshouse. And I, the heir, that should have been even now walking that park as its actual possessor—that should have been even now maturing plans of economy and improvement, to realise, eventually all the former affluence of the family—what was I but the guilty author

of all this devastation; for I could not conceal from myself—
and bitter was the reflection—that, like the last feather to which
the uncomplaining camel succumbs upon the sand, it was my
own imprudence, added to my poor father's extravagance, that
had necessitated my exile from the home of my ancestors. Once
before, and not so long ago, in the rosy hues of early morning,
I had surveyed that glorious scene, and turned from it in disgust,
because I deemed myself destined never to share it with her I
loved; now, I looked my last upon it in the mellow radiance of
a declining sun, and how would the sensations, which I once
thought misery, be now courted for tumultuous happiness!
Then, what was I but the spoiled child of prosperity? Now,
fame, fortune, all were blighted for ever, and Flora as hopelessly
removed from me as if she had never been.

'Great bore, an old family-place,' said Levanter, with a well-
meant attempt at consolation. 'Were it not for the rents, I really
think you would be well out of it!'

'There is no accounting for tastes,' was my reply; and I
mentally added, 'willingly would I give the best part of my life
if I might but die the real possessor of that estate to which I
was born.'

As we neared London, by the perilous and rapid transit which
custom has rendered so commodious, I found my companion's
manner becoming more and more absent and '*distrait*.' If I had
thought him pre-occupied at Haverley in the morning, his demeanour in our *coupé* of the fast train, as we neared the terminus,
was constrained in the extreme. At length, as we jolted and
clattered in a hack-cab through the lamp-lit streets of London
on our way to his suburban residence, he could stand it no longer,
but proceeded to make a clean breast of the disclosures which
had evidently worried him for the last six hours.

'I have to ask a favour of you, Grand,' he began, with an
affectation of carelessness, 'which is, that you will take no notice
of the name by which I am known at Fulham; in fact, if you
would not object to calling me "Mr Smith," you would be
conferring a kindness on me, for reasons which I will explain
to you.'

'Mr Smith be it,' said I; 'nor do I wish to pry into your

x

affairs; but I do think I should have chosen a more distinctive patronymic.'

'Ah! that is just the beauty of it,' said Levanter, apparently much relieved at my want of curiosity. 'But, jump out, old fellow; here we are.'

And out we bundled, accordingly, into a comfortable and airy second floor, over a baker's shop. Whilst I was arranging the curtailed wardrobe which Mortmain had rescued for me from the fangs of the enemy, Levanter came into my clean little apartment, half-dressed, as for an evening party, with a note.

'Just got an invite to a late dinner, three doors from this, Grand,' said he, struggling with the folds of a well-starched neckcloth. 'You will be most welcome, if you like to come. I know you are a quick dresser; so, jump into your dinner things, and let us be off.'

I had by this time arrived at that state when man is surprised at nothing—ceases to be a free agent, or to speculate on what is to come next; and yields unhesitatingly to the tide of circumstances, with a drowsy conviction that, when things are at their worst, any change must be an improvement. Had Levanter desired me to step up the chimney, instead of three doors off, I should have probably complied without the slightest hesitation; and ten minutes had not elapsed, before we were picking our way in the dark up the mimic avenue which led to a cosy little picturesque residence, with French windows down to the ground, and all the necessary accessories of laurels, roses, horse-chesnut trees, and damp, which make up a London country-house; whilst Levanter explained to me, in a most mystifying manner, that we were going to dine with '*that* Lady Burgonet— Miss Jones, you know,—who is living here in retirement whilst Sir Benjamin is in India.'

That the lady was surprised to see me I gathered from her contracted brow and flush of astonishment, which, however, on the exchange of a meaning glance with Levanter, gave place to the smooth and graceful demeanour that becomes a courteous hostess. Fanny Jones had learned her lesson to perfection, and did the great lady, only with a little *too much* dignity. Everything was extremely well done, and quite in the quiet, unostentatious style of an affectionate wife pining for her husband's return. Pictures of Sir Benjamin multiplied the person of that corpulent warrior in unlimited profusion, and a bust of the absent one quite blocked up one end of the little dining-room. A miniature of Fanny lay on the drawing-room table, with the drooping ringlets, the sweet girlish expression, of 'auld lang syne.' My heart ached whilst I gazed on it, and thought how changed we all are now.

'Dinner' and 'Mr De Tassells' were announced at the same instant; and as I offered my arm to our hostess, the 'Little Nell' of the K. O. Dragoons, now rolling out into a strapping, handsome young fellow, seized my unoccupied hand with a grasp of cordial affection, and whispered in a tone that reminded me of my escape from Canterbury, 'You here, Dandy!—this is, indeed, no end of a go!' Could I do less than take the first opportunity of making inquiry after the health of 'Jenny Jumps,' who was, as usual, in strong training for a private match.

I have already said, I was not in a mood to be surprised at anything; but as dinner progressed, I confess I began to open my eyes wider and wider. The first thing that struck me was the excellence of the wine, far more choice in its flavour than would be provided by the most confidential wine-merchant for a lady's consumption, and of which Mr De Tassells, thereto incited by Levanter, filled and emptied more bumpers than is usually considered decorous at a lady's table. Then my fair hostess and her former admirer seemed to have the most perfect understanding of each other's plans and arrangements; and were both warmly hospitable to 'Little Nell,' and obsequiously polite and deferential to myself. The young one, between drinking and talking, was getting almost 'uproarious,' whilst a stolen look, interchanged occasionally between Levanter and Fanny, appeared to evince their mutual satisfaction at the whole proceedings. 'What can it all mean?' thought I. *Excussus propriis, aliena negotia curo.* I resolved, having managed matters so *cleverly* for myself, to devote my talents to the observation of my friends' affairs. Lady Burgonet retired, with an injunction to Levanter to take care of his friends. And the Cornet, what between claret and cordiality, reminiscences of what he, poor boy! called old times, and mighty potations of what our host assured us was a 'perfectly pure and harmless vintage,' got gradually ripe for any and all kinds of mischief, readily provided, according to Dr Watts, by a certain contractor 'for idle hands to do.' Coffee and curaçoa, cut the jolly subaltern short in a hospitable invitation addressed to myself, 'to come and stay six months with him at his father's place,' backed by an apocryphal assurance 'that the Governor would be *delighted*.' And with all my faculties on the alert for what was to come next, I accompanied the unsuspecting lad and the wary experienced man of the world into the drawing-room.

Lady Burgonet was winding silk near the pianoforte, and an *écarté* table was conveniently laid out and lighted at the further end of the room. I began to see my way now. And when, after a preliminary farce of drinking tea and turning over caricatures, her Ladyship addressed me with, 'Would you mind, Sir Digby, holding this skein for me to wind,' adding, with the old glance, that had found its way through many a scarlet-clad bosom, 'you *used* to do it so well;' and Levanter, or Mr Smith, as De Tassells called him, yawned over the green table, and, listlessly cutting a pack of cards, asked the Cornet whether 'this sort of thing bored him more than doing nothing?' adding, 'only don't let us play high,' the conviction came full and strong upon me, that the whole party was a scheme of swindling from beginning to end.

It was evident that Levanter and our hostess understood each other; that the former, unable to appear under his own name, had picked up a pigeon in some of the haunts of dissipation too much affected by our young warriors, and that I, his old captain, and now a man with a sort of title, had been asked to fill the complimentary office of 'a bonnet,' and to degrade myself by standing by and lending my presence to inspire with confidence the open-hearted boy that was to be robbed before my face.

For once in my life I *was* angry, the more so, as I saw no possible method of saving my *ci-devant* Cornet without a scene. I ground my teeth in silence as I held Lady Burgonet's silks, and the breath of that handsome Delilah fanned my burning brow.

The game went on. The Cornet lost 'a pony.'

'Too bad,' I thought, as I revolved every possible method of breaking up the party.

They staked 'double or quits.'

Levanter turned up a king.

'Little Nell' remarked, 'There goes a fifty.'

I could bear it no longer, and, marching up to the astonished boy, I laid my hand upon his arm and walked him out of the room ere he had time to remonstate, nor, till I had him safe outside the house, did I explain to him the cause of so unusual a proceeding. Levanter interposed his person to bar our egress, with a furious oath, that confirmed my suspicions. But I had known my man for years. Though of powerful frame, he was a *cur when collared;* and though he shook with wrath, he ventured upon no personal violence, and we walked out unmolested. Never shall I forget Lady Burgonet's face of shame, consternation, and dismay, as she stood in the corner of her drawing-room, a second Arachne, contemplating the web that had failed in its odious purpose. Besides, she felt she was found out; and, true to her woman-nature, that was the bitterest drop of all. I can see her now; the pale face—the deep-set flashing eyes—the sneering nostril—the quivering ashy lip. She was beautiful even then; but it was the hateful beauty of a fiend.

Of course 'Little Nell,' being up for a fortnight's leave from his regiment, 'hung out,' as he called it, at Limmers's, which is some considerable distance from Fulham; and as the night air sobered my former subaltern, and the whole truth dawned upon him by degrees under my elaborate explanations, the good-hearted lad's gratitude knew no bounds, and, but that I was ashamed to be indebted for assistance where I had just conferred a benefit, I might have found a home wherever the Cornet had a roof to cover him, or, as he metaphorically expressed it, 'a crib to get his health in.' But I was too proud to confess my indigence, and taking leave of my *protégé* at the door of his hotel, I started to walk back again to Fulham, revolving many troublesome considerations in my mind. Remain as Levanter's guest, of course I could not, although, under the circumstances, I felt it was imperative on me to be in the way, should he think well to call

me to account for my late proceedings. Truly I had little anxiety
as to the consequences; my antagonist was not a thoroughly
good-plucked one, and if he were, life had but little charm for
me. But my slender stock of money would soon be exhausted,
and what was to become of me then? In the meantime, I was
fagged out, and a good night's rest became a primary consideration. I would make the best of my way back to Fulham;
bakers never go to bed, so I should not be locked out, and in
the morning I would face Levanter at once—demand the proceeds of those shares in his mining concern to which I had
a right, and then, repudiating all connection with the sharper,
start afresh in any line of life which promised an honest livelihood.

Tired and exhausted, I slept till noon, and my first inquiries
when I was up and dressed were for my temporary host. Mr
Smith had left at eight, and was gone out of town.

'Any address?'

'No, sir; Mr Smith left no address—but maybe they could
tell at "the Laburnums."' To 'the Laburnums' I accordingly
betook myself, and found it to be the villa of the previous evening's exposure. Here likewise there seemed to have been a late
departure. No tall footman, no portly butler, answered my
summons, but *the* old woman in a black bonnet, who with the
moth and the spider shares the solitude of all deserted houses in
and around the metropolis, made her appearance, and was as
sparing of information as that female anchorite when put to the
test invariably proves to be :—

'Did not know Mr Smith—had never heard of Captain Levanter—there was a Major Stopper over the way, but of course it
could not be him—this was Lady Burgonet's 'ouse—her Ladyship
had left at half after eight this morning—did not know where
the family were gone—believed it was either Scarborough or
Southampton'—and slammed the door in my face. Though
vague, this was conclusive, and I had nothing for it but to
trudge into the city to Levanter's offices, upon the hopeless
chance of saving something from what I felt to be a general
wreck. Of all toilsome pilgrimages, none is to me so painful as
a long walk upon the hot unyielding pavement, a fitting substi-

tute for the glowing ploughshares of the ancient ordeal. Take it easy, and you seem to make no progress, whilst the living stream flows by you in an uninterrupted volume; try to put on the steam, and an inevitable collision with some hurrying fellow-passenger is the result. Your pockets are insecure on the *trottoir*, and your life is endangered at the crossings. Nor are these pleasures enhanced by the fact, that you are hurrying into the city to present a bill at a house that has 'stopped payment,' or to pick up the few remaining crambs of a losing concern, in which your partner has bolted, and your own substance melted away like a dream. Ere the distance was half accomplished, I encountered St Heliers, leisurely wending his way towards the clubs, on the easiest of ponies, and in the airiest of attire. Shall I confess that my first feeling was one of shame at my own faded habiliments and shabby appearance?

As he drew near, I half resolved to make an application to my former friend for some assistance, either in procuring me an appointment, or recommending me to such a situation as a gentleman could accept; but the cool, though good-humoured manner in which, without stopping, he gave me two fingers to shake, and the matter-of-course tone in which he said, 'How are you, Grand? Thirsty weather, isn't it?' as if we had met every day for a month, quite put it out of my power to unburden my mind to one who would scarcely have listened to the recital; and, as we went our several ways, he to the cool sedulously-screened bow-window that I knew so well, I to the smoky, busy, broiling city, I said to myself, 'Can these be the men that the children of fashion are proud to call their friends?'

At Levanter's offices, all was as I expected,—the whole concern had failed, and the place was shut up; nor, as may be supposed, was I able to get more intelligence of the proprietor's whereabouts than at Fulham. One thing was clear, that not a farthing should I ever see from the speculation: the bubble had burst; nor was I the only sufferer; but that was small consolation. A few pounds were all my remaining stock, all my substance in the world; and, as I sauntered listlessly along, I found myself gazing on the 'outward-bound' vessels that throng the wharfs of commercial Wapping, with a vague idea, like that of a child, of seeking my fortune in some foreign clime. As I turned the matter over in my own mind, I bethought me of ' the Diggings,' the very place for a ruined spendthrift to recover, in abundance, the dross he had squandered so freely, or hide his head in an unhonoured grave. ' California for me !' said I, and I felt my step become brisker, my bearing more erect, as I fancied I had now *an object* before me. I would change my name, of course : I was strong (for the education of an English dandy makes him no milksop), I was healthy, and I would work my passage out. I was resolved, and was hurrying forward to ascertain the proper localities in which to make my inquiries, when my attention was arrested by a figure before me, that I thought I recognised. It was that of a powerful, strong-built man, inclining to corpulence, though, by his light step and active gestures, evidently still far on the sunny side of middle age, with a well-to-do air about him, and a nameless something in his dress that marked the substantial British merchant—it was highly improbable—it could not be—and yet how very like ! Two steps more brought me alongside my old friend, Tom Spencer.

No more California for me, at least for that day. Ere we had exchanged the cordial greeting due to our schoolboy friendship, it was evident to me that Tom was completely unchanged. The unfortunate bill that had cost me so many bitter reflections, and my friend his degree and preferment in the Church, he declared had been the making of him. He had gone into business as a wine-merchant, which suited him infinitely better, and was making a ' capital thing of it.' ' He was that instant going to the docks to taste sherry,—I must come with him, and dine with him after that ; where was I staying in London ? why not put up at his place ?' In short, casting care and reflection to the winds, I was easily persuaded to have at least one more day of enjoyment, one cozy evening, to talk over old times, with the faithful friend of my early youth.

CHAPTER XXIII.

THE SCENE SHIFTED.

THE Roman Postumus must have been a gentleman of a sadly unreflecting turn of mind, if we are to judge from that Ode, addressed to him by his harmonious friend, in which the somewhat obvious truism, that 'years glide swiftly by,' insisted on for the edification of the listener, is made by the minstrel a peg whereon to hang some half-dozen of the most graceful and deep-thinking stanzas that ever flowed even from the lips of Horace. The image of the cypress weeping over the grave of that departed lord, to whom the other trees of the forest owed their glorious existence, but which alone, amongst all those towering ingrates formed, as it drooped in grief, the one connecting link between the Dead and his Creations, is not more poetically beautiful than is that consideration true to human nature which follows immediately in the next stanza, where the jovial bard, with a quaint sympathy, that shows how deep is his feeling for all parallel cases of thirst, regrets that those choice cellared stores, worthy of a prelate's swallow, which the late Amphitryon had so carefully laid down for his own drinking, should bathe the thankless marble, and crown the overflowing goblet, alas ! but of the heir-at-law.

And this brings me back to my own concerns. Time had paid no more respect to me than it did to Postumus, or to the mortal tenement of him who has made Postumus immortal. (What a reason for asking poets to dinner !) And I, too, was occupied in hoarding up streams of liquid wealth, in the shape of port, sherry, and curious Madeira—not, indeed, for my own drinking, but for the gratification of a discriminating and thirsty public. My whole mode of life, my demeanour, my very appearance, had undergone a total change at the period when I again take up the thread of my narrative ; the loose attire, the lavender gloves, the jaunty hat, and swaggering gait, had been dismissed to make room for that sober costume and staid air which the world considers indispensable to ' a respectable man.' The flowing locks had been shorn of their honours, the luxuriant whiskers pruned down to a mercantile pattern. How seldom do you see a stupendous pair of these auxiliaries east of Temple Bar, and when you do, ten to one they are the property—often the only property—of some scapegrace come into the City to borrow money. My habits, too, had become as regular as my outward appearance would seem to indicate. Shaving-water at seven, breakfast at eight, office at nine, the Docks from twelve to four; then a stroll across London Bridge for the air, dinner at five, *tête-à-tête* with Tom Spencer, and occasionally, as a great treat, half-price to the play when a farce happened to be performed that was written by any of the young Templars, or other clever 'business men' with whom we associated. No more prize-fighters in the mornings (occasionally Tom and I indulged in a 'set-to' in private, but this was a dead secret, and he kept 'the gloves' locked up with Julia Batt's letters in his own bureau), no more hacks in the afternoon, dinners at Greenwich with the 'slang aristocracy,' or breakfasts at Richmond with pink bonnets and liberal damsels; and, above all, no more betting, horse-racing, or gambling. Forbid it, Cocker! Let the British merchant invest his own and other people's capital in the wildest bubble that ever ruined its thousands—let him blindly purchase share upon share to show his enterprise, and recklessly throw good money after bad to 'keep up his credit;' but let him not be discovered to have ventured a five-pound note on 'the Two Thousand;' and if he should be seduced to go to the Derby, it must be on the clear and oft-proclaimed understanding that he 'cares for none of these things.' No. Business is business; and I think no one will confound it with pleasure : and to business I attended as though I had been born a wine merchant, and acquired a taste for straw-coloured sherry with my mother's milk.

When, in the depth of my distress, at the very turn of the tide, I had been fortunate enough to meet Tom Spencer at Wapping, it required little persuasion on the part of my old friend to induce me to forego my golden visions of California, and I grasped eagerly at the offer of employment which he kindly and generously placed within my reach. Assiduous labour, constant drudgery, and many avocations, doubtless distasteful to the former dandy, were indispensable in my new career ; but it was 'now or never,' and putting my shoulder to the wheel, I was backed by Fortune, who seldom fails to assist those that assist themselves. From small beginnings, I managed before long the whole active part of my friend's business ; and a lucky venture 'coming off' with unlooked-for success, enabled me, partly thanks to Tom Spencer's generosity, partly thanks to my own diligence and efficiency, to become a partner in the concern. After this, things went on swimmingly ; and ere Time had streaked my locks with more than a silver line here and there—ere he had robbed me of all my youthful spirits and elasticity, Hope again shed her rosy hues over my prospects, and the future, like some mountain scene, from which the mist has at length cleared away, smiled all the more beauteous for the departing clouds which had so long shrouded its promise from my view. I was never so happy before—not so thoroughly and peacefully happy. In my boiling youth I had more thrilling excitement, more varied pleasures ; but the constant hurry in which I lived gave me no time to enjoy the delights of the passing hour, and the future was perpetually over-drawing the present. Now I had an active occupation, that kept my mind continually at work with the actual business in hand, I had no leisure to fret about what was to come, or brood over bygone times. Every day brought its duties, and every day brought, too, its relaxations ; for, to the stirring trader, ceaselessly immersed in his employment, the half-hour's stroll, the weekly excursion, the social meal in the company of a few friends, are, one and all, amusements gratifying in proportion to their rarity, and their contrast to those scenes in which he is usually engrossed.

Albeit in the heart of the city, our joint lodgings were airy and comfortable (for though partners, Tom Spencer and I lived together as brothers). Here, when the day's toil was done, we sat and talked over our still-increasing business, or planned our rare and economical recreations. Here Tom would confide to me the oft-recurring receipt of a letter from Julia Batt, who still clung faithfully to her old love, in defiance of the Rev. Amos,

and read to me touching portions of the warm-hearted missive
—ill-expressed, indeed, and hampered by no strict rules of
orthography or grammar, but breathing throughout the pure
constancy, the unselfish devotion of a woman's love. Here
would I sometimes, though this was a luxury I seldom permitted myself, brood upon the unforgotten image of my lost
Flora, or build castles in the air of which she was equally the
origin and the ornament. Need I say this was indeed a useless
occupation—a sad waste of time—an enervating indulgence?
And yet I clung to the dream all the more fondly, from the
hopeless impossibility of its realisation. But the comfortable
first-floor, with its many conveniences, was not exclusively
devoted to solitary musings or *tête-à-tête* confidences. Far from
it. Occasionally some of our best customers from the West-end
did not disdain to form here a snug, small dinner-party, enrolled
to discuss those good things which can only be had in real
perfection in the City, and afterwards pronounce their fiat of
condemnation or approval (we were utterly careless which) upon
those costly fluids which were to them the welcome elixir of
enjoyment—to us the stream of life.

My former career of London dissipation had done me one good
service—the last I ever expected to reap from its follies—and
this was conferring upon me a numerous and tolerably intimate
acquaintance amongst a class of persons whose reputation for
taste and well-know fastidiousness make them the wine-merchant's
best customers. Long ago, putting my pride in my pocket, I
had called upon Lord St Heliers to leave, not the little oblong
piece of shiny pasteboard owned by Captain Grand of the
Guards, but the wide respectable card that blazoned forth
boldly in capital letters how it was the escutcheon of 'Spencer,
Grand, and Co.,' and how 'the firm were qualified to supply
the choicest wines at the lowest rates,' &c., &c., &c. And in
many a succeeding interview with his Lordship, I had induced
him to deal principally with Messrs Grand and Spencer—need
I say I had dropped the title?—and to feed his gout diligently,
which, to do him justice, he was nothing loth to do, at our
hogsheads. Often had he promised to make one of our snug
little business parties, but it was not till a long period had

elapsed since our last interview, that the consignment of several casks of a peculiar dry and curious sherry, the colour of weak toast-and-water, with a strong flavour of boots and shoes, which we had imported with incredible difficulty and at an unheard-of expense, drew a special epistle from his Lordship, proposing an early dinner at our joint residence, and asking permission to bring an old friend with him, a particular connoisseur of sherry, and an exceedingly good judge of wine.

The proposed visit was respectfully accepted ; and the arrangements, in which constant practice had made us peculiarly skilful, for a comfortable *plain* repast, such as wine-bibbers most relish, had been completed with unusual care, as Tom and I sat waiting the arrival of our noble customer, once our familiar associate. *We* had spent the day in minute calculations and laborious occupation ; papers without number filed in the counting-house, and four broiling hours of rigid attention at the docks ; after which we were only able to afford a short twenty minutes, to catch all the air that was going, on London Bridge—little enough there was, and that little not over fresh, in so crowded a locality—ere it was time to return and dress for our commercial banquet. How different, in all probability, had been the pursuits of our guest, since his valet called him at twelve, in his shady dormitory in Park Lane. St Heliers was, beyond most men, learned in the art of keeping himself cool, body and mind, and doubtless *his* day had glided by in luxurious indolence, fanned by gentle airs, artfully wooed from Venetian blind and craftily devised thorough-draft, soothed by a quiet cigar or sedative ' hookah,' and diversified by a drive to his club after his valet had been sent forth to report upon the temperature of the outward atmosphere ; and yet, with all his wealth and all his luxury, I think either of us would have been exceedingly sorry to change places with St Heliers.

' What a wreck he has grown !' said Tom to me, as we watched him emerge from the well-appointed brougham that had brought him into the City. And, sure enough, despite the boot-maker's efforts and the tailor's skill, the ravages of time and pleasure were but too obvious on that once Herculean frame. The low broad shoulders were shrunk and wasted, the square muscular

figure bloated and obese, the well-turned limbs swollen and distorted; the small foot, once the only personal advantage on
which its owner piqued himself, now withdrew from observation
beneath the long, loose trousers, that only half concealed its
gouty deformity; whilst enormous shirt-cuffs and massive rings
called attention to the hands, powerless from chalk-stones which
they were meant to hide. The whole man was made up and
artificial, and looked as though if you did but untie his neckcloth the entire fabric must fall to pieces; and yet, with all
this, there was no mistaking St Heliers, even now, for anything
but a gentleman. The charm of his manner still remained un-
impaired; and although his memory was failing him, and his
good stories were repeated oftener than is fair upon any anecdote,
however amusing, he was still, when 'in the vein,' undoubtedly
pleasant company.

Close upon his heels followed a stout military-looking personage, in a blue coat, and 'lion and unicorn' buttons, whom it
was needless to present to me as Sir Benjamin Burgonet, but
whose surprise at finding his scapegrace aide-de-camp metamor-
phosed into 'Grand, Spencer, and Co.,' was so unmitigated as
completely to stultify any opinion which the military Bacchus
might pronounce on his first glass of sherry. He got over it,
however, after much chuckling and many inquiries as to my late
proceedings, interspersed with divers interesting and problematical stories connected with his Indian career; but as, in his
narrative, he never mentioned Lady Burgonet's name, I was
compelled to forego the gratification of my curiosity as to the
eventual fate of that enterprising dame; for, although her
husband's costume did not warrant the presumption that she
was dead, there are so many other ways in which that sort of
spouse may be lost, that I was too discreet to hazard a direct
inquiry.

Dinner passed over agreeably enough. The fish was perfect;
the beefsteaks tender, and brought in hot-and-hot, to the admiration of St Heliers, and reminding Sir Benjamin of a curious
circumstance that occurred to him at Dumdum, but of which
he had probably forgotten the details, as he left his story
unfinished.

'Capital wine this,' said St Heliers, turning up a goblet of 'the extraordinary.' 'Give me some more sherry. Burgonet, a glass of wine!'

'Delighted,' said the General, lifting his glass to the light, and watching the little motes in the golden liquid dancing towards the surface. 'Driest sherry I ever drank in my life, and, without any exception, the very best. 'Gad, sir, I think I understand sherry. I've worked the thing out, and I tell you this wine is superlative.'

The General's praise was the more liberal, as it so happened this was the very wine which he had condemned a fortnight previously as not fit to be drunk by the 'Amalgamated Veterans,' and on the merits of which, as one of its committee, and special taster to that fastidious club, it had been his duty to report.

'Try that claret, my lord,' said Tom Spencer, whilst our second course of 'Scotch pigeons' was being taken away. 'I should like your opinion of it before I get any more.' (O Tom, Tom! you know we bought all we could lay our hands on as 'light dinner-wine.')

'Falernian! real Falernian!' said his Lordship, setting down his glass empty. 'So pure—so silky. Send me some of this forthwith, Spencer. Never mind about price—it's cheap at any money; and now let me have one more glass of the old sherry.'

So we went on. The shades of evening grew darker and darker upon our symposium. Devilled biscuits filled the place of dessert, and such a substitute for fruit in the dog-days naturally entailed sundry additional supplies of the much-admired claret. The bottles waned—the two venerable Bacchanalians got more and more prosy and confidential; cigars were offered, but the old school never smoke, and more claret was ordered instead. St Heliers told us some capital stories twice over, and old Burgonet related several diffuse anecdotes of love and war, of which he had been the hero; and truly his escapes in the one, and successes in the other, were equally astounding, when the General's corpulent proportions were taken into consideration. At length the warrior's utterance became thick and husky. St Heliers was getting quiet and cautious, which I knew of old betokened his own conviction that he had drunk enough; and the brougham

having been ordered, we assisted our 'two customers' into its
recesses, carrying away with them each a very liberal sample as
to quantity of those wares upon the merits of which they had
been invited to pronounce. St Heliers retained his self-command
to the last, and although Tom and I, assisted by a Patagonian
footman, had some difficulty in keeping him on his legs, preserved the quiet unmoved demeanour of one who was merely a
very helpless invalid. Not so Sir Benjamin; his legs were perfectly capable of doing their duty, though in a somewhat tortuous
manner; but his ideas had become none of the clearest, and his
articulation was peculiarly husky. He had informed me during
the evening that my old friend Cartouch had just returned from
India, and had invited me to meet him at dinner on some early
opportunity, and this invitation he was now pressing with a confusion of time and place that was ludicrous in the extreme.
' You'll be sure and come, Digby,' hiccoughed the General, as he
stumbled up the steps of the brougham. 'Excellent business
yours—capital mess—walk about, sentry!' (to the astonished
footman, who was holding the carriage-door in an attitude of
respectful attention). ' St Heliers! where's St Heliers? Now,
you'll be sure and come. Take care of yourselves—you have a
long way to go home. Good night, lads! Always glad to see
you at Government House.' And away rolled the good-humoured
and mystified old commandant, and was probably fast asleep
long before the brougham reached Temple Bar.

' I think they enjoyed their dinner,' said Tom, as we parted
for the night on the threshold of our respective dormitories.
' What a lot of wine these old fellows hold! Don't forget to
send his Lordship a hogshead of that claret he liked so much,
Digby. I told you it ought *not* to be too cool, and you saw
how he sucked it down! I daresay he will not like it half as
well out of his own cellar—but that is no affair of ours.' And
so Tom yawned, shut his door, and went to bed with a good
conscience.

Can it be supposed that I suffered any long interval to elapse
between my first intelligence of Cartouch's arrival, and an early
visit to that old and well-tried friend? Even a flourishing
wine business admits of an occasional half-holiday; and with a

light heart and brisk step I quitted the office at an earlier hour than usual one sunny afternoon, in the height of what the *Morning Post* and those whose deeds it chronicles term 'the season,' to wend my way westward, and endeavour to discover the whereabouts of my old Colonel (a piece of intelligence which Sir Benjamin had striven in vain to impart), by inquiring his address at that Temple of Janus which moderns call the 'Amalgamated Veterans' Club.' As I strolled leisurely along the Strand, despising the tempting advances made by 'two-penny omnibuses' and 'penny steamers,' how amusing was it to mark the difference, becoming gradually more and more distinct, between the bustling traffic of the opulent city and the equally bustling, though far more showy and less substantial, crowds that throng the West End. The two phases of life are as distinct as light from darkness; and the dress, looks, and air of the inhabitants of these neighbouring localities are as different as the outward appearance of the shops and houses themselves. As you leave the haunts of Business, and near the abodes of Pleasure, the pavement widens, the buildings expand, the passers-by stroll more leisurely along, and the sunny side of the street is rarely occupied. And when you again emerge into the sunshine, the street-sweeper calls you 'my lord,' and you feel that you have left the retreats of the grub far behind you, and are at length entering upon the domains of the butterfly. Now, for the first time, you begin to experience sundry anxieties and misgivings as to your personal appearance, compared with those whom you meet, unworthy a man of your sense and respectability. But let not these depreciating comparisons irritate your vanity, or wound your self-love. This gorgeous apparel, these careful toilettes, belong generally to a class that is now fast dying out; and though your raiment may be not quite so glossy, your demeanour not quite so assuming, yet thank your stars that you are a useful member of society, and have never been by habit or repute a dandy. That a man should walk erect, with his face to heaven, and feel himself possessed of no one redeeming quality in the world save that he puts well-fitting clothes upon a faultless exterior, is a splendid absurdity, that in these days requires no demonstration—that any human being can devote his manly

Y

strength and his god-like intellect to no better purpose than that of riding, day after day, three-quarters of a mile backwards and forwards over the dusty surface of Rotten Row, and dancing attendance, night after night, in a suffocating crowd, whenever a foolish woman chooses to advertise that for that particular evening she means to remain in her own house, is a painful truth, that, alas! must be acknowledged by all who look upon society as it is. But the fault is not with the young. No; the rising generation are more manly in their pursuits, more rational in their employments, than that which immediately preceded them; and in several glorious instances, those who, had they lived twenty years ago, might have been empty coxcombs, or, at best, but harmless idlers, are now, thanks to the wide-spreading spirit of Christianity, and the increasing progress of the age, the welcome ministers of charity, the benefactors of their species, and the ornaments of a class whose pride and privilege it should be ever to lead their fellow-creatures in the path of virtue or the career of honour. The days of coxcombry are gone by; the sun of dandyism is set. Brummel died a prisoner at Calais; and I, Digby Grand, am a wine merchant in the City—*Sic transit gloria mundi!*

'Hence, avaunt! 'tis holy ground,' appears to be a sentiment carefully impressed upon the burly Cerberus who keeps watch and ward at the portals of the 'Amalgamated Veterans.' Stately the architecture, and massive the furniture, of that Temple of Indolence. Doors swing noiselessly on their hinges, and a waiter with creaking shoes is instantly discharged. Instead of a jovial resort of the living, and of those whose 'hairbreadth 'scapes,' and hard services have taught them the advantages of 'living well,' these silent halls would rather appear to be a mausoleum of the dead. Should a newspaper be unadvisedly rustled by some thoughtless recruit, whose twenty years of campaigning make him feel a mere boy in the presence of these Nestors of the sword, a dozen wrinkled foreheads frown down this breach of decorum on the part of the careless juvenile, and stern glances, at which hosts have trembled, remind the cowering culprit that the sons of Mars value peace and quiet all the more for a lifetime spent amid the turmoil and loud alarums of war. Need I add how the provisioning of this stronghold is conducted upon the most scientific principles of luxury and good cheer—how the old campaigners' fare—and well do they deserve it—consists of every delicacy yet devised by the culinary art, and all at cost price—how their sherry is older, their port drier, and their mutton more tender than that of any other club in the metropolis? Is it not enough to know that Sir Benjamin Burgonet chooses the wine, and Colonel Curry controls the cook?

It is doubtless not reassuring to a bashful man to reflect that, as he ventures cautiously up the steps of the 'Amalgamated,' to call upon a military friend, he may unknowingly rub shoulders with some celebrated warrior, whose deeds, chronicled on the page of History, have been his own admiration for many a long day, or jostle against some fine old admiral, a word from whose lips, in the event of a French invasion, would blow the whole Gallic fleet into a thousand shivers; nor, though his astonishment increases, does his confidence return when his gallant friend kindly takes the trouble to 'show him over the club,' and, walking through vaulted libraries, and spacious dining-rooms, he sees the celebrities of Europe writing shaky epistles or consuming half-pints of sherry—nay, even modicums of barley-water, like any other feeble old gentleman. On the contrary, he feels that he is an intruder, and wishes himself gone as heartily as his cicerone, who will probably have more pleasure in showing him the door than any other exquisite arrangement of this commodious club.

But, in the meantime, I humble myself before the porter, and timidly request to know Colonel Cartouch's address. For a time the over-worked functionary has great difficulty in calling to mind whether Colonel Cartouch is a member or not, as he has only enjoyed that privilege for the last seven or eight years. At length, by a violent effort of memory, and with the assistance of a venerable-looking junior, he manages to recollect that the Colonel is even now in the library, and informing me of that fact in a hoarse whisper, despatches the junior aforesaid to summon my old friend from his literary occupations.

'I have been inquiring about you everywhere,' said the Colonel, after our first greeting was over, 'but the only man that could give me any intelligence of your doings was old Burgonet, and even he had forgotten your address.'

'I am not surprised at the General's want of memory,' I replied; 'nor would you be if you had seen the dose of claret with which he refreshed it when we last met. But here we must not stay, we are blocking the heroes out of their hive. Where are you going? I came all the way from the City on purpose to see you, and now I am your man for the whole afternoon.'

'Of all places in the world,' said the Colonel, 'I am on my way to Newgate. The fact is, I have had a very disagreeable business on my hands lately. An unfortunate rascal has been convicted of forgery mainly through my instrumentality, as, amongst several cases of a like nature, he chose to borrow my not very lucrative name, and overdoing the "unappropriated," got found out accordingly. My evidence settled him, and he is now under sentence of transportation; and writes to me, begging to see me, as he has circumstances to disclose of the utmost importance to myself and family, whoever *they* may be.'

'To Newgate or anywhere else, my dear Colonel,' said I. 'We will stroll quietly along, and talk over old times. And first tell me what has become of Lady Burgonet?'

Cartouch was discretion itself on all matters where the fair sex were concerned, and was, moreover, a man of singularly placid and immovable exterior; but the prolonged whistle with which, as he stopped short, turned round, and looked me full in the face, he gave vent to his sensations as I put this simple question, spoke volumes as to his opinion of her Ladyship's proceedings, and his knowledge of her character.

'I am glad you have not heard what I thought all the world knew,' said he; 'but there never was such a mess as old Burgonet made of that business. We had scarcely been three months in India before we heard such accounts of her Ladyship's doings as made it imperative on the General to take *some* decided step. That scamp Levanter was more to blame than any one, and he behaved not only like a scoundrel, but a cowardly scoundrel as well. Old Burgonet came to me in a state of mind you can hardly conceive, for, strange to say, at his time of life, he was absurdly in love with his wife. He talked of throwing up his command, going straight home, and doing everything that was foolish when he got there; but, fortunately, some disturbances on the frontier made it impossible for him to resign his appointment just at that critical moment; and I talked him over and soothed him down till he thought better of it. From what I gathered during his first burst of anger, it appears to me that there was some hitch about his own marriage to this seductive lady; and since I came home I have been given to understand that she had a husband still living, by name Dubbs, who was once a bandmaster in my old regiment. If I recollect right, he left us about the time you joined. Well, be that as it may, the most sensible arrangement, as is generally the case in these matters, was what is called, "an amicable separation;" and that I managed for him without any very great difficulty. The fact is, the others were so thoroughly ashamed of themselves that they were glad to come to any terms. And old Burgonet is again loose upon the world, a *garçon volage*, and, I am afraid, much given to take advantage of his liberty.'

This off-hand account of Cartouch's tallied so exactly with all that I had myself witnessed at 'the Laburnums,' Fulham, next door to which Levanter was living under an assumed name, that I could not forbear relating to him the whole proceedings of that evening, indelibly impressed on my mind as the day on which I had left the home of my fathers, and found myself in London, a beggar and an outcast.

We agreed that on that occasion I had doubtless saved young De Tassells from being 'pigeoned,' and that, in all probability, our amiable hostess and the astute *Mr Smith* had decamped in company the following morning. And this very natural conclusion brought us to the forbidding walls and frowning portals of the far-famed Newgate.

We have classical authority for presuming that there was no *free* entrance to the great lock-up below, and that Charon was as venal as his corresponding functionaries in the realms of day. Certain it is that the Colonel had to put his hand in his pocket for the production of the customary *complement* ere a jovial rosy turnkey, leaving his occupation of discussing a pot of postprandial porter, in the company of a stout smiling woman, probably his better half, and two or tree chubby children, could be prevailed on to act the part of guide to the new-comers. No sooner, however, did his astonished gaze rest upon the Colonel's commanding figure, than he drew himself up to that rigid attitude of 'attention' which marks the old soldier's acknowledgment of the presence of a superior; whilst the simultaneous exclamations of 'The drum-major, as I live!' and 'Dubbs, by all that's wonderful!' gave vent to our surprise at this unlooked-for recognition of the military Orpheus in his judicial capacity.

CHAPTER XXIV.

THE COLONEL'S DAUGHTER.

HOW shall I describe Newgate? Had I the pen of a 'Boz,' how could I thrill the reader's heart, whilst I brought before him, with an almost painful vividness, the gloomy shadows and the mocking sunbeams of that spacious dungeon, the dreary walls and the loaded atmosphere, the narrow strip of sky, which, to the prisoner, belongs to another world, the touching contrast of a bunch of wild-flowers with the massive iron stanchions against which they lean, drooping and withering, those children of the wilderness, as though they, too, were pining for the southern breeze, which is even now dallying with their fellows on open moor and smiling upland! How pale the face that hangs so wistfully over their fragrance! how far away the captive's soul, roaming abroad in the free air of heaven! If desire spring, indeed, from separation, how must images of unspeakable beauty crowd upon his brain! The purple mountain and the dashing torrent, the graceful feathering birch, that scorns to flourish save in freedom, and dies outright when transplanted and circumscribed in the boundaries of a pleasure-ground,—the weeping alder, kissing the faithless ripple as it dances by, as though it, too, were fain to share in the wanton's sparkling career,—the broad surface of the wind-swept lake, the deep dark shade of its fringing woods, and the bonny heather-bells ringing in the pure mountain air. Perchance the tide of thought is bearing him, even now, in fancy over the glad wild ocean-wave; again the briny spray is leaping and dashing in his face, and the white sea-bird screams her shrill welcome, as she mounts the freshening breeze, and soars at will towards the far horizon. Perchance he is walking once more by the well-known woodland path towards the stile, in the mellow twilight of a summer's eve; and though the shadows are momentarily deepening and darkening around, his heart leaps within his bosom as through the gloom he descries *her* figure at the trysting-place before him. Perchance he is once more a merry urchin culling roses in his mother's garden, and offering her a lapful of the gathered treasures, as he stands before her, in healthy infantine sturdiness. Parting his clustering curls, she prints a kiss on that fair unfurrowed brow—a mother's kiss—and the captive wakes from his dream, whilst husky emotion grips the strong man's throat, and warm tears fill his eyes, bloodshot though they be with vice, and haggard with crime. Now, the whole misery of his lot bursts upon him for the first time, in all its unmitigated hideousness; now, the yearning for liberty, if only for a day, an hour, becomes uncontrollable. Priceless would be the privilege of drawing but one more breath of the outward air, of standing once again in the crowded street—how near, and yet how far removed!—of holding but for five minutes a place amongst his fellow-creatures in that world with which he has done for ever. What a prospect is his, for one who has still alive within him the hopes, the affections, the pride, and the weaknesses of man,—before him misery, behind him guilt—a noon of punishment to redeem a morn of crime,—the felon's existence, and the convict's grave!

As the Colonel and I paced the corridors of the gaol, and were admitted by the rosy Mr Dubbs, for whom, indeed, 'stone walls did not a prison make, nor iron bars a cage,' through here a clamped and iron-fastened door, there a jealous and strongly-wrought wicket, our guide, though he showed a certain cor-

diality of manner, and made sundry respectful inquiries as to his
old corps—an idol for which the retired soldier entertains a
veneration quite out of proportion to the concern which he
seems to take for its respectability when doing duty in its ranks—
betrayed, at the same time, a reserved manner and fidgety
demeanour, which showed that he was not quite at his ease.
And this peculiarity was the more obvious when Cartouch good-
naturedly touched upon his domestic relations, and presumed
' that good-looking woman was the present Mrs Dubbs.'   The
drum-major quite startled, and coloured violently, as he replied—

' Yes, Colonel ; no, Colonel,—that is, yes, Colonel. She has
been promoted, Colonel, as I might say ; ' and the rosy Cerberus
became more and more confused. Doubtless, the possibility of
an indictment for bigamy, a prophetic view of the bar of the Old
Bailey, and a ghastly phantom of his jolly self undergoing the
passive instead of the active part (which makes all the difference)
in the process of ' locking up,' flitted across the mental vision of
the uxorious turnkey.

' Depend upon it,' whispered Cartouch to me, as our guide
strode before us to unfasten a particularly complicated series
of contrivances for security, ' depend upon it, he knows his first
wife is alive, the rascal ! I see it all now, Digby. This is the
whole mystery of Fanny Jones's marriage to old Burgonet
being kept so dark. She ran away with this fellow, I recollect
perfectly, though we at headquarters could not conceive why ;
and must have left him as soon as she could do any better, by
entrapping the old General. I always supposed Dubbs was
dead, and could not conceive why neither she nor Sir Benjamin,
who never was able to keep a secret in his life, were ever
known to allude in any way to their marriage. And now she's
gone off with Levanter. What a bad one she must be ! By
Jove,' added the Colonel, in that reflective tone in which a
bachelor always thinks it necessary to couch his observations on
the sex, ' when a woman is a trump there is nothing like her ;
but when she does go to the bad, she goes altogether, " stock,
lock and barrel." '

' I quite agree with you,' said I; ' but if you knew as much
of her history as I do, you would think that, bad as she is,

her affection for Levanter is the only redeeming point in her character.'

'Very likely,' said the Colonel; 'but Dubbs has no occasion to be alarmed; you are not the man to lodge an information against him; and as for me, I have had quite trouble enough with the fair sex in my younger days, and I wash my hands of them. I hope I may have nothing more to do with the gentle creatures.'

This was the first time I had ever heard Cartouch allude to his early follies, or express himself so strongly upon a subject on which he generally preserved the most guarded silence.

We were now on the very threshold of the cell which the Colonel had come to visit; and it seemed as though the wish he had just uttered were almost prophetic; for, as Dubbs, drawing himself up to 'attention,' opened the strongly-fastened door, and ushered us into the small but by no means inconvenient apartment provided by the law for those in whom she takes an interest, the first object that caught my eye was the tall, graceful figure of a woman, closely veiled and enveloped in long dark drapery, with the whole light afforded by the narrow casement streaming full upon her, standing in the middle of the cell, and listening, with a haughty impatience, too evident from her gestures, to a stream of continuous reproach, addressed to her in a low, concentrated angry voice, from the darkest corner of the surrounding gloom.

I could see the bosom heaving beneath the dusky folds that concealed its outline, and the small foot beating the ground at regular intervals, as though in sheer vexation and despite, while I recognised in the symmetrical bust and graceful head thrown back in an attitude of untameable defiance, such as her finest piece of acting had never displayed before the foot-lights, the wild, peculiar beauty of Coralie de Rivolte! Our entrance appeared to have interrupted a fierce altercation, in which doubtless the roused woman had the advantage, for the proper owner of the cell, emerging from his lair, out of which his keen black eyes glittered like those of some imprisoned wild beast, came forward to welome his visitors with an ironical courtesy that

ill-concealed the bitter sense of shame, the sting of powerless
hatred that was rankling at his heart.

'You are welcome, Colonel! I hope you are gratified with a
sight of your handiwork,' he began, with a foreign accent, and
in a tone quivering with humiliation and malice. 'I hardly
expected you would have brought a visitor, but you too are
welcome, Sir Digby!—the wealthy baronet that pawns his watch
in a gambling-house—the brawling bully that strikes and swag-
gers in the street—the *friend* of this virtuous lady, this pattern
of a wife. I may have some business to do with you, sir, as
well, before we part, and the name of Grand will not gain much
credit in the City, from certain papers in my possession to which
it is appended.' And as the convict's features writhed into a
sneer of diabolical malice, whilst he uttered this meaning threat,
I recognised at once the pale scowling face that years before had
gone down before my blow at the door of the Opera House, that
I had seen borne out of the fencing-room to all appearance
stamped with the seal of death, and that glared upon me once
more in fiendish malice when I walked, a beggar, out of the
silver hell near Leicester Square. It was Sarmento—the bushy
beard was gone, the raven locks cropped to the prison cut, and a
plain, coarse jacket and trousers replaced the gaudy attire, the
vulgar, tawdry jewellery that had heretofore adorned the low
gambling-house keeper, the foul, insatiate bird of prey; but the
small glittering eye, the forbidding sneer, the quickly-averted
glance were unchanged, and save that the costume was different,
the features drawn and sallowed, and the frame wasted with
agitation and imprisonment, it was the Sarmento of former days
who now stood before me.

'I sent for you, Colonel,' he went on to say, 'that I might
repay you, as far as lay in my power, for the manly and straightforward evidence, as the dotard on the bench was pleased to
term it, which has placed me here, and is to give me an opportunity of enjoying another climate at the expense of your
country; and although I did not expect the honour of a visit
from *Sir Digby*, it is better that he too should be a witness of
my unfailing gratitude to those who have conferred on me a

kindness. I have known you long, Colonel, though you were not aware of the interest I took in your proceedings. I have watched your career for years; I have always been prepared to lay my hand upon you, though I hardly expected we should meet at last in such a place as this. Ay! you may well look surprised, but the high-minded soldier, the boasted man of honour, the punctilious scion of a stainless descent and an unblemished family, has convicted and sent to the hulks his daughter's lawful husband, his own son-in-law! Colonel, you smile,—you disbelieve me; have you forgotten the grove of chestnut-trees at Buenavista, the fair kneeling girl, the flash of steel in the moonlight, the glorious black-browed Nina?'

Cartouch started as if he had been shot. Hitherto he had listened to Sarmento's rhapsody with a calm, incredulous smile, but now the expression that came for a moment over his high manly features was positively awful; he was a man of the world as well as a proud and gallant soldier, and self-command had been the lesson of his lifetime in many a trying scene. In a calm and self-possessed tone, with the old determined look I knew so well, marked only by the keener glance of the eye, the firmer compression of the lip, he begged I would remain as a witness of this unexpected scene.

'I have no secrets from my friend,' he said, coolly, as if he were in his own orderly-room; 'whatever communications you may think proper to make, Mr Sarmento, I am ready to hear now upon the spot, as I presume it was for that purpose you wrote to me requesting an interview.'

'As you please, Colonel,' replied Sarmento, somewhat disconcerted. 'You are, I know, an immovable man, and you have commanded too long to be turned from your purpose by any such foolish considerations as family ties, worldly reputation, or a woman's tears. Had you attended to the communications I made to you before this mockery of a trial—had you but condescended to visit in prison the unfortunate man whom two words from your lips, nay, whom your silence even, might have restored to liberty and respectability—had this interview taken place but one short week ago, you might have been spared the degradation that will bow that haughty head into the dust, and

crush the seared heart that hath never felt for another's woes,
and scorns to acknowledge its own. Look at that woman,
Colonel—ay! look at her, as she stands there, clothed in the
beauty which to her has been a curse. Look at her as you have
done many a time with as much delicacy and respect as though
you were criticising the voluptuous graces of a picture, or scan-
ning the animal beauties of a horse. Little did you think, as
you lolled in your stall, or levelled your ribald jests from the
recesses of your opera-box, *whose* bearing you were canvassing
with such indifferent freedom, *whose* character you were blackening with idle tale, and wafting to shame in the unfeeling breath
of scandal. Little did you think of *whose* heart it was the
bloated *roué* boasted to you he had made his purchased conquest, or *whose* smiles you congratulated the vain frivolous boy
whom you now term your friend on winning so readily; blind
must you have been in your arrogance, and deaf to the voice of
nature in your heartless isolation, or I had not needed to tell you
what you must now hear when it is too late. Listen to me,
Colonel, as I take Heaven to witness for the truth of what I
say. The celebrity of Europe, the paid opera-dancer, the public
mountebank that sells her beauties and her graces to be gazed on
by the vulgar for hire—is my wife and your daughter!' And
Sarmento folded his arms as he concluded, with a sort of drama-
tic air that never deserts a Frenchman, whilst his small dark
eyes seemed positively to glitter in triumphant malice. I had
watched Coralie with a natural interest, whilst her degraded
husband was proceeding with his disclosures, and could not but
admire the stern self-command which she too seemed to possess when required. At first she shook like an aspen leaf, and I
fancied bent involuntarily towards myself as though for support
—it must have been only fancy, for the next instant she drew
up her slight graceful form to its tallest proportions, and fixing
her eye upon Sarmento, like some lion-queen controlling the
tyrant of the forest by the mere majesty of beauty, seemed absolutely to chain him in her glance. What a picture she was, as
she stood in that semi-obscurity, an unsupported woman, but
confident in her own high heart, her gallant fearless spirit; and
as I looked from one to the other, I could not but be struck by the

strong resemblance which she bore to Cartouch, that 'family like-ness' which, dormant in the every-day torpor of life, flashes out with startling vividness on occasions of excitement like the pre-sent. In an instant I felt convinced of the truth of Sarmento's story—all I had heard of the dancer's antecedents strongly cor-roborated the suspicion that Coralie was the undoubted daughter of my old Colonel and his ill-fated Spanish wife; and now, as they stood opposite each other, bending upon the same object the same look of haughty defiance, chastened in the man by a lofty sense of self-respect and a lifetime of self-control, but wild and flashing in the woman, as though the spirit within acknow-ledged no subjection to its mortal frame, the same keen, fearless glance in the dark eye—the same curl of the well-chiselled lip, as though despising the enemy it defied—the same lines of dauntless resolution round the small compressed mouth, argued —how forcibly!—that the same blood was coursing in the veins of each, of the high-minded chivalrous soldier and the spirited unprotected girl who stood opposite to him, in the grace of her womanly beauty and the energy of her fearless heart.

But Cartouch was, of all men, the last to make what is called a 'scene.' If the every-day occurrences of life were a little more like those picturesque developments which we witness on the stage, the 'world we live in' would be much more lively, though, doubtless, much less comfortable, than it is at present, when one very essential part of a gentleman's education is to impress upon him a holy horror of anything in the shape of 'a fuss,' to endue him with that enviable Saxon temperament which veils the keenest pleasure and the deepest grief under the same placid and somewhat sleepy exterior, and to give him the Sybarite's inward relish for enjoyment with the outward apathy of a Red Indian's stoicism. We all know that, in the jargon of that arti-ficial class of conventionalists which we most absurdly call 'the world,' it is bad 'ton' to laugh; so is it, too, we presume, bad 'ton' to cry. A daughter's wedding or mother's death must produce no greater visible symptoms of emotion than the failures of a cook or the elopement of a canary; the most un-looked-for success must only be acknowledged as 'rather lucky than otherwise;' the direst misfortune modified into the confession that it is 'certainly a bore.' And yet this affectation of indifference hides many a sensitive spirit, many an affectionate heart. 'The fine ladies' themselves, inexplicable as is their public behaviour, and ill-judged the manner in which they overact their parts, are as good wives, as fond mothers, as stanch friends, as any other woman in any other sphere or any other nation. The 'fine gentlemen,' who acquire that honourable designation by studiously 'snubbing' the ladies aforesaid on every available opportunity, are as gallant, as frank-hearted, and as generous as any other class of men whose destiny it is to go down to battle daily with the world; and that superficial dreariness which makes society in England the most disagreeable of all such gatherings of our fellow-creatures, is but superficial after all, acquired with infinite pains, worn with obvious discomfort, and put away thankfully in private, whenever the happy hour arrives that allows the actor to take off his mask amongst his few *real* intimates, and show himself in his own personal character, how superior in general to the stilted part he thinks it necessary to support. And why should a man take all this trouble to seem what he is not? why should he run the risk of becoming eventually as unamiable as he is hourly striving to appear? why, in short, does every passing hour, every incident of life, more and more impress upon us the truth of the well-known adage, 'One fool makes many?' Cartouch, however, had been educated in 'the world,' and the second nature of habit had rendered him as immovable as his own real nature was fiery and demonstrative. Quietly, as though conversing upon the most unimportant topic, though in an even more measured tone than ordinary, he addressed the excited Frenchman, now blanched and foaming with the rage into which he had worked himself.

'If you can prove to my satisfaction that this young lady (with a kind and courteous bow to Coralie) is bound to me by any ties of kindred, I shall be most happy to assure her of my regard and protection.' This was almost too much for the poor girl; the revilings of her husband, the incredulity of the Colonel, she had borne with unbending fortitude, but the voice of kindness from him whom she now almost hoped might prove her father, unnerved her completely. I saw her lip tremble, her eyes fill with tears, and her whole frame shake as if she must have fallen, whilst her brutal husband burst into a mocking laugh, as he exclaimed—

' Proofs, Colonel, proofs ! I can show you her mother's picture —I know old De Rivolte's will. Take her ; she is a child to be proud of ! If she is as good a daughter as she has proved a wife, *·e vous en félicite, mon Colonel*. In every theatre a hireling, in every capital of Europe a——'

' Hold !' shouted Cartouch, in a voice that brought Dubbs hurrying back to the cell, and for an instant, as the majesty of the natural man flashed through the artificial restraints of education, I thought he would have struck the convict to the ground ; but he mastered himself, as, offering Coralie his arm, he said, ' Whatever claims this lady my have upon me, she has at any rate that which is due from every gentleman, of protection from insult and annoyance ; any further communication with me, Mr Sarmento, must be held through the authorities of the prison. I have the honour to wish you a good morning.' And drawing Coralie's arm within his own, he supported her out of her husband's cell, and reached honest Dubbs's lodge just as the high-couraged girl's strength gave way, the over-worked spirit failed, and Coralie de Rivolte fainted in her father's arms.

At such a time I thought my companionship, old friends as we were, would prove irksome to Cartouch, and leaving him to communicate unreservedly with his child as soon as she should recover, which, thanks to Mrs Dubbs's care, I trusted might be at no distant period, I took my homeward way, revolving in my mind the many strange coincidences, the unlooked-for combinations that chequer our every-day life. Here was a clue to the whole career of my old friend and former colonel, only discovered after I had known him, as I fancied, intimately for years. Here was the woman by whose preference I had been flattered, whose talents I had admired, and whom, despite her education and profession, I had once almost loved, now proved to be the lawful wife of one of earth's vilest reptiles, an acknowledged sharper and a convicted thief ; and, more unlooked-for still, the daughter of that high-minded soldier, who was himself the very mirror of honour.

'Poor Cartouch!' I thought; 'what must be his feelings when he is convinced of the truth of Sarmento's story, when he is satisfied, as I am myself, that the child of that wife who "loved not wisely, but too well," has been at length restored to him, a blighted flower, truly—for had she not lacked the shelter of a father's roof? —but still his own!' Knowing him as well as I did, I was convinced that, though he would feel deeply the degradation—for to him it would unquestionably appear such—of his daughter's public calling, yet his strong affectionate nature would derive more pleasure than pain from recovering her, though even in such a manner as this. And then I began to speculate on the causes of Sarmento's extraordinary conduct. Why had his secret been kept so long? Why had the Colonel not been made aware of their relationship at any one crisis of the many in which the sharper must have found himself without the means of obtaining a livelihood? In all probability he had been so well supported by the allowance derived from his wife's exertions, that it was not until he took to a course of systematic swindling that he bethought himself of his father-in-law, and he then forged the Colonel's signature, in hopes that, should he be detected, their relationship would bear him harmless. In this scheme, as we have seen, he utterly failed, and the drama which he had just thought fit to enact must have been for the double purpose of revenging himself upon the man he had injured, at the same time that he took the chance (a hopeless one, had he known with whom he had to deal) of inducing him to exert his interest for a pardon or mitigation of his merited punishment. And then I recollected the expression of his countenance as he alluded to the unfortunate documents which had found their way into his hands from the possession of Mr Shadrach. That worthy had behaved with unprecedented liberality at the time of my father's death, but this was to a certain extent explained by his unaccountable disappearance within a very short period of that event, connected in a mysterious manner with the sudden death of a minor, who, had he lived six months longer, would have come into an enormous property, and the well-known crisis which occurred at about the same time in the Ring, when 'Deceiver' went back so unexpectedly to twenty to one. By the assistance of Mortmain, and the sacrifice of everything I possessed in the world, I had satisfied all claims on the part of Mr Shadrach, except that with which he had parted to Sarmento, and I now felt that the clog was still round my neck, and that I had not even yet expiated the follies of my younger days. I resolved to communicate with kind old Mortmain forthwith, and trusting in my uncertainty as to the state of the law, that a felon could possess no property, I dismissed that subject from my mind.

Then I began to think of Dubbs and his comfortable-looking wife, and the strange career his must have been, since his impudence and his whiskers tempted him to run away with a lady, who in her turn ran away from him. I reviewed, in fancy, my early soldiering days, my boyish love for the irresistible Fanny Jones, the perfidy of that damsel, and all her escapades, up to the final scene at Fulham ; then, by an easy transition, I began to moralise upon the many shrines at which I had worshipped, and to feel how there was but one at which I should ever wish to kneel again—how there was to me but one woman in the world that had a woman's truthful heart, and how I knew not what had become of *her*, and how improbable it was that Flora Belmont and I should ever meet again on this side of the grave ; and having arrived at this disheartening conclusion, and the narrowest part of the City at the same moment, I was roused from my day-dream, by what an intelligent young Londoner, about two feet high, with a face expressive of ludicrous malice and precocious humour, was pleased to term 'a jolly smash'— and a jolly smash it undoubtedly was, consisting as it did of a four-wheeled cab, a lady's chariot, and a baker's cart entangled together in a manner that threatened the destruction of each and all of them, whilst a red-faced coachman in convulsions, and a bay horse plunging violently and rearing straight on end, completed the confusion of the scene and the discomfiture of the foot-passengers.

'You a coachman !' swore the exasperated cabman, anxious to have it out in abuse before a policeman should make his appearance ; 'ain't fit to feed pigs—and come runnin' right across my old blind 'oss 'ow was I to pull on the pavement agin' the lamp-post ?'

'Take his number, John,' vociferated the Jehu, himself apoplectic with excitement, to his fellow-servant, a gigantic footman, pale and helpless, in utter bewilderment; whilst the baker, who was a wag in his way, and whose cart, not his own, but his master's, had been the original cause of all the difficulty, stuck his hands in his pockets, and roared out fits of laughter at the anger of the belligerents.

Meantime, the whip-lashes were going, the wheels grated, the panel of the carriage crashed, and a tremulous female voice from within was heard to exclaim, in piteous accents of mingled terror and entreaty,—'Take me out! take me out! I'd rather walk—I'll get out, if you please—I should much prefer walking ;' and seeing that John was infinitely too helpless to venture upon any decided step, I took the liberty of opening the door and offering my arm to assist the terrified prisoner in her escape. Rouged and wigged, flounced and furbelowed, dressed out as splendidly as ever, but light and wasted to a skeleton, in the withered frame that I now lifted as easily as that of a child, I could scarcely recognise the rounded form, the symmetrical proportions of the once beautiful Mrs Man-trap. Frightened as she was, she knew me immediately ; and recovering her self-command as soon as she was out of the jaws of danger, she accosted me with the old *empressement*, all the lively coquetry that were once so fascinating in the blooming enchantress, now so ridiculous in the withered dame that was clinging to my arm.

'Always the *preux chevalier*, Sir Digby,' she croaked, with nodding head and shaky voice, as I placed her in a cab, called for me by the wide-awake young friend who had first directed my attention to the collision, and to whom I presented a shilling in token of his services—'always prepared to serve the ladies ; pray take me home, and come in to tell me all about yourself—what you have been doing, and where you have been all these ages.' And so we rattled and jolted on together towards the snug little house near Park Lane, just as we might have done years before, when life was young and the gloss was still untarnished on the wings of the butterfly. How she screamed and laughed, and chattered above all the noise and clatter of the cab, which was driven, as cabs always are, through the least macadamised streets! How she gossiped and rattled on in the little boudoir near Park Lane, in which I found myself once more sitting in the well-known chair, with my very hat in the accustomed spot. All was unchanged save the lady herself—the choicest flowers, blocking up as of yore the carefully darkened windows, intercepted the blacks and shed their fragrance around. The rarest china, the quaintest oddities, crowded every corner of the apartment; the walls were covered with exquisite water-colours, and further decorated with cupids and posies, skirting the cornices, in the brightest colours and the most ingenious groups. A kit-cat of Mr Man-trap, like Love among the roses, occupied an honoured position where he could least escape observation; and although now in his grave, and even in the days when he sat for it a very artificial old gentleman, that portrait was made the subject of many a high-flown sentiment and romantic allusion by the lady who had deceived him as a *fiancée* and divorced him as a wife.

The weather was like the dog-days, yet a fire blazed and crackled in the grate, whilst a summer sun deepened the hue of the rose-tinted draperies and lined muslin curtains into a tone highly becoming the complexion of the human face. Alas! that Calypso herself should have been past all such adventitious aids! In vain for her to study how the upholsterer's art might assist the dressmaker's taste; in vain to sit perseveringly in that subdued light, which exposed fewest wrinkles, and modified an inch of rouge into the peach's bloom. There was no concealing the fact—despite teeth and hair purchased with a secrecy that is the more surprising as the lady's-maid must necessarily be an accomplice in the fraud—despite caps and flowers and mechanical little coiffures which keep everything in its place—despite the graceful outline of horse-hair, and the rounded proportions of starch, with all the accessories of light and attitude and *prestige*,—there was no disguising the unwelcome truth, that Mrs Man-trap was an old woman, and, sharper still the pang, an ugly old woman to boot!

And is it to this, young ladies, you will be satisfied to come? Is this an image of age that youth can dwell upon with feelings of affection or respect—can think of imitating without a smile of mockery or a shudder of disgust? How different from the dear old grandaunt or grandmamma, whom you can all look back to as the patroness of your infancy, the recipient of all your little childish schemes and schoolroom sorrows—the busy, kind, affectionate old body, whose eye was as bright and whose laugh was as hearty as that of the youngest and merriest in the little troop that gave such boisterous welcome to her presence! How well you remember every item of her neat old-fashioned toilette! You were too young, perhaps, to appreciate all her good qualities, her patience, her piety, her gentle, unselfish disposition; but even in your thoughtless childhood you found yourselves wishing, though you knew not why, that if you should ever live to her advanced age, you might be even as she was; and now, though in the full, fresh bloom and confidence of youth, with the rosy light of morning brightening all around you, and the clouds of sorrow that must, sooner or later, gather round your human lot, still far below the horizon, unthought of and uncared for, you go once or twice a year to weep over her grave—think you that her girlhood was devoted to the round of frivolity, her maturity wasted in the labyrinth of fashion? Far from it. An evening of contentment and repose can only succeed a day of laborious usefulness and self-denial.

And you, affectionate mothers and cautious chaperons, who watch over your respective fledglings with such undisguised solicitude; who detail, not without covert smiles of triumph, the hard-won victory in which papa was worsted (papa, it must be owned, is very ridiculous about the horses, and the number of times by day and night that they and the carriage are required); who sow cards so judiciously and reap invitations so successfully; who would pay morning visits to the Queen of Sheba, if she were going to give a ball, and let the Crown-Prince of Congo marry your daughter, if he would take a house in Grosvenor Square—

have you ever reflected for what you are taking all these pains, and encountering all sorts of rebuffs and annoyances? the *cui bono* of all your visitings and your inquirings, your dressings and your crushings, your jaded days and suffocating nights, your milliner's bills (which, to be sure, are papa's affair), and your own failing health and exhausted spirits, when August releases you from your labours, and young 'Desiré' starts unceremoniously for Caithness, without so much as a visit for leave-taking, far less a proposal in form? There it is—this is the will-o'-the-wisp that glimmers through 'the season,' and goes out at its close. This it is that smoothes Jane's ringlets, and trims Maria's gown. Dinner, concert, and breakfast; ball, opera, and French play, instead of being the pastimes of an idle hour, are the great business of life, the markets which the fair spinsters of England think it no shame to frequent 'on view.' 'Jane is a handsome girl, the image of mamma,' says old Cœlebs, 'and should be done justice to. Maria is getting on in the twenties, and must not throw a chance away.' So Maria and Jane toil on, night after night, in the labours of Hercules, to the fading of their roses and the attenuation of their figures; whilst young Desiré, who smokes cigars at his club, and comes into society smelling strongly of those vegetables, thinks Mlle. Gavotte of the French play more charming than either of them; and very likely ends by marrying the parson's daughter in his own parish.

And even should the triumphant matron, undeterred by repeated failures, succeed at length in fixing some reprobate peer, who wants an heir to his title, or some antiquated millionaire, who requires a nurse for himself, as the constant Damon of her unsophisticated Phyllis, is such a lot the one that, in her moments of reflection, she would desire for the child that has gambolled round her knees and nestled in her bosom? To be the plaything of the one, and the slave of the other; to be neglected for a mistress by the *roué*, when his fears are set at rest as to the failure of his line; or kept a close prisoner by the peevish valetudinarian, a martyr to the whims and caprices engendered by half a century of self-indulgence; or, worse still, exposed to the dangers that surround a wife who cannot love, and who has never learned to respect her husband.

And then, when years have glided down upon the stream of
time ; when *you* are laid at rest in your grave, and the darling
whom you now cherish has grown old and faded, to think that
she should subside into such an artificial wreck, such a skeleton
in roses as poor, made-up, chattering Mrs Man-trap, whose
lovely boudoir and withered self have given rise to my tedious
reflections !

But, weak as might be the frame, the spirit of the woman of
fashion was volatile as ever. As though the twig she grasped
and carried on with her could stay the tide that was bearing her
too surely downward, she seemed to cling to every passing hour,
to fling herself heart and soul into that world of which every
moment was now becoming so precious. Such a flow of gossip,
such an insight into every one's motives and actions, such scandal
of celebrities whom I had known, and stars risen since my time,
with whose private history I was made acquainted ! When at
last she suffered me to depart, and I took my homeward way
into the City, Fleet Street was quiet by comparison ; and I felt
like a man who, having lived for a week in the neighbourhood of
a water-mill, wakes to a luxury of repose which is positively
startling on the Sunday morning, when, to his comfort, he ascer-
tains that the wheel has stopped.

CHAPTER XXV.

HASTE TO THE WEDDING.

ONCE more I was on the road to Haverley—this time in the
depth of winter ; yet how much brighter was all within
than when I last took leave of my home on a glorious summer's
afternoon.   Then, I was reckless, degraded, and miserable ; now,
I felt that at least I was fulfilling my destiny as one of the
labourers in this toiling world—and that, though there was much

behind me I regretted in vain, much I would have given anything
to undo, yet for me there was still a future; Pandora's box had
indeed sent forth many a misfortune, but Hope, the sweetener
of our cup, was at the bottom after all. The day was clear and
bracing; a sharp white frost had crisped and powdered the leafless
twigs of the stately old trees above me, and gemmed the rustling
grass under my feet with a thousand brilliants. It was just the
day for a walk, when the blood glows with exercise, and the
spirits rise as you inhale the pure oxygen of the rarefied air.
The sun shines brightly down upon your path, and feels hot
against your tingling cheek as you emerge into his beams; but
the hoar-frost sleeps undisturbed on the shady side of rail and
gate-post, and the north banks under the fences are white as snow
and hard as iron. If you are addicted to hunting, you congratulate yourself on not having sent 'Favourite' on to the place
where the hounds were advertised to meet; and, striding away
upon your trusty supporters, you exult in the superior elasticity
of your own action to the constrained, tottering motions of a
high-conditioned horse, who feels each of his four legs gliding
from under him in a different direction, and is obliged to restrain
his inclination for a gambol, in fear lest it should terminate with
a slide. The waggon bell on the high-road, two miles away,
comes tingling on your ear, sharp and distinct through the thin
atmosphere—the distant spires are clearly defined against the
sky; and you feel man enough to visit each and all of them, and
scour the intervening country before sunset, early though it be.
This is the weather for five miles an hour, heel-and-toe; and if
you can indeed accomplish that distance within the given time, I
honour you as a pedestrian and respect you as a peripatetic.

It was quite a day for a walk, and leaving my 'impedimenta'
at the station, I determined to foot it to my destination, taking
the well-known bridle-way that would lead me right across the
park of Haverley. As I traversed the acres that ought to have
been mine, and looked around upon the Eden I had forfeited, I
could not but confess that the hand of improvement, the care of
a judicious landlord, was everywhere apparent. How different
from the waste and negligence of my poor father's time! The

present proprietor was no high-bred gentleman, for whom horse
and hound were objects of far greater solicitude than the
tenantry and cottagers, whose welfare it should be his privilege
to ensure; no scion of an old family, despising the *canaille*, and
esteeming 'blood' 'the one thing needful,' as though a long nose
and a small foot were effective substitutes for all the cardinal
virtues. No; he was a painstaking, practical man, who by his
own unremitting exertions had amassed a large fortune, which
he was now expending for the benefit of his fellow-creatures.
Capital judiciously applied, I could not but see was an advantageous exchange for all the wasteful excesses and empty state
of the old family; nor do I think the obtuse cottagers and thick-
headed farmers ever regretted the coach-and-six, the Norman
descent, the condescending courtesy, and the rack-rents of the
Grands. As I swung on, invigorated by the exercise, and
marked how well this farmhouse had been repaired, how systematically that plantation had been thinned, I came to the very
spot where, in my early youth, I had ridden the four-year-old,
afterwards immortalised as 'Sir Benjamin,' out of 'Haverley
cow-pasture' into the London road; and many as were the
years that had elapsed, changed as was the whole world around
me, and myself more changed than all, I confess to a thrill of
boyish exultation as I perceived my exploit commemorated by a
strong oaken rail placed across the gap established by our egress,
and which would effectually debar any daring equestrian from
a repetition of the feat.

Vanity is of all ages, and I have heard even a woman, and a
very pretty one to boot, aver that she would rather be complimented upon her horse than her looks. Can we then wonder at
the biped man, albeit when old enough to know better, clinging
to the fame of his successes as a Centaur rather than to a reputation for wisdom, morality, or science in the graver and more
important pursuits of life? The four-year-old brought back to
my mind the General from whom he took his designation, and
saddened my retrospective triumphs as I remembered that he
too, the thoughtless, kind-hearted old warrior, had passed away.
His name is now a blank in the Army List; the place that hath

known him knows him no more; his clasps and crosses have been returned to the Sovereign from whom they emanated, and Sir Tartar Trim, who succeeded to his vacant command, is countermanding his orders and revoking his regulations. The Dead March in Saul—the crape-covered charger—the cocked-hat, sword, and epaulettes of the senseless corpse—two regiments under arms—a deafening salute that cannot wake the dead—and a lively quick-step melody, cheering the troops as they return to barracks—is this all that is left of half a century of war and pageantry, the thrilling excitement of the bivouac, the seductive pomp of the parade—a life of alternate idleness and danger, hardship and dissipation, and all those varieties of scene and society that make soldiering so dear to a careless mind? Poor old Burgonet! with all your faults you had indeed a warm, kind heart, and it is not for me to pry into the motives or pass judgment on the conduct of another.

'If you please, good gentleman, to spare a trifle for a poor woman,' said a voice close to me, as I bounded over the stile that terminated my bridle-way in the high-road.

There was something in the accent that smote upon my ear, a glance in the wild large eye that went straight to my heart. Poor thing! poor thing!—that shrunken form, that pale wasted hand thrust out for an alms, can this be Lady Burgonet—can this be Fanny Jones?—a desolate tramp walking the high-roads, and bearing with her a wretched sickly infant, wrapped in that scanty shawl, of which, cold as is the day, she has deprived herself to shelter her child. Frivolity and vice, sin and misery, have made sad havoc with their victim, but she is a mother still. And that child's father, what has become of him?—the origin of all her misery, the first, the only love of that abandoned heart!

'O Sir Digby! Sir Digby!' cried the emaciated woman, blushing crimson over face, neck, and hands, as she recognised me; 'have pity on me—lost, ruined, degraded—have pity on me—I am starving! It is God's truth; I am starving, and my child will die upon the road for want of a morsel of bread!'

Poor creature! the first kind words she had heard for many a

long day brought on a fit of hysterical weeping, and a scene
extremely unusual on the Queen's highway. She knelt before
me on the cold ground; she covered my hand with kisses; she
showered blessings on my head almost as volubly as the
beggar who has been brought up to the trade, and whose beati-
tudes are of surprising eloquence; but her's came direct from
the heart, for our timely encounter had saved the life of her
child. She told me of Levanter—she called him Richard—
there was no concealment now. She described to me all she
had borne with him and for him; how they had cheated and
swindled together, and lived first in one place then in another,
on their dishonest profits; how they had been now in affluence,
now in extreme want; and how, whilst Richard was kind to
her, she had been happy through it all; how at last, when ill-
luck seemed to pursue everything they undertook, he had become
first morose, then savage; how he had cursed her as a clog round
his neck, when she bore him the child that was even then in her
arms; how he had struck her for going to old Burgonet's funeral;
and her tears flowed afresh as she sobbed out, 'for the old man
was indeed kind to me!'—and how the bitterest drop in her
cup was the assurance that Richard hated and wished to get rid
of her. How the gang to which he had attached himself was
discovered and broken up, and he was at that very moment
crossing the high seas, a transport for life; and even now, could
she find the means, despite his neglect, despite his crimes, his
false-heartedness, and his brutality, she would fain go out and
join him once more in another hemisphere!

Woman is indeed a wondrous creation. Had this one any
single redeeming quality but those which are inseparable from
her sex? Wanton, reckless, and deceitful, had she been a man,
she would have been the basest of her kind; but she was a
woman; and sunk, degraded as she might be, she was true to
her first love—she would have died for her child. Need I say
that I did all in my power to soften her wretched lot? But it
was with a slower step and a saddened, chastened heart that I
walked on to my destination, where a very different scene awaited
me—a scene of mirth and merrymaking, cordiality and good

wishes. What a mocking contrast to the sobs and anguish of that shame-stricken outcast!

I presume all weddings are much the same in detail, how different soever may be the causes that lead to such ceremonials. The one to which I was now hastening had indeed reason to be a joyous gathering. After years of probation, much opposition from papa, and all sorts of obstacles which proverbially ruffle the course of true love, my friend and partner, Tom Spencer, was about to be united to the faithful Julia Batt. The Rev. Amos himself was to give the bride away at the altar; old Doctor Driveller, assisted by two strapping curates, was to perform the ceremony; and the part of bringing the bridegroom in good order to the post, and then ' giving him a knee ' during the match, was to devolve upon myself; an office, I may remark, *en passant*, which, when often persisted in, is apt to stamp the scared bottle-holder a bachelor for life. In all well-regulated establishments, that sacred period which immediately precedes the irrevocable union of two fellow-creatures is treated by the females as a kind of saturnalia, during which, probably to guide the future conduct of the spouse, male authority is set utterly at defiance, and the grosser sex are carefully excluded from all those mysterious preparations and arrangements which seem indispensable to the occasion. Great gatherings are there of aunts past praying for, and pretty cousins on their promotion, matrons skilled in the science of wife and motherhood, damsels not yet released from the back-board and music-stool, to say nothing of old maids whose concern for all matters tending to marrying and giving in marriage must necessarily be of the most disinterested nature. Bonnets and shawls gather from the four winds of heaven. Silence flies terrified to take shelter in the clubs, and a hundred tastes pronounce their voluble decrees on the innumerable changes of raiment which custom has rendered it imperative to provide for a young lady about to be married.

When I arrived at Owlthorpe Rectory, the keen white frost of the morning had subsided into a dull, grey atmosphere, with a drizzling rain, and I found my friend Tom, the exulting bridegroom, whose shield I was to bear on the morrow, smoking a disconsolate cigar under the shelter of some dripping larches that overhung the Rectory gate.

'The lawyers are in the library with Mr Batt,' said the intended, with rather a woful air for so happy a man. 'The bridesmaids are upstairs with Julia—eight of them, all to be dressed alike, my dear fellow, and I don't know one from the other as it is ; there are seventeen ladies at cake and wine in the drawing-room ; Julia's new maid, over whom I feel I shall never have the slightest authority, has turned me out of the study, which is besides completely tapestried with clothes ; it is washing-day at the farmhouse, where I have got a lodging in the cheese-room, and this is the only place I can find to smoke a cigar and wait patiently till dinner-time.'

Encouraging, truly ! At dinner it was not much better. A family party is seldom a very lively *réunion,* and I think I may say, without self-conceit, that my arrival was most acceptable to all the relatives assembled at the Rectory. Old Mortmain, who of course had the entire management of settlements, was the only other disinterested person present ; and though the Rev. Amos pushed his bottle of port round vigorously after dinner, and held forth as usual concerning his shooting, from which increasing blindness did not seem to wean him, I firmly believe the lawyer and myself were the only two people present that had the slightest idea of what we were drinking or what we were talking about.

A peal of bells awoke me on the morrow, and with a lively impression of the responsible office I had undertaken, and an indistinct feeling of relief as I reflected that I was only the second, and not the principal, I proceeded to endue myself in the gorgeous attire without which it is unlucky to attend either weddings or christenings ; and after a hasty cup of tea, provided by the kind attention of 'Julia's new maid,' all the rest of the female domestics being at sixes and sevens, I proceeded to the farmhouse to look after my man.

Tom was nervous, undoubtedly nervous. His breakfast stood untouched upon the table, and his hand shook as he fastened the tie of his blue neck-cloth, and gave his whiskers their farewell twirl. All the females of *his* establishment were likewise on the move. The old dame that reigned over the farm eyed him with severe scrutiny as he left her threshold; and the blowsy maid-of-all-work forgot the ribbons with which we had presented her, in her infatuated eagerness to 'get a look at the bride-groom.' The village, too, of which we had to traverse the whole length, was up in arms; and still caps and gowns predominated over the male creation. Doubtless, there is something in a wed-ding that speaks directly to the sympathies of woman, reminds her of what has been, or kindles hopes of what may be, in her gentle bosom. Certainly she misses no opportunity of witness-ing the fatal ceremony.

In the church, the same 'ministering angels' thronged loft, aisle, and chancel, with inquiring countenances of every age and every hue; whilst many a whispered comment and open-mouthed stare did homage to the magnificent apparel of the bride. The men admired her beauty, the women her dress. The pen of fiction must not presume to describe the sacred ceremony; enough to say that the venerable clergyman, the quaint old church, the respectful congregation, were in harmonious keeping with the holy office then and there celebrated; but when the bride faltered out, as brides will do, the important words, 'I will,' a burst of weeping broke forth from the assembled fair, as violent as it was unaccountable; there was not a dry eye in the church, if we except the clerk and the half-dozen males who found themselves thus, as it were, swamped in tears. Even the old gipsy-woman from the common, who could scarce be said to belong to the parish, and had not set eyes on Miss Batt twice in her existence, sobbed as if her heart would break. One would have supposed a second Andromeda was bound for sacrifice, and that Tom Spencer, looking more meek, not to say sheepish, than I had ever seen him in his life, was the odious sea-monster, gaping to devour his victim. Had each and all of these sympathising Niobes been then and there about to be united in marriage to the Sultan, and shipped off for Constantinople and captivity on the spot, their grief could not have been more general or more inconsolable.

The knot is soon tied, however dilatory may be the legal process of untying the same. Again the old tower rocks with a
merry peal, and the ringers, refreshed with beer, and incited to
further exertions by the prospect of that favourite beverage in
still greater profusion, moisten their strong large hands and pull
away vigorously ; white-headed old men, the 'forefathers of the
hamlet,' bless the handsome bride as she passes. Tom Spencer
walks by her side, erect and smiling, and tries to look quite at
his ease with indifferent success. There is always a startled
look about a bridegroom, as if he had only just awoke to the
responsibilities of the office ; and Tom can hardly realise to himself that the lady whom he has adored so many years as Miss
Batt, is now handed in at her father's door as Mrs Spencer—
a new and strange designation, which somewhat destroys the
identity of that very charming person. May he love her as well
under her lately-acquired title ! and in the meantime we all go
to breakfast.

Now begins the triumph of the bridesmaids. Hitherto those
uniformly-dressed young ladies have been so occupied with the
various onerous duties of their position, that they have had but
little leisure for idle thoughts or worldly speculations. They
have accompanied their charge to church with the gravity becoming their years and office ; they have marched up the aisle
two and two, with a touching expression of sympathy for the
martyr clouding their pretty faces ; they, that is to say, two of
them, told of for that especial duty, have gravely mounted guard
over her gloves and pocket-handkerchief, whilst the others have
disposed themselves around, in groups so picturesque and attitudes so graceful, that it is difficult to believe they are so
thoroughly unstudied and inartificial ; but now they have their
reward, now they vie in interest with their principal—*Le roi est
mort—vive le roi!*

The Derby is over,—the favourite has won, and speculation is
rife as to the forthcoming event that day twelvemonth—for man
lives in the future. So the bride is now a wife, and as such has
just begun to lose the least shade of that enthusiasm with which
she was regarded half an hour ago. But these charming young

ladies in gauze and smiles are still on their promotion. You or
I might marry any one of them, but perhaps we are too cautious
to try—perhaps we are confirmed old bachelors, and have not
entirely forgotten a prettier face than any of these, at least to
our mind, that was dressed in smiles for us some forty years
ago. However, we may still look kindly on at the pretty faces
here, and, doubtless, though our hearts be not quite so susceptible, our appetites are infinitely better than when we were lads,
and fancied ourselves in love!

The Reverend Amos has provided a sumptuous breakfast.
Champagne at noon would make an anchorite lively, and a wed-
ding has been from time immemorial a fair subject for a certain
number of stock jokes and clumsy innuendos, which never fail to
obtain encouragement and applause. We sit down readily
enough, and there is a good deal of confusion about places, and
rustling of dresses which require liberal space in their arrangement. I sidle into my chair, so as not to compress pretty Miss
Glover into the slim nymph which I believe her to be when
divested of all those muslin outworks, and rally that blushing
damsel upon the killing appearance of herself and sister bridesmaids. There is a vacant place on my other hand—a lady in
half-mourning glides quietly into it. Her dress touches me as
she sits down, and turning round, I behold the pale, sad face,
the gentle, chastened beauty of Flora Belmont.

How changed from the laughing girl that I first met, kindling
with enthusiasm at the review! how changed, and yet how
inexpressibly lovelier! The deep blue eye was heavy and
sorrow-laden, yet its glance was soft and winning as ever. The
smooth cheek had lost something of its roundness and its
dimples, yet the outline was faultless as a sculptor's model
still; the low pale forehead had a shade of care, and a line or
two of silver already streaked those masses of dark-brown hair;
yet for spiritual beauty, for that indefinite indescribable something which makes woman *lovable*—there is no other word for
it—how superior was the Flora of to-day to the fresh rosy girl
of—it is needless to say how many years ago! Not that I perceived this all at once; not that I turned round and took an

inventory of Miss Belmont's charms, as of a portrait in the exhibition. Far from it; our greeting was indeed of the briefest and most formal; to a stranger it would have seemed 'something less than kind.' I am not sure that we shook hands. And it is more from conviction than memory, that I am aware Flora was residing with an aunt not five miles from Haverley, or three from Owlthorpe; that she had lost her father scarcely a year, and had been over-persuaded by Julia to come to the wedding breakfast, though her sable attire prevented her witnessing the ceremony in church.

To say truth, I have but a confused notion of the events of that morning. I have a dim recollection of much shouting and rapping of the table when we drank the 'health of the new-married couple,' and Tom Spencer's breaking down sadly in a suitable reply. I know that I was much laughed at for absence of mind and dereliction of duty in permitting Mr Mottles, now an excessively garrulous old gentleman, to take upon himself my office of proposing the bridesmaids' health, a duty which he performed in a speech of astonishing eloquence, comparing those laughing damsels to everything that was charming, animate, or inanimate, and bringing 'Lemprière's Dictionary' into play, with extraordinary research, for classical metaphors and examples illustrating their extreme loveliness; they were 'spring flow'rets,' they were 'budding roses,' 'satellites shining round the silver queen of heaven,' 'nymphs dancing in the train of Diana,' 'laughing Hours attendant on the rosy Morn,' they were 'the three Graces and the nine Muses' (there were just eight of them), and, in conclusion, he wished them 'all sorts of happiness, and one husband a-piece at least, and more afterwards, if that was not enough.'

My toast could not have fallen into abler hands. I *think* the bride retired for an unconscionably long time to change her dress for travelling—they were to spend the honeymoon at Maltby's place, in Yorkshire—and reappeared in a costume of surprising magnificence, surmounted by a bonnet, the like of which I have never seen before nor since. I am persuaded that I shook hands repeatedly both with her and Tom Spencer at un-

certain intervals, and for no obvious reason; and the impression
is strong upon my mind that either I or Mr Mottles threw an
old shoe after the carriage as it drove off, to the imminent peril
of 'Julia's new maid' on the dicky; but I do know that I
walked home on that afternoon alone with Flora Belmont, and
that the early winter sun set not the same evening upon a
happier man than the bridegroom's assistant.

Love has been written up by enthusiasts and sneered down
by cynics, till the very nature of that mysterious phase of the
human mind has become shrouded in contradictions and confusion; inflated into folly on the one hand, and scouted as madness on the other, the noble unselfish passion that, hand-in-hand
with honour, beckoned the knights of old along the path of fame,
is now sneered at as the fond imagining of a romantic boy, the
vain delusion of a silly girl. 'Such an one is in love,' is at once
an excuse and a reason for any act of folly, extravagance, or
self-conceit of which the patient may be guilty. 'They are
both very young; they will know better in time,' says Middle-
age, shrinking back into the coat of mail that Self has for years
been hardening for its defence, and the kindliest instinct of our
worldly nature is ridiculed as a fantasy, or denounced as an
absurdity. Surely this must be wrong; the very essence of
true affection for another is a total abnegation and forgetfulness
of ourselves; and perhaps the noblest attitude of man is that
in which he casts from him the idol to which his fellow-creatures
are too prone to bow, and throws off his allegiance to the tyrant
Self, whose chains, growing with our growth, and strengthening
with our strength, become daily and hourly more galling and
more unrelenting. When two people can live for years apart,
and never forget—can undergo toil, privation, perhaps cutting
sarcasm, and stern rebuke, each for the other's sake; when the
watches of the night bring back only the one image; when a
strain of music, a glance of sunshine, or a scene of beauty recalls
the one loved face; when they are prepared to confront the
battle of life under every disadvantage, and take the inevitable
journey, weary and afoot, so they may but go hand-in-hand;
depend upon it there is something more than human in the

instinct which prompts such self-sacrifice and self-denial—depend upon it that when we scout Love from the face of the earth, we are casting off the one last link that connects us with the angels in heaven, we are doing our best to wither 'the flow'rets of Eden;' nor can we complain that it is the fault of any but ourselves, if we find, indeed, that 'the trail of the serpent is over them all.'

CHAPTER XXVI.

SETTLED AT LAST.

HOW different looks the little room in the City now. 'Tis true that Tom Spencer has deserted me, and is living in a perfect paradise of strawberries at Fulham ; that my solitude is darkened by the gloom of a London noon, and refreshed by an atmosphere compounded of gas, dust, and large particles of soot, whilst my view is bounded by a dead wall, not ten feet from the window, and the 'blue vault above me bent,' reduced to a narrow strip of lurid leaden sky ; and yet what rosy hues pervade the interior of the small dingy apartment. The dream is at length to be realised. Hope is at last to become fruition, and Flora Belmont has promised, at no very distant period, to share the broken fortunes of the ruined dandy, to superintend the humble establishment of the struggling tradesman. How St Heliers will laugh, if, indeed, that wasted frame have energy enough left to indulge in merriment. How Mrs Man-trap will sneer at the eventual fate of that pretty Miss Belmont, who was voted a beauty even in London, and came out of the ordeal unscathed and uncorrupted ; who might have married Sir Angelo, and given the very ball which is advertised to take place to-night at his house in Belgrave Square. True, Sir Angelo is old enough to be her father, and, in addition to a somewhat repulsive exterior, is afflicted with a temper such as woman's nature is the least of all able to cope with—violent, sarcastic, and unforgiving—but then she would have had the best carriage-horses in London ; and what a salve must be a box at the opera to a wounded spirit and a disappointed heart! And the gentle girl (for is she not still a girl to me ?) has chosen to forego all these advantages for my sake. And what have I to offer her in return, save the homage of a sincere, and I hope an honest, heart ? Nor has her choice been made without a struggle, without the endurance of many a cutting remark and well-meant reproof on the part of her father's friends.

The Colonel died, leaving his only daughter, contrary to expectation, but ill-provided for; nor were his latter hours divested of anxiety for her comfortable settlement in life. Many a wealthy home was offered to the handsome Miss Belmont; many a true-hearted gentleman knelt at my pretty Flora's feet; but each and all were courteously and gently declined; nor does it become me to dwell upon the motives which could induce her to forego the substantial realities of comfort, if not happiness, for that which her friendly advisers could not but consider as a dream of the past. One scene only will I describe, as a specimen of the importunities to which woman is subject on a matter of which surely she ought to be the best judge; and I may observe, *en passant,* that I became acquainted with its details through my friend Tom Spencer, who gathered the particulars from Julia, who overheard the conversation by accident; and having herself sworn eternal secrecy as to the whole proceedings, only confided them to her husband under the same sacred and inviolable pledge.

It was some six months after Colonel Belmont's death that Flora, who was staying on a visit to her friend at the Rectory, was taken to task by the Reverend Amos, one of her father's executors, and his oldest friend, as to her repugnance to a comfortable settlement in life—the battered, worn, and calculating man of the world thinking himself, no doubt, capable of fathoming the depth of that priceless heart. Even Julia, who is every inch a woman, allows that she never saw anything so beautiful as the orphan in her deep mourning, bending, pale and sad, over the inevitable needlework, that soothes and beguiles the cheerless hours of many a weary spirit.

Oh, that needlework! with its provoking intricacy and slow-growing design—what hot tears have fallen on those crossing threads—what sorrow-laden eyes have gazed dully and unconsciously on that dazzling web, whilst the fingers plied their mechanical task, and the heart was far away, basking in the sunny visions of the past, or yearning in hopeless misery for the irrevocable ! From the village maiden, who sits at the cottage door and hems her father's shirt through blinding tears, as memory invests John, late 'listed for a soldier, with endearing qualities of which that faithless rustic is altogether guiltless, to the peer's daughter, drooping over her embroidery, and inhaling with the fragrance of the conservatory memories of him who is even now presenting the same bouquets and vowing the same vows to another, aggravated by that distant strain of music from the schoolroom, where her little sister is practising the very waltz that wafted his love-whispers in her ear,—the canvas is the refuge and the confidante of woman's memories, woman's hopes, and woman's sorrows.

What smoking is to man, needlework is to his helpmate—the same soothing sedative—the same idle occupation. How much more needed by the gentler spirit, whose feelings must be more carefully concealed in proportion to their greater violence !

Well, even Julia says Flora looked beautiful as she sat in the cheerful drawing-room at the Rectory, with the noonday sun brightening her calm, sad brow, and glancing from the waves of her glossy hair, busied apparently with her stitches, and totally unconscious of the presence of her host, who was watching her with alarming intensity. The Reverend Amos was a short-sighted man, mentally and physically; but when he was determined to see a thing, he brought both corporeal and ideal vision to bear in a focus peculiarly his own, and the abstracted sempstress quite started when he addressed her, in his abrupt and jerking manner, on a subject not generally entered upon without certain preliminary observations.

'Refused him again, Miss Flora, as I understand? Very ill-judged. What does it mean? Whom are you waiting for ?—what's the use ?' spluttered the angry divine, half ashamed of his hastiness and the calm surprise with which Flora looked up at him from her work.

'Really, Mr Batt, you must explain yourself,' she observed, quietly, after a lengthened pause, during which the gentleman paced nervously up and down the room, fidgeted with a flower-stand, and upset a geranium-pot—malicious Julia laughing in the garden the while.

'Explain! it can't be explained. Three before your father's—I mean last year, and two since. Never used to be so. Look at Julia—going to settle—quite right; so should you, Miss Flora. I asked Sir Angelo to dinner yesterday on purpose, and I told you myself to be civil to him.'

'Well, Mr Batt,' replied Flora, with a look of comic serious-ness, 'and I *was* civil to him—very.'

'Why didn't you accept him, then?' thundered out the divine, infuriated by his own disappointment in what he honestly thought a delightful arrangement for his fair charge. 'I saw him give you a rosebud; I knew he meant something by his coming in the coach with four horses. He took you in to dinner, and he sat with you the whole evening, and yet you refused him—refused him, as I stand here; and, for the second time, too.' What am I to understand? Once for all, will you marry him, Miss Flora? Be cool—for heaven's sake, be cool.' (This was a species of adjuration always addressed to himself and the public by the Reverend Amos, in moments of great excitement.) 'Once for all, and the last time of asking, *will* you marry him, Miss Flora?'

'Then, once for all, Mr Batt,' replied she, 'I will *not*.'

The Reverend Amos danced about the room; and Julia in the garden went into fits of laughter.

'It's no use my talking, Miss Belmont,' said he—'no use my pointing out the chances you throw away, the wilfulness, the blindness, the absurdity of your conduct. By all that's—extra-ordinary, it's too bad! Now, be cool! Capricious I knew you were—women are all so; headstrong I might have expected; for Julia is as self-willed as the rest of you; but ungrateful I never thought you would be, Flora—never: I, who have danced you on my knee a hundred times!'

The tears rose in poor Flora's eyes, as she besought him not to consider her ungrateful, or disrespectful to 'dear papa's oldest friend; but I cannot—no, I cannot marry Sir Angelo.'

'Very well, Miss Belmont,' said the rector; 'I see how it is.

Now mark my words, and be cool. You will live to rue this day; make your own choice; I wash my hands of you. I know what it is—you are waiting for a man who has never cared for you—that broken-down spendthrift, Grand; and for the chance of marrying him, you refuse nine thousand a year, and a house in London, with the best shooting in this country; and all for a man who has never asked you—a speculator, a tradesman!—Now, be cool!—a man without an atom of principle—a gambler —a *roué!*——'

'Not a word more, Mr Batt,' said Flora, rising with a calm dignity that, in spite of himself, made the adviser feel thoroughly ashamed. 'This is a tone to which I am unaccustomed; and, till you can speak of your own and your son's friend with proper forbearance, I shall retire to my own room; nor can I continue as a guest with one who presumes so much upon his position and my own forlorn and friendless situation.' And with these words, she swept out of the room with a calm dignity seldom assumed by that gentlest of women; but with which, when she chose, for all her pale face, and soft, sweet eyes, she could have 'looked a lion down.'

To her own apartment she marched, with measured, unfaltering step; and there, we may be sure, her dignity gave way; and thither, we may be equally sure, Julia followed; and the two women wept in one another's arms, and, doubtless, administered sal volatile and other remedies, and bathed their eyelids, and smoothed their hair; and made the Reverend Amos very uncomfortable at luncheon, and thoroughly ashamed of himself at dinner; and the skirmish ended, as usual, in the total rout and discomfiture of the master of the house; but yet to many such annoyances was Flora subjected, and still she remained faithful, unforgetting and uncomplaining, to the end.

Well, it is over now, I hope. Soon she shall again have a home—may it be a happy one! And, in the meantime, I people the little room in London with thick-coming fantasies and hopeful visions, in which a comfortable independence, a picturesque villa, and a smiling, happy wife, form no unimportant items; whilst, looming in the far horizon, I trace an indistinct prospect

of a fortune, acquired by diligence and self-denial, and au ancestral home repurchased by a vigorous old man, who has devoted
a lifetime to the endeavour of repairing the errors of his youth.
Castles in the air these may be; but such aërial edifices have at
least the advantage of an unlimited liberality of estimate, and a
boundless range of plan.

It is pleasanter, though perhaps less profitable, to look forward
than to look back. The reader has probably had quite enough
of Digby Grand and his autobiography; but to some amongst
those who may have glanced over these pages, he may say,
Mutato nomine, de te fabula narratur. How many a noble
intellect and gallant spirit is at this moment wasting its energies
on the most unworthy and unsatisfactory of all employments—
the pursuit of pleasure!—gaining nothing, hoping nothing, leading
to nothing, conjuring with the one word ‘society’ an excuse for
the neglect of all that is most dignified in humanity, all that is
most important to mankind; wearing out the body and corrupt-
ing the soul with labours that are worse than futile, pleasures far
more injurious than pain.

‘Push on, keep moving’—such is the motto of this world of
ours; and in this world nothing can remain stationary. Look
at your farm, dejected landowner; should you omit to sow that
corn which you have discovered to be so unremunerative an outlay, think you that mother earth will not bestow a supply of
weeds in choking profusion on the surface of your neglected soil?
Strip the favourite, noble sportsman, as you select him from your
costly string of race-horses, and say, statesman though you be,
can you keep him at his best for twenty-four hours? You know
you cannot, though thousands depend upon the result; if he is
not improving, he is going back. So is it with the human mind:
every day, every hour that passes, has its influence on the god-like
portion of man. If he is not storing his intellect from the past,
or training his soul for the future, depend upon it both one and
the other are imperceptibly but surely deteriorating from that
lofty ideal which, though unattainable here, should ever be in
view—are assimilating more and more with the grosser clay
which covers them, and sinking deeper and deeper to the debas-

ing level of the animal creation. Will you forfeit your birthright
for a few short years of that which, even under its most favourable aspect, can scarce be called pleasure? Are not her most
envied votaries, though exulting 'in joyous health, with boundless
wealth, yet sickening of a vague disease?' and will you enter the
lists, and strive with a vigour and assiduity that in other contests
might win an immortal crown, for a prize that when obtained is
utterly valueless, a victory more fatal than the most inglorious
defeat? Shall your youth be wasted in disappointment, your
manhood in disgust, your age in remorse? and all because you
have not strength of mind to break through the customs of your
kind, and embark upon your own career, in humble hope and
honest independence.

Look at the mighty names which stand inscribed upon the
roll of Fame—warriors, sages, and statesmen,—the beacons of
the present, the examples of the past : think ye that to them the
pastime of an hour could be the engrossing business of life?—
that those vigorous minds could be concentrated upon idle
follies and seductive pleasures? No. Taking the world as it
came, they might here and there step aside to pick up the
flower chance threw in their way ; they might enjoy—none so
much—the passing moments of amusement and relaxation ; but
the step was quickened after each refreshing pause—the mind
more braced than ever for the glorious object still held uninterruptedly in view. Shall you, then, be content to make the
giddy round of pleasure your all-in-all—to sink health, fame,
and fortune in her Lethæan wave ? Should such be your choice,
repine not when you find, as I did, that your life has been spent
in the pursuit of a shadow—that your treasures are but dross,
your gods but clay. Rather be thankful should the bracing
effects of adversity, the pressure of necessity, recall you to that
career of toil, that laborious destiny which is the normal condition of man.

Exertion is the salt of our existence. Without it the blood
thickens, the frame droops, the mind stagnates. Happier is the
peasant, home-returning from his daily task—weary, indeed, in

limb, but fresh and gladsome in heart—than his lord, tossing restless and discontented on his bed of roses—a palled voluptuary, who has exhausted pleasure after pleasure, till his sated spirit yearns even for the languor of fatigue, vainly striving to deaden the aspiring impulse within—vainly hoping to escape from his accusing self—seeking rest and finding none. I cannot but believe that there are moments during which the men that we see about us every day—the thrifty bees that gather, and the careless drones that spend—must reflect and speculate on the ulterior object with which this immortal soul of ours is imprisoned for some threescore years and ten in its imperfect tenement of clay. It is not self-indulgence, for her votaries are most of all sick and weary of their engrossing task ; it is not self-aggrandisement, for the slaves of ambition have never yet reached the topmost round of the ladder, and the draught of glory but irritates their fever, gasping still for more.

In all times, the wisest of mankind have deemed our present condition to be one of preparation, of training—severe it may be, but necessary, for a loftier and less material state of existence ; and shall we, of all ages, virtually reject this noble prospect, and grovelling here below, in sensual indulgences or idle pleasures, forfeit the birthright of our race, the privileges of our station, only, 'a little lower than the angels?' We shall each and all of us see this clearly some day, when darkened rooms, and hushed whispers, and a wistful sympathy on the old familar faces, warn our shrinking senses that for us there will be no to-morrow. Who would put off the preparation for his journey till the eve of departure? Let us make up the accounts and strike the balance ere it be too late.

The farce is over; the long-suffering audience impatient to retire ; ladies are shawling in the dark recesses of the boxes, and attentive admirers picking their way on dandy boots to look for 'the carriage' in the sloppy streets ; the coachman lashes his unoffending horses, the footman is torn from his porter, and the performers are summoned to the footlights to give an account of themselves, ere the public take their departure.

The companions of my youth, the friends of my manhood, are scattered far and wide upon the surface of the earth. Is it not so with us all?

> For some are in a far countree,
>   And some all restlessly at home ;
> But never more, oh, never we
>   Shall meet to revel or to roam.

Mrs Man-trap thinks Bath will restore her charms. St Heliers votes Buxton the only place for his gout ; the fashionable beauty looks forward to the visit of her doctor as the gayest hour in the twenty-four ; the brilliant nobleman, the delight of clubs, the charm of dinner-parties, the vigorous *bon-vivant*, the athletic sportsman, is now a helpless cripple, wheeled about in a garden-chair. I don't think either of theirs is a satisfactory old age.

Of my earlier comrades, some are still daily attending parade, some have disappeared altogether from the Army List. Spooner has married a widow with five children—they say she bullies him. Levanter is a convict at Norfolk Island. Of Fanny Jones's fate, I shudder to inquire. Colonel, now General Grandison, may be seen at any of her Majesty's Drawing-rooms, covered with orders, the beau ideal of an officer and a gentleman. Maltby has sold out, and occupies the position for which Nature has best fitted him, a kind landlord and a hospitable country gentleman, doing good to all around him, and hunting the wild country he lives in with unparalleled success. Dr Driveller has been removed from his cure at an extremely advanced old age ; but his memory did not fail him when he bequeathed to me, in accordance with his long-made promise, the family picture of Sir Hugo le Grand, the only one of my household gods I have as yet recovered. Mortmain, active and clear-sighted as ever, was with me this morning, making arrangements for certain nuptials, in which I take a personal interest. He has ascertained that the present possessor of Haverley will not entail the estate. I dined with Jack Lavish the night before last, at his, or rather his wife's, house, in Tyburnia Proper. He has shaved off his mustaches, and is getting fat. Miss Goldthred, that was, is a sensible and charming person ; but I think I can trace in her manner a slight and not unnatural distrust which she entertains of her husband's old friends. She looks pretty sharp after Jack ; and I understand that he rides alone in the Park only under the express stipulation that he shall accompany none but his male acquaintances. Jack says he likes being kept tight in hand, it saves him so much trouble ; and, till he had some lady to own him, he never knew to which of his fair friends he belonged. A print of poor Hillingdon hangs in his private apartment ; and we talked together for hours about the sad fate of that beloved and gifted being,—his generous romantic spirit, his fearless heart, his endearing qualities, and his awful end.

Some men, like wine, improve with age. Lavish, whose faults were those of youth, and most excusable in the young,— a carelessness of consequences, a merry, thoughtless disposition, and a disregard for the affectations of society, which made him a highly popular companion, is becoming, under the influence of a regular life, and a well-judging intellectual woman, a highly useful as well as agreeable member of society. He is still as jovial as ever, but beneath his merriment runs a vein of strong sound sense ; and his frank and still somewhat dandified exterior conceals a warm and benevolent heart. Of Cartouch and his daughter he had much to tell me. The Colonel was at first enchanted with the recovery of his child. To the tired, worn soldier, weary of barracks, and *blasé* with society, the prospect of a quiet domestic home—such a home as can only exist under female influence—was refreshing to the utmost. He pictured to himself a life of calm pleasures and contented tranquillity, an interchange of thoughts and sentiments with that fascinating woman who had proved to be his daughter, that should make him amends for all the sufferings entailed upon him by her mother's unbridled passions, and the long, dreary years of loneliness that he had since worn through—a widower, though a husband. Alas ! that he should have been disappointed and deceived. Neither Coralie nor himself were adapted, either by disposition or education, for the retirement of a country life. In vain the Colonel sold out of the service, and taking a sweet little place in Hampshire, embarked largely in the cultivation of the soil, and encouraged his child to take charge of a garden, such as many a flower-loving daughter of Eve would have esteemed a perfect paradise. It was all charming for a while—but the training in which the *danseuse* had spent her youth was of a nature which made constant excitement absolutely necessary to her existence. At first, the novelty of a home and a father—such a father, too, as any girl might be proud of—was very pleasing; but, after a time, the country walks, the *tête-à-tête* dinners, the early hours, became monotonous and wearisome; she pined for the amusements to which she was accustomed—the lively professional society, the daily tribute of admiration, the constant change of scene, the flatteries of the green-room, and the ovations of the stage. Besides, our English ladies have certain wholesome rules of quarantine, to which they cling with meritorious tenacity; and the name of ' De Rivolte ' was quite sufficient to prevent the Hampshire matrons from subjecting themselves or their daughters to contamination in the society of a *figurante*. All this annoyed Coralie as much as it disgusted the Colonel. She was used to be courted and caressed wherever she made her appearance; and he had all his life been a welcome and admired guest in far higher circles than those which now affected to draw the cordon of exclusiveness to his prejudice. The rector of the parish was courtesy itself to the new-comers, but his wife gathered her brood under her wings whenever she caught sight of Coralie's little French bonnet in any of the walks and lanes surrounding the parsonage. Lord Overbearing, who spent a month every year in that one of his seven palaces, near which their pretty farm was situated, asked the Colonel to shoot, and came himself to luncheon, and remained to dinner, good easy man, delighted to escape a party of fine folks who were staying at his own house; but her Ladyship never so much as left her card upon the inhabitants of the cottage. Altogether it did not answer, nor had they any right to expect it would. The sacred relationship of parent and child is not to be tampered with, as in their case it had been, with impunity; and the previous habits and education of Coralie were made the means of punishing her father's original neglect of that wife whom, whatever may have been her faults, he had no right totally to repudiate.

The upshot of it all is this,—Coralie votes England very *triste*, and Hampshire particularly disagreeable. The Colonel, who has been too long in harness to sink contentedly into a quiet country gentleman, gets very tired of his red land and his southdowns, and out of all patience with the stupidity of the 'chaw-bacons,' to use the vernacular term by which the inhabitants of that beautiful county are distinguished; and there is a scheme in embryo which will probably be put in practice, of leaving the farm and cottage to take care of themselves, and indulging in a year's tour on the Continent, '*mon cousin*' making one of the family party. I think it not impossible that '*mon cousin*' may eventually aspire to a dearer title, though how such an arrangement will suit my old friend Cartouch, I leave to be determined by those who are conversant with the habits of a British officer, and the education and prejudices of an Englishman.

Reader, the play is played out, the characters have made their respectively awkward bows and curtseys, the box-keeper is covering up everything; it is time to go home. What you have witnessed is intended to be but a representation of that every-day life, the reality of which we need only open our eyes to see around us whenever we please. It is neither a magnificent melodrama, a thrilling tragedy, nor an amusing farce, at the best. Yet the slowest comedy may suggest materials for reflection and improvement. We have all seen flaming advertisements, in letters an inch long, that on such and such a night, Mdlle. Entrechat will appear in her celebrated character of *La Fée Fusillée*, and dance the much admired *Pas de Fascination*. Well, we have pestered Mr Sams for a stall, and added another score to the bill at Andrew's or Mitchell's. We have dined early, and, half-choked with the unseemly haste of our repast, we have donned our white kid gloves, and levelled with accurate range the miraculously magnifying opera-glass—in fine, we have been and seen it. Shall we confess to a slight feeling of disappointment at that widely-renowned measure? Shall we acknowledge that the *Pas de Fascination* on the stage, with all its accessories of dress, scenery, lights, and music, was not half so gorgeous a spectacle as that visionary *Pas de Fascination* which passed before our creative imagination in those capital letters an inch long?

So is it with that reality of which the stage and the novel are but a mimicry and a representation. The life upon which youth fancies itself entering, is very different from the life which age refuses to acknowledge it is on the eve of quitting. The Real can never hope to equal the Ideal. Is it not that the Real is but typical of Time,—the Ideal of Eternity?

THE END.